# PLAYING DEAD

# PLAYING DEAD

Short stories in honour of Simon Brett
by members of the Detection Club

Edited by Martin Edwards
Introduction by Martin Edwards

With stories by
Abir Mukherjee, Aline Templeton, Alison Joseph, Andrew Taylor, Ann Cleeves, Catherine Aird, Christopher Fowler, David Stuart Davies, Elly Griffiths, Frances Brody, John Harvey, Kate Ellis, L.C. Tyler, Liza Cody, Lynne Truss, Martin Edwards, Michael Jecks, Michael Ridpath, Michael Z. Lewin, Peter Lovesey, Ruth Dudley Edwards and Simon Brett

SEVERN HOUSE

First world edition published in Great Britain and the USA in 2025
by Severn House, an imprint of Canongate Books Ltd,
14 High Street, Edinburgh EH1 1TE.

Paperback edition first published in Great Britain and the USA in 2025
by Severn House, an imprint of Canongate Books Ltd.

severnhouse.com



Cover and jacket design by Piers Tilbury



*British Library Cataloguing-in-Publication Data*
A CIP catalogue record for this title is available from the British Library.

ISBN-13: 978-1-4483-1296-2 (cased)
ISBN-13: 978-1-4483-1297-9 (paper)
ISBN-13: 978-1-4483-1298-6 (e-book)



*All Severn House titles are printed on acid-free paper.*

MIX
Paper | Supporting responsible forestry
FSC www.fsc.org FSC® C013604

Typeset by Palimpsest Book Production Ltd., Falkirk,
Stirlingshire, Scotland.
Printed and bound in Great Britain by TJ Books,
Padstow, Cornwall.

The manufacturer's authorised representative in the EU for product safety is
Authorised Rep Compliance Ltd, 71 Lower Baggot Street, Dublin D02 P593
Ireland (arccompliance.com)

# Contents

# INTRODUCTION

*Playing Dead* is the latest book produced by members of the Detection Club, founded by Anthony Berkeley Cox in 1930 and the oldest and arguably the most prestigious social network of crime writers in the world. The Club has a fascinating history and continues to flourish as it saunters towards its centenary, even though now there are many other opportunities for crime writers to socialize and collaborate at festivals and other events in the UK and around the world.

The Club's survival is in some ways quite miraculous, given its modest size and even more modest financial resources. Because it's a small dining club rather than a professional or representative organization (such as the Crime Writers' Association, in which most members of the Club have been prominent figures), the number of members has of necessity always been limited. Yet it attracts great loyalty from those members, because there really is nothing quite like it, and our three meetings each year are always highly convivial.

The Club's history is fascinating. I wrote about it at some length in *The Golden Age of Murder*, and our archives now form part of the British Crime Writing Archives held at the wonderfully atmospheric Gladstone's Library in Hawarden, north Wales. But, right from the Club's inception, members have recognized that if it is to keep going, the dining needs to be subsidized by occasional publications.

In the early 1930s, Club stalwarts such as Agatha Christie, Dorothy L. Sayers, Ronald Knox, Freeman Wills Crofts and others collaborated in writing detective stories on behalf of the Club, the proceeds of which were devoted to the Club's activities, and this became an established tradition. Since my election as President in 2015, we have produced a collection of short stories, *Motives for Murder* (2016), and a book about the art and craft of crime writing, *Howdunit* (2020). The former featured four stories which were nominated for the CWA Short Story Dagger, including the eventual winner, while the latter was nominated for five awards and won the H. R. F. Keating Prize for best critical/biographical book in the crime genre.

Now comes *Playing Dead*. Over the years, the Club has produced anthologies celebrating the eightieth birthdays of several distinguished members, namely Julian Symons, Harry Keating and Peter Lovesey, while *Howdunit* was dedicated to Len Deighton, who has been a member of the Club for over fifty years. When I realized that Simon Brett, President Emeritus of the Club and my immediate predecessor, was approaching a milestone birthday of his own, I felt it would be appropriate to celebrate his wonderful contribution to the Club (and the genre as a whole) by compiling a collection of short stories in his honour. Happily, our members agreed, and this book is the result.

I was a fan of Simon's writing long before I met him. I remember attending a talk he gave in Southport when I was an aspiring crime novelist; he was witty and entertaining and once I got to know him, years later, I discovered that he is *invariably* witty, and extremely good company. His writing is notable for his mastery of dialogue, while its range is remarkable; in the crime genre alone, he has written novels, short stories, radio plays, and mysteries that have been adapted for television and film. He masterminded a 'round robin' novel written by Detection Club members, *The Sinking Admiral*, and has even written a crime story in rhyme, which I once watched him perform to a very appreciative audience at Gladstone's Library. I must add that, since I succeeded him to the presidency he has been, at all times, wonderfully supportive. Like other members of the Club, I owe him a great deal.

I encouraged the contributors to *Playing Dead* to write whatever kind of crime story appealed to them and the result is an eclectic mix which I hope and expect will delight many thousands of readers. Some of the stories, including my own, make references to Simon and his prodigious literary output in various ways, and I hope fans of Simon's writing will enjoy spotting these hat-tips. Nothing better illustrates the varied nature of the contents than Liza Cody's contribution, a haiku inspired by listening to one of Simon's radio plays. The first story that I received when I invited members to contribute came from David Stuart Davies.

Sadly, David was diagnosed with a brain tumour a few months later and did not live to see this book. Nor did Chris Fowler, who was during his all-too-brief membership a great enthusiast for the Detection Club.

In their stories, John Harvey, Lynne Truss and Ruth Dudley Edwards bring back favourite series characters, while Simon's own contribution offers an amusing glance back to his very first detective novel, *Cast, in Order of Disappearance*, which introduced Charles Paris. Simon's reminiscences about his time as a member of the Detection Club for so many years bring the book to a fitting conclusion.

All the contributors have kindly donated their stories in this book for the benefit of Club funds and I'm most grateful to all of them. My thanks also go to Simon, again, for his consistent support and encouragement, and to Georgia Glover, the Club's literary agent, and everyone at Severn House who has worked on this book.

Martin Edwards

# L.C. TYLER – CRIMES ANCIENT AND MODERN

## Part 1 Crimes Ancient

'Not much doubt about the cause of death,' said my sergeant, viewing the two bodies.

'The problem is,' I said, 'that the Leeches are celebrities. Well, they were until last night.'

'That makes a difference?' he said.

'It'll be all over the TV and papers by tomorrow morning. The neighbours who called us in are probably already on the phone to the *Sun*.'

'You think so?' he said. 'They were only crime writers. It's not as if they were seventeen-year-old Tik Tok influencers. But I agree, we'll look pretty stupid if we miss something.'

'Exactly,' I said. 'So, we're not going to jump to conclusions. We're going to do a proper job.' I surveyed the large, comfortable bedroom, now a potential crime scene. 'I know what it looks like, but we still need to rule out foul play. There were rumours they weren't getting on that well anymore.'

'Well, they're *both* dead. I can't see how they can have taken turns to kill each other. And certainly not like that. Odd way for an intruder to have killed them too. Anyway, there's no sign of a forced entry.'

'Let's gather the evidence, then make up our minds. The way the Leeches did it in their books.'

'You ever read one, guv? They were jointly authored under the name of Julia Adam. That's—'

'Their real Christian names combined. Yes, I've read some. Coppers in the Leeches' books just plunge in with both feet and root around for clues. Since this is real life, I think we'd better call CSI in. We can tape things off while we're waiting for them.

Then, we'll talk to the neighbours. After that, we'll go through mobile phone records, internet histories, emails, diaries.'

'That could be a lot of work for somebody, sir. Under the circumstances, maybe we should just jump to conclusions after all?'

'Nothing's too good for a dead celebrity,' I said. 'Let's go and fetch some stripy tape.'

'So,' said my sergeant, as we sat in the car, drinking take-away coffee from paper cups and watching the white-suited CSIs coming and going from the house, 'everyone round here says they were a devoted couple, never apart. They'd had a big row a few days ago – lots of raised voices – but had apparently patched things up since then. Been married for ages. They'd written about twenty of those Julia Adam books. Traditional crime novels with a modern twist.'

'I know,' I said. 'I've read some, remember? And by "traditional" I assume you mean hopeless on police procedure. Well, the Leeches' phones and computers are now bagged up and in the boot. We can get to work on them, as soon as somebody back at the station can hack into them for us. I'll also phone their agent. He's George Green of Green Associates, according to the Leeches' Facebook account.'

My sergeant was looking fairly smug. 'The computers yielded some interesting stuff. Nothing much in their emails, but they'd both done a few internet searches in the past few days – the sort you might expect from crime writers.'

'Such as?' I said.

'He'd searched for cyanide poisoning – amount needed to kill and how soon the victim would die.'

'Poisoning? Interesting,' I said.

'Except it doesn't look as if cyanide was used in this case,' said my sergeant. 'He also searched for Beachy Head and one or two other beauty spots along the coast round here. Were they planning a day out maybe? Trying to patch things up after the row?'

'Could be. Though the weather's not been good lately. And Mrs Leech's computer?' I asked.

'Rather different stuff. She'd googled "sexual asphyxiation" – a bit of strangling during sex apparently intensifies erotic pleasure. I didn't know that. It seems young people are heavily into it. It's known as "choking". Do you think it's worth suggesting to my wife? Just for a bit of variety?'

'Only if you want to run the risk of it being your very last night of pleasure. There have been a few deaths lately when one partner has overcooked things. Erotic asphyxiation used to be mainly a solitary affair, with the practitioner found alone and dead in embarrassing circumstances, a plastic bag over his head. Of course, in that sort of case, it's sometimes difficult to say whether the death was self-inflicted or whether somebody killed the victim and disguised it all as something else.'

'So, maybe she was researching it for a book rather than for their own bedroom? As you say, it would be a good way of bumping somebody off.'

'Very true – it is. Anything else in her search history?' I asked.

'Yes, she was looking at the Volvo manual online – how to turn on and turn off various safety features. Maybe they were having problems with the car?'

'Or more research for a novel. Crime writers' search histories, eh? Nothing at all in the emails?'

'Like I said, all fairly routine. A lot of spam. Newsletters from other crime writers. Some emails from readers. One from their plumber to Mr Leech, asking when he could come over and do the servicing.'

'Any reply to the plumber?'

'No. Maybe Mr Leech was distracted by other things? Something on his mind? Research for the next book and so on?'

'My wife,' I said, 'reckons men are easily distracted when it comes to things like sorting out the central heating. Well, I had a very interesting chat with their agent. As you said, "Julia Adam" has written about twenty books. The early ones sold respectably. But the last few have flopped. There was a feeling they'd run out of ideas. Their publisher hadn't yet committed to any more in the series. Our two authors brought very different things to the party, according to George Green. Adam was a great traditionalist – Golden Age plots. It was Julia who gave it the modern twist – she was the one who occasionally slipped in an actual sex scene when Adam would have written "dot, dot, dot" and left it at that.'

'Well, that fits in with her research,' said my sergeant. 'I mean the kinky sex, not the Volvo.'

'Green said that she was the one who wanted to go for the high-concept crime novel.'

'And Adam didn't?'

'He implied that Julia was much the better writer – more literary – capable of producing really original stuff. Adam was holding her back.'

'Holding her back? He actually said that?'

'I'm reading between the lines,' I said. 'I suppose it was more that he praised Julia to the skies and didn't say that much about Adam.'

'Did he indeed?' said my sergeant. 'Well, that's interesting, because the phone records show Julia had made half a dozen calls to their agent lately. Adam made none. I did wonder . . . in view of what you just said . . . do you reckon she and Green were an item, guv?'

'Not especially. You can read too much into call records – or the wrong things anyway.'

'I suppose so. Anything from the guys at the crime scene?' he said.

'Yes. Something's been buried recently in the garden. There's a pile of newly dug earth. They're investigating.'

'A body?' he said.

'Apparently it would have to be a very small one. There's also a funny milky residue in the flower bed, just outside one of the bedrooms. They're getting it tested. They thought, by the way, they'd found something good in the kitchen – there was a nasty smell from the waste bin – but it turned out that the Leeches had thrown some oysters away.'

'Why would they do that?'

'Kept them too long?' I said. 'Can't stand shellfish myself. We'll give forensics a call later to see whether that milky-looking patch is anything we need to worry about.'

'I've just called CSI,' said my sergeant.

'And?' I said.

'The thing that was buried – it was a cat.'

'I didn't know the Leeches owned a cat,' I said.

'They didn't. The CSIs got somebody to ask around and it turned out the moggy belonged to their neighbours. It vanished a couple of days ago.'

'What were the Leeches doing burying a cat that didn't belong to them?' I said.

'No idea. Complete mystery. We're checking now how the cat died. Oh, and they're still testing to see what the milky stuff in the flower bed was. It's probably not significant, but I said you were interested in it.'

'You'll never guess, guv,' said my sergeant. 'The cat died of cyanide poisoning. The stuff Adam Leech was googling.'

'Really?' I said.

'And get this,' said my sergeant. 'That milky stuff – coffee laced with cyanide.'

'Interesting,' I said.

'Oh, and those oysters in the bin – dangerously toxic. They did well to chuck them.'

'Well, I don't think it was seafood poisoning any more than it was cyanide poisoning,' I said. 'The colour of their faces suggested something else entirely. Still, I think I can now piece together exactly what happened. So should you, if you've been paying attention.'

'Should I? Sorry, guv, I can't see any of it adds much to what we saw when we first arrived at the house. To be honest, CSI think you were wasting their time calling them in at all. How they died is obvious – the rest is just a series of red herrings, isn't it?'

'On the contrary,' I said. 'Everything we've discovered is helpful one way or another. The problem, if we want to explain not only how but *why* they died, is that we've been viewing this case as a story told by Adam in the traditional style – a crime, a mystery, an enquiry and, hopefully, a conclusion. What we should have been doing is viewing this as a story by Julia. It's all about character rather than plot.'

'If you say so. How would Julia tell the story, then? She'd start from her own perspective, right?'

'No,' I said. 'I rather think she'd start from Adam's. And, though I've no absolute proof and probably never will, I think the story would go something like this . . .'

## Part 2 Crimes Modern

'We're finished,' Julia said. 'It's over, Adam. That's all there is to it. You have to accept it.'

'You can't really mean that?' I asked, stunned.

'The writing has been on the wall a long time,' she said, not unkindly. 'Not literally or you might have noticed it. But subtly and metaphorically, which is maybe why you didn't. The last three or four books we've done together simply haven't sold well enough. You know that, as well as I do. George thinks I should strike out on my own. Write the high-concept novel I've always wanted to write.'

'But we're a *team,*' I said. I sounded a bit like a five-year-old complaining of the unfairness of life. But that was how I felt about it.

'We've been a *great* team,' she said. 'Look at all those books along the shelves. Some of them were actually quite good – the first one anyway. Good enough to get into the bestseller lists. And it's been such fun. Getting up together, having breakfast together, working together in the study, having lunch together, working some more . . . together. And so on. Day after day after day. Month after month. Year after year. Absolutely wonderful. But now we have to do something different. For both our sakes.'

'So, what does George suggest I do?' I demanded.

'That's up to you.'

'George has no views?'

'He wouldn't be representing you anymore. He thinks you'd be better off with another agent. Somebody who really loved your work and appreciated your very special skills.'

'So, you're saying you and George have killed my career stone dead, but you're fine. And George will still represent you?'

'The last bit is right anyway. He's very excited about an idea that I pitched him over the phone the other day.'

'We could do it together,' I said. 'Whatever it is, Julia, we can do it together. The way we always do.'

'The way we always did,' she said. 'Honestly, I've had enough of Knox and his Decalogue and none of our characters ever swearing or having much fun. You can have too much of Christie and Sayers. And Allingham.'

'Too much *Allingham*?' I gasped.

'Yes,' she said. 'Too much Allingham.'

It was then that I realized she would have to die. I went to the study and googled cyanide.

OK. Maybe I shouldn't have said 'too much Allingham' to Adam of all people. I can see that now. He was in the study for a very long time. Once, I heard the printer rattle and then fall silent. In the end he got over his little sulk and came to bed.

When I awoke the following morning, my first thought was that it was a great day to start work on our next book. Then I recalled the new state of affairs. And my plan.

'Good morning, Julia,' I said. 'Just to show that I have no hard feelings, following our little chat yesterday, I thought I'd make you a cappuccino. Then I might go for a walk to clear my head.'

'Thank you,' she said, without turning over. 'A coffee would be lovely.'

I got up and collected something from my sock drawer, then headed for the kitchen.

Agatha Christie used to tell the story of having worked with a pharmacist who kept a lump of a deadly poison, curare, in his pocket because it made him feel powerful. In the same way I had, long ago, obtained a phial of cyanide, though I kept it more cautiously in my sock drawer. Now, having checked the correct dosage, I intended to use it in earnest. I poured the contents of the phial – enough to kill a dozen people – into the milky coffee. Then I took it back to the bedroom and placed it on Julia's table.

'Drink it while it's hot, my love,' I said. 'I'm off now. For a little walk.'

I paused in the kitchen to leave a brief note I had printed out the night before on paper that I knew already bore Julia's fingerprints. It said that Julia deeply regretted her rejection of me and, knowing that she did not deserve forgiveness, had decided to do away with herself using a phial of cyanide that she had possessed for some years. I signed it 'J' and propped it against the tea caddy for somebody to find. I set off on my walk.

I couldn't remember the last time Adam had made me coffee. I sniffed it cautiously, then went out to the kitchen, where I discovered my suicide note. So, that was his game was it? I went back to the bedroom and tipped the coffee out of the window on to the flower bed. I closed the window and drew the curtains again.

Later I thought I heard an animal lapping something up.

Adam almost jumped out of his skin when he returned three hours later and found me still alive and sitting up in bed reading *Blotto and Twinks*. He looked suspiciously at the empty mug.

'Sorry, my love. I was so engrossed in Simon's latest that I let the coffee get cold. Just couldn't put the book down. And I hate cold coffee, as you know. So, I threw it out into the garden.'

He went to the window and peeped out between the curtains.

'Shit!' he said.

'Is anything amiss, dearest?' I said.

'There's something I need to clear away . . .' he said.

'Can I help you at all, my sweet?' I asked.

'No, I'd better just get a shovel and deal with it,' he said.

There are more ways than one to skin a cat, I told myself, albeit that was an unfortunate analogy as things stood.

I've always thought that the surest way of killing anyone – Julia for example – without risk of detection was to take them for a walk along a deserted clifftop and push them off. So long as nobody sees you, there is no possible proof that they did not slip and fall, provided they do not survive to give evidence. The cliffs at Beachy Head are five hundred and thirty feet high. There was no way Julia was going to shrug that off. Of course, the problem is that there are always busybodies milling around in the car park. Using my computer, I worked my way along the coast, beauty spot by beauty spot, until I had the right combination of remoteness and vertical drop.

* * *

'Adam, dearest,' I said, 'The weather forecast is for heavy rain. Why would I want to take a trip along the coast?'

Adam muttered something about the romance of misty seascapes.

'Well, not today anyway,' I said. 'I'm going into town to do some shopping.'

He grumpily returned to the study. He'd have to do much better than Beachy Head to make me lower my guard. I think that was the point when I decided that you had to fight fire with fire. I could sit there tamely until he finally managed to kill me. Or I could just deal with the problem once and for all. As it happened, I had a perfect plan myself. We'd soon see who was the better plotter.

I visited a certain shop that I had occasionally glanced at as I passed by but never quite got round to visiting. There I purchased a number of devices and some nightwear that scarcely existed at all. This was going to be easy.

When I came to bed Julia was, unusually, sitting there dressed in some scanty lace garment. She looked chilly. On the bed were what I could only assume were bondage devices, including a length of silken rope.

'Just to say how sorry I am about everything,' she cooed, 'I thought I might spice things up for us a little tonight.'

'How?' I asked.

'Have you considered trying "choking"?' she asked.

'No,' I said.

'It's a way of increasing erotic pleasure.'

'Never heard of it.'

'In that case let me just assure you that you're going to love it,' she said somewhat impatiently. 'First, I tie you up. Then, as we make love, I just apply a little pressure to your throat. All you have to do is relax and enjoy it.'

And suddenly all became clear.

'Agatha Christie,' I said, 'would never – never in a million years – have stooped to a cheap plot device like that.'

'Gladys Mitchell would,' she said.

'Yeah, OK, maybe Gladys Mitchell,' I said.

'So, how about it?'

'I'm off to sleep in the spare room,' I said. 'I'll see you in the morning.'

'Who was that ringing the bell?' asked Adam.

'It was just Maggie from next door, asking if we'd seen their cat. It's gone missing, apparently.'

'And what did you say?' he asked.

'I said I hadn't. Have you?'

'Not today,' he said.

I was still somewhat miffed by last night's failure. I decided to try another way. In traditional crime novels, a surefire murder method was to saw halfway through a brake cable and make the mug drive down a steep hill. Modern cars are trickier in some ways, but offer different opportunities. I went online to check how to disable selected safety features from our Volvo. It was easy enough. Then it struck me that I was wasting my time. The problem of course was that Adam, hating every aspect of modernity, never relied on any of the technology our car was packed with and drove it just as he'd driven his first Mini many years ago.

But I was confident that, before long, a chance would come up.

One of the plots that Julia and I have always admired is Roald Dahl's oyster poisoning. You buy thirteen oysters and put one in a flower pot in the garden for a day or two to decay nicely. Then you drip lethal juice from it on to the six you are not going to eat yourself. An apparently accidental death ensues.

I visited the fishmongers. I put twelve oysters at the back of the fridge and one in the flower pot by the door. Twenty-four hours ought to be enough.

I was looking out of the bedroom window, when I saw Adam messing around with the flower pot by the patio doors. I waited until he had finished, then I sneaked out and checked it. So, he was trying to work the old Roald Dahl oyster trick, was he? We'd see about that.

It was the following day when he announced he was preparing oysters for dinner that evening.

'I didn't think you liked oysters much,' I said.

'I don't,' he said. 'But I know how much you like them, my darling.'

'So thoughtful, my pet,' I said.

That afternoon I dug up my oyster. Dahl's instructions were vaguer than I would have liked, but it smelled pretty bad. I separated the oysters in the fridge into two servings and dripped poison on Julia's.

Ha!

From my vantage point in the sitting room, I could see Adam messing in the fridge. Once he'd gone, I checked. Two separate portions now, eh? I switched them round and went back to *Blotto and Twinks*. If Adam could write half as well as Simon, none of this would be remotely necessary. But there we are.

We sat down together in the kitchen for what would be her last meal. She wouldn't be looking that smug for long. Outside the rain was lashing against the window, but the boiler was humming away and the radiators were heating up.

'Bon appétit, my love!' I said.

'Enjoy your oysters, dearest!' she said.

We looked at each other. 'Actually,' she said, 'I'm not feeling terribly well.'

'But you've eaten nothing,' I said.

'I'm beginning to feel queasy,' she said.

Then I realized that I wasn't feeling exactly right either. I was getting dizzy and I had a pain in my chest.

'I'm going to bed,' she said.

'You don't want the food?' I asked.

'Eat yours if you wish. Just throw mine in the bin,' she said.

I looked at the two plates. As I say, I wasn't entirely convinced Dahl knew what he was doing. They'd probably just have made her a bit ill and more on her guard. Perhaps it was as well things had turned out as they had.

I binned them and followed her to the bedroom. Once we were over this winter flu, or whatever it was, there would be other chances. I wasn't giving up that easily. She'd be dead before she knew it.

## Part 3 Authors' Tragic Death
## (*Daily Telegraph*, bottom of page 7)

Julia and Adam Leech, who died recently from carbon monoxide poisoning, were better known by their joint pen name, Julia Adam. They collaborated for many years on the popular Inspector Dumas series, which was twice shortlisted for the CWA Gold Dagger. Though there was a thorough police investigation into the circumstances of their deaths, yesterday's inquest confirmed the cause as misadventure. Their plumber gave evidence that he had been waiting for Mr and Mrs Leech to arrange a date for their boiler service, but they had clearly been busy with other things. A Fire Brigade spokesman added afterwards that it was vitally important that people serviced their boilers regularly and installed a carbon monoxide monitor in their kitchen. The Leeches' agent, George Green, commented: 'Amid the tragedy of their deaths, there is one great consolation – this devoted couple, whom one could not imagine apart, passed away together. It was, in a way, exactly as they both would have wished.'

# ANDREW TAYLOR – DEAD GROUND

'Shit,' I said.

The phone was buzzing in the living room. I pushed the laptop aside and went to answer it. I could hear bath-water running upstairs. It was the kids' bedtime.

'Sam?'

I didn't recognize the voice or the number on the display. 'Who's this?'

'Dave.'

'Dave . . .?'

'*Dave*. You know – from school? Davy Mac.'

For a moment I couldn't think of anything to say. Davy Mac – that's what we used to call him. It must have been fifteen years or more since we had talked, and that was at Charlie's funeral. The last thing I wanted to do was talk to Davy Mac from school. I had a work email to finish, and I hadn't even begun to make supper. 'Oh – hi,' I managed. 'How did you get my number?'

'Your mother,' he said.

'You went to see my mother?' Surprise made me blunt. 'Is she OK?'

'Yes . . . well you know, nothing's changed. I thought she'd have your number – or the people at St Simon's would . . . I think she recognized me. Your mother, I mean. I told her I wanted to organize a reunion. The old gang, twenty-five years on. Except Charlie, of course. Obviously. And maybe Jack.'

'A reunion? When?'

'Well, not exactly a reunion.' Dave sounded flustered. 'I suppose we could have one, but that's not why I wanted to call. The thing is . . . they've found it.'

'Found what?'

'You know.'

At last I realized what he was trying to tell me. 'Oh. I see.'

'There's something in the paper,' he said. 'The *Gazette*, that is. You can google it if you want.'

I said nothing.

'Anyway. I thought you'd want to know.'

He cut the connection.

There had been four of us originally. Now there were only three – Charlie had lost an argument with an articulated lorry on the M25. He'd been the bright one – he had just qualified as a doctor and was working all hours; they thought he'd probably fallen asleep at the wheel, but you never really know, do you?

That left me, Davy Mac and Jack. Jack was said to be in New Zealand or Thailand, though no one knew for sure, and I was in Manchester. Dave was the only one who had stayed. The four of us had been at primary school together and then went to the same comprehensive. We had gradually coalesced into a gang, an offensive and defensive alliance against the world. Naturally we squabbled among ourselves but we needed one another too. I remember thinking our friendship would last for ever. You think all sorts of stupid stuff when you're fifteen.

What made our friendship even better was that our parents and teachers disapproved of it. That year, in fact, we had been forbidden to see each other during the summer holidays because of an episode involving red paint on school property on the last day of term.

In those days the summer holidays seemed to last for ever. We were poised between childhood and adolescence. We were flirting with being Goths, unaware it was no longer a particularly cool thing to be.

We were too young for proper holiday jobs and too old to hang around in one another's homes doing the sort of things we used to do when we were twelve. So we found places where we could hang out together with a packet of cigarettes or a can of cider or even some vodka stolen from our parents. We played at being grown up.

The best place – in other words, the most private – was a triangle of ferns, bushes and trees with a housing estate on one side and a disused quarry on the other. It was dead ground, one of those patches of land with no obvious owner and with no practical use. It had been fenced off because of the risk it would slide into the quarry. There were warning signs around the edge. That was part of the charm of the place. It was dangerous, and for as long as I could remember our parents had forbidden us to go there. So we made a den among the ferns, and that's where we spent half the summer.

Literally. It was exactly halfway through the holidays when we found the body. We never went back after that.

One hundred miles.

Give or take the odd mile, that's the distance between where I lived now and the place I used to call home, the place that used to be both a prison and a refuge. I tried to go back to see my mother once a month, though usually it was nearer six weeks or even two months. A hundred miles is a long way, particularly when there's not a great deal to do at your destination and you don't really want to go there in the first place.

My mother, who was widowed by then, had sold our old house when I left to go to university. She moved into a bungalow, but after her stroke that had to be sold as well to pay for the nursing home fees. As far as I could tell, St Simon's looked after her well enough. She was effectively bedridden. At first she watched a lot of television and listened to audiobooks. She didn't talk much, and when she did it was an obvious effort to frame the words, and they came out in a muddled way.

We tried phone calls and video calls, but she couldn't get the hang of them. She needed me to be there, with her, in that overheated room with the hospital bed and the pictures of her grandchildren on the bedside table. I'd tell her how the kids were doing, and show her more recent photos on my phone. I'd talk about where we were going on holiday and how our jobs were going. She wasn't one of those people who wanted to be reminded about the past. She'd had enough of that. She'd always preferred to dwell on the present and future.

Gradually it got to the point where the few words she spoke dried up, and she was silent, at least when I was there. The staff said she occasionally spoke to them, but only a word or two. Sometimes she muttered, but that was almost worse than silence as the words were indistinguishable.

I went down there on the Friday evening after Dave's phone call. I was due a visit anyway. It was too late to visit my mother so I had booked into a Premier Inn about five miles away. The following morning I drove to St Simon's.

The staff said she was more alert in the mornings after a night's drugged sleep. They hadn't managed to get her out of bed. She was like a very old, very disgruntled doll propped against the pillows. Every time I saw her she seemed to have shrunk a little more.

'I can't stay long, I'm afraid,' I said, as I always did.

We talked about the usual stuff for half an hour. Or rather I did. Then, after a pause, I said: 'I hear you had a visitor the other day – Dave McMahon.'

She stared at me. And swallowed.

'You remember Dave – we used to call him Davy Mac at school. The tall one with big ears. His parents had the hardware shop in Pargeter Street. You could see the back of his house from ours. You remember?'

She murmured something I couldn't make out.

'He phoned me after he'd seen you,' I said, trying to sound casual. 'He's talking of organizing a reunion – did he say? Just a few old school friends. Twenty-five years on, sort of thing.'

My mother grunted.

'We were chatting – it's been a while – and he said there's been a bit of excitement down here.' Did my tone sound as artificial to her as it did to me? 'A sort of murder mystery. Have you heard?'

Her head gave the slightest of shakes. She used to love crime novels and true crime stories.

'Actually they're saying it could be murder but they don't really know. They've found a woman's body, been there a long time, at least twenty years. Apparently there's damage to the skull that could have been caused by a blunt instrument. Or she might have just fallen and hit her head, which is probably much more likely.'

I let her think about that for a moment. She opened her mouth and moistened her lips. Her room was too hot, too airless.

'They found it in that bit of waste ground at the back of Fethering Crescent, where it slopes down to the old quarry. Do you remember? It's been closed off ever since I can remember because of the risk of landslip. You and Dad made me swear never to go in there when I was a kid.'

My mother stirred in the bed. She tried to say something but gave up the attempt almost at once.

'It was a woman who found the body – she was walking her dogs and they ran off. They got through the fence somehow, and she after them. Two little spaniels. There was a picture of them in the paper. They're called Blotto and Twinks. Isn't it amazing what people call their dogs?'

Somewhere in the building, invisible pans were clattering, and I heard a snatch of conversation as two people walked past the door. I wondered what the dogs had seen, what had made them look more closely. Perhaps the whiteness of bone? A few rags? Surely there couldn't have been much more to see after all those years, and the smells must have been long gone.

'The paper said there was nothing in the pockets like a wallet or a phone. But the police can do amazing things these days, can't they? They'll probably identify them sooner or later with DNA or dental records or something.'

There was a tap on the door, and a woman in a pinafore poked her head inside the room. 'Time for our lunch, dear.'

My mother stared blankly at her.

I stood up too quickly. 'I'd better be off then.'

The day we found the body, it was raining. Not hard – more like a gauzy mist than rain. It was only after you'd been out in it for half an hour that you realized how wet you'd become.

The four of us had arranged to meet at the den after lunch. It was Jack's idea – he was the nearest thing we had to a leader. I'd suggested going to the cinema instead but as usual the others backed Jack.

We called it the den, though the word had come to seem a little childish, a word that didn't belong in the vocabulary of four almost adults who drank and smoked and sometimes talked about sex. We had propped up fallen branches around a central sapling to make a sort of tepee which was big enough to take all four of us.

Looking back, it's amazing how idle we were that summer. We had time to be bored. On the day we found the body, everything was as usual. We sat around and smoked. We gossiped about other people. Afterwards, we tried to list a complete alphabet of band names, beginning with Abba and ending (after some debate) with Frank Zappa.

I remember Dave kept interrupting. He'd had a telescope for his birthday and was yearning to boast about his astronomical research. Charlie shut him up at last by pointing out that Uranus was a planet, not a star, and then Jack started laughing about calling a planet after your arsehole and we all joined in, even Dave in the end.

After about an hour Charlie stumbled into the undergrowth, saying he wanted to piss. The whole area was dense, with brambles and ferns, nettles and saplings. You had to go carefully – not just because of the vegetation but also because the ground was pocked with holes. Perhaps they were left over from old mine workings or something. But if you were careful and knew your way you could move about even at this time of year when nature was doing its worst to make the place impassable.

He was gone a long time. In the meantime, Davy Mac brought out his poker dice, and we started a game. After a while, I was aware that Charlie was crashing through the bushes towards us. A moment later he appeared in the opening of the den.

We didn't pay him any attention as he shuffled inside. We were waiting for Jack to throw the dice, and there was one pound fifty in the pot.

Jack threw up his arms. 'Yes! Low flush! Beat that, suckers!'

'Guys,' Charlie said quietly.

No one paid him any attention.

'Hey listen. I found something.'

Davy Mac threw him a glance. 'What?'

'There's someone out there.'

That grabbed our attention. 'Who?' Jack said.

'I don't know. They're lying down.'

'What – sleeping outside?' Davy Mac jeered. 'In this weather?'

Charlie was always pale, but now he seemed almost transparent. 'I couldn't see the face properly. They're not moving.'

I didn't talk much to Charlie after that day, not properly. Obviously, we met at school and talked about things that didn't matter. But we never recaptured the old intimacy, the old easy friendship, the old closeness. I tried to pretend it didn't matter. But it did. Out of the three of them, I'd liked him the best.

After we'd all gone our different ways, I wondered whether what Charlie had seen that day had something to do with him wanting to be a doctor. In my darker moments I also wondered whether it had made him pull out without warning into the path of an articulated lorry on the M25.

Dave wanted to see me. He'd texted me a few days after his phone call, suggesting that the next time I was down to see my mother we should meet for coffee.

Why not, I thought? He suggested the Starbucks in Brett Street. I walked over there when I left the nursing home.

It was Saturday morning and Starbucks was crowded. I was a few minutes early but Dave was already in the queue. He was still tall but his ears no longer seemed so big, presumably because the rest of him had had time to catch up with them. His hair was beginning to recede and he'd put on weight in the wrong places since Charlie's funeral.

When he saw me approaching, his eyes widened but he didn't say hello. He just asked what I wanted and suggested I find an empty table.

He brought the tray over and set it down clumsily on the table, slopping some of his coffee into the saucer. He handed me my flat white.

'Well. Here we are,' he said in a low, urgent voice. 'What are we going to do?'

That was Dave all over, just like the old days when he was Davy Mac. No how are you doing, or it's been a while. Blunt as a sledgehammer. And asking someone else what to do.

'What about?'

'You know.' He jerked his head in the general direction of the dead ground. 'About what's turned up.'

'Nothing,' I said. 'What is there to do?'

'Listen, it must be the same one.' His voice was even lower now, almost a whisper. 'When we saw it, it looked . . . well, fresh. You know?'

I nodded. It was an odd word to choose but I knew what he meant.

'So if we told them, they'd know roughly when it was done, wouldn't they?'

*Them*. The police.

'They won't need us to tell them,' I said, affecting an assurance that came from watching too many episodes of *Silent Witness*. 'Forensics will tell them how long it's been there. It's only a matter of time. A day or two maybe, if they don't already know.'

Dave sipped his coffee. There was sweat on his forehead. Maybe I imagined his sour smell as well.

'I wish Jack was here,' he said.

'Why?' I snapped. 'So *he* could tell you what to do? He was the one who thought we should leave it, remember. So he wouldn't thank you, would he? Even if you could find him. And if you did, he'd just say the same thing.'

I watched Dave sink into his chair as if trying to make himself smaller. He cleared his throat. 'Yeah,' he said. 'I guess you're right. I just worry sometimes.'

'Then don't,' I said. 'How are Sheila and the kids?'

'We didn't have any kids,' he said. 'And Sheila walked out on me.'

Dave was right: the body had looked fresh. I don't remember it smelling either.

When Charlie stumbled back to the den with his story, I'm not sure that Jack believed there really was a dead person. Charlie was obviously upset, so he could see it wasn't some sort of joke. But Charlie was one of those nervy kids – bright as they come, but never quite at ease in his skin; too imaginative for his own good.

'Are you sure it wasn't just something that looked like a body?'

Charlie shook his head. He was on the verge of tears. 'It's a person. And they're dead.'

There was only one way to find out. Jack scrambled out of the den and asked who was coming with him. We all went of course, because we didn't want to lose face. There wasn't really a path. It was just a zigzag that Charlie had trampled through the undergrowth.

'We've never been down here,' Dave said. 'Why did you?'

'No reason,' Charlie said.

I guessed he'd chosen it for precisely that reason: because we never went that way. He'd needed a shit, and he'd wanted to go somewhere he wouldn't be interrupted.

Jack and Charlie struggled down the makeshift path, with Dave and me behind. It sloped diagonally downhill. I realized we must be approaching the place where the fence along the rim of the old quarry met another fence, the one that ran along the lane up to the back of Fethering Crescent. But we didn't get as far as that.

Charlie grabbed Jack's arm, forcing him to stop. Dave and I almost bumped into them. The four of us were very close together.

Immediately in front were the remains of a shed. Its roof and walls were made of rusting corrugated iron, and it was perched above a depression in the ground perhaps ten metres across and a metre or so in depth. I guessed it had once had something to do with the now abandoned quarry on the far side of this patch of dead ground. A clump of hazel grew thickly on a carpet of brambles and nettles.

'Look,' Charlie said in a voice that was much higher than usual, almost as it had been before his voice broke. '*There*.'

The first thing I saw was a long, dark coat spread out like a fan. The collar was turned up but I could see part of a white cheek with a thin streak of blood running down towards the corner of the mouth.

'Oh shit,' Jack said.

'Is he – is he dead?' Dave said.

'How do I know?'

Charlie cleared his throat. 'Shouldn't we check?'

'I guess we should.' For once Jack sounded at a loss.

'I'm not doing it,' Dave said, backing away.

Charlie blundered to one side and vomited noisily. None of us commented.

'Fuck it,' I said. 'I'll do it.'

The others looked at me. Their faces were sheepish and relieved. I'd like to say that I saw respect in their faces as well, but I think they were just glad that someone else had volunteered.

'Are you sure?' Charlie said.

'Of course I'm sure.'

I wanted to take the words back. But it was too late. I couldn't escape paying the price of bravado. I zipped up my jacket and tried to work out the best way to scramble down. I could see the body out of the corner of my eye but I avoided looking directly at it.

My mouth was dry, and I wanted to be sick. I had the sensation that I was rushing into a tunnel from which there was no escape, because the gap between the walls on either side was gradually narrowing towards what was inevitably going to happen.

Slowly, deliberately, I worked my way down the slope, clinging to hazel shoots for support and trying to kick the nettles out of my way. The bramble suckers wrapped around my legs and arms, and the spines hooked themselves into the fabric of my clothes. I almost welcomed them. They delayed the inevitable.

But at last I was there. I crouched down beside the body. It was partly buried in the mass of vegetation. I kept my eyes half closed and deliberately blurred my focus.

The black coat was some sort of waterproof. There were drops of rainwater on it. The coat had a hood, which had fallen forward, obscuring part of the face. I was grateful for that. Small mercies.

Jack called down, 'Is he dead then?'

I looked up at the three of them on the edge of the hole beside the rusting shed. 'I don't know.'

'Feel his mouth and nostrils,' Charlie suggested. 'See if he's breathing.'

'Don't you need a mirror for that?' Dave said. 'See if it goes misty.'

'I haven't got a mirror,' I snarled.

For the first time I looked directly at the face. The bit of cheek I could see was pale and waxy. The blood wasn't fresh – it had crusted and turned to a shade nearer brown than red.

'Maybe he's got a wallet,' Dave suggested. 'You could have a look in his pocket.'

'Or maybe you could fuck off instead.'

I picked up a twig and pushed up the hood an inch or two. Just in front of the ear, there was a shallow indentation about the size of a cricket ball. That's where the blood had come from. Just a trickle. To its right was an eye, partially open.

Just for the look of the thing, I put my hand under the nose. I waited but there was no sensation of moving air from the nostrils. The same with the slightly open mouth. I took a deep breath and touched the skin. It was cold, though the day was warm enough.

Shit, I thought, I'm not old enough to cope with something like this. I looked up at the three of them gawping down at me.

'He's dead,' I said.

Jack scowled. Dave shuffled his feet. Charlie gave a muffled sob.

I scrambled back to join them. Without a word we walked back to the den in single file. There were the dice on the ground, and the little pile of change, and Jack's cigarettes, and the empty lager tin where we collected the butts. They had been robbed of their significance. They were trivial and worthless.

Jack looked at us. 'We've got to figure out a plan.'

'Are we going to the police?' Dave said timidly.

'I can't. If my dad finds out . . .'

Jack didn't need to go on. He was meant to be minding his younger siblings. His father was free with his fists, and I'd seen his handiwork on Jack more than once.

'I've been grounded since they found the vodka,' I said. 'Anyway, they made me swear not to come here. Ever.'

Dave and Charlie looked at each other. Charlie said, 'I'm meant to be studying for the scholarship exam.' He swallowed. 'They'd kill me if they knew I'd been here. You know what they're like.'

'An anonymous phone call?' Jack made a face. 'Trouble is, with our luck they'd probably find out it was us. I can't risk it.'

The three of us looked at Dave, who looked at his feet. The tips of his ears were red. 'I can't do it on my own,' he muttered. 'It's not fair. Couldn't we . . . just not say anything? It wouldn't really matter, would it? Someone else will report it soon enough.'

'Yeah,' I said. 'You could be right.'

Dave flashed me a look of gratitude.

'OK,' Jack said. 'That makes sense, I guess. It's best just to forget this. Everything.' When he spoke, we all knew the decision had been made. He scooped up his cigarettes. 'Anyway, I'd better be off now. But we'd better clear up first.'

We didn't speak while we tore apart the den we had built. We stuffed our litter in a carrier bag. In ten minutes' time there was nothing left of us in the dead ground. We never went back. We might never have gone there at all.

On the day we found the body, there was no one at home when I got back. My mother worked as a nurse, and she was on a twelve-hour nightshift. Dad's car was gone – he was a car salesman at a dealership on the bypass and worked all hours. Even when he wasn't at work, he spent many of his evenings in the next town, where there was a theatre of sorts. He was keen on amateur dramatics.

Later, after he'd died, my mother told me in an unguarded moment that they would have divorced if it hadn't been for me. I think it would have been better if they had. I used to dote on my dad, probably because he was so rarely there. But when I was older I despised him. When I knew what he was like.

Anyway, when I got home that day, I turned on the TV and sat on the sofa with a jumbo bag of crisps. I was still there when my mother got back from work at six thirty.

'You could have emptied the dishwasher,' she said.

'Sorry,' I said. 'Didn't have time.'

I went to see my mother the following Saturday – much sooner than I had expected. That was because I'd had a phone call from St Simon's to say they thought it wouldn't be long now.

Luckily she was in no pain. I sat beside the bed and held her hand. I hoped she knew I was here. She must have sat beside a lot of deathbeds in her time. Despite everything that had gone wrong between them, she'd nursed my father in his last illness. I was away at university when he died at the age of fifty-six.

The room seemed hotter and more airless than before. I talked to her in case she was still aware of her surroundings. I tried to reassure her that I was all right, and so were her grandchildren, and that we cared about her and were grateful for what she had done for us. We had never been a demonstrative family and the words didn't come easily. But I tried.

'That other thing,' I said, almost in a whisper. 'The body they found in the dead ground near the quarry. They say it's a woman.

But they haven't identified her yet. They haven't said it was murder either.'

My mother's hand was warm in mine. It twitched.

'Nothing to worry about,' I said. 'It's all right.'

I kissed her when I left. I couldn't remember when I'd last kissed her.

At seven o'clock the following morning, my mobile rang. It was St Simon's.

'I'm so sorry,' the woman's voice said. 'Mum slipped away in the night.'

She wasn't your mum, I thought, she was mine.

It happened like this.

My mother was on nights all that week. Two days before we found the body, I got back before her. I'd spent the night at Charlie's, not that his parents knew. My mother knew I was having a sleepover with a friend but didn't ask questions.

When she came in she poked her head in the living room and found me eating cereal from the packet in front of the telly. 'Did you see your dad before he left?'

'He wasn't here when I got back,' I said.

'He must have gone into work early,' she said, but then she went upstairs.

My mother had died in the early hours of Sunday morning.

There was nothing practical I could do until Monday. Besides, I felt I needed a day at home to process it all. To be with my own family in my own home.

I was in the middle of a wildly competitive board game about dinosaurs when the doorbell rang. I found Davy Mac on the doorstep, his collar turned up against the rain.

'Hi,' he said as if it was the most normal thing in the world for him to turn up at my house.

'What are you doing here?' I said.

'I'm sorry about your mother.'

'Yeah – thanks. But . . . how did you know where I live?'

'It was in your mum's address book. Can we go somewhere? The café round the corner, maybe. I noticed it's open.'

By now I'd had time to wonder how he knew about my mother's

death. And to wonder why he'd been prying in her address book. 'I don't understand. How did you know she died?'

'I called St Simon's this morning. Just to see how she was. I've been giving them a ring most days.'

That was weird in itself but I let it go for now. 'Anyway why are you here now?'

He lowered his voice. 'It's about that body. You know. Let's go and have coffee.'

We looked at each other for a moment. Old certainties crumbled to dust. I called upstairs. 'Kids, I've got to go out.'

'But *Mum*! It's your turn!'

'Go and find Dad. I won't be long.'

'But it's not *fair*, Mum!'

I changed my shoes, took my coat and umbrella from the hook and followed Dave into the rain. We walked in silence to the café. I sat down at a table in the window. He went up to the counter and ordered, without asking what I wanted. He brought the cups back and set them down, slopping the coffee into the saucers just as he'd done before.

'One flat white,' he said with pride, as if he was hoping for a speech of thanks. 'No sugar. Just as you like it.'

I ignored that. 'Well?'

'I always fancied you,' he said.

'You *what*?'

'When we were at school, I mean. I suppose we all did. You were so cool.' The tops of his ears reddened, just as they did when we were kids. 'I used to watch you. You weren't like the other girls.'

'Why are you telling me all this?' I asked, stirring the coffee so I didn't have to look at him.

'You know we could see each other's houses at the back?'

I nodded.

'I used to watch you at home sometimes. Through the telescope. Quite often actually.'

'That's creepy,' I said. 'Really creepy.'

'I know. I'm sorry.' Dave sounded sincere. 'Looking back, I think I was obsessed. I was jealous, too. I thought you might be doing it with Charlie. But the thing is, I saw you. I saw you that morning because I was watching. You and your mum came out with something wrapped in a blanket. Something big and heavy. And you put it in the boot of her car. Then you both got in and you drove off. Two days later, Charlie found the body.'

'So? I can't remember any of this. I expect we were going to the dump or something.'

He let the silence lengthen. Then: 'The police issued a statement yesterday. It was on the local news. Did you see it?'

I didn't answer.

'That body,' he said. 'It was a woman. You were the only one of us who saw it up close. You said it was a man.'

I shrugged. 'Because it looked like a man.'

'But they haven't identified her yet. Nothing in her pockets or anything. Maybe there'll be dental records. You know. Or DNA. Or someone will remember something.'

I sipped my coffee. I glanced at my watch. 'OK. Thanks for telling me all this but I'd better get home now. I'm meant to be cooking lunch.'

'Just a moment.' He smiled at me. 'Your life's perfect, isn't it? Nice house. Kids. I bet your husband's got a good job.'

I pushed back my chair. It scraped across the floor. 'I really must be off.'

'One thing more.' Davy Mac reached across the table and wrapped a paw-like hand around my wrist. 'The thing is, I saw your dad too. You know he had a bit of a reputation? Everyone said he put it about. You know – played away from home. But this time he played *at* home, didn't he? I saw him, you see. He came back the evening before with a woman. He must have thought it was safe – your mum was on nights and you were staying with someone. Charlie, was it? So the house was empty. Remember?'

I remembered all right.

'They didn't even close the curtains, not at first, not at the back. And in the morning he left before you turned up. But she was still there. I saw her. I was watching, you see, waiting for you to come back. She opened the curtains in your parents' room. I wonder if she overslept? Then I saw you come home. Just after I saw her.'

He released my wrist and sat back. He smiled at me.

'Either your mum did it or you did,' he said. 'I'd put my

money on you. Not that it matters, really. And afterwards you both cleared up the mess. Must have made it easier, her being a nurse.'

'What do you want?' I said.

'Nothing much,' he said. 'Same as always, really. I want you, Sam. I want you.'

# ANN CLEEVES – SLEEPING BEAUTY

I signed up to the Tarset Players as a last resort. I was depressed but not so low that I didn't realize something had to change. Gerry had been very persuasive. He was my only neighbour and he'd been very kind to me over the past year. He was single too but divorced and we'd become friends of a kind. He was a great listener, and sometimes I had to stop myself pouring out all the details of Val's illness and death.

I'd been lonely for months but still it took an effort to plaster a smile on to my face and walk into the Holly Bush. Val and I used to go there every now and again. It's a small room. A couple of scrubbed pine tables and a range fire, with Marie behind the bar pulling pints. I wondered if she'd recognize me, but I'd lost a lot of weight and it had been a while.

I knew some of *them*. They were all sitting round the same table. At the other there were just two old gents playing dominos. Not speaking. There was a lot of noise from the Tarset Players though. The sound hit me as I walked into the pub, and I nearly went straight out.

Christine the vicar had the loudest voice. A tall angular woman with teeth too big for her mouth. I'd called her horsey once and Val had said that was unkind. Gwen Robson from the post office in Bellingham sat in the only comfortable chair. Flame red hair. Val had said she was fifty if she was a day and some of the colour must come from a bottle. I'd said *that* was unkind. Gwen could have been a model for those nineteen-fifties seaside post-cards. You know the ones: a buxom lass, head flung back and laughing, some off-colour joke printed in bold type underneath. Gwen was laughing now, but it sounded a bit forced, as if she didn't quite fit in.

A young couple I didn't know squashed together on the bench, although there was plenty of room for them to spread out. And

Gerry was standing with a couple of pints in his hand. I'd phoned him earlier in the day to say that I'd be there.

'Cuddy Milburn,' he said. He set one of the pints on the table in front of me. 'You timed it just right bonny lad.'

Gerry worked for what used to be called the Forestry Commission. It's probably been privatized now. Nearly everything is. He didn't manage the commercial forestry but was some kind of ranger. A wildlife expert. He could tell the different birds in the woods just by their calls. He was one of those wiry, older men, who can walk for miles without any sign of tiredness. Indefatigable in his social life too, he seemed to be on every committee in Tarset. Everyone knew him.

He lived in a cottage with a badger sett in the garden and even now in the pub he had a pair of binoculars strung around his neck. He often went away on wildlife expeditions to exotic countries. I asked once how he could afford the trips on a ranger's salary, but he explained that he was tour leader and he actually got paid for his travel. I thought I'd been in the wrong career all my working life.

I resigned from my job in Newcastle after Covid and Val took early retirement from the school where she'd been teaching for more than twenty years. We bought a rambling stone house at the end of the track, where the moorland meets the forest. It was a kind of dream, and we wouldn't have had the nerve to do it if the world hadn't changed with lockdown. It needed a lot doing, but I'd always been practical. I was used to fixing things. I couldn't fix Val though, when the cancer took hold, despite all my internet research, and shouting at the doctors that there must be something they could do. She died at home in the spring, when the first primroses were on the grassy bank by the burn and lambing had just started. It was April. They lamb late here in the hills.

We bought the house, imagining grandchildren damming the burn and climbing the trees. But Duncan moved to Malta with his kids for work, Sylvie lived in London more focused on her career than starting a family, and I was on my own, rattling around the place. I'd see the lasses behind the till in Bellingham Co-op once a week when I went shopping, and sometimes Gerry came in on Saturday evenings for a beer and to watch *Match of the Day*, once the footie started again. Most days I forced myself out for a walk to keep fit, but even that was starting to feel too much, and I was usually home alone, staring at the wall, as the garden, which Val had planned, grew up around me.

Gerry told me about the Players. 'You should join! The panto is always fun, and it'll get you out of the house.'

'I can't prance about on a stage!' The thought of it was enough to make me feel faint, to curl up in a ball to shut out the world.

'But you could make the sets and do the lighting.' A pause. 'They all want to be bloody stars, but nobody wants to do the backroom stuff.' He gave me one of his grins. 'I'm always the dame. I love a bit of prancing.'

And so there I was, in the Holly Bush, overwhelmed by the noise and the heat, listening to plans for the Tarset Players' latest performance, and wishing I'd stayed at home. Marie left the bar in charge of a young lad with film star good looks, who looked hardly old enough to drink, and she joined us.

Christine had written the script. Apparently, she always did, worried perhaps about smutty gags. This year it would be *Sleeping Beauty*. I thought again about my garden, the forest seeming to encroach closer to the house every day, the light fading. When Val died, she'd looked as if she was sleeping.

Christine looked across the table at me. 'Cuddy, a good Northumberland name. Cuthbert, I presume. Like the saint.'

I didn't like to tell her that I was conceived on Holy Island, before my atheist parents were married, that I'd hated the name Cuthbert since I was old enough to be mocked by school friends, that I'd always gone by Cuddy.

'Like the ducks,' I said. On Holy Island, where the saint had lived almost as a hermit, they call eiders cuddy ducks.

She smiled, her lips pulled back over her teeth, looking more like a horse than ever. I drank my pint, then moved on to Coke because I was driving. The rest of them stuck with alcohol, and I wasn't sure how any of them would get home. I've noticed that the drink drive laws seem to operate differently in the country. In the past, that might have made me angry, but nothing mattered now.

They'd all read the script and were talking about casting. I wasn't sure why I had to be there, though occasionally they would ask me a question. The performance was to be held in the village hall, and I'd need to see what tech they had before I could answer. Christine gave me a copy of the script and I marked the pages where they had queries.

The meeting broke up at ten and Marie went back behind the bar. I'm not sure what had been achieved. The young lass on the bench had been cast as the beauty, though I thought that Gwen would love the role. I offered Gerry a lift home.

'I can pick you up in the morning to get your car.'

He'd been drinking steadily all evening. I wouldn't have wanted an accident on my conscience.

He just winked. 'Thanks very much old chap, but I've got other plans.'

He and Gwen were sitting together at the bar, chatting to Marie when I left. I wondered which of the women he had his eye on. I'd picked up in the village that he had a reputation as a ladies' man, charming and sympathetic.

Rehearsals in the village hall became part of my weekly routine. I wouldn't stay all evening, but Christine seemed pleased with the sets I'd designed, and I managed as best as I could to sort out the sound and the lighting. Gerry had been right. The change was good for me, and the Players' appreciation was cheering. Some nights I'd go with them to the Holly Bush for a quick pint afterwards, but usually I'd head straight home.

The night of the dress rehearsal, it was so cold that the air had that winter smell of ice and iron. It was almost a year since Val had been given her diagnosis and I just wanted to go home to remember her, but everyone else was in high spirits and I said I'd go with them for one drink. The cast paraded into the Holly Bush still in full costume and makeup and the other customers – even the silent domino players – cheered. Marie was principal boy, dressed in tights and knee length boots, and looked remarkably fetching. Gwen was in a floaty frock with wings and a wand as the fairy godmother. She must have been freezing, and Christine, who was director and stage manager and prompt as well as writer, gave her a coat. And Gerry was got up as the dame, with a wig and false eyelashes and a ridiculous dress.

I offered him a lift home later as I often did. Usually he

accepted, but as on that first night, he just winked, and said he had other plans.

His body was found the next day by a shepherd on a quad bike. Gerry's car had slewed to one side of the track, but *he* seemed to have been tipped out, and the body was lying on a mossy bank under the trees. Billy, the shepherd, knocked on my door and asked to use the landline – mobile reception is non-existent in that part of the valley. He was so shocked that he could hardly speak, and I followed him out to wait with him for the emergency services. I couldn't make out quite what had happened. The track was slippery with ice, but even drunk, Gerry couldn't have been driving fast enough to be thrown from the car. He never wore a seat belt though. He was one of those people who thought the rules didn't apply to him, so perhaps it *was* a freak accident. I thought I'd miss our Saturday nights in front of the television.

There'd been a flurry of snow in the night and Gerry's body was scattered with white diamante flakes. He was still wearing the dress, but the wig had fallen to one side, and the effect was much less ridiculous than in the Holly Bush the night before. As soon as I heard the sirens on the main road, I left Billy to it. I had no desire to meet any of the professionals who'd have to deal with this death. It was the anniversary of Val's diagnosis, and I had my own mourning to do.

Despite myself, I couldn't help being curious, and the following day I went to the Co-op, the best place for gossip in the whole of the North Tyne. Everyone was talking about Gerry; about what fun he'd been and how he'd be missed. The police had put his death down as an accident – there'd been a lot of alcohol in his blood, the road was icy, and he'd not been wearing a seat belt. I could understand the assumption, but I'd worked as a senior detective in the city's serious crime squad, and I couldn't quite make the facts fit the theory.

It was none of my business of course, but I had Gerry's spare key in case of emergencies, and I thought it would be neighbourly to check out his cottage. The freezing weather might have caused leaks. The house had once been a gamekeeper's lodge, built for a grand estate before the land was taken over by the forest. It was surrounded by trees and the only access was down a narrow path. The architecture was unusual for this part of the county; it was built of red brick with a steep roof and a dormer window. There were mullioned windows, and it could have come straight from a child's picture book. I imagined it as the witch's house from *Hansel and Gretel* – that story had always given Sylvie nightmares – and shivered a little before I let myself in through the kitchen door.

The house wasn't cold inside though. Gerry must have left the oil central heating on low. I'd been into the house, but not very often and then only into the kitchen to drink a mug of bad coffee. He'd not invited me any further into the place. I'm not usually an imaginative man and I'm not sure what had triggered that moment of dread. What had I been expecting? Some kind of horror? The skeleton of a woman lying on the spare room bed?

I'd done some research, you see, and Gerry wasn't divorced. He hadn't even been married. Neither had he led any natural history tours to the places he'd claimed to have visited, despite his photos of elephant and tiger.

There was nothing out of place in the living room. It was a comfortable space with a log burner and attractive art on the walls. Gerry had been a man of more sophisticated tastes than I'd realized. Upstairs there were two bedrooms. The larger had a double bed, the duvet neatly folded back, and a wardrobe full of his clothes. There were a couple of suits, which surprised me, and a dinner jacket. I'd never seen him in anything so formal. The second room had been kitted out as an office. I knew that he worked from home, so there was nothing surprising about that. All the same, I spent a considerable time there, sitting at his desk, looking out over the frozen trees. His laptop wasn't password protected, which was an error, but I'm sure he never expected anyone to come snooping. He hadn't expected to die.

A week later, I had a call from Christine. The Tarset Players had cancelled the pantomime of course, but they were going to meet up in the Holly Bush to remember Gerry. They thought I might like to be there.

The cast was in the pub before me. It was much like that first planning meeting, although the young couple was absent. I'm sure they had better things to do with their time, or perhaps they hadn't been invited. They'd never really been part of the group. The others were sitting at the long table and they'd already starting drinking. Christine got to her feet.

'Cuddy, I'll get you a pint.'

If I'd been expecting a sombre atmosphere, I was mistaken. This felt more like a party. Marie and Gwen were sharing a bottle of Prosecco. Christine must have sensed my surprise.

'We decided that Gerry wouldn't have wanted this to be a gloomy occasion. We're celebrating his life, after all.'

I took the pint. I thought tonight I would get Ron of Tarset Taxis to drive me home. I could do with a few drinks. It was a weekday, and the weather was bad and nobody else was in the bar. Ron wouldn't be busy. Marie was sitting with the others. I found myself at the head of the table, furthest away from the fire. For a moment I felt as I had when I'd been leading the final briefing at the end of a murder investigation.

Carefully, I banged my glass on the table. This was good beer and not to be spilled.

'When did you all decide that Gerry had to die?'

There was a moment of silence. They stared at me as if I was mad, but I continued.

'I do know that he was blackmailing you all. I've found the evidence. He kept a record of the payments. They were beautifully judged so you could just afford them, but they must have added up over the years. And you all thought you were the only ones to be targeted. Until the night of the dress rehearsal, when one of you must have shared your secret.'

*Gerry had kept a record of all the luxury cruises to exotic places. And the photographic safaris. Gerry hadn't pretended about his passion for wildlife. But the travel hadn't come cheap.*

Still, nobody spoke.

'He was a good listener, wasn't he? We all thought he was such a good friend. But really, he wanted you to confess your sins and to share your gossip, so he could put the facts together and squeeze you dry.' I turned to Christine. 'I know what he had on you.'

She straightened her back. 'I had a life before I became a priest.'

'As an accountant who defrauded her clients.'

'I didn't mean to.' Christine paused. 'I became overwhelmed with the work. It was a kind of paralysis. I couldn't face the chaos, so I ignored it. The court understood and I received a non-custodial sentence.'

I knew that was true. Something else I'd checked. 'Of course, your parishioners might not have been so understanding. Some of your clients lost their life savings.'

'It was a relief to tell someone, and he was so easy to talk to.' She looked up at me. 'I played no part in killing him. I went back to the vicarage before it happened.'

'But you knew what the others were planning, and you didn't tell the police. You didn't stop it.'

She didn't answer, and I turned my attention to Marie. 'You were having an affair with your very young barman. Not illegal of course, but your husband might not have been very forgiving.' Marie's husband worked on the North Sea rigs and was away for weeks at a time. 'I thought Gerry was flirting with you, but he was only interested in your confidences. Sucking them out of you, like a leech.'

Still, she remained silent, but I could tell that I'd been right.

Flame-haired Gwen spoke then. 'I thought I loved him once. I was very young.'

'What did he have on you?' Christine asked. 'You never told us, even on the night that he died.'

'I was wild in those days. A country girl in the city trying to make ends meet. He was a student. Ecology at Newcastle Uni. He gave me stuff to make me feel better about myself.' She stared across the table at us all. 'I ended up dealing for him. He left the city with a degree, and I was left as an addict.' A pause. 'It took me years to sort myself out. And then he turned up here, reminding me of my past. Making me pay for the damage *he'd* caused.'

The room fell silent, and they all looked at me.

Christine was the one to speak. 'What will you do? Will you tell the police?'

I shook my head. 'That's a decision for you, not for me. You have to judge if you can live with what you've done.'

I left them then and drove home, not needing the taxi. I didn't want to know the details: how the secrets had spilled out and how Gwen and Marie had killed Gerry to make the murder look like an accident. After all, who was I to judge? I'd done what Val had asked and helped her to die with a little dignity on the day in April when the spring sunshine cast shadows on to her bed.

How close I'd come to confessing to Gerry. How easy it would have been then, to join the Players and commit cold-blooded murder myself.

# PETER LOVESEY – JUST A MINUTE

Peter Lovesey writes: *I grew up listening to the 'wireless', everything from Tommy Handley to Lord Haw-Haw. During the war years the BBC was as omnipresent in our home as blinds for the blackout. When peace returned and more staff and resources became available, the General Forces Programme morphed into the Light Programme, pledged to entertain. Numerous game shows aired and among these was* One Minute, Please*, which was rejigged and relaunched in 1967 for Radio 2 as* Just a Minute *and is still running. The first producer to work with the streamlined version was David Hatch and the second was Simon, whose groundbreaking radio career as producer and writer cries out to be celebrated along with his crime writing. He was in at the beginning of* I'm Sorry, I Haven't a Clue. *With David Hatch, he started* Week Ending*, which became the longest running audience comedy show. He directed the first six episodes of* Lord Peter Wimsey*, which incidentally inspired him to become a crime writer. He created more than a hundred scripts of* Frank Muir Goes Into . . . *He wrote the much-loved* After Henry. *And it was Simon who spotted the talent of Douglas Adams and invited him to write a science fiction series for radio and then persuaded the fusty old BBC to broadcast the outrageous* Hitchhiker's Guide to the Galaxy. *Listeners like me have enjoyed more hours of entertainment created or initiated by Simon than we can possibly calculate. The story that follows bears no relation to Simon except that the title is my way of thanking him for his innovative career in radio.*

The governor said, 'Is he ready to tell us where the bodies are? Is that what you're saying?'

The chaplain rubbed his chin. He didn't like being put on the spot.

'Honestly now.'

Neither did he like his honesty being brought into it, but he was on a mission, so he swallowed hard and said, 'That's my belief, Governor.'

Now it was the governor who was uneasy. 'I'm going to take some convincing. People have tried with him for almost twenty years and got nowhere. The police, psychiatrists, padres like yourself.'

'Kilroy is not a religious man.'

'Not many of them are, more's the pity.'

'Which is why I looked for an alternative way of reaching out to him, trying to find something we have in common.'

'Not much, I should think, you a man of God and him a killer.'

'We both listen to radio.'

'Ah.'

'And we both listen regularly to *Just a Minute*.'

The governor couldn't see the connection. 'I know the show, of course. I wouldn't say I'm a fan, but it's sometimes on of an evening when I'm preparing my supper.'

'Well, I make a point of tuning in at 6.30 every Monday.'

'So that's how he talked you into this. Are you sure the boot isn't on the other foot and he looked for a way to reach out to you?'

The chaplain reddened. 'It wasn't like that at all, Governor. The show is quite an obsession with him. He used to play it with his former cellmate, the Chinese fellow known to the prisoners as Left-wing Lo. When Lo was released last year, Kilroy was quite bereft.'

'Lo? I'm trying to place him. A Communist?'

'No.' The chaplain laughed. 'He had a slight deformity. You know how cruel nicknames can be. Actually, he was popular and rather gifted mechanically. Made and repaired radios in the workshop. After his release he went straight back to his old job in the nickel-plating industry. But I was telling you about Kilroy. He still listens to *Just a Minute* and reckons he can spot the repetitions before any of the players do. And he practises speaking for a minute and claims to be very good at it.'

'It's a way of passing the time, I suppose,' the governor said. 'We should be grateful he isn't thinking up escape plans.'

'He'd like to play the game himself, but it can't be done alone. He needs someone to suggest a topic and then stop him each time he deviates, hesitates or repeats something.'

'I'm aware of the rules. My worry is that he could be playing games with you – in another sense.'

'There is something else, Governor. Kilroy isn't well.'

'His heart. I know that.'

'The doctor told me in confidence that he may not even see the year out. This "Just a Minute" project could be a last request.'

Still unconvinced, the governor said with more sarcasm than sympathy, 'And our last chance to get the truth about the two people he murdered twenty years ago. Is that the deal?'

Lack of pity wasn't stopping the chaplain. 'Something like that. I know the victims' family want closure. They'd like to give their parents a Christian burial. I've told Kilroy that. Asked him to find some sympathy in his troubled soul.'

'He's heard that before and ignored it.'

'But this time he said something rather enigmatic.'

'Oh?'

'He wouldn't mind clearing the decks before his ship comes home.' The chaplain's eyes moistened.

The governor's eyes stayed stubbornly dry. 'He's stringing you along, Padre.'

'I'm not sure of that. I see this as a God-given opportunity. If we indulge him and play the game as he requests, he'll be in a cooperative state of mind.'

'I can't imagine it.'

'He wants us to join in. And he wants you to act as chairman.'

'God forbid.'

'With respect, Governor, the Lord might approve if it's the way to unlock this door Kilroy has kept shut for so long.'

'What difference does it make if I join in?'

The chaplain leaned forward in his chair in the way he leaned forward in the pulpit at the climax of a sermon. 'You get to choose the subjects.'

'Ah.' There was a glimmer of interest.

'He's ready to speak for a minute about anything and he wants it to be a fair test.'

'So, if I ask him to speak on where the bodies are, he'll tell us?'

'That's the general idea. We may have to frame it less obviously, like, er . . .'

'Spilling the beans?'

The chaplain didn't think much of the suggestion, but he managed a nod. 'Isn't it worth a try?'

'And what if someone interrupts before he gets to the point? There are usually other players in this game and they have buzzers.'

'I'll be the only other player. I won't interrupt unless he deviates.'

'And if his explanation takes more than a minute? Doesn't someone blow a whistle?'

'That will be your job.'

'But you said I'm chairman, not the whistleblower.'

'We're shorthanded. We need to double up. You're also the timekeeper. You can give him as long as he needs.'

'And blow the whistle when we've heard it all? It's asking a lot of me. And I don't possess a whistle.'

'That's not a problem in this place. Every prison officer has a whistle.'

'The buzzers?'

'Will be provided by his brother George. George is a techie, I'm told. Making a couple of shiny new buzzers is child's play for him.'

'It seems you and Kilroy have planned this in detail already.'

'He's set his heart on making it work.'

'I hope his heart holds out in all the excitement. Where do you propose to stage this performance? Not in my office, I trust?'

'No, no. I was thinking – if you don't object' – the chaplain cleared his throat – 'we might use the, er, spare room at the end of Block C.'

The governor shuddered. 'The old execution shed?'

'It's been empty ever since the death penalty was abolished. I can get it scrubbed and dusted and dress it up to look like a sound studio.'

'Pardon me, but this isn't worthy of you. We can't play games in an execution chamber. It's grotesque.'

'Some might say that leaving it untouched for so long is grotesque.'

A fair point. The governor shifted his argument. 'It's a parlour game, for heaven's sake. We don't need to pretend we're the BBC.'

'I'm sure it will be worth the extra effort, Governor. The right ambience is conducive to truth-telling, as any psychiatrist will tell you.'

'The execution shed?'

'Transformed beyond recognition.'

The governor took a moment to reflect. 'I've racked my brain for years to think of a decent use for that room.'

'I can take this on,' the chaplain added. 'I'm familiar with the inside of a BBC studio. I've done "Thought for the Day".'

The governor was still grappling with the extraordinary suggestion.

The chaplain said, 'I can furnish it at minimal expense. It will just be a mock-up, of course. Tables from the canteen, cardboard boxes painted up to look like audio equipment, that sort of thing.'

There was no response.

'And inside one of the boxes we can have a real tape recorder running and pick up every word he says.'

The governor shook his head. 'That's deception. We don't do things that way. It wouldn't hold up in court.'

The chaplain blushed. 'Very well. Let's forget the tape recorder.'

'I'm getting rather drawn to this, but only if we play fair with the man. You'll organize it yourself, you say?'

'I could enlist the help of one of the inmates. Biggins in Block A is a scene-painter by trade. And if you don't mind acting as chairman, that would really put the cap on it.'

The governor had never revealed much about his private life, and certainly not his membership of The Fair Players, an amateur dramatics society. His Gravedigger in the festival production of *Hamlet* had not gone unremarked by the theatre critic of the Middlesex Chronicle. '*The accidental loss of a vital prop, Yorick's skull, was the only moment of real tension in the evening, requiring improvisation that would tax any actors, let alone this amateur company. All credit to Cedric Hodgkinson as the Gravedigger for resourcefully removing his boot and using that instead.*' After praise like that, he knew he could play a convincing game-show chairman. He gave a shrug. 'All right, Padre. I don't have much confidence, but let's try it.'

You wouldn't have known the previous purpose of the room. It had been transformed and no detail overlooked. As the governor approached, a box above the door to the gallows lit up with the words ON AIR, an irony that must have passed the chaplain by. The bare walls and ceiling were now coated with soundproofing made from bubble wrap. Beige carpeting had been laid over the trapdoors. A broadcasting desk and audio console were in place where the condemned man had once been positioned. A studio microphone that was basically a packet of tea hung from the crossbeam.

'Amazing,' the governor said. 'Is it really just cardboard painted to look realistic?'

'Most of it,' the chaplain said. 'The mixer console once held tins of baked beans. The faders are cut-outs from the lids and they really do move if you want to try them. The processors are cornflakes packets. Only the headphones are real because we happened to have some sets here.'

'Has Kilroy seen it?'

'Not yet.'

'He'll be touched by all the efforts you've made.'

'Surprised, maybe. Pleased, even. Touched, I think not. If Kilroy has a tender side, it's well concealed. But I wasn't alone. Biggins did a lot. And Kilroy's brother George made the beautiful shiny buzzers. I collected them from him in the park this morning.'

'You don't say. What's he like?'

'I can't tell you much. It was cloak and dagger stuff. He was in dark glasses and a beanie hat and wearing an anti-Covid mask. Well, I think that's what it was. He also had a stoop that I think he was putting on for my benefit. He said very little. I gather he wants no credit and won't take any money for the materials. If you look closely, he's inscribed Kilroy's initials on one and a C for chaplain on mine. They have batteries inside.' He stepped to the desk and demonstrated. The sound was just like the real thing.

'Nice.'

'Yes, and between ourselves, I suspect he made them at work using parts paid for by his employer.'

'I think we can turn a blind eye considering he hasn't charged us anything. His secret is safe with me.'

'And me. Did you bring your script, Governor?'

'Committed to memory.' The governor added coyly, 'Did I ever mention that I've trodden the boards?'

'You didn't. What a bonus.'

'I'm ready. Shall we fetch him in?'

Jake Kilroy was a hard man who had lived off the proceeds of crime for the whole of his life. Apart from some short, sharp shocks in his youth, he had eluded the police until his retirement, largely by being security-minded. Soon after moving into a large house in leafy Worcester Park, he had murdered two elderly neighbours because he had thought they were spying on him. He was caught on CCTV gunning them down on their doorstep. Their bodies had never been found.

When he was brought into the revamped execution shed, he gazed in wonder at the chaplain's creation. His scarred, sullen features softened into a faint smile.

'What do you think?' the governor asked him.

'Not bad.' Praise didn't come higher from Kilroy.

'Let's make a start, then. I have the cards with the subjects.'

Kilroy raised a restraining hand. 'Don't tell me. I want to do this proper.'

'And we shall.'

They took their places on office chairs, the governor behind the main desk, the others facing him. They put on the earphones.

Kilroy said, 'Can't hear nothing.'

'Neither can I,' the governor said.

'They aren't live,' the chaplain said. 'They're just for effect.'

A sensible decision was made to manage without the earphones.

The governor produced the subject cards from his pocket, followed by a stopwatch, a whistle and a small cassette recorder.

'Whassat?' Kilroy asked in an accusing tone.

'Relax. It's for playing, not recording. It's the theme music. We're doing this properly, just as you asked.'

'Better be. I don't want no tricks. Is the door shut?'

'It is and we're ready to go. From now on, you must forget

that I'm the governor. I'll be using your first names and you can refer to me as chairman. Are we ready, gentlemen?'

The chaplain was looking tense. He gave a nod.

Kilroy shrugged.

The governor mouthed the words, 'One, two, three. Action.' Then he said aloud in a carrying voice, 'Welcome to *Just a Minute*!'

He touched the tape recorder. The opening bars of Chopin's piano piece sounded sharp and clear before reducing in volume. 'Hello, my name is Cecil Hodgkinson, and as the Minute Waltz fades away once more it is my pleasure to welcome you to the show that for almost sixty years has charmed and entertained audiences not just up and down the country, but around the world. Tonight, we have two talented and exciting players who in their different ways have made their mark in society. They are the Reverend Sam Parker, who has worked as a clerk in holy orders for many years and is well-practised in speaking for more than a minute, and Jake Kilroy, equally long-serving but in another sphere, a man of fewer words and deeds we need not go into, but much respected by his peers. Would you please welcome them both.'

The governor clapped enthusiastically and nodded to the others to do the same. The chaplain joined in, while Kilroy, stony-faced, kept his hands out of sight.

'This particular edition of *Just a Minute* is coming from a new studio in a location I'm not at liberty to name for reasons of security. As usual, I will ask our contestants to speak for a minute without hesitation, repetition or deviation on a subject I will give them. When the sixty seconds are up, I'll blow my whistle. And I'm going to ask Sam – if I may, Padre – to get us underway.' The governor knew what was on the card, but he cleverly made a show of looking at it. 'Ah, this is right up your street. Confessions. One minute, if you can, on confessions, starting now.' He reached for the stopwatch and pressed it. He was glowing with his achievement. The entire introduction had been delivered without notes.

The chaplain was so slow to start that he should have been buzzed for hesitation before speaking a word. Kilroy must have decided to cut him some slack in this opening round. 'I generally begin with a text and I cannot think of a better one than Proverbs twenty-eight, verse thirteen: "Whoever conceals their sins does not prosper, but the one who confesses and renounces them finds mercy."' He paused and looked hard at Kilroy, who yawned, but didn't press his buzzer for the hesitation. Perhaps he didn't want to take over the subject.

'But I am not here to deliver a sermon,' the chaplain resumed. 'That wouldn't be appropriate in a game like this. I don't feel any holier than anybody else. Sinning is a universal failing. Each Sunday morning in the part of the service known as the General Confession, I admit to my own transgressions and ask for forgiveness and I feel a better man for getting them off my chest. So, I heartily recommend the process of shriving, as it is known. Em, how am I doing, chairman?'

'Hesitating, I would have thought,' the governor said, 'and if I were a player I would have buzzed, but as I'm not, I can inform you, you still have seven seconds left.' He turned to Kilroy. 'It's not for me to tell you how to play the game, Jake. Is your buzzer working?'

Kilroy said, 'Me bruvver made it, so it works, OK?'

'Very well. Seven more seconds, Padre, starting now.'

'Oh, my word. I wasn't expecting –'

The governor blew his whistle. 'Whoever is speaking when the whistle goes gains an extra point. On this occasion, it was Sam Parker, who also gets a point for speaking for a minute without interruption. He interrupted himself, but I think we can overlook that. At the end of that round, he is in the lead with two points. But it's early days, of course. So, we're going to hear from you now, Jake, and the subject on the card is Happy Endings. Can you speak for a minute on Happy Endings, starting now.'

Kilroy was far better at the game than the chaplain. All the hours of practice came into play. He launched immediately into his turn. 'Happy endings is what you get in fairy tales. "And they all lived happily ever after." Most of the dumbos in this place think there's gonna be a happy ending when they serve out their stretch, like their girlfriend will be waiting for them and they get a job straight off. That's horseshit. The woman has moved in with another bloke and no one wants to employ an ex-con. The truth is, there's no such thing as a happy ending.' He stopped.

The chaplain had pressed his buzzer. 'Isn't that deviation? He's not talking about happy endings. He's talking about unhappy endings.'

'A correct challenge,' the governor said. 'Deviation isn't allowed, so you gain another point and the subject passes to you with only twelve seconds remaining. 'Happy Endings, starting now.'

'Oh, er. I'd forgotten I have to take it on. Well now, er, every follower of the true faith can look forward to a happy ending and I advise the members of my flock who may not have much time left in this life to make absolutely certain their conscience is clear before they meet their Maker. It could be just a matter of unburdening themselves of some secret they have nursed for too long. The sense of relief can be a joy. I've seen it myself and I think I'm running out of steam.'

The whistle blew.

'Another point to the padre,' the governor said. 'I may have blown the whistle a few seconds late, I was so impressed by what you were saying, Sam. However, I'm surprised you didn't buzz, Jake. There was definite hesitation when he started. You are familiar with the rules?'

Jake grunted something that may have been an answer.

'Is your buzzer working?'

'Got to be, hasn't it?' Jake said.

'Because your brother made it? He's a mechanic, I understand. Shall we put it to the test?'

'Please yerself.' Jake slid the beautifully crafted device across the desk.

'I've been wanting to give it a try,' the governor said. 'I believe this is how it should be done.' He pressed his thumb down.

The bodies of the governor, the chaplain and an inmate called Kilroy were discovered late the same evening lying on the floor of the old execution shed. The interior had been dressed up bizarrely as if it was a stage set of a radio studio. On the advice of the doctor who first attended the scene, breathing apparatus was issued to everyone who entered, which was a good thing because the victims were later found to have inhaled cyanide. A broken vial of it was found inside a contraption made to look like a buzzer.

A second buzzer, similar in appearance, was harmless. It worked from a battery. The police made extensive enquiries and failed to discover who had provided the buzzers. A prisoner called Biggins thought it may have been Kilroy's brother George, but he was mistaken. The records showed Kilroy had no brother at all, no family other than ex-convicts and most of them kept in touch out of fear. His tentacles reached far outside the prison walls.

In hours of questioning, Biggins admitted he had been asked by the chaplain to build the secret cardboard studio, but he insisted he was ignorant of its purpose and innocent of any serious involvement. The police were forced to conclude he was speaking the truth.

The joint inquest into the three deaths was unable to reach a firm conclusion. A suicide pact was thought to have been unlikely. There were strong suspicions that Kilroy, who had a serious heart condition, had contrived an elaborate plot to kill himself and take the lives of the governor and the chaplain at the same time by smuggling the murderous buzzer into the prison, but nothing could be proved. An open verdict was eventually delivered.

'The fumes of cyanide are lethal,' a toxicologist explained at the inquest. 'They set up a reaction that prevents the body's cells from using oxygen and anyone who inhales it will die quickly. Cyanide is an agent commonly used in gas chamber executions.'

'How would anyone planning a murder acquire it?' the coroner asked.

'It's used in certain industries. Electroplating is the obvious one. You'll have noticed the buzzers were nickel-plated.'

'I see. And you say the victims will have died quickly. How quickly?'

'Difficult to say. There are various factors.'

'But the quickest possible – how long is that?'

'Just a minute.'

# KATE ELLIS – LOOKALIKE

I needed advice. My agent wasn't answering her phone – she rarely does these days – but, by good fortune, I spotted an old acquaintance in the bar. In his time Charles Paris had explored most of the possibilities the acting profession had to offer from voice-overs to corporate videos and rain-soaked open-air performances. He knew a thing or two about the ups and downs of theatrical life.

The least I could do was buy Charles a scotch, then one drink became two and then three, which in my current impecunious state, I could barely afford. But I told myself to look upon it as an investment.

The advice Charles gave after downing his third drink could be summed up in three words. Go for it. Yet I still felt a tingle of uncertainty as I replied to the anonymous email. The payment mentioned was generous for what sounded like a very easy job. After all, I'd imitated Kris Collins in a pantomime two years before so the challenge was nothing new. I would be impersonating a celebrity at the opening of a fete. What could possibly go wrong?

The mysterious nature of the correspondence reminded me of a TV spy thriller I'd starred in when I was a good-looking thirty-year-old with the acting world at my feet. Although there'd been no TV work since the *incident*. I replied in the affirmative and now all I had to do was await instructions.

A week later a parcel arrived containing clothes, a blond wig and details of the event; a garden fete at Gartenford Hall in rural Kent. I was to arrive at eleven o'clock precisely and open the proceedings at eleven thirty. In the package I found a typed speech which I was to learn by heart and deliver in the voice and manner of Kris Collins. Then, once the speech was over, I was to return to the house, remove my disguise and leave by the back entrance. For this I would be paid a thousand pounds in cash once the job was done. Everything seemed straightforward but I still couldn't help feeling uneasy.

Apart from Charles, the only person I told about this mysterious piece of good fortune was Caroline. After the *incident* she'd asked me to move out of our Dulwich house and since then I'd been surviving in a series of bedsits, hoping that one day she'd relent and let me home. The hoped-for reconciliation never happened but she hadn't demanded a divorce so I nursed a hope that all wasn't lost. And surely this new job would impress her; a thousand pounds for twenty minutes' work.

I'd married the twice widowed Caroline when my career was at its height. Until two years ago I'd been a regular in *Magnolia Road,* one of Britain's best-loved soap operas, playing Billy Star, the suave millionaire yacht owner. But stardom had backfired badly when I began to confuse fiction with reality. Like my fictional character I'd partied hard and drank far too much until one fateful evening I'd told the director in colourful language exactly what I thought of him and my co-stars. This disastrous mistake led to my character meeting a horrific fictional end in an accident involving an inflatable unicorn and after that my career took a dive, along with my bank balance. I was labelled as a troublemaker and forced to survive on scraps of acting work, including the occasional engagement as a Kris Collins lookalike. The thousand pounds in cash would be a life saver.

On the appointed day I drove the old VW I'd swapped for my beloved Porsche when times became hard, to Gartenford Hall. I'd been told to park around the back by the stables and, as I steered slowly down the winding drive, I saw posters bearing pictures of a grinning Kris Collins with his mop of blond hair and his trademark dark glasses. Collins had shot to fame when he'd won *Test of Character*, a peak-time show in which celebrities underwent gruesome challenges. Before this he'd been a bit-part actor and male model, until he'd hit middle age and his looks began to fade. Now, however, he was a household name and in high demand as a TV personality and presenter. I still wasn't too sure why I was there. I could only assume that someone had seen my three-minute pantomime performance as a Collins lookalike and thought I'd be the cheaper option.

I did exactly as I was instructed and drove past the field in front of the grand Georgian house where crowds were milling around the stalls. There was a dais at the edge of the field nearest the house, complete with microphone and bunting, presumably where I was intended to deliver my speech. I'd become rather good at imitating Collins's whiney Essex accent and I was sure I could pull off the deception. Also, it is a well-known fact that people on TV look rather different, and often smaller, in real life so I didn't anticipate any problems.

When I reached the back entrance to the house I heard a woman's voice.

'Bartholomew Smythe?' The curt question made me jump.

'That's me.'

'Have you got the clothes?' The speaker was an earnest young woman dressed in black as though she was attending a funeral rather than a charity fete.

I tapped the holdall I was carrying. 'All ready. Just one question. Why the secrecy?'

'I'm not allowed to say,' she snapped before whisking me through plain downstairs corridors, through a baize door and into the main house, ending up in a drawing room filled with modern furniture that seemed out of place in the elegantly proportioned room. The curtains were drawn so it took my eyes a moment to adjust. And when they did, I realized I wasn't alone. A man was sitting on the edge of the low sofa, nervously gnawing at his fingernails.

When the man looked up I recognized him at once. 'Kris, isn't it? Kris Collins?'

He nodded and I could see that he looked terrified.

'I'm Bartholomew Smythe,' I said, hoping to put Collins at his ease. 'I thought I was hired as a lookalike so I didn't expect you to be here.'

Collins appeared to relax a little. He cleared his throat before saying 'Pleased to meet you. Sorry, I'm just a bit . . . nervous.'

'No need. I'm doing the hard part.' I smiled encouragingly, hoping Collins would give me some answers.

'I expect you're wondering what the hell's going on.'

'I am a bit.' I felt that a spot of British understatement was called for.

'It was my publicist, Phaedra's idea. She thought if we used a decoy . . . To put her off the scent.'

'Decoy?' The word rang alarm bells in my head.

'Phaedra's mother saw you imitating me in some pantomime. She said you were good.'

'Thank you,' I said, acknowledging the compliment. 'Er . . . What do you mean – put her off the scent?'

'My stalker. She turns up at every gig I do; tries to get near me and bombards my social media. Phaedra says we might have to take out an injunction against her.'

'Would that put her off?'

Collins shrugged his shoulders.

'Has she threatened you?'

Collins looked sheepish. 'Not exactly. But she makes me uncomfortable.'

'Does she have a name?'

'Dolly Grey like in that old song. She's a big woman with bright red hair. You'll see her in the front row when you give your speech. Can't miss her.'

'Is she likely to do anything?'

'She hasn't so far. But there's always a first time.'

'If I'm here taking your place, I'm surprised you've bothered to come.'

'Harriet, the organizer, is a friend of my agent's so I couldn't be seen to let her down. Hopefully she won't realize our little deception.' He gave the smile familiar to his millions of fans. It lit up his face and made him appear ten years younger. 'I'll sneak away once you've done your bit out there. Thanks, Bartholomew. You're a life saver.'

I thought of the money. 'I should thank you. I . . . er was told I'd be paid in cash.'

He waved his hand, unconcerned with such mundane matters. 'Phaedra will see you right.' He glanced at the clock on the marble mantelpiece. 'Time you were becoming me. Break a leg.'

He hurried out of the room, leaving me alone. I'd had a good opportunity to study the man at close quarters and, as I changed my clothes and donned the blond wig, I was confident that I now had Collins's mannerisms off to a tee.

Ten minutes later an unsmiling Phaedra walked in and handed

me an envelope stuffed with cash. After I'd put it in my holdall, she announced that it was time to go on.

The performance went without a hitch but, after Collins's revelation about his stalker, I was only too aware of the large woman with the bright red hair in the front row gazing up at me adoringly. I'd definitely seen the light of obsession in Dolly Grey's eyes. And all my instincts told me that I needed to get away as soon as possible.

However, I hadn't counted on Harriet Sumner, the owner of the house, organizer of the fete and friend of Kris Collins's agent. Just as I was sneaking away into the house, doing my best to avoid Dolly Grey, Harriet collared me with gushing enthusiasm.

'Mr Collins – or may I call you Kris? It's so good of you to help our little cause, it really is.'

'My pleasure,' I said, doing my best to maintain the accent and hoping she wouldn't notice that my wig had begun to itch badly in the heat of the sun.

Harriet didn't leave it at that. 'You must have tea. The ladies from our local WI will be most hurt if our VIP guest doesn't sample their delicious cakes.'

She linked her arm through mine and almost dragged me towards the largest marquee. I had no choice but to smile weakly and go with the flow, hoping Harriet's presence would deter Dolly Grey. Although I feared that such a fanatical devotee wouldn't be put off that easily.

It isn't easy to make polite conversation while pretending to be someone else but I was careful to stick to the general rather than the personal. After half an hour I thanked Harriet for her hospitality and said that I needed to get back to London for an appointment.

I hurried back to the house breathing a great sigh of relief. The job was done and, after a quick change of clothes, I could drive away with my fee safely stashed at the bottom of my holdall. It had been easy money and even Dolly Grey hadn't given me a moment's trouble.

There was no sign of Kris Collins when I returned to the drawing room so I presumed he'd sneaked away while I was doing my performance. It was now time to remove my disguise, leave by the back entrance and drive away.

I hummed to myself as I checked my reflection in the mirror above the fireplace. Perhaps acting as stand in for Kris Collins might become a regular thing. A nice little earner. I experienced a fresh rush of optimism. Maybe my reputation would soon be restored. Maybe Caroline would take me back. By the time I headed for the door I was feeling quite cheerful. Until I spotted something protruding from the back of the sofa. A pair of legs encased in pale trousers. Exactly like the pair Kris Collins had been wearing when we'd met.

All hell broke loose. The police weren't allowing anybody to leave the fete and statements were being taken. The worst part was that my cover was blown; I'd had to be completely honest about my arrangement with Collins. I'd had no choice.

As I sat in what had once been the butler's pantry guarded by the very young policeman who'd written my account of events in his notebook, I realized that Harriet must know the truth by now and I felt very bad about deceiving her.

'You say this woman.' The constable consulted his notebook. 'Dolly Grey was stalking Mr Collins.'

'That's what he told me. I stuck with Harriet, the organizer, so I could avoid her while I was dressed as . . .'

'You claim that Mr Collins asked you to imitate him because he was frightened of this woman?'

'That's right. Ask his publicist, Phaedra, if you don't believe me. She made the arrangements.'

The young man looked puzzled. 'How do you spell that?'

As I was spelling out Phaedra's name we were interrupted by a man in plain clothes. He was medium height with short brown hair and piercing blue eyes. And he looked as though he was in charge.

'I'm DCI Mungo Tay, Senior Investigating Officer. I just wanted to tell you that we've arrested a woman on suspicion of Mr Collins's murder. She's been identified as Dolly Grey. What do you know about her, Mr Smythe?'

'Only what Kris Collins told me. I only met Mr Collins for the first time today. Phaedra will confirm that.'

'Phaedra, wife of Theseus of Athens. Not a fortunate name,

as I recall. I acted in Racine's version in my student days.' He smiled at the memory and I couldn't help being impressed.

Suddenly the DCI leaned forward. 'Aren't you the Bartholomew Smythe who used to be in *Magnolia Road*? My mother never missed an episode. She was quite upset when your character was killed in that terrible accident with the inflatable unicorn.'

I smiled modestly. No actor ever tires of praise.

'I sense that your career isn't going too well at the moment.'

It was as though the detective had second sight and I hoped he wouldn't enquire about the unfortunate incident that had brought about my fall from grace. But, to my relief, the conversation returned to the recent tragedy.

'Our pathologist thinks Mr Collins was struck on the head several times with one of the silver candlesticks from the mantelpiece so we're treating his death as murder. We're working on the theory that Dolly Grey found him in the drawing room and that he said something to upset her. She's denying everything but she seems very . . . volatile. Your statement tallies with what his publicist told us so you're free to go, although we might need to speak to you again. Thank you for your cooperation.' He smiled. 'And I hope to see you on TV again soon.'

'Thank you.' I felt genuinely grateful. After being shunned as an actor for so long any scrap of encouragement is like water in the desert.

It seemed like an open and shut case, as the detective I once played in a corny whodunit in Cleethorpes would have said, and I was anxious to leave. I was just opening the car door when I heard Phaedra's voice.

'Are you going?'

'The DCI said I could leave. Thanks for the cash, by the way.'

'No problem. Pity our little deception didn't work. She's still denying it, you know.'

'Dolly Grey?'

'That's right. But I actually saw her creeping into the hall. She was hard to miss.'

'Look, I'm sorry about Kris. He seemed a nice bloke.'

'You didn't know him,' she said before marching away. Perhaps there was more than one person who wanted Kris Collins dead.

* * *

The following day I decided to call Harriet Sumner. Phaedra had given me her number and I thought it only polite to get in touch because I hadn't had a chance to apologize for deceiving her at the fete. Besides, I imagined the woman must be in shock; having a murder in your home is a terrible thing.

Harriet accepted my apology graciously, saying she now understood Kris's fears. She seemed glad of the opportunity to unload her thoughts, even if it was to a stranger she'd only met once.

'It's good of you to call,' she said. 'Most people are avoiding me. I presume they don't know what to say.'

'Have the police told you anything?' I couldn't resist asking.

'Oh yes. Mungo's very approachable and, as I'm not a suspect, he seems to treat me as one of the team,' she said with a little giggle. The DCI had clearly made an impression and I detected a hint of flirtation in her voice

'He said the woman – Dolly Grey – admits that she entered the house to look for Kris but she claims she saw a woman wearing black creeping about near the drawing room.'

'Phaedra?'

'No. She said this woman was older and a brassy blonde. It could have been anyone, I suppose. One of the WI ladies looking for the loo perhaps.'

'Probably,' I said, thinking Dolly Grey might have made up this sighting out of desperation.

We chatted on for a few more minutes. Harriet was the widow of a brewery owner and a down-to-earth Yorkshire woman. I found her conversation refreshing.

The second I ended the call the phone rang again. 'Mr Smythe. This is Mungo Tay. Just a quick question. Can you think of anyone who'd want you dead?'

The question took me by surprise and my answer was a gasped 'Me? No!'

'It's just that Ms Grey's fingerprints weren't on the murder weapon and her DNA wasn't found in that room.'

'She must have worn gloves?'

'She had no gloves on her person.'

'Disposable ones? She got rid of them somewhere?'

'A thorough search has been made. No gloves. Besides, she

swears she'd never have hurt Kris Collins because she was in love with him.'

'Love can turn to hate. If he rejected her . . .'

'Possibly but I'm not convinced. Let's leave it there. I'll keep in touch.'

Tay's call made me uneasy. What if someone did want me dead for some reason? I'd been dressed as Kris Collins so what if the killer had got the wrong man?

When I went to bed that night I lay awake listing all the people I'd offended in the course of my life. The list seemed quite long, although I didn't think anyone hated me enough to want me dead. As for women with blonde hair, I've always preferred blondes and in my glory days there had been a lot of them. Even Caroline was blonde but I dismissed her from my list of possibles. She had no motive and I'd already told her that, if she did want a divorce, she could keep everything. The collapse of my career had been my own stupid fault and the house and most things in it were Caroline's anyway, bought with the money she'd inherited from her two wealthy late husbands.

Try as I might, I couldn't think of anyone who'd want me dead; not even the TV director who'd been the target of the drunken rant that caused my dismissal from *Magnolia Road*. Surely DCI Tay's theory was wrong. Kris Collins was bound to have more enemies than me. There are always people who resent success. Besides, only Charles Paris and Caroline knew where I'd be that day and the idea of either of them wanting to kill me was ludicrous.

I was drifting off to sleep when I heard a noise. A key in the lock of my bedsit door. I sat up, alert. If it was a burglar, they were in for a disappointment because I hadn't much to steal. Then I remembered the thousand pounds inside the holdall I'd stuffed under the bed. But who knew about that apart from Phaedra, Caroline and Charles? Somehow I couldn't imagine any of them breaking in to steal. Caroline had enough money of her own and I'd known Charles for years and trusted him. The only unknown quantity was Phaedra.

I held my breath as the door creaked open. In the darkness I couldn't make out the person who stepped into the room and as the figure approached the bed, my adrenalin suddenly kicked in. I rolled on to the floor and wriggled beneath the bed, trying to stop myself sneezing as the dust hit my nostrils.

I lay there perfectly still, too terrified to peep out from my hiding place. Then all of a sudden the room was bathed in light and I heard a familiar voice.

'It's OK, Mr Smythe. You can come out now. We've got her.'

I lay there for a few moments, confused. What was DCI Tay doing in my flat? And how had he managed to arrest Phaedra so quickly?

I rolled out from under the bed, blinking, and as I pushed myself up into a sitting position I saw a uniformed constable handcuffing a dark, hooded figure. Tay was standing over me, offering his hand. I grabbed it and he helped me to my feet. Then the hooded figure turned to look at me and I gasped.

'Sorry, I killed the wrong person at Gartenford Hall,' said Caroline harshly. She didn't sound sorry at all and I could sense her defiance. 'It was you I was after, not Kris Collins.'

I wondered whether I was dreaming. This was Caroline who'd always been so calm, so reasonable; Caroline who hadn't even demanded a divorce when I'd screwed up badly. I watched in disbelief as she was led from the room.

I'd expected Tay to follow but he stayed behind and poured me a tumbler of Scotch from the bottle on the shelf.

'Here. For the shock,' he said as he handed me the glass. 'I suppose you want to know what's going on.'

I nodded, lost for words.

'After what happened I did some digging and discovered that your wife's first two husbands died in accidents, leaving her a very wealthy widow. I spoke to the officers who dealt with both cases and they confirmed that there had been suspicions at the time but nothing could be proved. Then I delved a bit deeper and discovered that she'd recently insured your life for an extremely large sum of money. When her attempt on your life at Gartenford Hall failed, she was planning to make it look as though you'd been killed in the course of a burglary. She knew you had a large sum of cash in the flat and she would have taken it to make it look convincing. Do you know what the inspector who investigated her second husband's death called her?'

I shook my head, still unable to believe what he was saying.

'The praying mantis. You were to have been her third victim.' He poured me another scotch and I downed it in one.

I was still shaken when I met Charles Paris in the bar a few weeks later. I'd been plagued by the media and, with Tay's help, I'd made a moving statement. Even though I say it myself, I played the perfect victim.

'Know your trouble, Bartholomew?' Charles said when I told him what had happened. 'You're a bad judge of character.'

My phone rang and I saw my agent's number on the caller display.

'Your story's been all over the papers and social media,' she began without asking me how I was. 'Do you realize how lucky you are? You couldn't buy publicity like that. I've had several enquiries already. Can you do a voice-over this Thursday? Good money. And they're auditioning for a new play in the West End next week. I said you'd be there.'

I turned to Charles and laughed. 'Seems Caroline's done me a favour.'

'There's always a silver lining in this business. At least that's what I keep telling myself. Another drink?'

# MARTIN EDWARDS – SANCTUARY

Martin Edwards writes: *This story was inspired by Simon's* Crime Writers and other Animals *and* A Crime in Rhyme.

Dear Chief Inspector Garfunkel

Now that I am safely out of your reach, perhaps I owe you an explanation. Don't get too excited, my conscience isn't pricking. You may call this a confession. But let me be clear – I am certainly *not* confessing to murder. Merely amusing myself by helping you to tie up a few loose ends. Clarifying some of the more obscure aspects of the Mott Manor Mystery.

As for my present whereabouts, forgive me for remaining coy. Suffice to say that I'm out of harm's way, and you don't need to fret about extradition; it's simply not possible. I'm glad to say that I'm very comfortable in the Sanctuary, as I call my new home. I am blessed to enjoy wonderful views, looking out to a tree-fringed lake. The sky is blue, the sun high. All very peaceful – and so far removed from the mayhem and murder at Mott Manor.

First things first. My real name is not Osbert Mint. Without wishing to be unkind, your failure to deduce my true identity typifies the hapless way you have conducted the investigation into the demise of the late Sir Ben Mott.

Not that his real name was Sir Ben Mott, of course. Having begun life as Ernst Tobim, he rose from humble and indeed highly obscure beginnings to enjoy both wealth and prestige, thanks to good old-fashioned hard work, generous donations to senior political figures, and a flair for money-laundering, using the apparently innocuous business of O.N.T. Timbers as a front for all manner of illegal (and sometimes violent) shenanigans.

From the start, your inquiries got off on the wrong foot. The fact that Sir Ben's corpse was found in the library of Mott Manor should have been the clearest possible indication that he was the victim of foul play. Admittedly, the only door to the library was locked and bolted, and the windows were barred. There was no way in from the wine cellars below the library, nor any means of access from the room above, a guest bedroom occupied that weekend by Tibor Sment, the enigmatic Hungarian businessman whose partnership with Sir Ben was the cause of such a vicious quarrel between the two men a matter of hours before the owner of Mott Manor met his end.

(Not that Tibor Sment was his real name needless to say. But that is, given Sment's long-ago involvement with the Hungarian secret police and the KGB, unquestionably a red herring.)

On Sir Ben's desk was a tumbler of whisky – almost empty – and a pearl-handled revolver. Your interpretation of events was predictable. It looked as if he had been intent on killing himself, but undecided about the precise means. The fact that analysis of the contents of the tumbler and the half-full decanter revealed traces of Veronal seemed to indicate that he'd poisoned himself. Had he intended merely to dull his senses or to consume enough of the sedative to take his own life? At first the question seemed academic.

When your long-suffering sergeant finally convinced you that Sir Ben had not been stabbed in the neck by an improbable accident or act of God, your insistence on exploring a variety of unlikely means by which the murder might have been committed was, I'm afraid, a profound mistake. Your extensive researches into lassoes, catapults, and whether the pet monkey belonging to the housekeeper, Mrs Bonetti, could have been trained to do the deed squandered valuable time, given that the small pool of water beneath Sir Ben's roll-top desk must surely have indicated the part played in the crime by a dagger made of ice.

As to the question of motive, I am surprised that you misinterpreted the significance of Sir Ben's announcement to his guests as they gathered for dinner on Friday evening that he intended to change his will. Flamboyant as ever, he took the melodramatic step of tearing up his existing will in front of everyone's eyes. He explained that he'd summoned his solicitor, the senior partner of Brent, Moist & Co, to come to the Manor on Monday. The way he disposed of his fortune, he said, would depend entirely on the behaviour of his guests over the weekend.

This development undoubtedly came as a terrible blow to the assembled family members, above all to Sir Ben's ward Tim Nosbert (to use his stage name), who had every reason to expect he would be the principal heir. Sir Ben made it clear that he disapproved of Tim's decision to pursue a career in the theatre, not to mention his rather more successful pursuit of his fellow thespian, Monti Brest. Nor was Tim the only hopeful beneficiary who had reason to despair at the prospect of being cut out of an inheritance.

As for the mysterious hooded figure seen in the grounds of the Manor that night which prompted Mrs Bonetti to have a fit of hysterics, that was of course not the ancient phantom of the Mott Martyr, the poor soul who was hacked to pieces in Elizabethan times after being discovered in the priest hole behind the grand fireplace in the hall.

A great deal of time, Chief Inspector, was wasted on investigating the underworld, namely that priest hole and the adjoining secret passage. At least this did uncover the large stash of cash that Sir Ben had kept from the prying eyes of His Majesty's Revenue and Customs, as well as from Mrs Bonetti, who had, together with her pet monkey, been searching high and low for it. Perhaps, however, your time would have been better spent on examining motive and opportunity in the case of those present in the Manor at the relevant time.

Take Sir Ben's glamorous ex-wife, Brit Montes, for instance. Might he have mentioned her in the new will? I must say, it seems unlikely. He had evidently summoned her for the weekend for the sole purpose of humiliating her and her partner, the ageing rocker T-Bone Strim, who was a one-hit wonder long before most of the other guests were born. Brit and T-Bone only accepted the invitation in the hope that they might be able to persuade Sir Ben to fund T-Bone's 'comeback tour'. All in vain, of course. He rejected their pleas for financial support with such loud mocking laughter that his contempt was heard by everyone else in the household. Might they have been driven to exact a terrible revenge?

Was it snobbery or merely an outdated taste in music that

prompted you to concentrate on other potential culprits? Was the particularly close interest you took in Storm Benit, the Scandi noir film star, attributable solely to Sir Ben's expressed determination to make her his next wife? Or did her striking resemblance to the blonde-haired member of your favourite pop group play a part? You were wasting your time, believe me; had you tried it on with Storm, you would certainly have met your Waterloo and issued an SOS in no time.

I noticed that you also took a close interest in the movements of Betti Morns. Sir Ben may have been her godfather, but she was also his latest conquest. Can Sir Ben really have been unaware that Betti was having an affair with his secretary, Rob Mittens? Mittens it was who disguised himself as the Mott Martyr as a prelude to conducting his assignations with Betti in the orangery. Certainly, their relationship was no secret to the retired military man who worked as Sir Ben's chauffeur, RSM Bonetit. An old hand at blackmail, he determined to squeeze the couple financially until the pips squeaked.

I can at least understand why you paid so much attention to Mrs Bonetti, surely the most voluptuous housekeeper to be found in any of the stately homes of England. Once you discovered that her references were forged and that she came from Palermo rather than the Clerkenwell side of Little Italy, it was perhaps inevitable that her Mafia connections should come to the fore. She'd arrived in England seeking recompense on behalf of those cheated in one of Sir Ben's shadiest business deals, involving O.N.T. Timbers' participation in construction projects the length and breadth of Sicily. As regards his murder, however, she is guilty of nothing more than tardiness. In other words, I beat her to it.

Committing the crime was, frankly, simplicity itself. You will recall that I raised the alarm late on Saturday evening when, as I explained, I took Sir Ben's hip flask to the library as he'd requested, but found myself unable to open the locked door or get an answer from him. Did you not wonder why, when the drinks cabinet in the library was so extensively stocked, he would need a hip flask? Or why I simply didn't use one of my keys to open the door?

However, those questions didn't occur to you, nor to anyone

else. I was accompanied to the library by Storm Benit, Tim Nosbert, Monti Brest, Brit Montes, Rob Mittens and Betti Morns. Rob, a hefty young fellow, broke down the door and he and I rushed in, urging the women to stay back. Sir Ben was slumped over his desk, having drunk from the decanter into which I'd previously poured powdered Veronal. When, predictably, Betti screamed, Rob rushed back to comfort her. I was still carrying the hip flask and in all the confusion it was easy enough to slip out the ice dagger and stab Sir Ben moments after pronouncing that he was dead and urging everyone to keep out of the library and summon the police. I'm afraid, Chief Inspector, that your unfortunate reputation precedes you. I was confident that you would insist on taking personal charge of the investigation from the start, with the customary disastrous results.

If only you'd paid more attention to me, you might have uncovered the fact that until taking the job at Mott Manor, I was known as Tom St Brien.

Not that this was my real name, naturally. In fact, I am the product of a brief liaison between Sir Ben and one of Mrs Bonetti's many attractive predecessors.

Yes, you've finally guessed it. I am none other than Mr Bettison, that meek and nondescript individual who swore to avenge his mother's death in abject poverty after being turned away from the door by Sir Ben when desperate for cash to support the dying woman's care.

But I was hungry for more than the taste of a dish served cold. I was determined to inherit Sir Ben's fortune. The destruction of the will meant that I am his closest heir. I heard yesterday from Brent, Moist & Co that the funds have been transferred to a bank account in a jurisdiction far from the prying eyes of the British police.

All in all, quite a triumph. If only you'd studied classic detective fiction, even you might have stumbled upon the truth behind this crime.

The butler did it.

'Awesome,' said Toni B. Merts, as she waved goodbye before closing the door behind them and turning to her companion. 'He really is quite far gone, isn't he?'

Boris M. Nett nodded. 'Such a shame. If anyone is guilty, I suppose I am.'

'You've nothing to blame yourself for,' she said as they walked down the corridor.

He hung his head. 'But I'm his literary agent. I'm responsible. Poor Bert . . .'

'His books about the Mafia simply weren't selling. All that macho, hard-bitten masculine stuff is so yesterday. There's no way we could continue to publish them, especially after the company rebranding. Our new logo with that awesome horse's head. I mean, we often say we are one big family, but there's a limit, right. Besides, St Mitborne Press is many things, but it isn't a charity.'

Those last words tripped off her tongue with the ease of long practice. Over the past few years, many authors had heard them, although in kinder moments, Toni opted for the polite formulation that their latest novel was 'not quite right for our list at this time'.

For all his track record as a one-time Amazon #1 bestseller (in those long-ago days when the number of writers boasting such an accolade was far below seven figures), Bert Timson had become publishing kryptonite. Hadn't *The Rat Pack* itself suggested in a review of his last novel that it was time for him to take a vow of omertà?

The solution, Boris had realized, was to move with the times and to give Toni exactly what she and other editors were crying out for. This was, they said, something new, fresh and innovative. In other words, something exactly like the books sweeping all before them around the globe, right down to the typeface and design on the book jacket.

So, Boris had begged Bert to adapt and move with the times. But it hadn't worked. The Mafia had sneaked back in to the work-in-progress. There was a gathering of the family and even a godfather. Before long the sheer effort of embracing unfamiliar tropes while crafting a subtle homage to the traditional locked room mystery (or, as Bert put it in dark moments, using endless clichés in the cause of shameless plagiarism) had simply proved too much for him to bear. The scale of his mental collapse was illustrated, Boris reckoned, by the fact that he'd ended up unravelling his wretched mystery through that hoariest of devices, the confessional letter from the culprit to the detective, which explains everything. The unmistakable sign of an author bereft of ideas.

The two of them walked out into the sunlight and stood on the terrace, looking over to the lake. Boris breathed in the warm summer air.

'Marvellous place, though.'

'Awesome,' Toni agreed. 'Lucky that Bert kept up his membership subscription to the Society of Writers. The Sanctuary's facilities are state of the art.'

'They truly are.' Boris pointed to a separate building, separated from the main development by a fast-flowing stream. 'What's that?'

'For cancelled authors,' she replied with a frown of disapproval. 'Complete with a seminar room for continuing education.'

Boris turned his back hurriedly. 'Bert was such a hard-living type, a real hell-raiser. But I must say, he seems happy here. Comfortable room, nice outlook, lovely setting.'

'I'm just stoked that he and his book have found the perfect home.'

'You're right.' Boris was brightening already. 'His life now is so much better than that dreary round of book launches and events where nobody turns up except family and friends. The horrific realization that your foreign sales are so much higher because the translator is a better writer than you'll ever be. The savagery of one-star online reviews, ranting that the book was delivered to the wrong address.'

'You know,' Toni said pensively as they reached the car park. 'I've never quite understood this desperate longing so many people have to become published authors. Anyway, ours not to reason why. Ready for lunch?'

'That would be . . .'

'Awesome. I've booked our usual table.'

She cast one last, lingering glance back at the Sanctuary.

'You should be proud.' Her eyes were shining. 'Your client may not be writing any more, but frankly, that's a bonus. This is the perfect place for his reinvention. What's happened to him *is* truly awesome. And we've seen it for ourselves.'

'You mean . . .?'

'Bert Timson is *cosy*.'

# ALISON JOSEPH – MURDER AT MOUSECOMB

*(with grateful thanks to Rosy Fordham)*

Ladies and Gentlemen. People. Welcome to this lovely theatre. And, welcome to Murder at Mousecomb. My name is Angela Murtagh. Miss Murtagh, the famous detective.

We find ourselves at the beginning of the story. The prologue to a murder mystery. And as the play unfolds before you, I shall lead you through all the peaks and troughs, the nuances, the little lies, until we find the truth – the truth at the heart of the mystery.

The story so far is this: There is a body found in the library. A mysterious figure was seen earlier, lurking behind the hydrangea bush. A terrible shout was heard soon afterwards. And poor Colonel Blight was found dead, among his own priceless leather-bound books and cases of rare beetles. But – and I did warn Riccardo, our wonderful director about this – at this stage I'm going to depart from the script. Because the odd thing is, I'm only here because of a mystery – back there. My wonderful, marvellous companion Irene should have been playing the lead, and I'm sure that's why you're all here, no, don't be polite, I'm only the understudy, you've paid good money for tickets to see the great Irene Sullivan. So, I'm just going to take a little of your time to explain, it's only fair isn't it? You see, poor Irene. Well . . . she died. Yes. Terrible. You'll have heard about it, last week, we had to cancel of course, none of us could go on after that, found at the bottom of a ladder by the back stairs, here in this very theatre . . . but as they say, the show must go on. So – here I am.

She was my friend. I don't really know how to carry on without her. Stepping into her shoes. She used to have a right go at me, one of these days I'll be found in a heap and you'll get your moment in the spotlight . . . we had no idea it would come true. If I'd thought for one minute . . .

Anyway, the play's the thing, isn't it? So, at this stage, Miss Murtagh, the detective, does the Prologue. And at the end of her setting it all up, she steps back, and she says, Enjoy the Play. And then it's curtain up. So, here we go. It all happens at Mousecomb House in Cornwall. Colonel Blight, he's played by the lovely Philip, he and his wife Laetitia retired there five years ago, so that he could concentrate on his entomology, that's the insect collection. He's rather an expert, in fact, always writing letters to the South Kensington museum. He has a butler, Merrick. And two days ago, an old colleague of his, Professor Macintyre came to stay. Well, I say colleague, but in fact it's no secret that over the years they've locked horns several times, with accusations of plagiarism in learned pamphlets, and also that rumour about the Professor and the Colonel's wife . . .

And I can see, looking out at you all, that you're a sharp lot. I bet you're already having a bit of a think about whys and wherefores, and who would have wanted the Colonel dead. That's part of the fun of it all, isn't it?

Irene used to say, there's enough here who would want me out of the way. Rubbish, I would say. Don't be a twit. We love you.

Oh, and there's the police. In the play. A local copper called Inspector Finch. As in all these things, he sees his chance to make his mark, what with a real live murder in the village . . . but he ignores Miss Murtagh at his peril.

The police were here. When Irene was found at the foot of the ladder. It was on Monday. Anthony, our stage manager, he found her. An awful lot of blood. He called an ambulance, but it was too late. We all knew it was, really. Game over. Next thing we know, a real crime scene, blue tape and them all talking into radios, and then the questions, did she often have fainting fits, that kind of thing. Fainting fits, I said, she was tough as old boots, it would take more than a tumble at the top of the stairs to carry her off . . .

The policeman looked at me. What do you mean, Madam, he said. I looked back at him. She was my best friend, I said.

It's not the first time I've been up here, of course. A long run like this, Irene and I both started in this production eight, no, nine years ago now. Such a successful play, as you know, full houses even now . . .

So, yes, I've had my moments here as Miss Murtagh. Cases of flu. Irene with her dentistry . . . she's always encouraged me, oh Jan, of course you can do it, buck up old girl . . .

Friendship, you see. Having each other's backs.

And now . . .

Last Monday she died. The theatre's been dark ever since. But now it's Saturday, and here I am. Georgie, he's our company manager, he said, enough is enough. The play must go on. 'It's what she would have wanted,' he said. Of course, it'll be re-cast, they need a name in the role, lots of talk backstage here about who it might be . . .

This is her coat. The rest of the costume, I insisted on having my own, I may be the understudy I said, but at least my clothes will fit. But the coat . . . it will do, they said.

A murder mystery. A caper. Such fun.

I don't know how we'll manage without her.

She played the role so well. I used to watch her sometimes, from the wings. I mean usually we understudies sit in the dressing room, knitting, people say, although, I've never met an understudy who knits, one of those myths about the Theatre that people love to tell isn't it? Reading. Listening to podcasts. My current favourite is one about astrology, it's all in the ascendant, it turns out, not your sun sign at all, that's just the basic building blocks. But the ascendant is how you appear to the world, how you stand here and say, this is me. Here I am.

I never knew Irene's ascendant. I knew her sun sign, obviously, it couldn't have been more clear. But how she appeared to the world . . . You need the time of birth for that, not just the date . . .

Five past five last Monday afternoon. That was the time she died.

CCTV. Police all over it. Never thought those cameras were working, you think they'd have broken long ago and no one had noticed. Two cameras, one on the stage door, one near the back stairs. They've been going through it all, they told us. Even took our phones off us, though I've got mine back now.

It's like those TV cop shows. We did one, once, me and Irene, soon after drama school. Such fun. Only small parts but it felt like the beginning of something.

Which it was.

Anyway. The Prologue. Miss Angela Murtagh. She's quiet, and English, and knows how to behave. But she watches all the comings and goings. The police are always several steps behind dear Miss Murtagh, and even then they don't believe her, who would listen to an old lady like that . . .

A bit like last Monday, actually. Police swarming everywhere, and then one of them took me on one side and said to me, your friend Miss Sullivan, what about her private life? Had she made any enemies, he asked me, I mean, you theatre people aren't known for your loyalty, are you, he said.

I didn't say anything. I wanted to say, don't disrespect my friend. But instead I said, maybe just concentrate on the CCTV, it might tell you more.

In the play there's no CCTV. Just Miss Murtagh, watching, waiting. The Colonel is married to Laetitia, who comes from a very old family and thinks she's married beneath her. And Laetitia is played by a wonderful colleague, Estella Spinks. You'll have heard of her, I'm sure, lots of telly she was in, as she never tires of telling us. She played the barmaid in that soap, no, not that one, the other one, oh you know. Always goes on about it. Then they wrote her out, her character eloped to Melbourne with the guy who owned the garage . . .

We did telly too. Our cop show – it was good. Gritty, you know. Set up north. The main detective, he was troubled, a drinker, like they all were in those days, believed rules are made to be broken . . . He had a catch phrase. Police work, it's a game of chance, he'd say. Sometimes you win, sometimes you lose. And sometimes, just sometimes, a mystery is revealed.

The Prologue. That's what I'm supposed to be doing. So, where were we?

The Colonel had invited an expert from the Natural History Museum to see a particular specimen that he'd just acquired, a very rare kind of locust. Biblical, you might say. Like when there was a plague of them, in punishment for some wrongdoing by humanity. We're always at it, aren't we? Always need our knuckles rapped from time to time. So, the Professor turns up. Played by dear Howard. He's the old rival of the Colonel, but he says the chap he invited was indisposed so he's come instead. And then the Colonel is found dead. And Laetitia, his wife, is strangely upset. She keeps saying, I don't know how I'm going to manage without him.

I've not had a life like that. Dependent on someone. Probably for the best.

So, that's set the scene for you. Oh, and there's the butler, of course. There's always the butler. Merrick. A faithful servant of the family. In fact, he came from Laetitia's side, her mother said, if you're going to marry trade at least have proper staff. So, he joined them on their wedding day. A good-looking man. He's played by James Feather. Very good casting if you ask me. We all adore him. Irene in particular. They were very close. You'd expect him to be more upset, come to think of it. But he's a bit like that. Stiff upper lip. English. It all happens on the stage.

There are rumours that he's seeing Alice, our costume lady.

I wonder what his ascendant is.

There are lots of pockets in this coat. All sorts of hiding places. I like investigating them, when I try it on. You never know what you'll find. Ooh – look. An old lightbulb. Wonder why that's there.

When I was young, I was always hiding things. Used to drive my mother mad. Pencils. Rubber bands. She took me to a doctor once. I must have been about seven. I think she was hoping for a long word, a diagnosis. A mania. The doctor was a kind man. I was standing by his desk, and he put his hand on my shoulder. And he said, children often hide things when they don't feel safe. Mother got very angry then and snapped her handbag shut and jumped to her feet and said, 'We're going, darling, no point listening to this charlatan.'

I remember the word. Charlatan. I looked it up, we didn't have many books but there was a dictionary I used to read. I thought about the doctor. He had those half-spectacles that people had in those days. Kind blue eyes. I looked at the word and I decided that whatever he was, it wasn't a charlatan.

After that I raised my game. Whole tins of sweets. New, larger spaces, under the floorboards. And after a while, jewellery. Money.

Planning my getaway. My mother would search and search but I was cleverer at hiding than she was at searching. It made her very angry.

Kleptomania. That was the word she wanted the doctor to say. But all he did was rest his hand on my shoulder.

There was only me and mother. And then there was only me.

On Tuesday a copper from the team called us all together to keep us abreast of their findings, that's how she put it. DS De Souza she's called. It could almost have come from the play. She said that Irene might have survived the fall, except that she was also stabbed with a pair of scissors. That explains all the blood, I thought, but I didn't say anything. The scissors were embedded in her side. The stabbing seems to have happened at the same time as the fall. She told us the scissors had been taken from the costume department. I saw Alice exchange a glance with James.

She asked us about Irene's life. She was married, Howard said, to the ghastly Jeffrey. Thank God he's not here to see it, it would be all about him, he said, and Estella laughed. I thought, you two can shut up. It wasn't a conventional marriage, but Irene adored Jeffrey while he was alive, and I didn't see why this rozzer chick had to hear that kind of gossip now.

Then there was another copper. Stuart, he said his name was. DS Stuart. He wanted to know more. About Irene being my best friend. He sat me down, just there, where those chairs are. It was quiet in there, no one around. All that blue tape across the back stairs. He said, how well did you know Miss Sullivan? I said, where do you want me to start? Drama school? Before that?

He said, did you know about this relationship with Mr Feather? I just smiled.

He tried again. 'Did you know that Miss Sullivan had received threats. This letter, for example? And he produced a big folded sheet of paper, and there was a scrawl across it in big black letters. It just said, 'I know what you did.'

It was in her dressing room, the policeman went on. Who would have written an accusation like that to Miss Sullivan?

I took a deep breath. It's a prop, darling. That's why it's in big letters. So the audience can see it.

In the play, the Colonel's wife is accused, by his brother Arthur . . . but I'm not going to give away the plot.

That's all very well, he said. But we've traced the pen that was used. And it was hidden in your dressing room. Under the floorboards.

I had a moment, then, to make a choice. To say, someone else must have hidden it. Or to be honest. Kleptomania, I said. I suffer from it. Since childhood. Half the time I don't know what I'm doing. But pens, in particular. A trigger. I must have seen the pen and . . .

Your fingerprints, he said. The only ones on it.

Well, I said, the prop people would be wearing their gloves when they get everything ready. Even Miss Murtagh in this play draws that conclusion very quickly, when the Professor – oh, dear, I shouldn't give too much away. Irene always said, when you do the Prologue, stick to the script. Don't give too much away.

The policeman looked at me like I was lying. In the play, Inspector Finch thinks he knows more than Miss Murtagh. But he's wrong.

I left home when I was fifteen. But the hiding things . . . that stayed with me. I used to think about the nice doctor with his kind blue eyes, and wonder what would have happened if he'd taken me under his wing. Maybe there'd have been a treatment for it.

It's got me into terrible trouble in the past. Almost a trance state. I'll pick something up, shiny things, and stash them away. And food. Saving things for later. Old habits.

When I was little, I would tuck myself away, and open the hiding place, and gaze at the things there. And I would dry my tears, and think about a future time when I would take those things and be somewhere else. Somewhere away from it all. I would think about the doctor in his nice warm house with his wife and his children and how he would rest his hand on their shoulders and talk about feeling safe the way he did with me just for that moment and it would feel as if perhaps everything would be all right.

Still, it's made me what I am. I have no complaints. Friendship, that's been my great strength in life. Like Irene. That's what I tried to tell DS Stuart. We went through so much together, I wanted to say. But he said, don't you mind being her understudy, and I just laughed. The oldest cliché in the book, I said. That and the knitting.

As if I'd want her dead. Standing here in her coat. With all the lovely pockets. How I've wanted to wear it. And now I can.

But that doesn't mean I'd kill her, does it? I know what it's like to want someone dead. And it doesn't feel like this. Oh no.

So, I sat there with DS Stuart, with all the blue and white tape everywhere, and I took a deep breath, and I said, isn't there a possibility that it was just an accident? Irene was holding the scissors, and was up the ladder, and just slipped? A terrible accident.

He gave me that look, again. He said, 'We have to explore all possibilities, Madam.'

I wondered if he'd seen the play, actually. The detective, Finch, says almost exactly the same thing.

Of course, in the play, I know far more than he does. But Irene's death . . . it's just life isn't it? Sometimes you win. And sometimes . . .

Jeffrey, Irene's husband. He despised the theatre. He'd say, it's just people dressed up. Why did you marry an actress then, I wanted to say to him, if that's what you think? But I didn't want to cause trouble between them.

He died. Some years ago now. Heart trouble.

Howard said, a while ago, he said, I remember you two, at Jeffrey's funeral. I watched you both, standing by the grave, chalk white with grief. And I thought, Howard said, how in death we mourn people we never liked in life.

Can't think what made me remember that now.

Anyway, the thing about the Colonel, it turns out he was much wealthier than anyone realized. And at the start of the play, they've found his will. And now his estranged brother, Arthur, is due to arrive at the house.

It's not true, of course, what Howard said. Jeffrey was a difficult person, but I didn't dislike him. Howard is a bit of an amateur psychologist, he says that's how he starts with a new character, pretends to be their analyst. Not my way of doing things. When I start with a character, I just think, what would it be like to be that person? When I was little, I'd watch people, neighbours, kids in the street. I'd copy their walk, feel my way into being them. Walking with their mother, holding hands.

Howard once said my dependence on Irene was about replacing the abandoning mother. I said, for Christ's sake, Howard, she's only two years older than me, and anyway, I had one mother, that was quite enough for me, I'm hardly going to start looking for another one.

I was Irene's bridesmaid, at the wedding to Jeffrey. When they walked down the aisle, such a handsome couple everyone said, he had her arm in a grip. Like that. On her wrist. It left marks.

Only I could see it.

Oh, the tales I could tell you about Irene and me. We met in Queensway, working at a casino there. I was just sixteen. Lying about my age, living in a shabby rented room. Irene was applying to drama school, staying with an aunt in Stanmore. 'You could do it too,' she said. 'You're a natural. You should follow your dreams.'

Dreams don't keep you safe. That first night on the streets, when I got off the train at Paddington and thought, here I am. London. One night on the streets was enough for me. That sleepless, bone-chilled dawn, I gathered up my stuff and walked. Knocked on doors asking for work. The man at the casino eyed me up and down, asked my age. I lied. He said I could have a try out. Croupier. Dealing cards, you know. He gave me a so-called uniform, tiny skirt and blouse. Watched me change into it.

I was like, just try it mate. After that he was OK, Carlos. He showed me how to do the cards, twenty-one, blackjack.

I slept in the cloakroom there for the first few weeks, crept back in after they closed up. No dreams. It's enough to be safe.

Once, Irene asked me, you must have had a father too? I told her I never knew my father. He left when my mother found out she was expecting me. She always blamed me, my mother did. I couldn't expect Irene to understand, an only child of devoted parents, a kind aunt in Stanmore.

One night, Irene caught me tucking the casino biros into my bag. She said, right, that's it. That's the end of that. So, she made me fill in the forms, we both auditioned, we both got in.

We cried tears of joy. Well, she did. I'm not one for crying.

Three years of drama school. Still working in the casino, I had to eat, didn't I? But I moved in with Irene and her aunt Sheila. She was kind, Sheila. Funny. Didn't believe in breakfast.

Two cups of coffee and a cigarette. We didn't believe in breakfast either, so we all got on.

And maybe Irene was right, about dreams coming true, in those days, anyway. Desdemona. Lady Macbeth. Legally Blonde. Not bad for a teenage runaway, I said to her. You're my friend, she said. Irene Sullivan and Jan Reid. We keep each other's secrets.

Irene Sullivan. It's dactyls, you see. She was a bit taken with them. Obsessed, I'd say. Da da da, da da da. It's the syllables. She said it was a surefire sign of success if you had a name like that. She'd get cross if people called her Ireen. It's Irenee, she'd say. Three syllables. Think of them, darling, she'd say, to me. Marcus Aurelius. Margaret Rutherford. Michael Ignatieff. It has a ring of achievement, that metre. I said what about Judas Iscariot? She said, oh darling, there's always one bad apple.

I thought, more than a bad apple, that Judas Iscariot. A terrible betrayal. A whole barrel of bad apples in one man if you ask me. But I didn't say that. Instead I said, Kourtney Kardashian, and we both laughed.

Once I said, that's why I'll always be the understudy. Not da da da, da da da. Jan Reid. No ring of achievement in those two syllables. Nonsense, darling, she said. What about Clark Kent?

He was fictional, I said. After that, she'd say two syllable names, randomly. Mae West. John Wayne. Once she said, King George. I said, that doesn't count, one's a title, not a name. Also, you need a number. The first, the third?

We left royalty out of it after that.

I suppose Queen Anne might count. There was only one of her. But not sure about surefire success.

Jeffrey never understood. How it's all make believe. Like all of this. That wood panelling, just painted on. That window, the pretend garden outside, recorded birdsong. Our make-believe world. And yet real enough. Bearing witness. Shakespeare knew. A rag-tag company of people bringing to life stories of thwarted love, and fairies and donkeys and Romans. And kingdoms. And vengeance.

He knew. He knew what it was like to want someone dead.

But Jeffrey would say, you're all just pretending. He'd get angry. He'd say, 'I stick with the facts, I do.'

He was obsessed with facts. Dates. The Boer War. Which battles we won when. Once Irene said, who is this 'we', Jeffrey? The English of course, he said. Well, she said, and who's that? Can't be you, Jeffrey, as you're partly Dutch and before that you were probably a Kazakh or something, a Scythian out on the Russian steppes. And me, she said, I'm definitely not 'us'. A grandmother who changed her name from Goldstein, and on the other side a grandfather who stood with the Irish in Ulster? Don't go telling me about wars we won, she said to him.

I was sitting there, in the corner of their nice lounge, they lived in Finchley by then. I knew she'd overstepped a mark. He went a kind of grey colour. A flush on his cheeks. His hands in fists. He said, 'We'll talk about this later,' and he left the room.

There was a silence, and then she did a kind of laugh. Oh dear, she said. Jeffrey.

But the next day I saw the bruises. Not for the first time. And certainly not the last.

DS Stuart asked me about Jeffrey. I gather it wasn't a happy marriage, he said. I thought, he's been talking to Estella. All marriages have their secrets, I said to him. It's a line from the play, actually, Laetitia says it when Finch asks her about the Professor and how they seem rather close . . . oh dear, giving things away again. He wouldn't give up, DS Stuart. He said, I gather that Irene Sullivan was rather close to James Feather, recently. And that perhaps other people in the company weren't happy about it.

Definitely Estella. She's a terrible gossip. And James is a lovely man, that's the thing. Charming. Not surprising people fall for him. Alice is very keen on him.

Jeffrey didn't like Irene being called Sullivan. You're a married woman, he'd say. You're Mrs Amherst now. To start with, she'd just smile, and take his hand. But he wouldn't give up. It became one of his things, one of the subjects he'd start on, over tea, or drinks, if it wasn't Sebastopol or Waterloo or something. 'To have a wife called Miss, it's not respectable.' The theatre has never been respectable, she'd say. Once she got cross. She stood up, and said, I've fought hard to be Irene Sullivan. I'm not going to give it up. Amherst is one syllable too short and I won't have it. She left the room. Jeffrey followed her.

After that, I thought, she will leave him. There is no other way.

But still she stayed. There was a time, soon after that, when I was there as usual, and Jeffrey had found fault with the dinner, the carrots were undercooked, he'd had a lot of wine, too much I felt, it always made him worse . . . and I found her in the kitchen, sobbing. Don't tell me to leave him, she said. I am defeated by it, she said.

I tried to say, no one defeats you Irene Sullivan. Buck up old girl. 'Marcus Aurelius,' I said. 'Angela Lansbury.' She smiled, and dried her tears. I held her for a bit, and then we went back into the lounge as if nothing was wrong.

Once Estella said, why did she marry him? They've nothing in common. I tried to explain. How we met him, on a cruise. A brief holiday. Sights of the Rhine valley. We weren't doing telly then, we were in the West End, Noel Coward revival, our photos in the foyer – but hand to mouth as ever, renting in Stoke Newington . . . and Jeffrey took a shine to her. He'd join us at our table. He was in insurance, he'd worked his way up, ran a whole department now. Very keen on his work, talked a lot about it. The thing about insurance, he said, is that it protects people from harm. We turn tragedy into a minor inconvenience.

I almost said, I can't see that working with King Lear, but Irene laughed, and I didn't want to spoil things.

Jeffrey made her feel safe. They got engaged, soon after the holiday, when we were back in London. Married soon after that. A short honeymoon in Rome.

She said, some months later, you're different from me, Jan. You're brave. I said, I don't feel brave. And she said, that's the point. You don't even ask to be brave. You just are. It's what I liked about you when we met, when we were young. You didn't expect life to be safe. You'd learned it wasn't. Whereas me, she said, I was always craving safety. I'd always say, but what if? When we were in that farce, where I had to fall through a door, do you remember, with that drop on the other side – every night I would say to myself, what would Jan do? Because you, you'd just take that step and think, either I'll land safely, or I won't. You'd think, if I fall, I fall.

Jeffrey looked like a place of safety. A future. A roof over her head. A nice house in the suburbs. 'I won't be able to work for ever,' she'd say.

My wife is an actress, Jeffrey would say. I allow her to continue in her chosen profession. The fact is, he needed the money. He'd taken early retirement from the insurance firm, and his pension wasn't all he thought it would be.

You'd think he of all people would have made sure of that. Mind you, most of what he earned he drank.

And then it was Wednesday, and the police still wouldn't give up. Who would have a motive to want Irene dead, they kept asking. So, there's me, because I want to step into her shoes. There's Alice the costume lady, because she wants to be with James and she was jealous about his attachment to Irene. It's true that Alice lent her scissors to Irene on the morning of her fall, but that's because Irene wanted to trim the thread on her costume, Alice was supposed to do it, but she was off that morning . . . and Irene was only up the back stairs because that's where we were storing the evening gown for Act Three because there was a rail in the loft up there where things could hang nicely.

On Thursday it all went quiet. And then yesterday, Friday, DS Stuart asked to see me. He sat me down, and said, Jan, I think you're right. We're beginning to conclude that it was indeed an accident. On the CCTV, the only person who goes through that back door is Irene. And the initial post-mortem findings show that the only way the blade could have struck Irene is from her own grip, as she fell. A funny angle, apparently, not one that anyone would make deliberately. And then he smiled and he said, you were right about the threatening letter too, Josh in the props department said he wrote it, he didn't know about the pen going missing but he says, round here nothing's safe unless you chain it down.

It's what I've thought all along. An accident. No mystery. No motive. No villain. Just real life.

But still a tragedy. For me, anyway.

DS Stuart said the coroner might release the body next week. I thought about funerals and stuff. There's a funeral director down the road so I called in. A nice woman, very sympathetic. Will you want to see her again, she asked me. She talked about embalming, making Irene look peaceful so that I can sit with her.

I said I'd think about it. I've never seen anyone dead. Anyone I love, I mean.

They do a good job on the Colonel here, they get old Philip to lie there all waxy-faced with a trickle of blood, 'My star turn old love,' he says, after the curtain comes down and he takes off his makeup and nips off to the pub for a wee dram or two . . .

I did see my mother after her death. I had to pay for her funeral. There was no one else. She lay there, looking as she'd always looked. Tight faced. Unfeeling. Philip looks better dead than she ever did.

Oh, and Jeffrey. I saw him.

Heart attack. Carried him off.

Things got worse with Jeffrey and Irene. I was worried about her. She got thin, there was less merriment. One day at their house I caught her with his heart medication, packets of tablets, gripped in her hand. Look, she said, jabbing her finger at the writing, it says here, do not exceed the stated dose. I took the packet away from her, sat her down, said, Irene, when you leave him, it will not be like that. You don't need to think that way. One day, you will walk away. It will be all right. But she shook her head. Jan, she said, it's not a play. It's real life. There are no neat endings in real life.

I don't know how she managed those years. On stage, every night, being sharp and witty and forthright . . . It's what we do, isn't it. Think about what it would be like to be someone else. Someone happy.

And then, at home, those awful nights with Jeffrey. Reading the packet of his heart pills. Do not exceed the stated dose. 'Do not mix with alcohol,' she said once, as she poured Jeffrey his nightcap of brandy.

We keep each other's secrets.

It was six years ago. That spring.

Irene called me late at night, in a panic. He's gone, she kept saying on the phone. He's gone.

I thought she meant he'd left her, I had a wave of relief. But then I realized what she meant. He's here, now, kind of lying across the bed, oh Jan, darling, it's awful, come quickly.

I hurried over to their house. It was about one in the morning, all quiet, their nice suburban street. I thought about people behind those doors, living their lives.

I'd been there earlier, I often called around tea time when we weren't working, Irene liked me to be there, it kept him on his best behaviour, she'd say. That afternoon, when I got there, Irene was a bundle of nerves. She grabbed my arm, and started going on about Jeffrey, and his habitual after-dinner brandy. She said, it works in the play. Perhaps it will work in real life.

I calmed her down. I said, you have to leave. We don't need to talk about heart pills. You simply have to pack a bag.

She was shaking her head. I can't do that. He'll follow me. He'll track me down. There is no way out, she said.

That evening, she served his dinner. He complained that the steak was overcooked. He said he'd deal with her later, he was drunk, as usual. She went back into the kitchen. I followed her. She was crying. I said, Irene, come and live with me. But she wouldn't listen.

Later, after supper, she set his brandy glass in front of him. I could see it was a bit more full than usual. He drank it all, complained about the taste, ranted at her a bit. Then said, he was tired, and he was off to bed.

When he'd gone upstairs, she held me. Then she said, you go off home now. Nothing will work, she said.

I left, reluctantly.

It was later that night she rang me. He's gone, she said. I was amazed, in fact. I wondered how . . . But I felt nothing but relief.

I got there. We stared at him. His eyes were all red, his skin all kind of flat and greasy. Horrible. Foam around his mouth. We held each other, shaking. Then we called an ambulance. Lovely ambulance man, he said, I'm so sorry Mrs Amhurst, there's nothing we can do. Irene wept, as a grieving widow should.

Heart trouble, the post-mortem said. Made worse by alcohol. One of those things.

Irene blossomed. Her performance grew lighter, she laughed more, she seemed taller, more beautiful. Every so often she would hug me. Clark Kent, she'd say. King Charles.

We had six wonderful years.

And now she's gone. An accident. One of those things.

Irene always said, remember to keep to the script, for God's sake. Make sure you don't give too much away.

That spring afternoon, six years ago, I walked up to their house from the tube station, and I thought, he's got to go. It wasn't the first time I'd thought of it. Irene had rescued me, and I thought now it's my turn to rescue her. I owed her so much. I owed her everything. Still do.

Anyway, that afternoon, beautiful weather, everything was going so well, we had just transferred to this very theatre . . . and I thought, I can't face it any more. I can't face sitting there smiling while he goes on about the Crimea, telling me that Irene would be a pauper if it wasn't for his pension and how she's never grateful . . . I thought, it has to stop.

She knew, of course. She knew, when she was sobbing in the kitchen. She heard me go upstairs, she heard me opening the medicine cabinet. And then, when they were both in the lounge, and the brandy glass was waiting in the kitchen . . . I went into the kitchen, quickly, with the heart pills. Lots of them. Crushed them up. Topped up the glass. No wonder it was more full than usual.

No wonder it tasted funny.

We never spoke of it. At the funeral, both of us, clutching each other. Chalk white.

She saved me. And I saved her. And now she's gone.

Last night, Georgie, our company manager, said, we open tomorrow. Saturday. He turned to me and said, Jan, I hope you know your lines. Patted my arm, like that. 'Good girl,' he said. Estella started on about the re-cast again, we need a name, she said, a real star, as it is they're only turning up because of the notoriety . . .

Georgie said, shut it, love. We're a company, he said. The show must go on.

And so, here we are. Saturday.

And here you are.

I loved her. I don't know how I'm going to . . .

Mae West. Clark Kent. Jan Reid.

The lights will fade. Soon it will be curtain up.

Look. Her shoes. Gorgeous. A perfect fit. As she always said they would be.

Jeffrey thought you could reduce the tragedy of King Lear to a minor inconvenience. He knew nothing. About theatre. About life. About love.

And now, here I am. It turns out, Irene was right. I just take that step, and I think – if I fall, I fall.

She was my best friend.

I don't think I've given too much away, have I?

A murder mystery. A caper. Such fun.

Enjoy the play.

# MICHAEL RIDPATH – SILVER FOX

## 1.

Óskar Davídsson sipped his coffee and surveyed his place of work.

A posse of horses bucked and skipped across the lush green meadow, their manes flashing in the low morning sunlight, which was squeezing itself between the wall of mountains behind him to the east and the pink-edged clouds above. Beyond the fields, the crater of Eldborg squatted, a formidable rim of rock thrusting up sixty metres out of its thousand-year-old bed of lava. This was a much better view than the car park and the rubbish bins of a fast-food chicken restaurant that he used to stare at from the window of his old office in Reykjavík when he worked in marketing for an auto dealership. It was almost four years to the day since he had been fired from that job.

His gaze drifted to the west, where the sea glistened silver and far beyond that the near-perfect, glacier-topped cone of the Snaefellsjökull volcano shimmered at the end of its peninsula.

A gentle, cool breeze caressed his cheeks. He sniffed his freshly ground Sumatran coffee and grinned. Óskar was at peace.

'Óskar! Will you get your lazy arse down to the bottom paddock and fix that fence! We can't use the field till it's mended. And you promised you'd do it yesterday.'

Óskar turned and smiled benignly at the approaching figure of his wife, Anna Glúmsdóttir. She was one of those women who was even lovelier when she was angry. Tall, with long blonde hair that flew about her face in the wind, she had poise when motionless, and a vibrant energy when on the move. It was her money that had bought the horse farm when Óskar had been fired those four years ago, money that had partly been provided by her wealthy father, Glúmur, who was in oil distribution, but mostly from the sale of her own successful insurance brokerage business.

She was an intelligent, hard worker who loved horses and who had realized her dream by buying this farm on the west coast of Iceland.

'I'll do it this afternoon, darling,' Óskar said. 'I just need to analyse the A/B testing on the Facebook ads I've been running.'

Óskar was responsible for marketing the riding expeditions they provided for tourists, almost all of it online. Anna knew nothing about digital marketing.

'You're just waiting for me to do it, aren't you? Well, I won't! You know how to mend a fence and you can bloody well mend it!'

'Of course, my love,' Óskar said as he watched his wife marching off towards the stables.

Then she hesitated. Stopped. Turned. Walked back towards him head down.

She lifted her bright blue eyes, smiled and gave him a quick kiss on the lips. 'You are a lazy bastard,' she said, taking the cup from his hands and sipping from it. 'I don't know why I put up with you.'

'I make very good coffee.'

She smiled. 'You do make very good coffee.'

Óskar returned to the farmhouse and climbed the stairs to their son's old bedroom, which had been turned into his study. He logged on to his Facebook advertising page, stared at it for a minute and then logged off.

With a smile, he accessed the photo library on his computer and found the pictures from their holiday the previous year in India.

Most of the pictures were of him. Anna was a good photographer – naturally – especially now she had her new Nikon that Óskar had bought her the previous Christmas.

Anna took the best photos, but Óskar made the most use of them. Increasingly, it was images that sold online, be it a day's expedition on horseback through the magnificent Icelandic countryside, or, well, anything really. Óskar was good with images.

For his current project, he needed to choose five, he decided. He examined the photographs. He didn't look bad, he had to admit. His shorts and polo shirt were neat, his thick silver-grey hair nicely trimmed, his pale Icelandic skin turned a light golden colour by the harsh Indian sunlight. His favourite was taken outside a palace hotel in Rajasthan, where he and Anna were drinking cocktails beside a water fountain draped in bougainvillaea. Anna had managed to snap him smiling at her, he a little drunk, a little sentimental.

She gave him a hard time, but she was worth it. She was definitely worth it. It was their twenty-fifth wedding anniversary in three weeks. That, he wouldn't forget.

He selected that photograph. Now he needed four more.

## 2.

Bonnie: Hey! Are you there?
Chuck: I'm here.
Bonnie: What time is it there? I get so confused. Isn't it late? It's eight in the evening here.
Chuck: Five thirty. In the morning. It's so late it's early. It doesn't matter. I can't sleep.
Bonnie: Abigail?
Chuck: Yes, Abigail.
Bonnie: How's she doing?
Chuck: OK, I guess. No worse.
Bonnie: That's good. I guess
Chuck: Cheer me up. How are you doing?

Bonnie sat back from her computer. How was she doing?

Well, she was a fifty-eight-year-old woman living in a house that was falling down in Allentown, Pennsylvania with a husband who was a jerk and who beat her up every now and then. She had a daughter who wouldn't speak to her because she hated her father just as much as Bonnie did, and a grandson whom she never saw as a result. She was lonely. She was angry. She was miserable.

Bonnie: Fine. I guess.
Chuck: Bonnie?
Bonnie: I think my husband knows. About this. About us.
Chuck: About what? We're just talking.

Bonnie: I know, but he'd be furious if he found out.

Chuck: He hasn't hit you again, has he?

Bonnie: No. No, he hasn't. And he knows nothing about computers so he'll never see these messages. I can just tell he knows.

Chuck: Be careful.

Bonnie: I sent the money. It should be in your account tomorrow.

Chuck: You did? Bonnie, that's amazing.

Bonnie grinned to herself. It was amazing.

Bonnie: Didn't you think I would?

Chuck: I knew you would. You said you would, so I knew you would. It's just incredible, though! I'll book the flight tomorrow. With luck Abigail will be at Sloan Kettering Hospital in New York by Monday.

Bonnie: That would be cool.

Chuck: I can't believe how kind you are. I should be able to pay you back by the end of next month. The real estate broker says there's an offer of seventy thousand bucks for one of our fields. The buyer has cash.

Bonnie: That's good.

Chuck: Hey. Would you like to come up to see the farm in Vermont? Maybe I can give you the check in person?

Bonnie felt a rush of blood to her fingers as she typed.

Bonnie: Yes. I would like that.

Chuck: Can you get away? Will your husband suspect anything?

Bonnie: I've got an old friend from high school in Upstate New York. I'll tell him I'm going to see her. He won't know.

Chuck: Great! That's great. Listen, I've got to go now. Thank you so much for sending that money. I truly think it will mean the difference between life and death for Abigail . . . I don't know how I can ever thank you. I'm just . . . overwhelmed.

Bonnie: I'm happy to do it. Bye, Chuck. Speak soon.

Bonnie leaned back in her chair and looked out at the patchy grass in the backyard. She was happy to do it. She was *so* happy to do it.

She gazed at the picture of Chuck on her computer. It wasn't as if he was strikingly good-looking, not one of those guys you would stare at in the street as he walked past. He was unassuming. About her age – maybe a couple of years younger – medium height, slim, thick silver-grey hair, kind blue eyes. There was something calming about him, something reliable.

They had met online, in a word-puzzle chat room of all places. One thing led to another, and now they talked every day. Chuck was a widower with a horse farm in Vermont. His daughter lived in India with her husband and their own two-year-old child, Chuck's granddaughter, Abigail. The poor little girl had been diagnosed with a rare form of leukaemia, which Bonnie had googled and googled. Chuck had flown out there to help his daughter look after the child. Chuck said that the health care in India was better than you might expect, but Abigail's prognosis wasn't good. The only hope was hospital back in America, which would cost money, money he didn't have.

Bonnie was happy to help. Especially since it was only a loan for a couple of months until Chuck had sold one of the fields on the farm.

They had exchanged plenty of photos and followed each other on Instagram. Bonnie's favourite was the one she could call up with a couple of keystrokes on her computer any time she wanted.

Chuck, sitting in front of a fountain draped in purple flowers, a cocktail by his right hand, staring at her, with those warm, understanding, kind eyes.

'Wanna beer?'

Kevin had his head stuck in his refrigerator. Kevin had been divorced three years, lucky guy. There was more beer than food in his refrigerator. A lot more.

'Sure,' said RJ. 'Got any Troegs? I like that stuff.'

Kevin took two bottles from the fridge, expertly removed the caps and handed one to his friend. He took a seat in front of his computer screen. Kevin was a plumber, RJ a carpenter – they frequently worked on contracting jobs together. But as well as boilers and toilets, Kevin knew his way around computers.

'Are you sure you want to do this, man?' he said.

'I'm sure I want to do this.'

'You don't know what you're gonna find.'

'I know what I'm gonna find.'

Kevin was taken aback by the menace in his friend's voice. He began to wonder whether it had been such a good idea to suggest coming back to his apartment from the sports bar so that they could check out RJ's wife's online activities.

He typed a few keys. Wiggled his mouse.

'OK, I need a password.'

'She uses one of three,' said RJ. 'Holly, Molly or Piggles plus the year of her birth – 1966.'

'Holly, Molly and Piggles?'

'Names of her pet dogs when she was growing up.'

Kevin tried them out. 'Piggles1966 it is,' he said. 'Let's take a look.'

He took a look. 'Oh,' he said. 'Uh-oh.'

'What is it?' said RJ, pushing Kevin out of the way so he could see the screen. 'The bitch!' he hissed.

RJ scrolled. And scrolled, to a litany of unimaginative swear-words. His face reddened. Even the top of his shiny scalp turned pink. But he wouldn't let go of the mouse.

'It's not like they're doing anything,' said Kevin, trying far too late to defuse the situation. 'They haven't met, I don't think.'

'Of course, they're doing something!' said RJ. 'Look, dude! It's right in front of your eyes. Wait . . . There's something about me. The bitch!'

Kevin tried to regain control of his mouse, but RJ was having none of it.

'Oh, oh. Look here. She's giving him money. For his dying granddaughter. Or who he says is his dying granddaughter.'

'It's not his dying granddaughter,' said Kevin.

'Jesus! Thirty thousand bucks. She's only gone and given him thirty thousand bucks! And she's sent it to an account in Panama! How dumb can this woman get?'

'That doesn't look good.'

'I didn't even know she *had* thirty thousand bucks. I knew she had her own savings account, but I just thought it was a few hundred dollars' Christmas money.' RJ flung the mouse across the desk in disgust. 'Who is this guy?'

'You can bet his name ain't Chuck,' said Kevin.

'You mean it's a scam?'

'Damn sure it's a scam.'

'I don't believe it!' yelled RJ, slamming his fist down on the desk so hard that pens and papers danced a little jig. 'I s'ppose there's no way to discover who this jerk-off really is?'

Kevin frowned. 'There may be,' he said. He quickly googled the term 'reverse image search'.

He pulled and pushed and pummelled his computer until it divulged a name and an address.

'Hey, RJ. You wouldn't believe where this guy lives!'

## 3.

Óskar watched as Anna led the group of six tourists towards the lava field and the crater at Eldborg, with Turid, who helped out on the farm, taking up the rear. It was a good day for it, with sunshine picking out the subtle oranges, yellows and greens of the mosses and lichens growing on the lava. The mysterious crater looked at its best: bold, proud and faintly dangerous. Two of the tourists – two women from Scotland – had excellent posture and clearly knew what to do with a horse, whereas the other four were sacks of potatoes from Dortmund, slopping and slouching on the backs of their steeds. It didn't much matter; the horses knew the way, and Anna knew how to match horse to rider. And they all paid the same money.

Óskar's task for the day was to drive into Borgarnes to pick up some feed supplements. He would combine that with a nice lunch. It should take care of the day quite pleasantly. He had, after all, fixed the fence.

He was heading back into the farmhouse when he saw Gúdrun's red post van approaching. He waited for her. She always liked to stop and chat – to flirt a little. She was in her late forties, a beefy woman, but she had a good line in cutting gossip.

This time, though, she was in a hurry. Needed to get home as soon as she could because her daughter was off school sick with a cold. Could it be Covid? She didn't want to test – she'd rather not know.

Óskar had been expecting the parcel. He took it inside and opened it. He grinned as he examined its contents. He was pleased.

Before he went to Borgarnes, he had to finish the crossword. He poured himself another cup of coffee, picked up *Morgunbladid*, and sat down to work.

He was stuck on 26 across when he heard a car approaching outside. He resisted the urge to check who it was because he suddenly realized the answer to 12 down. As he pencilled it in, the doorbell rang.

A big, burly man stood in front of him, head shaved and shining, little grey goatee jutting forward, undecipherable tattoos on his bulging forearms. The temperature was a bit on the cool side to be wearing a T-shirt, frankly, but this guy had the bravado of many a young Icelander. Except he wasn't young – he was probably in his late fifties – and he wasn't an Icelander. He was carrying a shopping bag from Húsasmidjan, the hardware store, containing something heavy.

Sure enough, when he opened his mouth, English came out of it, English with an American accent.

'Hello, Chuck.'

The man took a step closer to Óskar and looked down at him.

'May I come in? Chuck.'

'I'm sorry, sir, I'm not Chuck,' said Óskar in English. 'I think you have the wrong house.'

'I have the right house. Chuck. Cos, you see, I recognize you. Chuck.'

The man had hard brown eyes, almost black. Although his voice was low and even, it was also menacing. This guy was angry. And he appeared to be angry with Óskar.

'Now. I asked nicely,' the man said. 'May I come in?'

This stranger was making Óskar nervous. 'I don't think so,' he said, raising his hands ineffectually.

The man raised his own hand, the one not holding the shopping bag, and pushed Óskar rapidly backwards into the little hallway. Then he kept pushing and Óskar kept retreating, until he was in the living room.

'What is this?' Óskar protested, trying to summon righteous indignation to replace the fear. 'Who are you? And what do you want?'

'My name is RJ. I'm Bonnie's husband. And I want her thirty thousand bucks.'

'Who's Bonnie?'

Anger flared in those dark eyes. 'Don't give me any "who's Bonnie" crap. You know perfectly well who she is. You've been talking to her for months on the internet.'

Óskar shook his head. 'I don't remember anyone called Bonnie.'

The man hit him. Hard. On the cheek.

Óskar staggered backwards and raised a hand to his face. 'That hurt.'

'It's going to hurt a lot more the next time I hit you.' The man pulled a small mallet from the shopping bag: a short wooden handle with a solid chunk of iron at its head.

'You're not going to hit me with that?'

'I sure am. Unless you give me back the thirty thousand bucks Bonnie gave you.'

'I tell you, I don't know anyone named Bonnie! Please leave. Now.' Óskar raised an arm and pointed towards the door, with as much authority as he could summon up. But his arm was shaking.

Óskar was relieved to see the man turn and place the mallet on the coffee table behind him. But then he swung round and a fist rushed towards Óskar's face.

Anna walked up to the farmhouse from the stables. She was worried about Hrafn's left foreleg. They had only been two kilometres out when Turid had spotted a slight limp. Anna hadn't wanted to risk it getting worse, and so had swapped horses with the tourist riding Hrafn, and taken the black gelding back to the farm.

She didn't like the look of that leg. More vet's bills.

There was a black car parked about thirty metres away from the farm. A small woman was sitting in the passenger seat, staring at Anna. Óskar should have been on his way to Borgarnes by now, but his pick-up was still outside the front door. He must be entertaining someone.

Who?

Anna frowned. She knew that Óskar had been up to something recently, something involving his computer that he didn't want her to see. Could this woman and whoever was driving the car have something to do with that?

It didn't make any sense.

She hurried into the house and the living room.

There stood a large man, arms hanging in fists by his sides, staring at the floor on which lay her husband. Out cold.

'Óskar!'

She rushed over to him.

'Wake him up, will you?' the man said in English. 'I think I hit him too hard.'

Anna stroked Óskar's cheek and glared up at the man. 'I'm calling the police!'

'No, you're not, lady,' said the man. 'Because if you do, I'll kick Chuck here's head in, and you'll need to call the funeral home.'

Anna couldn't believe what she was hearing. But he was a big guy, and he was wearing boots and his expression suggested to her he was willing to use them in exactly the way he was suggesting.

'Why have you done this? How do you know my husband? And who is Chuck?'

The big man folded his muscular forearms and grinned.

'You don't know anything, do you?'

'No,' said Anna. 'Does Óskar owe you money?' she guessed. But she had no idea how or why. Could it be internet gambling? Was that what Óskar had been so secretive about?

'Let me explain it real clear. Your husband Óskar Davídsson has been pretending on the internet he's called Chuck and he has a horse farm in Vermont in America. He has made friends with my wife – she's the gal in the car outside. And my stupid wife has given thirty thousand bucks to him to fly his granddaughter from India to New York for specialist cancer treatment. Except your husband ain't got no granddaughter in India does he?'

Anna shook her head.

'And if you have grandchildren, they ain't got cancer, do they?'

Once again, Anna shook her head. 'We don't have any grandchildren,' she said, although as she said it, she knew it didn't matter.

Could this be true? Could Óskar really have lied to this man's wife and persuaded her to part with all that money? Óskar could be a little secretive, in fact, he lied all the time to her. He could happily sneak in a cup of coffee at a café when he should be driving straight home and not tell her about it. But they were all little lies. Weren't they?

That kind of internet fraud? Could he do that?

'I can see the doubt in your face,' the man said.

Then he pulled out a phone from his trouser pocket and sent a quick text.

Bonnie watched the tall woman stride into the farmhouse.

She was gorgeous. If that was Chuck's wife – or Óskar or whoever he was – Bonnie stood no chance.

Of course, Bonnie knew she stood no chance. Ever since RJ had come home and shown her the photographs of Óskar Davídsson on the website of his horse farm in Iceland, and on his Instagram account, it had been crystal clear that Chuck was not a widower, that Chuck did not own a horse farm in Vermont, that Chuck did not have a sick granddaughter in India, that Chuck was not, in fact, Chuck.

And she had sent him thirty thousand dollars! Most of her savings. How could she have been so stupid?

She had stared blankly at her husband, whose fury had temporarily abated at the sight of her distress, to be replaced by a cruel grin.

Then she had burst into huge, uncontrollable sobs.

RJ had booked a flight from JFK to Reykjavík the following evening and insisted that Bonnie come with him. She had meekly agreed. She had been such a fool. She deserved his anger.

She was angry herself with Chuck or Óskar or whatever his name was. She wanted her money back! And if RJ roughed Chuck up a little bit, good for him.

Yet, as she sat in the car, she realized that part of her was secretly hoping that it had all been some mistake. That Chuck really did love her, or at least like her. That he would be pleased to see her.

That she would be pleased to see him.

And then she had seen his beautiful wife, which somehow rubbed the reality of his cynical lies in her face.

There were so many reasons for her disappointment. But she now realized that one of the most important was that however unlikely it had seemed, she had hoped that Chuck might have provided her with an escape from RJ.

So much for that idea.

There was no escape from RJ.

Her phone pinged.

She checked it. Three words from her husband. *Come in now.*

She hesitated. She couldn't resist checking her makeup in the rear-view mirror. She opened the car door and walked towards the farmhouse, shoulders slumped, head down.

But her heart was beating rapidly at the knowledge that she was soon to meet Chuck in the flesh.

And there he was, lying on the floor, eyes closed, the tall woman who was his wife kneeling beside him.

'What have you done, RJ?'

'I hit him a bit harder than I planned, is all,' said her husband, flexing the fingers of his right hand.

The man on the floor groaned. His eyelids fluttered open. He looked up at his wife and then across at RJ and Bonnie.

'Chuck!' exclaimed Bonnie, before she could help herself.

The woman glared at her. 'My husband's name is Óskar.'

She had a strong, kind of husky, Icelandic accent.

'Yeah, we know his real name is Óskar,' RJ said. 'But for months he has been lying to Bonnie, grooming her so he could get her to send him money. Show her your phone, Bonnie.'

They had planned this. All the messages between Bonnie and Chuck were ready on her phone. She handed it to the woman.

The woman took the phone and began scrolling through the messages, her frown deepening. RJ looked on with a half-smile.

Bonnie watched as the poor woman at first couldn't believe what she was seeing, and then could believe it. On the floor, Chuck/Óskar groaned and forced himself up on to his elbows.

Jolly Reyes expertly guided his Honda Genio scooter through the tangle of Manila traffic and into the parking lot behind the squat concrete cube that was his place of work.

He climbed the flight of stairs to the first-floor office and greeted the half dozen of his co-workers who were already plugged into their computers, tapping and mousing.

From his backpack, he pulled out his latest purchase from the second-hand bookstore, a romantic comedy by the American author Curtis Sittenfeld. Jolly was twenty-five with a degree in English Literature from De La Salle University. He enjoyed books for their own sake, but he had also found that the knowledge he gleaned from reading works from Jane Austen to Colleen Hoover via *Fifty Shades of Grey* was invaluable in his job.

He took a swig of Royal Tru-Orange, logged on to his computer and started work.

Bonnie noticed a slim hardbacked volume on the coffee table. It had *that* photograph on the front, the one with which she was most familiar – Chuck by the fountain in India. The words *Anna og Óskar 1999–2024* were superimposed on the photograph.

The woman was Anna. She wasn't dead. And she had been married to Óskar for twenty-five years.

Despite herself, Bonnie picked up the book and leafed through it. It was one of those custom-made albums that you can get produced from a set of digital pictures you send in. So many of the photographs Bonnie recognized. Óskar on horseback, Óskar in front of the Taj Mahal, Óskar with a happily smiling young woman who may or may not have been his daughter. No small kids, though.

And then, at the back, Óskar in a suit and his wife in a white dress standing outside a white church. Actually, she had seen that one before too; Chuck's dead wife was the same woman as Óskar's living one, Bonnie had just not recognized her at first.

'See?' said RJ to Anna, who was still scrolling through many of those same pictures on Bonnie's phone.

Anna glanced up at RJ in anguish. Then she passed the phone to her husband and said something to him in Icelandic.

Óskar/Chuck blinked, looked at the phone, stared at Bonnie and shook his head. 'Nei,' he said.

The disavowal pierced Bonnie's heart.

'Oh, yes, you do,' RJ said. 'You know her. And you have our thirty thousand bucks in a bank in Panama.'

'Panama?' Óskar blinked again. 'Anna, what is this man talking about?'

Anna didn't answer. Bonnie could see she was doubting her husband. Been there, done that.

'You got electronic bank transfers in Iceland, don't you?' RJ said. 'I want you, lady, to transfer thirty thousand dollars back to my account now. You got that?'

'But we never received thirty thousand dollars,' Anna said.

'You might not have done, but he did.' RJ nodded towards Óskar. 'Didn't you, Chuck?'

'No,' mumbled Óskar.

RJ kicked him hard in the shin and Óskar let out a yelp. 'Don't lie to me, buddy. You got the thirty grand and your lady is going to transfer it to me now.'

'No,' said Anna.

RJ picked up the mallet and clasped the heavy block of metal that was its head. 'Yes. Or I'm gonna kill him right now. It's that simple.'

'You're bluffing,' said Anna, her eyes alight.

'Watch me,' said RJ with a grin. Bonnie believed him. And Anna did too.

Óskar's blue eyes focused with fear. He mumbled something in Icelandic to his wife. It looked like he was telling her to do it. She frowned, her face ravaged once more by doubt.

Jolly logged on to his computer to see how the dozen or so 'Daisys' that he was responsible for were doing. He glanced up at the four clocks on the wall. Seven p.m. in Manila, nine p.m. in Sydney, noon in London, seven a.m. in New York. The Daisys could be anywhere in the world: seven p.m. to seven a.m. Philippines time were the best hours for communicating with them in Europe or North America.

Jolly felt a firm clap on his shoulder. 'Hey, Jolly, my man. The thirty thousand bucks is in the account. Nice work!'

'Yes!!' Jolly raised his fist in triumph and grinned up at Carlos, the boss, a thirty-two-year-old entrepreneur who had started the business six years before and recruited Jolly. Carlos understood women – and he could identify other men who understood women just as well as he.

Jolly was the second-best performer in the team. Other members passed the Daisys on to him, once they had been hooked on Facebook or Instagram or, most effectively, the online chat rooms attached to games sites. Word puzzles was a good area – the kind of game that women of a certain age might play online. *Grand Theft Auto* not so much.

So that was it. No more Bonnie. The rule was that once the Daisy had paid, the handler went dead. No goodbyes, no letting her down gently. Just silence.

But Jolly always went through the message trail one last time. Partly for professional reasons – to review the chat and learn from any mistakes he may have made. But partly to let himself down gently.

This was always a moment of mixed emotions for Jolly. He loved the money he was earning – he almost had enough for a second-hand BMW. But he put something of his soul into cultivating each Daisy. He liked Bonnie and felt genuine sympathy towards her. Her husband was clearly a nasty piece of work. If he ever found out what she had done, she would be in *so* much trouble.

Oh, well. That's life. No space for guilt in this job.

He switched windows to Shelley from Adelaide. They were using the same picture series, silverfox15, for her as they had for Bonnie. There was something about the Icelander that all the Daisys seemed to fall for. The only one who came close in effectiveness was silverfox9, who was a building inspector from Brescia in Italy, with salt-and-pepper hair and warm eyes – brown this time.

Jolly got himself another can of Royal Tru-Orange – he was powered by the stuff – and tapped out a quick message. silverfox15 was now known as 'Larry'. American again – Jolly was almost perfect at American style and usage – but this time a schoolteacher from a small town in Minnesota.

'Hi Shelley. India's great. Here's a picture of me having a cocktail with my daughter. She's worried about little Taylor – we're waiting for the tests to come back – but I'm sure it'll turn out to be nothing. Have you ever been to India?'

He attached the silverfox15 picture by the fountain and pressed send.

And then he realized he had sent it to the wrong woman.

Oops.

* * *

'You know, he will do it,' Bonnie said. 'He will kill Óskar.'

She *hated* the idea of RJ killing Óskar, whatever Óskar had done to her, however much he had stolen from her. But she realized that unless Anna believed RJ's threat, that's exactly what would happen.

Anna believed him. She glanced at her husband, who had pulled himself into an armchair. He still looked groggy, but he seemed to be following what was going on.

He nodded.

'I'm going to have to use my computer to transfer the money,' Anna said. 'I need to switch funds from my savings account first.'

'Where is it?' RJ asked.

'Right there.' She pointed to a desk beneath a window on which lay a laptop.

'OK. Go ahead. Here are the routing details for my account.' He handed over a slip of paper he had prepared earlier.

Anna returned Bonnie's phone to her, took the slip and walked over to the desk.

Bonnie's phone pinged.

For several seconds Bonnie didn't understand what the message meant.

And then she did.

'RJ?' She showed him the message.

'What the hell is this?'

Bonnie muttered into RJ's ear. 'It's a guy called Larry. And he's talking to a woman called Shelly. And he's claiming that that photo of Chuck or Óskar or whoever the hell he is, is really him.'

RJ frowned. 'So what does that mean?' he whispered back.

'It means someone has stolen Óskar's photo and used it as part of a scam. They've probably used it over and over again. Óskar really doesn't know anything about it.'

RJ glanced at the Icelander sitting in an armchair, trying to focus on what they were saying.

'Jesus!' he said.

'So what do we do?'

'I dunno.'

'Should we apologize and leave?'

'No way! I've just beaten up an innocent guy. They'd have me in jail in no time.'

'So what do we do, then?'

RJ thought. Anna was logging into her bank. Óskar was frowning at them.

'They don't know we know this. They're scared we really believe Óskar is Chuck and I'm gonna off him. We let them go ahead and transfer the thirty thousand bucks to us.'

'And then?'

'Then . . .' RJ hesitated, frowning. 'Then I finish them anyway.'

'RJ!'

RJ nodded to himself, decision taken. 'We got no choice. We kill them. We get out of the country. There's no link between us and them. No one has seen us here. We'll be OK. Otherwise, we go to jail. This way we get the thirty grand back. No way I'm leaving here down that thirty G.'

'*You* go to jail, you mean?'

RJ grinned nastily. 'I'll take you with me, Bonnie.'

Anna interrupted their whispers from her computer on the other side of the room. 'OK, I'm about to make the transfer. Do you want to watch?'

RJ took a couple of steps towards her.

He had put the mallet back down on the coffee table. Bonnie saw it.

If she picked it up and whacked him, RJ wouldn't kill Óskar and his brave wife. Bonnie wouldn't go to jail for their murder. And she would be free of her husband forever.

It was a huge decision. And she only had a couple of seconds to make it. If RJ turned and grabbed the mallet, she'd never have another chance.

She snatched up the mallet and brought it crashing down on her husband's skull.

RJ barely made a noise as he crumpled to the floor.

There was silence in the room as Óskar and Anna stared at Bonnie, and Bonnie stared at her husband's sightless eyes.

'Why did you do that?' said Óskar.

Bonnie turned towards the oh-so-familiar face of the man with the kind blue eyes.

'I don't know,' she said. 'But I sure would appreciate the help of the both of you figuring out a good answer to that question before we call the police.'

# ELLY GRIFFITHS – THE WOMAN IN WHITECHAPEL

Elly Griffiths writes: The Woman in White *by Wilkie Collins is universally acclaimed as a masterpiece. The rest of this story is fictional.*

'And what did she do, this . . . woman in white?'

'She disappeared,' replied Wilkie, rather sulkily.

'Disappeared, eh?' Charles leaned back in his chair, smoothed out his beard and prepared to enjoy himself. He was entertaining in these moods as long as you were not the subject of his ponderous irony. Wilkie feared that he was in for it.

'So . . . a dreadful scream rends the night. A beautiful woman, clad all in white, appears at the door of a respectable Regent's Park house. She looks around her in terror and then flees, seeming to float rather than run.'

There was a hint of parody here, a suggestion of Wilkie's rather nasal vowel sounds. Also 'clad' was taking things too far. Wilkie was sure that he had said 'dressed'. He had used the floating line though and was now rather regretting it.

'The three men look at each other in wild surmise. Who is the mysterious woman? From what peril is she escaping?' He was overdoing it now. Charles was a good actor but seldom a subtle one. Wilkie first met him when they were cast in the same play. He played Charles's valet. Which said it all really.

'Ask my brother Charlie if you don't believe me,' said Wilkie. 'Or Millais. They were both there.'

'What were you three doing? Staggering home from a Dionysian orgy?'

'Walking back from a dinner party at mother's. In Hanover Terrace. We all saw the woman. We were struck dumb by her.'

'I'm not sure any of you are reliable witnesses,' said Charles, doing some more beard stroking. Charles had taken against

Wilkie's dreamily romantic brother Charlie, partly because his favourite daughter Kate had once said she found him handsome. Millais, being a pre-Raphaelite, could always be accused of overheated imagination.

'If it were me,' said Charles, 'I would have run after the woman and clasped her in my arms. I'm sure she was fleeing from a wicked husband and needed the comfort of a good man.'

Was Charles a good man? Wilkie sometimes doubted it. He was certainly a married man and the father of ten children. Wilkie liked Charles's wife, Catherine, a stolid woman who seemed to exist only to provide a domestic setting for the great writer, but he thought she was probably deeply unhappy.

'I tried to follow,' said Wilkie. 'But she was too quick for me. She ran like a gazelle.'

'A white gazelle,' said Charles. 'A rather beautiful image.'

'I am capable of the odd piece of imagery, you know.'

'Of course I know, dear fellow. One day, I am sure, you will write a really fine book.'

It would make an arresting start to a book, thought Wilkie. The moonlight, the white dress, the sense of urgency and danger. He hadn't told Charles the whole story. He never did. Because, of course, he had run after her. What did Charles think he was? Wilkie wasn't going to let a beautiful woman get away from him, not without hearing her story first. Besides, the look she'd given the three men, one composed of entreaty and a certain glint of challenge, seemed directed chiefly at Wilkie. He'd given chase. He'd been a good runner in his youth and the pipe of opium that preceded the dinner gave him a godlike belief in his ability to catch the gazelle.

But then again, she didn't make it too difficult.

She was standing in an alleyway between gardens. One of those secret pathways known only to errand boys and scullery maids. Her white skirts shimmered in the moonlight and provided a spotlight as effective as any conjured by Charles's theatricals.

'You've caught me,' she said. That look again.

'My dear lady,' said Wilkie. He was panting slightly. Laudanum can only do so much. 'You seem in distress. Let me know how I can serve you.'

'Serve' was pushing it but something about the woman made chivalrous language seem appropriate. Although she was older than he first thought, she was even more beautiful, with large regular features like an Italian Madonna, although her hair, which was loose, was Anglo Saxon blonde.

'I had to get away from him,' she said. 'He thought he could . . . oh it's too horrible . . . he thought he could somehow control me, control my mind.'

'My dear lady,' said Wilkie again. He paused, delicately, for her to insert her name.

'Caroline,' said the woman in white. 'Caroline Graves.'

'My dear Caroline, you must allow me to escort you to my lodgings. They are not far from here. A respectable widow keeps house for me. You need not be afraid of being alone with me.'

Caroline turned her lamp-like eyes upon him. 'Oh I am not afraid of that.'

Which was just as well because the respectable widow existed only in Wilkie's imagination.

'Has he gone?' asked Caroline, peering around the door.

'Yes, departed to ruin someone else's day.'

'Mr Dickens is a hard man,' said Caroline. 'I've known dangerous men and he's one of them.'

'My dear.' Wilkie held out a hand. 'You are quite safe. Sit beside me and let us decide what to do.'

She was still wearing the dress, a little creased now and dusty around the hem, but an impressive garment nonetheless. It caught the light as she swayed across the room and came to sit on the sofa beside him. All Caroline had told Wilkie yesterday was that she had been kept a prisoner in the Regent's Park house by a man called Ransom. Wilkie hadn't pressed her for more information but had offered his bed for the night. He had slept in his dressing room, acutely aware of the presence next door. Charles had made one of his inconveniently early morning calls, so this was Wilkie's first chance to solve the mystery.

'Tell me about this Ransom,' said Wilkie. 'If it isn't too distressing for you, that is.'

Caroline shivered but there was something rather mechanical about it. If Wilkie had been writing the stage directions, he would have described it thus: SHE SHIVERS AT THE MEMORY.

'He's a mesmerist,' she said. 'He can control the thoughts of others.'

Wilkie had heard of mesmerism. It was the invention of Franz Anton Mesmer, a Swiss doctor who trained at the University of Vienna. He claimed to be able to cure people by putting them into a trance and channelling the psychic ether in their bodies. When Mesmer, a broodingly attractive man, visited London, hundreds flocked to his demonstrations where he unveiled an apparatus apparently designed to distribute magnetic energy to the crowd.

Wilkie and Charles had been present at one such display because Mesmer was a protégé of Charles's great friend, Dr John Elliotson. After attending the demonstration Charles decided that he, too, could mesmerize. Sure enough, a few weeks later, at a party, Charles put a woman called Augusta de la Rue into a trance. The whole thing had been very dramatic. Madame de la Rue lay on a sofa, apparently asleep, her eyelids flickering. When Charles asked her what was troubling her, the woman replied, in a guttural voice quite unlike her own, that she was being pursued by a phantom. 'Begone foul fiend!' bellowed Charles in a voice so loud that it extinguished several candles. When Augusta opened her eyes again, she declared herself much refreshed. 'The spectre has left you,' Charles told her and Augusta was very grateful, despite not knowing of the creature's existence until a few moments ago. Charles repeated this trick several times but always, Wilkie noted, with attractive young women. It was, apparently, more difficult to hypnotize men or older ladies.

'How did you meet this Ransom?' Wilkie asked Caroline.

She didn't answer. Instead, she held a handkerchief to her eyes.

OVERCOME, SHE HIDES HER FACE.

'What did he do to you, my dear?'

'He would put me into a sleep but it was as if I was awake the whole time. Awake but unable to resist him. He made me stand up and sit down. Eventually he made me discard my clothes . . .'

SHE SOBS.

Wilkie waited a few seconds before saying, 'Let us be practical.

You are free from this monster now. Are your belongings still at the house in Regent Park? Would you like me to fetch them for you?'

'No!' This was almost a shout. 'Please don't go back there. I never want to think of the place again.'

'Are you quite alone in the world?' asked Wilkie. It was not an unpleasant thought. But Caroline raised her eyes to his and said, with a note of defiance in her voice, 'I am a widow with a young daughter. We live in Whitechapel with my mother-in-law.'

It was a depressingly respectable answer and, for a moment, Caroline looked less like a wronged heroine and more like a tired woman in a crumpled dress. But then Wilkie imagined a child running through the apartment, smiling up at him, maybe even calling him 'Papa'. Watching Charles, who was an energetic if inconsistent father, playing boisterous games with his progeny, occasionally evoked a sharp pain which Wilkie treated with laudanum before realizing that it was longing. The problem was that Wilkie was deeply opposed to the institution of marriage. Could Caroline provide him with a wife and daughter without the interference of church and state?

'Bring them here,' he said. 'It would be cheering to have a young person about the place.'

That afternoon, Wilkie hired a carriage to convey Caroline to Whitechapel and she returned with her daughter, Harriet, and her mother-in-law, Mary Ann. Before the day was over Caroline was Carrie and Harriet, an engaging child who loved answering doors and announcing visitors, was 'the butler'. The living arrangements had to be revised, of course. Wilkie's dressing room became a bedchamber for Mary Ann and Harriet. Caroline and Wilkie occupied what Wilkie, in ironical quotation marks, called 'the marital bed'.

Two days after the flight from Whitechapel, the four of them were in the drawing room. Carrie, dressed in leaf green, was busy with her embroidery. Mary Ann was nodding over a book and looking indulgently at Harriet, who was arranging her dolls for their daily rote learning. Although the girl herself did not attend school, she was strict about her toys' education. Wilkie was scribbling in his journal. A loud knock on the door made Harriet leap up in excitement.

'Your butler,' said Wilkie, with a smile at Carrie.

A few moments later, Harriet was back, announcing proudly, 'Mr Diggins.'

Wilkie rose from the sofa with what felt like deadly sophistication.

'Charles, my dear fellow, can I introduce Mrs Mary Ann Graves and Mrs Caroline Graves? You've met the butler, I see.'

Charles bowed but his eyes, when he raised them to Wilkie's, were alight with curiosity. He conversed with the ladies, employing his usual charm, drank a cup of tea and, when he rose to go, asked if Wilkie would escort him into the street.

On the pavement outside the house, Charles turned to his friend. 'Was that *her*?'

'The woman in white?' said Wilkie. 'Yes.'

'And you are living with her? As husband and wife?'

'As civilized people, yes.'

'But . . .' This was a moment. The great writer was actually lost for words. Wilkie wished that he had one of the new heliographic devices so that he could capture the image forever.

'What do you know of her?' was the best Charles could manage, after a few moments of throat clearing.

'She is a widow,' said Wilkie. 'She was held prisoner by a man called Ransom. He performed mesmeric experiments on her.' He looked Charles squarely in the eyes. The man had the grace to look slightly chastened.

'How barbaric,' he murmured.

'Yes, indeed.' Wilkie was enjoying himself. In fact, he wondered if this was the best day of his life. 'I have rescued her. I think she is the love of my life. I think she is my muse.'

'Your muse?'

'Yes. Didn't I tell you? I have had an idea for a new book. It begins with a man crossing Regent's Park at night. He feels a hand touch lightly upon his shoulder. He turns and sees a beautiful woman dressed . . . *clad* . . . in white. She asks him the way to London and they talk for a while until she hears a carriage approach and runs away in alarm. In the vehicle are two men who are pursuing her. Two wicked men.'

Wilkie smiled up at Charles who was, once again, speechless.

'A good beginning, don't you think?' said Wilkie.

Of course, he was curious about the mysterious Mr Ransom. Wilkie hadn't overlooked the strange name, which sounded as if it had been invented in response to the story that was unfolding. Kidnap, hostage, ransom. So, a few weeks after Carrie, Mary Ann and Harriet joined his household, Wilkie made the journey to Regent's Park. He recognized the house, one of those white edifices that looked as if it had been spun from icing sugar. It was here that Caroline had stood, on the steps by the door, poised for flight. Or was it? The events of that night had become mythical but that made them harder to recall. Wilkie couldn't now remember if the door opened and then Caroline emerged. Or was she already on the steps or even in the garden? The woman in white had become a different person from Carrie, the companion who fetched his nightly sherry and was in the process of embroidering some slippers for him.

It was a beautiful spring day and the trees in the front garden were bridal with blossom, pale pink against the pale blue sky. Wilkie approached the black front door. The knocker had been removed as if the house were empty. Undeterred Wilkie tapped on the wood with his cane and, a few minutes later, the summons was answered by a man in old-fashioned livery, accessorized by a green baize apron. Wilkie asked for Mr Ransom.

'No one of that name lives here, sir.'

'Indeed.' Wilkie considered. 'Would you mind conveying my compliments to whoever is in residence?' He proffered his card.

'I'm afraid the house is shut up, sir. We have holland covers over all the furniture.'

'I was passing a few weeks ago,' said Wilkie, 'and I met a lady leaving here.'

'There's no lady at this address, sir. The house has been closed for many months. It is owned by Mr and Mrs Vanstone but they are *abroad*.' He gave the last word a very sinister emphasis.

Wilkie wondered if this butler, unlike his own, would be impervious to bribery but, after the exchange of a coin, he was allowed to enter the house. It was, as described, swathed in white linen. Even the chandeliers had become monstrous clouds hovering over the ghost furniture. Watched anxiously by the servant, Wilkie climbed the stairs. He opened doors leading to many bedrooms but there were no signs that any of them had been occupied recently, covers were stripped from beds and the curtainless windows reflected a cloudless sky. The only possible clue was a thread of white material caught in a doorframe. Wilkie put it in his pocket.

Wilkie descended the staircase and, at the foot, he stopped. There was a stain on the floorboards, irregular in shape and dark brown in colour. Wilkie poked at it with his cane.

'Nothing can shift that mark,' said the butler sadly. 'The housekeeper is quite distraught. I don't know how it can have happened. As I say, the house has been empty since January. Mrs Betteridge and I only returned a few days ago.'

'Try a rug,' said Wilkie, pressing another coin upon the man.

He walked away, enjoying the May sunshine. A line came into his head, 'nothing in the world is hidden forever', but he dismissed it, thinking instead of drinking sherry with Carrie that evening, while Harriet played with her dolls, one of whom was now called Mr Diggens.

## *Author's note*

According to John Millais' son, his father, accompanied by the Collins brothers, did meet a woman in white fleeing from a house near Regent's Park. Millais and Charles Collins were transfixed by her beauty but Wilkie gave chase. This is corroborated by Katy Dickens, who later married Charles Collins.

The woman was Caroline Graves. Wilkie and Caroline lived together for many years, Wilkie treating her daughter Harriet as his own child. This idyll was interrupted by Caroline's marriage to Joseph Charles Clow and Wilkie's liaison with Martha Rudd, with whom he had two children. But Caroline and Wilkie were soon cohabiting again, although possibly upon different terms. Harriet's childhood nickname was 'the butler'.

Charles Dickens did perform mesmerism upon Augusta de la Rue.

# JOHN HARVEY – CRISS-CROSS

The body was discovered a little shy of six, the light a gracenote on the horizon. A dog walker, walking early. Dew on the grass and the promise of rain. The dog, a German Shepherd, moving close then backing gradually away, growling low in its throat. One step, one careful look and the man reached for the mobile in the folds of his waterproof jacket.

The phone resting beneath the edge of Alex Hadley's pillow vibrated and, already on the edge of sleep, she slowly swung her legs from beneath the duvet and, careful not to disturb Rachel, steadied herself to her feet. The polished boards struck cold.

6.49.

Chris Phillips, her number two in the Major Investigation Team, one of twenty-four within the Met's Homicide and Serious Crime Command.

'Fatality, boss. High up on the Heath.'

'Where exactly?'

'The Tumulus. You know . . .'

Hadley knew. A supposed burial ground midway between Hampstead to the west, Dartmouth Park to the east. Everyone from Boudica on was rumoured to have been interred there, none of it, apparently, true.

She glanced at the time on her phone. 'Twenty minutes, thirty tops.'

Behind her, Rachel stirred and muttered something in her sleep. What could have been a name. Not Alex. Hadley leaned down to kiss her cheek and, still in sleep, Rachel's face turned away, a small sound of discontent.

When Hadley stepped outside, the rain was falling in continuous lines, undisturbed by the wind. Stair rods, her father would have said.

What kind of a summer was this?

Thirty became thirty-five, became forty. The rain intensified. At the entrance to the Heath a uniformed officer raised the barrier to let Hadley drive through, one hand briefly touching his forehead in a gesture that was part salute, part wave. Joggers grudgingly stepped aside. Where the path narrowed small stones spun up against the under carriage; mud freckled the windscreen. Hadley pulled over behind a small convoy of parked vehicles: ambulance, two area cars, an IRV. A Range Rover she recognized as belonging to the medical examiner. The immediate vicinity was already cordoned off with tape, a tent raised over the body.

At either end of the tumulus a pair of large oaks dwarfed the spindly spread of fir trees at its centre; gorse pressed up against the surrounding railings. As she cut upwards across the grass, Chris Phillips strode down to meet her, takeout coffee cup in one hand.

'Not as hot as it was.'

Hadley nodded thanks, prised off the lid, sipped, swallowed, handed it back. 'What've we got?'

'White male, fifties, thereabouts. Nolan's looking at him now.'

'ID?'

Phillips shook his head. 'Empty wallet, chucking distance. Up among the trees. Could have been his. Initials CF on the outside.'

'No sign of a phone?'

'Not so far.'

Nolan came out of the tent to meet them, murmuring something disparaging about the weather. He and Hadley shook hands.

'Before you ask, I'd say dead between four to six hours. Blows to the side of the head with something heavy and sharp the most probable cause. None of that admissible as yet. Expect more tomorrow. But now let's get this body moved before it floats away.'

Hadley's phone rang. Alistair McKeon, Detective Superintendent with overall responsibility for N. W. Homicide Command. 'Quick update, Alex . . .'

Hadley told him what little she knew so far.

'Mugging, that the way you're thinking?'

'Possibility, sir, of course.'

'Keep me up to speed.'

'Sir.'

As Hadley turned away a flurry of crows rose up, squawking, from the centre of the trees, beaks jabbing at a piece of discarded food wrapping, tearing it this way and that, until one snatched it away and rose up towards the higher branches of the nearest oak, a card that had somehow become attached, fluttering back down towards the ground.

Phillips retrieved it.

Carl Ferguson, Private Security. Website and mobile number. The initials, CF, silver against a gold background.

'Crows working Scene of Crime now?' Hadley remarked.

'Avian patrol group, boss. New initiative.'

'Cheeky!'

Phillips blushed.

Along with the expected self-promotional guff, Ferguson's website provided an address, a small thirties apartment block with partial views back across the Heath. Ferguson's flat was on the top floor of three.

At first glance you might wonder if anyone lived there at all.

Everything from bed linen to sofa cushions neatly in place; glasses, crockery stowed away. Perhaps the cleaner had been in the previous day.

In what an estate agent might have described as a generous second bedroom, a high-tech exercise bike shared space with a laptop and printer; weights on racks along one wall.

The living room had a faint air of polish; a few books and magazines. An empty flower vase. A bottle of Jameson's and, beside it, a solid bottomed glass, wiped clean. Little or nothing personal at all.

Hadley turned away, crossed to the window and looked out through the tops of the trees in the direction of the tumulus, wondering if Ferguson had been walking away or returning when he was attacked. Where he might have been going, where he had been.

* * *

The necessary authorization from RIPA obtained, the team began accessing the contents of Ferguson's laptop, chasing down email connections, compiling as accurate an internet search history as possible. The area where his body had been found continued to be cordoned off while SOCA officers scanned the ground, cursing the rain that continued to fall in slow waves, washing any distinguishable footprints away.

The post-mortem results confirmed the cause of death as blunt force trauma to the head. Severe haemorrhaging, fractured skull. Two blows in particular, delivered with force enough to slice through flesh and splinter the bone beneath. Elsewhere, bruising to the upper arms and body, the skin unbroken.

Two different weapons? Hadley wondered.

Two attackers?

'Boss!' Hadley's thoughts were interrupted by the arrival of Mark Foster, the youngest member of the team, flush-faced at her office door. 'Ferguson, boss. He's only ex-Job. East Midlands Special Operations Unit. DS. Resigned, 2009.'

'Jumped before he was pushed?'

'Not clear, boss. Need to double check.'

'Double check, always a good idea. Check and check again.'

Foster scuttled away.

The basic pieces continued to fall into place. Ferguson's work had ranged from advising worried home owners about personal security to a sideline as bodyguard-come-driver for a small selection of minor celebrities. He had contracts with a number of pubs and clubs, guaranteeing to supply them with trained and properly supervised doormen and bouncers. It was one of these – a club in Hampstead with a licence for live music and a kitchen that stayed open till midnight – that he had been returning from on the night he was attacked.

Hadley was checking back through what they had – what they were still lacking – before making a report to Homicide Command HQ, when Foster returned, bright eyed, the words tumbling out one over another.

Prior to his resignation, Ferguson's estranged wife had applied to have a restraining order against him, on the grounds of coercive and threatening behaviour. That had been in early 2009. Towards the end of the following year his wife had died from smoke inhalation when a fire spread through the house in Nottingham where she'd been living. Arson was suspected, Ferguson questioned, never charged.

'Connection, boss?'

'Big leap,' Hadley said. 'Small steps, remember? One after another.'

'That would be alongside the double-checking?'

'Precisely.'

He was along the corridor when Hadley called him back. 'The fire in Nottingham, do we know who was leading the investigation?'

Foster took a quick look at his notes. 'SIO . . . let me see . . . Resnick, boss. DI Resnick.'

Hadley found that she was smiling.

It had been a joint investigation, Notts and the Met. Hadley a young DC, just her second posting. Since then she'd moved away, moved on, returned. Resnick had seemed affable, open to ideas, however cockamamie; for a bulky man, Hadley remembered, he seemed surprisingly light on his feet. It was at his suggestion, after the case came to a satisfactory conclusion, that celebrations in the local pub continued in Soho, half a dozen of them just in time to catch the last set at Ronnie Scott's.

Georgie Fame and the Blue Flames.

'Night Train'. 'My Girl'. 'Walking the Dog'.

Hadley leaned back and closed her eyes, remembering. He must be well retired by now, she thought, Charlie Resnick. But with any luck still around.

One hand firmly gripping the banister, Resnick stood at the top of the stairs. No sense in rushing, whoever it was would ring again. Less than six months back his former DS had hurried to respond to the front door bell, lost balance and tumbled down a full flight of stairs, resulting in triple fractures and blurred vision. Now he walked with a stick, if he walked any distance at all.

Since retiring from the force a good ten years ago, Resnick had, on occasion, been called in to divisional HQ in the role of civilian investigator: taking statements, processing paperwork, watching the real business of police work pass him by. Set against daytime TV with its constant ads for stair lifts, health insurance and problems of an erectile nature, it just had the edge.

Otherwise, he found ways enough to occupy himself: a little self-conscious gardening; attempting, yet again, to make the perfect borscht; continuing a correspondence with one of his junior DCs who was now a senior officer in Morecambe on the Lancashire coast; filing his Monk CDs in chronological order. Most days, he took a slow walk down into the city, a coffee at Cartwheel, sometimes a glass or two in The Peacock, and then walked back again.

He was at ground floor level, midway between kitchen and living room, when the phone rang again.

'Resnick.'

'Charlie, it's Alex Hadley. I don't know if you'll . . .'

'Holmes Road MIT. What? A dozen years back now?'

'Near enough.'

At least his memory wasn't yet atrophying, along with the rest of him. 'How can I help?'

'Carl Ferguson. Ring any bells?'

Bells and whistles, sirens, flashing lights.

'What about him?'

'He was murdered. Late last night, early hours of this morning.'

Good bloody riddance hovered on the edge of Resnick's tongue, unspoken.

'He was suspected of involvement in his wife's death. Arson? I think you were in charge of the investigation.'

Resnick said nothing, waited.

'I'd like to come and talk to you about all that if you're willing, see if there's any connection.'

Still nothing.

'Charlie?'

'Yes, of course. When were you thinking?'

'Tomorrow. Tomorrow morning.'

'Fine. Call me again when you're close. I'll give a think to where we can meet.'

When he turned away his eyes were smarting from the acrid smoke that seemed, suddenly, to have filled the room.

* * *

They sat at one of the tables outside Nottingham Playhouse, around the corner from the Central Police station. Coffee and cinnamon buns. Sunlight bouncing off the Anish Kapoor sculpture and lancing their eyes.

'What is that?' Hadley asked, pointing up at the bright blue of the sky.

Resnick grinned. 'East Midlands microclimate. Summer all year round.'

Hadley gave a quick smile back. Small talk enough.

'The fire,' Resnick said, 'no doubt it was arson. Petrol poured through an opening in a downstairs back window and set alight. Small terraced house, two up, two down, didn't take long for the whole place to be ablaze. By the time we got there, folk both sides had been evacuated, fire crew doing their best to bring it under control. Went in as soon as was safe. Brought out a woman. Scarcely touched by the flames, it seemed. Declared dead later, smoke inhalation.'

He reached for his coffee, a quick double swallow. 'All the while the neighbours kept shouting there's a kiddie. A kiddie inside. Two men went back inside, found no one, just made it out again before the roof caved in. The girl, Mia, eight years old, she was on a sleepover at a friend's.'

'And your thoughts went to Ferguson straight away?'

'He was the obvious suspect. From when they first got together, four or five years back, before the restraining order, seems like he was threatening her with this and that pretty much the whole time. Small stuff at first. Once in a while, a tap – that was how he characterized it – to keep her in line. And for stupid things, little things. Could be nothing more than putting the knives back in the cutlery drawer the wrong way round.'

'And four or five years, you said? Not his daughter then?'

'Father legged it long since. Ferguson seemed to have tolerated her at best.'

Hadley whispered something beneath her breath. 'She was brave to get away, the mum.'

'Women's refuge first, then, back in work, benefits – considerate landlord, one of the few – found a place of her own. Her and Mia.'

'Made them a target.'

Resnick looked back at her, didn't reply.

A couple of teenagers went past on skateboards, narrowly missing a group of Japanese tourists taking photographs of the Kapoor sculpture.

'He was arrested back then,' Hadley said, 'but never charged.'

'According to the CPS not enough evidence to presume a likely conviction.'

'You disagreed?'

'At the time, yes. Looking back . . .' He shrugged. 'The only physical evidence, petrol on the shoes he'd been wearing that evening. Small amount splashed up on to his trousers. Claimed it had happened when he was refilling his car earlier. CCTV from the garage seemed to bear that out. Plus, the woman he'd been having a thing with testified to them spending the night together while her old man was away.'

'And there were no other credible suspects?'

'Not really. Some rumours of a feud between Helen and the family a few doors down. She'd complained about them not keeping their dogs under control, reported them to the council, to the police. Then there was a pair of youths seen hanging round in the ginnel that runs along behind the houses, but that came to nothing, prospecting for a bit of B&E at best.'

He edged his chair back from the table. 'What happened. That woman dying like that. I wanted someone to be found guilty. Needed it, I suppose.'

'And the girl? Mia, I think you said . . .'

'Taken into care. After a year, maybe a bit longer, her friend, Katie's parents applied to foster her. Seemed like a perfect solution, perfect as it was going to get, couple of responsible adults, caring, another girl her own age, brother just that bit older.'

'Perfect's hard to come by.'

Resnick nodded. 'All right for a time and then she started cutting herself, self-harming. Feeling guilty for not having been there when her mother died. When it got worse there was therapy, short spells in hospital. Last I heard, she'd been sectioned . . .'

Resnick's breath seemed to drain away.

Hadley looked directly into his face and for the first time since they met earlier that morning he looked old.

'Ferguson, you still believe he was responsible?'

'I do.'

Back down in London, it was still raining. Nothing fierce, sudden. Just a slow drizzle that began then faded, began again. Most of Hadley's afternoon had been spent battling with what Resnick had told her, pushing it into place; going over what little development there'd been in her absence.

Ferguson's recent clients and others he would have come into contact with in the course of his work were in the process of being contacted, looking for anyone with serious grudges, harbouring any kind of festering dissatisfaction. What little private life he seemed to have had was difficult to decipher and what had been uncovered so far offered little or nothing. Up on the Heath, the search area had been widened and widened again; the question of divers being brought in to scour the ponds was on hold, a matter of budgeting.

By the time Hadley left the station it was dusk, darker by the time she arrived home. The lights in the flat were on, turned low; Radio Three quietly playing. The emptiness was palpable.

She poured herself a glass of wine, drank too quickly – slow down, slow down – poured herself another. Rachel was off seeing something or other from a season of Taiwanese cinema, the programme lay open on the living room table.

At the university where they'd both been undergraduates, Rachel had studied Film and Psychology, stayed faithful to them ever since. Faithful – how did the song go? Faithful to you, darling, in my fashion; faithful to you, darling, in my way.

The first time they met, if meeting was the right word, Rachel had been in the student bar with friends and Hadley had just stumbled out of a screening of Satyajit Ray's epic of poverty-stricken life in rural India, *Pather Panchali*, having mistaken it beforehand for some kind of Bollywood musical.

'Jesus!' she exclaimed, launching herself into the only space at the bar. 'What a waste of fucking time that was!'

When she looked she found she was pressed close alongside Rachel, whom she'd only previously seen from a distance. Chair of FilmSoc, GaySoc, fine boned and unattainable. To her surprise, Rachel made no attempt to move away.

* * *

That night and the next Resnick was woken by the sound of fire engines, the smell of burning timber. The sight of a slight body covered with a white sheet, being carried to the waiting ambulance. When it couldn't be shaken he got up, made tea, put a CD of Bill Evans' solo piano on the stereo, hoping that peace would follow.

Some chance.

At first light he went downstairs, made coffee, decided doing something was better than nothing. A quick call to Alex Hadley, letting her know what he had in mind, making sure he wasn't muddying any waters.

Norma Davis was hanging out the washing in the yard back of the house nearby Lenton Rec. With Katie up in Newcastle at uni and Michael down in London – an apprentice electrician with HS2 – she didn't know where it all came from.

She was pegging up the last of her husband's work overalls when she heard the bell at the front door.

It took but a moment to recognize him. 'Mister Resnick. Caught me in my apron. But come in, come in why don't you? Give me an excuse to stick kettle on.'

A good hour to spare before setting off to her job as a dinner lady at the local primary.

When she came into the living room, mugs of tea and biscuits on a tray, Resnick was staring at a framed black and white photograph on the wall. Two girls and a boy. Mia, Katie and Michael. Somebody's birthday.

'Our Katie,' Norma said. 'Her thirteenth.'

It wasn't Katie that Michael was looking at. Gazing. Mia looking back at him with a shy smile.

'Thought the sun shone out of her eyes for a while, Mister Resnick. Katie were right jealous at times. But then, you know, puberty and she started shutting herself away, Mia. Cutting herself. Near tore us apart, I don't mind saying.'

'Do you still see her, Mia?'

Norma took a pack of cigarettes from her apron pocket and set it down again by where she was sitting, unopened. 'When she first went into hospital, we'd visit regular, me and Katie together.'

'Not Michael?'

'Upset him too much he said. Though he did go a few times, back in the beginning.'

Resnick broke off a piece of biscuit, drank some tea. 'Lately, you've not been going so much?'

Norma shook out a cigarette, lit it, turned her head aside as she released a slim wand of smoke.

'She'd been staying at some kind of, I don't know, halfway house. Hanging out with all sorts. Once in a while she'd turn up here, one or two in the morning, half out of her head and of course we'd take her in. Then . . .' Quick drag on the cigarette. 'We hadn't seen her in a while, thought maybe she'd pulled herself together . . . but she . . . she got this can of petrol, poured it over herself, tried to . . . tried to set herself alight.'

A cry broke from Norma's throat and the mug of tea that had been balancing beside her went to the floor. Resnick reached over and took the cigarette from her hand. Held her. Tears wet on his shirt front, one of her hands clinging to the lapel of his coat.

After some minutes, she prised herself away, accepted Resnick's handkerchief and dabbed at her face.

'I'm sorry, I'm sorry.'

'No need.'

From out on the recreation ground, the sounds, faint, of young children playing; music from the radio next door, or was it the television? A song Resnick faintly remembered.

When she spoke again, Norma's voice was little more than a whisper. 'After the business with the petrol, she was sectioned for her own safety. I went to see her, just the once, back in the Priory. Katie was up in Newcastle so I persuaded Michael to come with me. Mia stared at us as if she didn't know who we were. Didn't say a word. Not to us, not to anyone. Nonverbal, that's what the nurse in charge called it. Taken it upon herself not to speak again. When we got outside Michael . . . I don't know, I'd never seen him like that before.'

'Upset? Uncomprehending?'

'Angry. The look on his face. As if the only thing he could do was to break something. Tear it to pieces. And his hands like fists. I was frightened, I don't mind telling you. And then, just as soon as it had started, it was over. Took my arm and said, 'Let's go home.'

Travelling down on the train, an echo of Norma's words kept rising and falling among the surrounding sounds: the tinny jingle from a child's computer game; a man talking too loudly, almost angrily, on his phone; the rattle of the refreshment trolley as it made its way slowly down the carriage; the constant announcements – If you see or hear anything that doesn't seem right . . .

Earlier that morning, the woman who had provided Ferguson with an alibi for the night of the fire, safe now from whatever threats he'd made against her, had presented herself at the Central Police Station and said she'd like to change her statement.

Through the window, the landscape hardly seemed to change. Rain swept across bare fields, leaving patterns on the glass. As they neared London the buildings became taller, more frequent. Passengers anxious to be first on to the platform reaching down their luggage, fastening their coats, shuffling towards the doors.

Resnick had arranged to meet Michael Davis on the forecourt of St Pancras International Station, a short walk from the HS2 works at nearby Euston. At first he thought he wasn't there and then he saw him, the face easily recognizable from the photograph on his mother's wall, body thickened out, taller, a man not a boy.

They turned out of the station and walked along by the canal, the rain now little more than an afterthought, the sun breaking through the clouds.

'I'd gone out with a bunch of the lads,' Davis said, 'this club over in Camden, some band one of them was keen to see. On the way back from the bar I near enough bumped into him, Ferguson. Nearly dropped the ale I was carrying. If he recognized me he gave no sign. Seemed like he was working there, one way or another, and when I asked the bloke behind the bar he said, security. There and a few other places, apparently. Hampstead, Kilburn. I don't even know why I was doing it at first, but I took to, well, not exactly following him, but finding out which nights he was where. Sometimes he'd turn up, sometimes not. Always full of himself, talking loud, laughing, shaking hands. I couldn't help thinking of Mia, the last time I'd seen her. Unable to say a word. And there he was, free and easy. Not a care in the world.'

They walked on, not hurrying, Resnick happy to let the young man take his own time. The rain had now stopped completely and the sun was reflecting back brightly from the surface of the water.

'What I wanted . . . all I wanted to do was get him to own up to what he'd done, the consequences. Just once. Just to me. I wanted him to look me in the eye and acknowledge who I was and what he'd done.'

'So you followed him . . .'

'Yes. One or two nights a week, he'd take this walk home late across the Heath. Then, this one time, the last time, I stopped him. And he knew, knew what I'd been doing. What the fuck d'you think you're up to, he said, following me around like shit stuck to the sole of my fucking shoe?'

He pushed his hand up across his face, through his hair.

'I told him what had happened . . . to Mia. What she'd tried to do . . . And he laughed, just laughed and said if she gives it another go tell her come and see me, I'll show her how it's done. That was when I went for him. Charged him, head down, and he grabbed me and swung me round. Mud everywhere underfoot we both went flying. I fetched up against those railings by the trees and one of them, it must've been loose already, came away in my hand. And he was still laughing. Fuck off, he said, fuck off back to your pathetic little girlfriend. And before I really knew what I was doing . . . the railing, it was in my hands . . . and I swung it at him hard as I could. And I kept . . . kept hitting him until he was down. Down and still.'

Broken-breathed, Davis lowered his face into the cradle of his hands. Sobbing.

He leaned forward against Resnick and Resnick held him, his face against Resnick's shoulder, his breath, fast and ragged, against his chest.

When he had calmed down enough to move his head away, Resnick said, 'You didn't mean to kill him.'

'No. I didn't mean to kill him.'

They sat there for some time, not speaking. Over the young man's shoulder Resnick could see Alex Hadley and another officer slowly approaching.

Standing, Resnick rested a hand on Davis's shoulder, as much to steady himself perhaps as to offer consolation.

The lights were showing through the partly drawn curtains when Hadley finally arrived home, stepping in out of the rain. What was surely Mozart on the radio, some piano concerto or other. Weren't they all more or less the same?

When interviewed, calmer now, Michael Davis had repeated what he had told Resnick, but little more. When it came to court, Hadley thought, his defence were going to find it hard to reconcile the picture of someone being driven to strike out in a fit of righteous anger with that of somebody who, not so long later, was capable of setting things up to look like a run-of-the-mill mugging and launching the murder weapon into the nearest body of water, which is what he confessed to have done.

Hard to reconcile didn't necessarily mean untrue.

It was only after she'd poured herself a glass of wine and softened the radio still further that she noticed the note attached to one side of the grey stoneware bowl they'd bought on their last visit to the Leach Pottery in St Ives.

Might be late back. Don't wait up.

And then, hastily across the bottom, almost as an afterthought.

We need to talk.

Signed R with a flourish and a single kiss.

Resnick slid an old vinyl album down from the shelf and set it in place. The track he was searching for was the third on side one and, with a slightly shaky hand, he lowered the stylus as carefully as he could. *Criss-Cross*. Recorded, New York City, 27 February, 1963. Some ten, eleven years after he was born.

Michael Davis sat on the narrow bed, leaning back against the rough surface of the cell wall, legs drawn up to his chest, worn blanket loose across his knees. Eyes closed. Mia was singing. If he listened carefully he could hear it. Her voice, small and clear. A song from their childhood. Something that had become lost . . . a yellow basket?

Outside, the rain continued to fall.

# CATHERINE AIRD – DEAD IN DEPTFORD

The Off-Beats was the informal name enjoyed by the Retired Police Officers Association of the Calleshire County Constabulary. Members met once a month on a rotating basis in a hostelry of their choice to discuss old murder cases. Today the venue was the Bellingham Hotel in the market town of Berebury – a place where they understood what a man needed in the way of food and drink. Nobody ever asked the one lady member, Mrs Brenda Price, what she needed in the way of either.

The town of Berebury was also where tonight's speaker, old Inspector Wilkinson, lived. This was important. Because of his eyesight not now being what it had been once upon a time, he no longer enjoyed driving long distances at night in the dark. Naturally this was not discussed, but it was rumoured that Traffic Inspector Harpe, of F Division, Berebury, had been warned and asked to see that old Wilkie didn't get into any trouble. The implications of this request weren't discussed either.

Coffee having been served the Chairman called the meeting to order in the time-honoured way of tapping his glass with a spoon. He introduced the speaker by simply saying that they all knew who Wilkie was anyway and that tonight he was going to talk about a very old case indeed.

'Not Jack the Ripper, I hope,' complained someone. 'If they didn't know who the killer was then, then they're never going to find out now.'

'No, not him,' said old Inspector Wilkinson, setting down his own glass and struggling to his feet with the help of his neighbour. 'Before him. Long before.'

'Not something in the Bible either, I hope,' said another man, a retired detective sergeant. 'Cain and Abel are all too easy when it comes to murder.'

'To say nothing of Romulus and Remus,' chipped in another old sergeant. He'd been a graduate entrant to the Force but had never had the promotion he thought he deserved. 'You know what it is with brothers as young men.'

'Sibling rivalries are what they call the Cain and Abel complex these days,' added a former inspector called Steve.

'Not that woman – Judith somebody – who chopped a man's head off?' asked Bob who had spent his working days in Drugs.

'No,' snapped Inspector Wilkinson, losing patience. 'Not her. The murder I'm going to talk about tonight is one that's never been solved. That is, they know who killed the man and how he died all right but not all the whys and the wherefores.'

The oldest member shook his head. 'Gives too much scope to a Defence Counsel, that does. Much too much. He'd make mincemeat of the Prosecution.'

'What has always been missing, gentlemen,' the speaker carried on regardless, quite forgetting the presence of Mrs Price, who didn't like being overlooked, 'is the real motive.'

'Did you know,' intervened a man who was sure he'd have made a better solicitor than some he'd seen in court, 'that not knowing the motive doesn't have to be a factor taken into consideration in an English court of law?'

'All I know is that this famous murder has never been really and truly explained even though it's been written about time and time again over five hundred years. Except by me, that is,' he added with a regrettable lack of modesty. 'I've solved it for sure.'

'Good for you, Wilkie,' said a man at the back of the room.

'This victim died from a stab in his eye,' the speaker went on, adding, 'If victim is the right word. I'm not so sure about that now.'

'Ah, *1066 and All That*,' declared Alan, the one really genuine reader among them.[1]

'No,' said Wilkinson flatly. 'Not Harold with an eye full of arrow, on . . .'

'On 'is 'orse with 'is 'awk in 'is 'and,' Alan, one time detective superintendent, completed the quotation for him.[2]

1 W. C. Sellar and R. J. Yeatman, *1066 And All That* [1930]

2 Marriott Edgar (1880–1951), 'The Battle of Hastings'

'No, not him,' said Wilkinson testily. 'Later than that. It happened in a brawl in an alehouse in Deptford on 30 May 1593, and the deceased was a famous playwright.'

'Professional jealousy?' offered Bob, a former police sergeant noted for his ready wit.

'Certainly not,' retorted Wilkinson. 'There was no one to touch him in England at the time. Not even William Shakespeare.'

'We all know what goes on backstage in the theatrical world,' volunteered a retired inspector called Fred. He didn't really know himself, but he'd read all the Charles Paris novels and so thought he did.

'Christopher Marlowe,' divined the Chairman. He'd had to read Marlowe's play *Edward the Second* at school and hadn't liked it.

'That's him,' responded Wilkinson. 'Said to have been stabbed in the eye by one of his drinking mates, name of Ingram Frizer.'[3]

'Either he was, or he wasn't,' said Steve truculently.

'Oh, he was stabbed in the eye all right and by Ingram Frizer too, like they told us,' replied Wilkinson. 'No doubt about that either. They all carried daggers in those days.'

'Boys' toys,' murmured Mrs Price, not that anybody took any notice.

'So, what's the problem then, Wilkie?'

'What I think, Steve, is that Marlowe himself egged him on to do it,' said Inspector Wilkinson.

'You having us on, mate?'

'No, I'm dead serious and dead is the operative word. To begin with, it seems to me that Marlowe lets Ingram Frizer get his hands on Marlowe's own dagger suspiciously easily.'

'That's a very good point,' conceded Steve, hoping the double entendre would be noticed. It wasn't.

'Are you sure?' asked a senior man who had served his time in the police station in the Minster city of Calleford and never let anyone forget what a superior patch it was. He made a point, too, of always being addressed as James rather than Jim.

'Dead sure and also,' insisted the speaker, 'by being aware of Frizer being assisted by Marlowe putting himself in an unusually

3 William Urry, Christopher Marlowe and Canterbury [1988]

vulnerable physical position that made the stabbing in the eye very easy.'

'How come?' asked somebody else.

'He laid down on a bed that was just behind the table that his three mates were all sitting at,' said Wilkinson. 'They had their backs to him, with Frizer in the middle. Asking for trouble, I call doing that, making himself vulnerable in that way.'

'Why should he do that?' asked Steve.

'Look at the evidence and you'll see. The man's under great pressure because he's just been summoned to appear before the Privy Council. In other words, there's a warrant out for his arrest and in those days that meant you were as good as dead from then on.'

'I always said there was a lot to be said for the death penalty,' put in the oldest member.

'We know you did, George,' said the Chairman wearily, 'so there's no call for you to go on about it now.'

Before he lost his audience Inspector Wilkinson said firmly that in those far-off days an arrest warrant usually ended up in public execution, evidence not coming into things that much. 'I reckon Marlowe had decided he'd rather end up dead in Deptford instead. And in a pub brawl with someone else getting the blame.'

'Make a good title, that would, for that young fellow Simon Brett who writes all those stories about the detective on the stage,' observed Bob.

'He writes about a woman, too,' volunteered Mrs Price, intent on keeping her end up. 'A Mrs Pargeter.'

Nobody took any notice.

'Dead in Deptford.' The speaker rolled the phrase round his palate, savouring it as if he was a Master of Wine. 'Make a good title, that would.'

'What had this Marlowe been and gone and done then, Wilkie?' Frank had spent his working life in the industrial town of Luston and its argot had made its mark on him. He felt that speaking in the demotic ought to help him get through to the villains more easily, but it didn't.

'He uttered homosexual, irreligious, and subversive remarks that were bound to be heard in high places. Tantamount to committing suicide, that was, in those days.'

'Downright dangerous at any time, if you ask me,' put in another officer bitterly. He was convinced that it was only his well-known personal outspokenness to authority – speaking Truth to Power they called it these days – that explained his own lack of promotion. It wasn't, actually.

'Not today, surely,' said James from Calleford in his superior manner. 'Even subversion isn't what it was. Happens all the time now. You've only to go on social media.'

'Some people will do anything for good PR,' put in an officer often called on to speak to the press on behalf of the Force and equally often affronted by what they'd done with what he'd said.

'Dead in Deptford,' repeated Bob. 'I like it.'

'I can tell you for starters,' said Inspector Wilkinson, 'that the Coroner didn't. Not one little bit. And you know what Coroners are like.'

A general murmur of assent rippled round the room. The assembled company without exception all knew what Coroners were like, especially the former Coroner's Officer present. 'I could tell all you lads a thing or two. . .' Bill began and then thought better of it and fell silent.

'That meant there was an inquest,' concluded someone else.

They all knew about inquests, too. 'Must have been.'

'Oh, yes, there was an inquest all right but what is given in evidence at an inquest isn't always evidence, is it? Or the whole truth, come to that.'

There was an audible snort this time from the former Coroner's Officer, but he didn't utter a word.

'If you ask me, at an inquest it's what you choose to say,' insisted the speaker.

'Or been briefed to say,' muttered an old sergeant darkly.

'And there isn't always a jury there either,' continued Wilkie, 'so you don't have to mind what you say as much.'

'I've been to some funny inquests in my time,' remarked the man called Bob.

'It was all very odd,' went on Wilkinson before Bob could elaborate. 'They put the death down to a load of young men arguing with the landlady, a Mrs Eleanor Bull, about the bill of fare – the reckoning, they called it at the time – after a long day drinking in an alehouse and its garden and things getting out of hand as usual as time went by.'

Mrs Price stirred. 'Like in real life now,' she said. She hadn't liked attending pub fights in her time, especially if there were wolf whistles when she arrived. 'You can't arrest a man for wolf whistling.'

'The way things are going, you'll be able to any time soon,' said the bitter man gloomily. 'Harassment or something.'

'But the death wasn't either a fight or an accident, was it?' observed the Chairman to hurry the speaker along. He wanted another drink, and he was sure he wasn't the only one who felt the same way. 'Is that what you're saying?'

Inspector Wilkinson shook his head. Since his head was starting to shake anyway these days nobody took a lot of notice. 'No,' he said. 'You see he would have known all about poor Tom Kyd. Bound to have done.'

'Who he?' asked Steve.

'An old roommate of his who was another playwright.'

'Professional jealousy, like I said before,' put in Bob immediately.

He was ignored by the speaker who carried on. 'And knowing what had happened to poor Tom Kyd he knew what might be coming to him once he fell into the Privy Council's clutches. You could say he was as good as dead then anyway and he knew it.'

'What was it that happened to Tom Kyd, then?' asked someone. 'Tell us.'

'Tortured until he was in so much agony, he would confess to whatever they wanted him to. Which in Kyd's case they reckoned had meant shopping his old mucker, Chris Marlowe.'

'What for?'

'You name it – heresy, atheism, treachery, spying. The chap in charge of their M15 in those days, Sir Thomas Walsingham, wasn't above bending a few rules to get a confession.'

'Nothing changes,' said someone cynically.

'No recorders or cameras in their interview rooms in those times, of course,' observed Frank from Luston.

The speaker, Wilkie, didn't know if it was his imagination, but he thought he detected a touch of wistfulness there and said hastily that all that would have been quite enough to put the wind up any man, let alone a man of the theatre.

'There was a nasty piece of work around at the time, too, called Topcliffe who was known as a rack master,' Inspector Wilkinson went on. 'He was good at putting the frighteners on.'

'I don't like the sound of that, Wilkie,' said Mrs Price. 'Not at all nice.'

'That's to say nothing of the two other men in the room at the tavern. I daresay we'd have called it the snug if we'd been there at the time.'

'I'm glad I wasn't,' shuddered Mrs Price.

'A rum lot, they were, too, I can tell you. Besides this Christopher Marlowe, there were Ingram Frizer and Nicholas Skeres, who were as wicked a pair of loan sharks that you would ever come across and one Robert Poley, not a man to trust at any time, least of all in that company.'

'You can tell a lot about a man from the company he keeps,' remarked James sanctimoniously. He himself was always very careful with whom he consorted in Calleford.

'I get your drift, Wilkie,' the Chairman said, 'Although what I want to know is why on earth didn't the man Marlowe just take his own life and be done with it?'

'I can tell you that, Chairman. In those days suicide was considered the way to eternal damnation,' replied Wilkinson briskly. 'That's why. Although, come to think of it, Marlowe was an atheist so it shouldn't have bothered him, should it?'

'Didn't think it through,' concluded Bob.

'Oh, yes, he did,' said Wilkie with unaccustomed vigour. 'Ingram Frizer was sitting between Skeres and Poley and all Marlowe had to do was to give him a dirty great shove in the back to annoy him, add a few insults and there you are. Job done. What we would call these days "death by police".'

'Suicide by cop,' put in Frank less elegantly.

'So, Wilkie,' said the Chairman, one eye on the clock and the imminent approach of closing time, 'you think it was a clear case of Marlowe egging on Ingram Frizer to kill him so that Frizer would be getting all the blame for his murder?'

'Beyond reasonable doubt,' said Inspector Wilkinson firmly.

'What happened to Frizer?' asked Steve.

'Not a lot,' said Wilkie.

'Rather proves your point, doesn't it, that?' said he who would have liked to have been a solicitor and who was used to checking incongruities.

'I thought that, too,' said Wilkinson, breathing a sigh of relief and sitting down rather abruptly. He waved at the barman as he did so, pointing at his empty glass. 'I may be mistaken, of course,' he added, but he said it without conviction.

# CHRISTOPHER FOWLER – THE LUNCHEON

Last time they went to Étienne's; it's expensive enough to keep out the riff-raff, although God knows that's no guarantee these days, and the intimidating menu has not changed in fifty years, but Étienne's is closed for refurbishment, its bilious pink and grey walls to be replaced with something hopefully less French, so instead they're going to La Trahison, tucked away in a backstreet, a restaurant so new that even *The Times* hasn't managed to send its food critics there yet and they normally get in everywhere, like rats.

They haven't seen each other since Étienne's, the two women. That was three years ago. Everything has changed since then.

Amanda arrives first, and her initial impression is not good. Pale green walls, beige rattan, wicker and raffia, folk-horror knick-knacks like corn dollies and naïf art, but the napery is reassuringly thick and white – like her husband, she always jokes – and there are plenty of interesting wineglasses to fill.

In places like this she's used to being the only black woman in the room, but it still startles her to think that if her mother had ever entered a place like this it would have been to work in the kitchen. She wears her green suit like armour, to make up for her lack of confidence.

A handful of middle-aged male diners are seated behind fine linen, children waiting to be fed by nanny. Most are playing with their phones. It's coming up to one o'clock. She doesn't usually drink before six but today she's prepared to make an exception.

Her companion has never been on time in her life, so Amanda goes ahead and orders sparkling water and a glass of Puligny Montrachet while she's waiting. She flirts with the idea of a gin and tonic, but gin blunts the tastebuds and she plans to enjoy the food even if the meeting proves difficult. Of course, she rather hopes it will be, if only so she can enjoy the drama. She's married to an actor, after all, so daily performances can be sparked by anything from lost car keys to accusations of infidelity.

Madeline is very good at making entrances. She's simultaneously discreet and showy, dressed in a classically cut light grey woollen suit with a beige leather handbag on a gold chain that's probably real. And a hat, no less, small and simple, hiding her pinned-up red hair. Not many women can pull off that look in daytime.

'Darling, am I late? I'm so sorry if I am. Or were you early? I make it . . .' she squints and attempts to perceive the miniscule bauble on her wrist, '. . . just coming up to one.'

'I'm always early,' Amanda tells her. 'At bedtime I'm like a dog in a basket, it takes me an age to get settled.'

Madeline hands her hat and jacket to the Mâitre D' without catching his eye. 'Richard had to rush off to a council meeting, something about a new swimming pool with cracks in it, and took the car. I should never have got rid of my little runabout. Let me look at you. Flawless. I haven't seen you in . . .'

'Three years,' says Amanda.

'Has it been that long?'

'October the seventeenth.'

'You remember the date?'

'I could hardly forget. We were settling my dismissal.'

'I'd forgotten about that. At least it never had to go to court. I admitted I was wrong, didn't I? And you did make a lot of money out of it.'

'I was owed a lot of money.'

'Well, let's not dwell on the past. I'd better order myself a drink, it looks like you're already half a glass in.' She flags a waiter. 'I like the look of this place. It makes a change from those ghastly bling restaurants oligarchs eat in. At least nobody here looks like they spend their evenings strangling hookers.' As she looks around, her voice changes to soft, pleasing and faintly flirtatious for the benefit of the staff. 'I'll have a glass of what she's having, and some still water please, with two slices of cucumber on the side.'

'For your eyes?' asks Amanda, amused by the way in which restaurants encourage pretensions.

'God, are they baggy? Everything's drooping, I hate getting old.'

'I was going to say how well you look.' She examines her old opponent closely. 'Have you had something done?'

'Why, does it look like I have? It's just my usual regime. Actually I can't be too long today. I have to prepare for a product launch this afternoon.'

'What are you blinding rabbits with this time, lipstick or moisturizer?'

'Some kind of vegan paste that gives you a breast lift. At the moment the stuff still smells like sprouts. It's more the sort of thing your company would be interested in. I hear you're doing very well for yourself.'

Amanda had used her settlement to set up an online ethical makeup company. Now she's worth considerably more than her old boss. 'A lot of people feel more comfortable with cruelty-free products. Of course, our clientele tends to be younger and better educated.'

Madeline waves the idea away. 'We're an old established organization. You cater to a different market sector, that's all. I never think of you as a rival. I'm glad I was able to give you the opportunity to get started.'

*And you'll never let me forget it*, thinks Amanda. The women have placed their phones face down to the right of their plates, like a pair of duellists setting aside their pistols. Madeline is forty-four, and although she's lived in the city for twenty years, she still has a touch of countryside about her. Amanda is more worldly, thirty-five, urban to the core.

'Anyway,' says Madeline pleasantly, 'enough about work. I think there's something else we need to discuss. I understand you've been sleeping with my husband.'

### First Course

**Hay-smoked sea trout tartare in pink fir jus**
**Carrot tartar with black garlic and bitter orange**

Amanda puts a pause on the conversation while her companion's wine is being poured. Why they always stop speaking until the waiter is out of earshot remains a mystery to her.

'I'm not sure *sleeping with* really covers it. We do quite a lot together.' Amanda concentrates on keeping her tone light.

'Well this is all news to me.' Madeline raises her glass. 'I can't imagine where Richard finds the time. He barely sleeps with me, let alone other people. I'm surprised you're his type.'

'Perhaps we can avoid talking about an absent man over luncheon and discuss how *we* feel instead,' Amanda suggests. 'After all, we're the only ones affected.'

'Are we?' Madeline adopts a look of surprise. 'I can imagine there'll be all sorts of repercussions. Richard is a politician, after all. The press have been on his case for years. It's different for you, being married to an actor, they're expected to behave badly.'

'You're being remarkably calm about this,' Amanda says, unfolding her napkin as her starter is set down. 'I was worried that you'd be upset.'

'Darling, I've had plenty of time to grow used to the idea that he would one day betray me. I just didn't think it would be with someone I knew. You must admit it's fairly insensitive of you both.' She raises a fork over a splinter of trout on a thick, white plate the size of a manhole cover. 'I assume you want something from me.'

Amanda smooths the napkin across her lap. 'Only your permission.'

'I'm not sure it's something that can be retrospectively granted. As you've already done the deed. When was that, by the way? Not when I had to go to Bahrain?'

Amanda tries to think. How long ago was that? 'It's not a new thing, Maddie.'

'Which means he's been lying to me on a regular basis. I'm listening without prejudice, just trying to get this clear in my head, you understand.'

'I assumed you must know. He says he talks to you all the time.'

'Well yes, men talk, but it's usually about house insurance or whether the car needs a service. After a while you stop having sex and settle for having a companion. It's either that or a dog. Speaking of which, how is your marriage?'

'Hard to tell. Jericho's so busy getting into character for his next audition that we barely get to talk anymore.'

'So you decided you needed back-up and took my husband.'

'I didn't kidnap him, Maddie. He likes being with me. He was always very clear about that.'

'Darling, he likes a lot of things. Shiny new cars, Caribbean holidays, adoring women. He's not much of a catch. Completely self-centred, in love with the sound of his own voice, never thinks to ask about anyone else, zero empathy. The perfect politician.'

'Perhaps that's just with you.' Amanda examines what's on the end of her fork. 'Carrot tartar is just raw carrot. A bit rich for fifteen quid.'

'Why do you need my permission, anyway?'

'We want to get married.'

Madeline bursts out laughing. 'Why? You can't possibly be thinking about having children.'

Amanda bristles. 'I'm still capable.'

'You'd better pace it up, darling. Anything above thirty-five is considered a geriatric pregnancy.'

'They don't use that term anymore.'

Madeline is not prepared to leave the subject alone. 'I know older women can give birth but their children are hardly ever right in the head. We think we can have it all but we're quite deluded. We don't get to have everything, that's the deal.' She plucks a bone from a morsel of trout. 'How is this going to work? I agree to a quick divorce, you book the church and we carry on as normal until the next lovely luncheon? Or should I make a date with Jericho instead? Where did he get that name? I imagine the only thing that came tumbling down was his career.'

'I'd like to think we can be civilized about this.'

'Ah – that word. Whenever Richard returns from a cultural tour of Rwanda he always tells me they were so *civilized*.'

There's a hint of something so unpleasant just behind those perfect bleached teeth that Amanda chooses her next words very carefully. 'Neither of us wants anyone to get hurt.'

'It's a bit late to think about that, isn't it?' She sets down her cutlery and sits back to let the waiter remove the plate. 'How long have the two of you been – together?'

She thinks for a moment. 'Six years.'

'Six years?' Madeline repeats in amazement.

'It must be,' says Amanda, 'because my daughter is nearly six.'

**<u>Main Course</u>**

**Pan-seared Lincolnshire duck with truffled celeriac and mint raita**

**Stonebass confit with Cantabrian anchovies and seaweed doughnut**

The great Saturn-like plates have tennis ball-sized indentations in which the ingredients, mostly cut into neat sticks, huddle together like soldiers in a ditch waiting to be shot. Their forks hover but struggle to alight anywhere. Instead, they order an austere, almost frozen bottle of Chenin Blanc and concentrate on demolishing that.

'Are you telling me – claiming – that Katie was fathered by my husband?' Madeline asks, swirling her glass.

'It happened the first time we slept together.'

'Only I'd hate to think that as well as being an adulterer Richard was also trying to undermine me by seeding my staff.'

And there it is, thinks Amanda, that's what she thinks of me. I'm still *staff*. 'Maddie, I know you can't have children and that Richard wants them, but Katie wasn't planned. If you must know, he used a condom.' Her voice drops on the last word.

'Of course he did. Whenever I found a packet in his pocket I put holes in them with a needle.'

Amanda does not allow an eyelid to flicker. 'Then you only have yourself to blame. It's a miracle I didn't have more than just one. I didn't tell him Katie was his, not then. We didn't stay in touch. Richard wasn't around for the birth. I didn't see him for years. One day he called me out of the blue, very upset, said he'd made a mess of his life. We met up and everything changed between us.'

'How do you know he's the father and not your Jericho?'

'I'm not an idiot.'

'You're a lot of things but no one could accuse you of that.' She prods at her meal. 'The chef's got a nerve. This duck's body fat ratio is lower than mine. How on earth did Richard hide all this from me for so long?'

She wants to point out that it was probably easy; Madeline notices no one else, not really. She skims conversations and issues standard replies but if you question her she's hardly able to recall a meal, a meeting, a party, a face. She exists on life's surfaces. Well, perhaps this will make her pay a little more attention.

'What does Jericho think about it all?' she asks.

'I wanted to talk to you first,' says Amanda.

'Before confronting your own husband? I'm honoured.'

The scrap of confit fish on Amanda's fork looks like something you'd find in the sink after washing up. She sets down the utensil. 'I'll give my husband very favourable terms in the divorce. That's all he really cares about.'

'But you've made one mistake,' says Madeline. 'Richard will never leave me. He's broke. He gets his allowance from me.'

'You mean his consultancy comes from your cosmetics company. I think he can learn to manage without it. I supported a penniless actor for years. If you think Richard will stay with you, why don't you call and ask him?'

'He's probably learning about the tensile strength of diving boards right now but why not?' Madeline snatches up her phone and speed-dials. 'He knows which side his bread is buttered.'

Amanda tears a piece off her seaweed doughnut and chews it ruminatively. Madeline listens and impatiently rings off.

'No answer?'

'Straight to voicemail.'

'That's because right now he's heading to the airport with our bags. He said he was going to get something to eat in the business lounge and meet us later.'

Madeline attempts to absorb this fresh news with good grace. 'Oh. Anywhere nice?'

'A boutique hotel in Greece.'

She pushes her plate away rather too brusquely. 'It sounds as if you've thought of everything.'

'We both felt it was better if we were out of the country for a while, to give you a chance to think things over. Richard never had a meeting about a swimming pool. He was trying not to hurt you.'

'Please spare me the respect for my feelings. I can't eat this. It tastes like a spicy inner tube.' She summons the waiter to take away her eviscerated duck while she does some mental arithmetic. A swift calculation tells her that each mouthful cost £8.32. This tallying up is a habit Madeline has had ever since she made her first million.

She generously tops up their glasses. 'Do you have any other surprises for me or are you done?'

'Maddie, I'm sorry it turned out like this but I have to think about my own happiness as well.'

'Well, I can't let you have it all your own way. There are a few things I need to tell you. I was going to sit here looking surprised through the rest of the luncheon but keeping one's eyebrows permanently arched is simply too exhausting.'

Amanda is confused.

Madeline leans forward in a conspiratorial pose. 'First of all, thanks to the condoms, obviously, I knew Richard had affairs. He's a politician, for God's sake, they're like footballers, they can never resist taking their tops off after a victory. Every thought my husband has is visible from space. At first I was insulted by his inability to lie convincingly. I knew for quite some time that he'd narrowed down his playing field to just one patch of grass. He's so pathetically in thrall to high earners that screwing a shop girl is out of the question. Most of the people he meets in Parliament are scholastically bright but incredibly ugly, so it was likely that I had introduced him to someone at a social event. Once I realized it was you he was sneaking off to see, I did a little digging. Actually, I'm quite pleased it turned out to be someone I knew.'

'You are? Why is that?'

'Oh, I've always felt a little proprietorial towards you. I gave you your first break, after all. I gave you visibility.'

'Not much, though. Just the events where the press were present.'

'It played well for both of us.' She waits while the waiter sweeps away non-existent crumbs with a strigil that looks like a silver windscreen wiper. 'I won't give Richard up without a fight. You see? Here we are talking about a man again. If I can still bring myself to call him that.'

'I really don't see what you can do about it, Madeline.'

There's something secret in her smile. 'I didn't at first. But I treated it as a creative problem and gave it some careful thought. And I've taken care of Jericho for you.'

Amanda's fork pauses in mid-air. 'What do you mean, taken care of him?' She thinks of her embittered husband teaching drama to another classroom full of rowdy children in a coastal town. His stage career faltered thanks to a nervous breakdown brought on by two years of touring in *Cats*. He's trying to work his way back, step by step.

'Let's face it, he was never much of an actor,' Madeline says. 'Having him out of the picture just clears the decks and makes things easier for everyone. I'm not terribly good with computers but I know plenty of people who are. I think if you call the school this afternoon you'll find he's been arrested for harassing young girls online.'

'You're bluffing.'

'Once the police start poking around they'll find all sorts of incriminating bits and pieces planted in his online history, most of them involving underage girls – I think we put in a couple of boys for variety.'

'Why would you do that? He hasn't done anything to you.'

'No, but you have, so he's fair game. When you hurt other people, the people around you are bound to get hurt.'

She tops up their glasses and asks for the dessert menu, then squints at her watch. 'Speaking of which, your daughter is due to be collected from Sunnyside school around now, isn't she?'

**<u>Desserts</u>**

**Jivara mousse with sake-soused goji berries and orange jelly**

**Dulce de leche crème brûlée with shiso and pineapple granita**

Amanda feels as if a hole has opened-up in front of her. 'I told them I was sending a car for her.'

'So you did. I wanted you to enjoy your lunch so I arranged for her to be picked up. Katie is already on her way to a place where she'll be safe. As soon as you cancel your plans with Richard you can have her back.' Madeline glances distastefully at her plate. 'Meanwhile, if you want to ensure that nothing untoward happens, just carry on as normal and enjoy whatever the hell it is you've ordered.'

Amanda is forced to crack the top of her fussy little crème brûlée. She looks like a child faced with her first boiled egg. 'If anything happens to her . . .'

'It won't so long as you talk to Richard and tell him you're finishing with him. Katie is my insurance. To make sure you return Richard to me in one piece. He's not much but I don't like giving away things I've already paid for.'

'You could go to jail for this.' She feels as if she's ageing five years. 'Where have you taken her?'

'You don't have to worry, Amanda, just make the call.'

'I have no control over him. Richard does whatever he wants. You know that.'

'He'll have read my letter by now, so I think you'll find him amenable. When was the last time you wrote anyone a letter? I'd forgotten how much fun they are. I felt like sealing the envelope with wax and ribbons.'

Madeline refills her glass. She finds she's rather enjoying herself. She nibbles on teaspoons of mousse while she waits for Amanda to have the conversation with her husband.

Amanda's hesitancy makes her look weak. 'I don't know what I'm going to say.'

Madeline permits herself a triumphant smile. In truth, she can't wait to get rid of her husband. He's been a big, fat burden around her neck for years. But she needs to prove to herself that she can win him back, so that she can sue for divorce on her own terms.

She worries that she might have overplayed the deserted wife routine, but Amanda seems to have been taken in by it. She almost feels sorry for her old friend; caught between a deadbeat actor and a disappointing politician. Now both of them will leave her. Well, as she said, you can't have it all. Amanda will be a lot better off as a single mother.

Madeline is close enough to hear the call, which is answered on the second ring. It's so typical that Richard will talk to the one he wants and run away from the one he can't speak to anymore. The only reliable thing about men is their unreliability.

Amanda dutifully explains what has happened. She listens to a drone of limp excuses and half-apologies. Richard sounds as if he's answering awkward questions at the House. He feels so ashamed. He has let them both down. After reading his wife's letter he realizes how badly he's behaved. It's better for both of them that he goes his own way. For a politician there's no such thing as good publicity, et cetera. He wishes them all the best. It's not them, it's him, and so on ad nauseam until she finally hangs up on him.

'You probably heard all that,' she says. 'He found your letter and has given it a lot of thought.'

Amanda sets her phone down with great care. She looks as if she's about to burst into tears.

'Coffee?' Madeline suggests.

**<u>Après</u>**

**Cortado with foamed Oatley Barista non-dairy cream**
**Decaf flat white microfinished with skimmed milk**
**Petits fours**

The waiter sets down their coffees and a plate of tiny macaroons on a bed of pebbles painted in bilious fairground colours.

'And the bill, I think,' says Madeline sweetly before leaving to go to the bathroom. Amanda notices that when she returns her makeup has been refreshed. She's ending a phone call.

There's no indication that eating ever took place at the table, but then it hardly had. Resuming her seat, Madeline says, 'I've kept my end of the bargain. Katie will be with you as soon as you get back. Is that convenient? Or do you have some shopping to do after this? Now that you're staying at home by yourself instead of going to Greece? To be honest, you can get a kebab anywhere.'

Amanda mutely accedes.

As she sips her coffee, Madeline can't resist one last little dig. 'Don't be too hard on yourself, darling. You were never going to win this.'

'You didn't win. He's not coming back to you either.'

Madeline looks at her with something amounting to pity. The poor girl still doesn't get it. 'Don't you see? It's like your company. It's a lovely little idea, all the ethical sourcing, and it reflects your caring personality, but it's hopelessly naive. And it makes your products too expensive. You didn't think it through. You don't have the killer instinct to get invited to the grown-ups' table.'

'There is no grown-ups' table online, Maddie, that's the point.

Being successful isn't meant to be an act of revenge. That just makes you bitter.'

'It's not just about success, it's about being with the right people. And I'm afraid your face doesn't fit.'

Amanda should have known it would end like this, the way it has always ended in this country. With the discreet closing of ranks.

The empty coffee cups are replaced with a bill that arrives inside a Victorian farming calendar. The figure at the bottom is enough to have fed a Victorian family for two years, but Madeline takes out her gold card with a generous smile.

All Amanda wants to do now is be there for her daughter. It occurs to her that the whole kidnapping thing was a ridiculous bluff, an empty hand played by a desperately unhappy woman. So was that story about compromising Jericho. Madeline is a great poker player.

'You said my face doesn't fit.' She fixes Madeline with an accusing look. 'My *face*.'

'Really?' Madeline tries to laugh it off as she hands the bill tray back to the waiter. 'Are you going to play the race card? Because it seems you've done very well because of me.'

'I've done well in spite of you. Let's talk about your face. You had a botox appointment just before coming here.'

Now it's Madeline's turn to look surprised. 'What are you talking about?'

'Do you know how I know?'

She takes out a compact and passes it across the table. Madeline's face has broken out in a mask of crimson blotches that show through her makeup like patches of damp under paintwork. Horrified, she pulls out a tissue and dabs, turning the paper pink.

'An allergic reaction, I imagine. The wrong dosage, far too high.'

'That's impossible,' Madeline sputters, clutching the mirror and mopping at her face. 'My little man is one of the most expensive in the business. I've been going to him for years. He would never make a mistake.'

'I'm sure he followed all the correct procedures. But you have definite signs of suffering from a massive overdose. My goodness, it's all over your neck. Of course, botox is just botulism. In a high dosage it's usually fatal.'

'How do you know what the dosage was?' Madeline asks, noisily trying to push her chair back. The other diners look less alarmed than irritated that their expense account lunches are being disturbed.

'I have no idea what it was,' says Amanda offhandedly. 'I have no clue as to where you went. Richard told me the appointment was in your shared diary, that's all. But I know how much there was in the coffee. They'll blame it on your doctor because they won't be able to tell that you had a second dose.'

Madeline can no longer hear or see her. Her skin feels as if it is on fire. She starts frantically, noisily scratching at her neck. It's an off-putting sight when you're trying to eat a crab salad. After a minute or two she's leaving bloody streaks. The Maître D' is looking horrified. Perhaps they can bundle her back to the bathroom.

Amanda pockets the luncheon receipt from the returned tray, rising to get her coat. 'My friend isn't feeling very well,' she tells their host. 'I'll call her an Uber. Perhaps you would be so kind as to see her into it.'

She gives Madeline a concerned pat, as if comforting a dog, and pouts at her. 'Poor thing. Wishing you better. Although there's really not much point.'

As she leaves the restaurant, she's aglow with the thought of spending two weeks in Greece with Katie, just the two of them on an empty beach together. Outside, she calls the taxi and barely a minute later a white Toyota Prius pulls up on the other side of the road.

Looking back through the restaurant window she sees a pair of legs wriggling about on the floor. One shoe has come off. Those heels are far too high for a woman of Madeline's age.

Perhaps she should take the Uber instead. Looks like Madeline won't be needing it now.

Amanda won't be going back there again. The confit stonebass was extremely overrated. Taking the restaurant receipt from her pocket, she gives it a careless glance before crumpling it and dropping it down the drain.

**Thank you for visiting La Trahison**
**We look forward to welcoming you again soon**
**Your waiter's name today is JERICHO**

# DAVID STUART DAVIES – AN OLD-FASHIONED MURDER MYSTERY

Captain Brian Eastbourne called upon his friend Pierre Leroux, the famous French detective, at his Chelsea apartment one morning in the autumn of 1935. The captain found him in a state of excitement; the detective's little cherubic face alight with pleasure. 'You come at a most crucial time, mon ami. I am just about to depart for Dreadnought Manor in the county you call Buckinghamshire.'

'Off to some sort of house party, eh?' responded the captain, slapping his fine leather gloves against his thigh.

'In a manner of speaking, Eastbourne. The kind of house party that greatly appeals to me.'

'Ah, one in which a murder will take place.'

Leroux beamed. '*Has* taken place.'

'Already?'

'Oui.'

'Not in the library?'

'Exactement. The victim was clubbed to death with a volume of the *Encyclopaedia Britannica*. Volume 3: E to F.'

'Great Scott. Who was the unfortunate fellow?'

'That is yet to be established. He was a guest of the owner of the house, Sir Percival Parker.'

'The industrialist.'

'The same.'

'I presume there are other assorted house guests who make up a pleasing array of suspects.'

'Of course. As well as Sir Percival and his wife Prunella, there is Sylvia Stratton, the film star, Daniel Dangerfield, the notorious man about town, Wilhelmina Waters, Sir Percival's impoverished cousin, the crime novelist A. A. Ayers and a strange fictional character called Roger Ackroyd.'

'Ah, my money's on him.'

'Why so, mon ami?'

'Well, because he's the only one whose name is not alliterative.'

'Oh, Eastbourne, you squat to conclusions so easily.'

'Jump.'

'Pardon?'

'I jump to conclusions, not squat.'

'Oh, you and your English idioms.'

'Have you discovered a motive?'

'Just a very simple one.'

'Good man, Leroux. What is it?'

'The murderer wanted his victim dead.'

'Bravo. You are halfway to having solved the case.'

'Would you care to accompany me down to Dreadnought Manor and witness how brilliantly I bring the murderer to justice?'

'Will there be lots of lengthy interviews with the house guests, a spot of clue-giving, revelatory eavesdropping, another murder, a deliberate red herring and a final rally of survivors in the drawing room for your overdramatic unmasking of the culprit?'

'Inevitably.'

'Then I'll come,' said Eastbourne with a facile grin.

They travelled to Buckinghamshire in Leroux's ancient roadster. 'You will be happy to be sleuthing again,' cried Eastbourne from the passenger seat, above the roar of the engine.

'Oh, yes,' responded Leroux. 'I have been unemployed for too long. It seems that no one wants the great Leroux to investigate their murders for them anymore. Even Inspector Sap from Scotland Yard has stopped calling for advice. Times have been very hard. But when times are hard, one has to be inventive.'

'I understand,' said Eastbourne, although Leroux knew very well that he didn't.

After passing through Little Piddling in the Bowl, Leroux observed, 'Not long now, mon ami. I shall be glad to take off these goggles.'

'Why on earth are you wearing them?' enquired Eastbourne.

'To protect my mascara, of course,' came the reply.

Very shortly Leroux pulled up outside a dilapidated looking cottage set amid a wild overgrown garden. Attached to the rickety gate of the property was a piece of white card on which someone had scrawled the words 'DREADNOUGHT MANOR'.

'This can't be it,' observed Eastbourne snootily.

'Oh, yes, it is, mon ami.'

They entered the premises. To Eastbourne's eyes, the place looked decrepit and deserted. Leroux, who seemed unperturbed by the surroundings, led him into what must have been the front room. Assembled there in a semi-circle were six human life-sized cardboard cut-outs.

'These are the houseguests, mon ami. This is Sir Percival Parker and here is his wife. No doubt you are familiar with Sylvia Stratton. You could not fail to recognize that outstanding décolletage. This fellow is Daniel Dangerfield and here we have poor little Wilhelmina Waters. Last, but not least, is crime novelist A. A. Ayers, whose last book, *Murder on the Penge Railway* was a stinker.'

'What about Roger Ackroyd?' asked Eastbourne tentatively.

Leroux grimaced. 'It turned out that he couldn't make it. A close friend of mine said she needed him urgently.'

Eastbourne was bemused by this bizarre scenario, but assumed it was some kind of comical charade dreamed up by Leroux to fend off ennui.

'What about the dead body?' he said.

'Ah, I'm glad you asked,' replied the detective.

Eastbourne had just time to turn sideways and glimpse a large brown volume hurtling in his direction – *Encyclopaedia Britannica*. Volume 3: E to F – before it connected with his skull and he lost consciousness and crumpled to the floor.

Sometime later the little plump detective stood astride the corpse of Captain Brian Eastbourne, as he addressed the collection of cardboard cut-out house guests. 'So you see,' he began in his magisterial manner, 'while Sir Percival and Lady Parker were in the kitchen supervising the making of the cucumber sandwiches, Daniel Dangerfield was upstairs on the telephone to his bookmaker. At the same time, Sylvia Stratton was in her room staring at the mirror and admiring herself. Poor little Wilhelmina Waters was somewhere else making herself scarce and being very successful at it. That only leaves A. A. Ayers. Where were you, sir? Ah, you remain silent. Let me elucidate. You see I know you were in the study attempting to write a new detective novel. I discovered the discarded pages in the wastepaper basket. The work is called *And Then There Were Only a Few Left*, I believe. And so, mes amis, while you were all occupied elsewhere, the villain came in here and clobbered this poor devil to death.

'And now I come to the moment where I reveal the identity of the murderer. The mastermind behind this cunning and devious crime. I have to tell you . . . it is I. I, the brilliant Pierre Leroux, criminologist extraordinaire. Yes, yes, I did it. I planned it, carried out my clever plans with splendid precision and committed the murder.' He laughed in an unstable fashion before rushing to the back of the room. Reaching into the shadows he retrieved yet another cardboard cut-out and brought it forward to join the others. 'This is Inspector Sap of Scotland Yard,' he announced grandly. 'And he will now arrest me and take me into custody.' He laughed again, more hysterically this time, while tears ran down his cheeks and his body shook with maniacal merriment. His laughter echoed through the empty house.

# LYNNE TRUSS – BELLS AND WHISTLES

***October 1957***

For a good half-hour after his live broadcast on the Home Service, it was Inspector Steine's weekly custom to linger in the reception area of Broadcasting House, under a somewhat artless pretext.

'He's doing it again,' the smartly dressed ladies on reception would mutter as they nudged each other, pretending not to look. 'Angling.'

Regularly checking the time on his pocket-watch, the inspector would give every appearance of a man impatiently – even agitatedly – waiting for someone, and only vaguely aware of his surroundings. Whereas, as the smartly dressed ladies were well aware, Steine was simply acting on the knowledge that if he stayed long enough in that famous marble-floored lobby, with its grand Deco doors and busy reception desk, he would eventually snag the notice of prominent individuals passing through.

'Strike,' the reception ladies noted, shaking their heads, whenever the ruse paid off.

Of late, it had paid off handsomely. Actresses, government ministers, and the great philosopher and mathematician Bertrand Russell (twice) were among those in the past month who had stopped in their tracks, asked themselves a mental question ('Is it him?') and then come across and warmly shaken the inspector's hand. Because he was nowadays quite famous. Not only was his Friday afternoon talk on 'Law and the Little Man' an institution; he had become a national hero for taking down (that is, shooting dead in cold blood) a notorious London crime boss during a riot at a Brighton milk bar. By rights, he should be facing a judge and jury, or at least an inquiry. Instead, he was riding a wave.

'Really? A hero? That's very kind, but honestly, I'm just waiting for someone!' he would protest, as the admirers flocked. Two weeks ago the great Richard Dimbleby, no less, had forced his way through the throng to say, 'Good show, Steine.' Back in Brighton, he had reported this remark not once, not twice, but nineteen and a half times before the station charlady Mrs Groynes stopped him mid-sentence and threatened him with an all-personnel walk-out if he ever mentioned it again.

This week, however, he felt oddly self-conscious as he lurked in his usual spot. And the reason was: he really was waiting for someone. He was waiting for Twitten. His eager young constable had often asked to accompany him to London, and this week Steine had unwisely relented – and this was how his kindness was repaid! Once inside Broadcasting House, Twitten had noticed that a children's serial – and this bore repetition, a *serial for children* – was due for live transmission immediately after 'Law and the Little Man', and had begged to be allowed to sit in and 'watch the magic happen', before making the journey home.

'It was one of my favourite programmes when I was a child, sir,' Twitten explained. 'And each episode is only ten minutes. The Spiffing Six solve all sorts of mysteries. Four children in East Anglia, the youthful Aunt Rosemary and their dog Sammy, who literally has a *nose for crime*.' He waited for a response. 'That's the six, sir.'

Steine had refused to be impressed by the arithmetic.

'So, I just popped my head in, sir, and asked a chap if I could observe, and he was the writer apparently, quite drably dressed and sort-of starving-looking, and he said that he had no say in anything around here so it was up to me. So, can I, sir? I'd really like to meet the actor who plays Sammy the dog. He's so lifelike. And, of course, the whole purpose of the series is to make children more law-abiding!'

Steine had wearily assented, so now here he was, genuinely waiting, waiting, waiting; awkwardly crossing and recrossing his legs; flicking through his script again and again, trying to look casual.

'Something's different,' observed one of the ladies at the desk, tilting her head in his direction.

'Gosh, sir. So you're really the writer of *The Spiffing Six*?'

Twitten didn't often experience envy, but looking through the plate glass into the brightly lit studio from behind the control desk, he couldn't help thinking, 'I would love to do this.' In front of two standard microphones, limply holding scripts, stood four bored-looking middle-aged actors, one of them with a black eye and a bandaged forehead. Surrounding them were umpteen functional green baize screens and walls soundproofed with cream-painted peg-board. Cables snaked across the floor. Twitten couldn't hear the conversation beyond the glass, but a tweedy Oxbridgey young man with floppy hair was pointing at passages in the script while an hourglass-figured female assistant stood pressed against him, making notes.

Anything less breezy than this airless environment would be hard to imagine, yet Twitten knew it to be true: from this unpromising scenario – one of the actors vacantly tugging at his grubby bandage with arthritic fingers; one consuming a flaky sausage roll – would emerge in less than ten minutes' time an exhilarating story of childish adventure and fun, with wholesome children calling to each other under cloudless Norfolk skies, 'Susan! Timothy! Come and see what clever Sammy has found in the corner of Old Jacob's Meadow!'

The writer held out a hand for shaking. 'Nigel,' he said, distantly, and took a swig from a coffee cup.

'Not Nigel *Barnes*?' Twitten gushed.

'You've heard of me?'

'Of course, sir. I love this programme. I grew up on this and *Pirate Island*, which was better but bally terrifying. You're a bit of a hero to me, sir. You and Charles Prescott, you know, who wrote *Pirate Island*. I would say him first and you second, but still.'

'Oh.' Blinking with surprise, Nigel produced an old torn hanky from his trouser pocket and blew his nose. He was terribly pale. Twitten wondered if he ever saw the light of day.

'The producer and the BA,' the writer explained, 'have just popped in for a word with the actors. Although I don't know why he bothers.' Twitten took a breath to ask a question, but Nigel anticipated it. 'Broadcast Assistant,' he explained, pointing to the curvy woman. 'Barbara.'

'Thank you, sir.'

Nigel sighed. 'Favours port and lemon.'

'Gosh, if you say so, sir.'

'But only if someone else is paying.'

Nigel assumed a faraway look, then pulled himself together. 'The producer is Guy. She thinks he's a genius, of course. Pah. Upper-class pillock. He won't stay long on *The Spiffing Six*; they never do.'

Despite his determination to enjoy this experience, Twitten was gaining the unfortunate impression that Nigel – despite being a household name for writing a popular long-running show on the BBC – had tragically mislaid any of the pizazz or verve he was surely born with.

'Tell me about the actors, sir. How do they manage to sound so jolly convincing as children?'

But if Twitten hoped this would be a safe topic, he was wrong.

'Right. Well, the only one who's been here since the start is James there cramming all the sausage rolls and not leaving any for the rest of us; he plays Timothy.'

'Oh, he's excellent, sir. I love Timothy. I sort-of identify with—'

'Talentless shit.'

'Oh.' Twitten was covered in confusion. 'Oh. Ooh, perhaps we shouldn't—'

'And he earns double what I do!'

'Well, that doesn't sound fair, sir.'

'Maureen in the mauve coat plays two parts – Aunt Rosemary and young Susan – and mixes them up *all the bloody time*. Fred plays Peter and all the character villains, which is why they sound identical. And Gerald in the hat – well, he's all right actually—'

'Thank goodness.'

'Yes, he's all right. He plays Georgie-Porgie and everyone else.'

Twitten struggled to take it all in, and account for the full complement of the six who were spiffing. He came up short.

'So does Gerald also play Sammy the dog?'

'Ah, no.' Nigel laughed a hollow laugh. 'No, no. That's *Val.*'

Twitten frowned. 'But which one is—'

'He's behind that screen at the back. Got his own little kingdom back there. Bloody Val.'

Twitten saw only a screen. 'Does he come out to do Sammy?'

'No, no. He has to stay back there with his own microphone. He's in charge of spot effects. You know: *ding-a-ling-a-ling* goes the bell at the shop, *clip-clop* go the horses, *crunch, crunch* go the feet on the gravel. A child could do it.'

'Oh, I see.'

'He's got a short flight of steps back there that's got carpet on one side of the tread and plain wood on the other, so characters can run up and downstairs. It gets wheeled about. I'm not joking. He does the sound of Sammy scampering down to say hello by yanking two little bags of sand down the steps – you know, *bumpety-bumpety-bump*. I keep saying it makes Sammy sound the size of a hippo, but as usual I'm wasting my breath.'

'I love all those effects, sir.'

'Well, don't tell him that.' Nigel had grown considerably more animated since the subject had turned to Val. Perhaps this was another person who was paid more than he was. 'Here,' he said, brightening. 'Do you remember in your beloved *Pirate Island* when Blackbeard hacked someone's head off with a cutlass?'

'Oh golly yes, sir. I had nightmares for weeks. My mother wrote in to the BBC.'

'Well, that was Val getting carried away.'

'Gosh.'

'Yes, now I come to think of it, they cancelled *Pirate Island* because of that! Funny how you forget these things. Last anyone heard of Prescott – ha! – he was rumoured to be living under the arches at Charing Cross!' Nigel chuckled to himself at the happy memory of a rival show being unfairly shelved and a fellow writer rendered destitute. 'Anyway, Val also does Sammy. For budgetary reasons.'

'But Sammy isn't an *effect*, sir.' Twitten objected. 'He's a major character.'

'I know. That's what I keep saying. But as I think I've already mentioned . . .' Nigel didn't bother to finish this thought. He looked up at the clock and took another swig of coffee. Just a couple of minutes to go.

Twitten made a decision. 'If I may say so, sir,' he said, earnestly, 'I think they should listen to you writers a bit more. And they should definitely pay you better.'

'Well—'

'And I know this will sound impertinent, sir, and it's arguably not my place, but that handkerchief of yours is a bally disgrace, sir, and I can't help noticing that your shoes are laced with string, and you really need a haircut and the alcohol you've quite obviously spiked your coffee with smells like paint-stripper. So, what I'm putting to you is this. Is it possible that working for the BBC all these years has not only dangerously depleted your Vitamin D but also destroyed virtually all your self-respect?'

Nigel, astonished, was just about to answer when time ran out. The producer swept in with his BA, both importantly clutching scripts, and ignoring Twitten as they sat down at the desk. From another door appeared a chap in an engineer's lab-coat who brought with him a miasma of tobacco smoke.

'Hello, Frank. Nice of you to come,' muttered Nigel.

The engineer said, 'Stand by studio,' into a microphone as he likewise sat down, while pressing a button on the control desk.

'Val, can you hear me?' said Guy, the producer.

By way of reply came the *tring-tring* of a bicycle bell.

'Excellent. Thank you, Val. Ready to go, studio.'

'Here we go,' whispered Nigel, opening his script for Twitten to follow it, and tapping a pencil.

Everyone looked up at the sweeping second hand on the studio clock, and as a brylcreemed BBC announcer silently entered the acting area, a green light was switched on and a red ON AIR sign illuminated.

'And now,' said the announcer, 'We rejoin the Spiffing Six for a new adventure, "The Castle of Secrets" by Nigel Barnes. Episode one, "Where's Sammy?"'

Twitten held his breath as familiar theme music played, and the actress called Maureen stepped forward, half-moon reading glasses balanced on her nose. The script called for her to be Aunt Rosemary, and Twitten closed his eyes to listen. He loved Aunt Rosemary. Her voice was like honey.

'Well, children,' she purred. 'What have you been getting up to this summer without me?'

'Another cup of tea, dear?'

'Ooh, thank you, Mrs G.'

'So, you enjoyed your jaunt on Friday, all in all?' Mrs Groynes the charlady took an appreciative drag on a Senior Service cigarette. 'Christ, that's better.'

She waved the smoke away and was about to sit down at Sergeant Brunswick's desk across the room from Twitten's when she remembered something. A large hold-all full of banknotes was sitting, open and bulging, in the middle of the floor of the office. 'Long night, dear,' she shrugged, by way of explanation, as she dragged the bag towards a cupboard in the corner of the room, shoved it in, and locked the door.

'Need I ask?' said Twitten.

'I wouldn't.'

'No, I didn't think so.'

'So,' she continued, sitting down, fag in hand. 'So, on the plus side, you got to see a real-life radio drama studio. And on the double-plus side, you discovered a freshly murdered bleeding corpse surrounded by – what was it, dear? An ironing board and a pair of coconut shells?'

Twitten flipped open his notebook. 'A tray of gravel, a tray of sand, a bicycle bell, a hand bell, a jolly good whistle, a copy of *The Times*, well, the list goes bally well on and on, but coconut shells most definitely.'

'What was the ironing board for?'

'Apparently that's how Val replicated the sound of a gate opening. You know, that grating metal noise.' He wrinkled his nose. 'I still can't quite imagine that one.'

Mrs Groynes made a face. 'And no one could have got in or out, you said?'

'That's right. That's what makes it so bally interesting. I mean, aside from the body being discovered during a live transmission. The first indication that there was something wrong was when young Susan rode up on her bike, you see, and Aunt Rosemary said, 'Here comes Susan,' and the script said '*Bicycle bell*' and nothing happened, but the actor playing

Timothy nevertheless said the line, "That's her bell all right! I'd know it anywhere."'

'Ah. Not very clever of him.'

'According to the writer, the actor playing Timothy is a – well, that's just Nigel. I couldn't help thinking, incidentally, that levels of demoralization in the BBC would make a jolly good case study, if only I had the time to conduct it. More specifically, levels of demoralization as expressed through alcohol dependence.'

Mrs Groynes gave him a look.

'Anyway,' he resumed, 'back with the bicycle bell that didn't go *tring*, they all looked a bit panicky and then one of the others started improvising about how, unlike Timothy, actually they *hadn't* heard the bell, and Susan explained rather unconvincingly that her bell had fallen off her handlebars the day before yesterday as she was riding over Harrier's Hill, and then somehow thank goodness everyone steered themselves back to where they ought to be in their scripts and Georgie-Porgie said, with relief, 'Here's Sammy, anyway! Good dog, Sammy! I've missed you!' And I'd been looking forward to hearing Sammy come galumphing heavily downstairs and start woofing, but golly, nothing happened *again*, so one of the actors said, 'Oh no, the poor dog hasn't got laryngitis? Poor Sammy!' and BA Barbara crept into the studio to look behind Val's screen and she screamed and fainted and that was that!'

Mrs Groynes, who tended to focus more on the mechanics of crime than on its fascinating incidentals, had waited patiently for all this stuff concerning ghastly piping middle-class children to pass by. 'But like I said, dear,' she said, tapping the ash off her cigarette into the open drawer of Brunswick's desk, '*no one could have got in or out*?'

'No. And you see Mr Val (I never learned his surname) must logically have been killed in the space of about three minutes because he was alive and well before the transmission! When Guy asked him if he was OK immediately before we went on air, he rang the bicycle bell. We all heard it.'

'Well, someone else could have rung that bleeding bell, dear. This Val bloke could have been dead already.'

'I agree, of course, Mrs G. But who? Everyone was in plain

sight. We searched behind all the screens and stuff, and there was no one there.' Twitten took a sip of his tea. 'Quite honestly, I'm stumped.'

If this Monday morning scene between clever young constable and friendly station charlady seems cosy enough, it conceals a relationship far more complex – as perhaps might be suggested by Twitten's strange lack of reaction to seeing Mrs Groynes' confident possession of a large bag of swag. On joining the Brighton Police just four months earlier, young Twitten had quickly deduced that this harmless-seeming Cockney woman was in fact a cunning career criminal, the head of an extensive gang responsible for most of the crime in Brighton. Initially, he had done his best to expose her, but he soon discovered that as well as being quite shockingly criminal by both nature and inclination, she was ingenious, devious, ruthless and – worst of all – just a great deal cleverer than he was. At every turn, he was outwitted.

It sounds intolerable. How could he stand it? But life is, if nothing else, a lesson in compromise, and quite quickly Twitten came to a strange accommodation with his ethical pickle, and the two of them became improbably close, considering their polar differences in relation to 1) the law and 2) abiding by it. One major factor was that, as a clever person himself, he couldn't help admiring the way she turned every situation to her own advantage. Also, he appreciated the wisdom of her early remark that the longer he pointed the finger at her, the more he hurt only his own credibility. Meanwhile, Mrs G had likewise grown to enjoy the fact that she had no secrets from Twitten: she relished having his reluctant complicity; she also wickedly delighted in his Cassandra-like predicament. Because the truth was: no one – not a single soul – would ever believe him. She so perfectly played the role of funny, harmless 'Mrs G' that all Twitten's colleagues – especially the hapless Sergeant Brunswick and the idiotic Inspector Steine – were utterly brainwashed into taking her at face value.

This meant they would never know, for example, that in the corner of their own office was a locked cupboard in which Mrs G stashed hot jewellery, sticks of dynamite, state-of-the-art safe-breaking equipment, a much-loved copy of *Rififi* on several reels of flammable celluloid, and countless bags of cash. But would they have smelled a rat if they *had* discovered this stuff? The answer, probably, was no. She'd have explained it away, or changed the subject. Take Sergeant Brunswick. Whenever a trace of suspicion passed through his mind, Mrs Groynes needed only to offer him a slice of gala pie, or a humble fig roll, or even just an extra spoon of sugar in his tea, and he instantly abandoned his train of thought. Twitten had witnessed it a hundred times. As for the inspector, she had once been struggling to load a box of gold bullion into a taxi outside the back door of the station when the inspector happened to pass by. Instead of saying something appropriate (such as 'Stop in the name of the law'), he had gallantly helped her to lift it in.

So, this was what lay beneath the cosy cup of tea and the friendly chat about a murdered sound-effects man up in London. The situation wasn't ideal, heaven knew. One day Twitten would find a way to call this wicked woman to account, and he would do it. But as things stood, Mrs G was Twitten's best friend in all the world, and it was possible that he was hers.

It was just a day later that the dog came into their lives. He was a police dog, unimaginatively named Bobby – but that was the only unoriginal thing about him. The inspector decided to forewarn his men, but gave them no time at all to get used to the idea.

'Men,' he said – ignoring the gender of Mrs Groynes, who was just handing him a cup of tea. 'For this week's talk I am considering the role of the police dog in modern detective work, so I have borrowed a dog called Bobby from the canine unit of the Metropolitan Police.' Here he was briefly thrown off course by Twitten's gasp of excitement. 'Are you quite all right, Twitten?'

'Yes, sir. Sorry, sir.'

'What was I saying?'

'Metropolitan Police, dear.'

'Thank you, Mrs Groynes. This dog is from the Canine Unit of Scotland Yard, where I believe he has established quite a reputation for *sniffing out crime*. Twitten, what's wrong with you?'

'Sorry, sir. Just a bit excited.'

'Well, try to contain yourself. It was that dratted children's serial of yours that gave me the thought. You are entirely to blame.'

'Yes, sir.'

Steine sighed. 'Here is my plan. Today you and Sergeant Brunswick are to take Bobby out and about on your investigations. Take note of his behaviour. Rate his effectiveness. I might as well tell you at the outset that my considered opinion is that dogs *do not* "sniff out crime". The whole idea is preposterous, and I intend to disprove it empirically.'

He stopped, and they all listened.

'Ah, here he comes.'

On the stairs outside they could hear the unmistakable tap of claws on lino along with the heavy footsteps of a regular human. Twitten gasped again.

'This is like a dream come true, sir,' Twitten just had time to say, when there came the expected knock at the door. Twitten glanced at Brunswick. Brunswick pulled a face. Mrs G muttered, 'Oh my good gawd', and sat down. Steine called, 'Come in!' And Bobby the dog trotted into the room.

His handler signalled at them not to address the dog, but it was unnecessary: Bobby's demeanour commanded silence. To Twitten's surprise, the animal was not a large Alsatian, but rather a smallish black-and-tan terrier with a confident, measured gait and head held high. Having entered the room as if he owned it, Bobby now stood absolutely still, sniffing the air.

'He does this,' whispered the handler. 'He never rushes. Good Bobby.'

'Does anyone else feel guilty all of a sudden?' whispered Brunswick, whose face was reddening.

'Shhh!' said Twitten.

Each man stood completely motionless as Bobby sniffed him thoroughly and methodically, shaking his head from side to side as he moved from one to the next. Then, finally, he took position in front of Mrs Groynes and commenced to bark the place down.

By the end of Bobby's awayday to Brighton, Twitten's initial excitement about the dog had been exploded. He was in turmoil. He wasn't sure whether he loved Bobby, hated him, or just felt overwhelming compassion for him, because Bobby persisted in identifying the criminality of Mrs Groynes by the only means at his disposal – by barking at it hysterically – and all day he was disbelieved, ticked off, and even reprimanded. It was pitiful to see. Watching a clever well-meaning dog go through this oh-so-familiar humiliation *for being spot-on about Mrs G* was somehow worse for Twitten than enduring it himself.

'What *can* this silly dog be thinking of?' was the general consensus.

'I'm sure he knows what he's doing,' pleaded Twitten.

*Bark bark bark*, said Bobby, with mounting urgency.

Profuse apologies were made to Mrs Groynes.

The barking started to edge over into whining and howling.

'It's unaccountable,' said the handler. 'He's never wrong.'

'Perhaps he doesn't like the smell of furniture polish?' offered Brunswick.

'That could be it,' said the handler.

'Why on earth does he keep scratching at that cupboard?' said Steine. 'I'm sure there's nothing in it. It's been locked for years and no one has the key. You see, Twitten? This is what I told you. This dog has no "nose for crime". He's just attention-seeking, that's what he is. Look at him! Good grief, what more proof do you need? He is obsessed with our harmless Cockney charlady!'

Eventually the affronted Mrs Groynes was allowed to take the rest of the day off, on account of the dog's irrational dislike of her. But when Brunswick took him out for a walk in the afternoon, Bobby dragged him straight to an address in Upper North Street and sat outside it, howling.

'And you know what, son?' Brunswick confided to Twitten afterwards, gravely shaking his head. 'It was the home of Mrs Groynes.'

Luckily Bobby did show his worth in other ways on that fateful day of his loan to the Brighton Police. Just in passing, he flushed out a Russian spy ring operating from the amusement arcade on the Palace Pier, and also uncovered invaluable new evidence in the case of the Brighton Trunk Murders. But sadly, what he would be remembered for was his unsupportable behaviour towards Mrs G. If ever Twitten had doubted the tragedy of his own predicament vis-à-vis his charlady nemesis, he now saw it played out graphically in the case of Bobby, and it made him wretched.

'You did your best, Bobby,' he whispered in the dog's ear when he had the chance at the end of the day. 'In some ways you're lucky. You go back to London tomorrow where everyone knows how clever you are, and no one doubts you and laughs at you. You can go back to being just like Sammy in *The Spiffing Six*. Sammy would have solved the crime of the dead sound-effects man like a shot!'

Which was when Twitten began to hatch an idea that really cheered him up.

'Well, if he'd been here a minute longer I'd have made sure he was picked up in a brothel in Little Preston Street accepting a backhander, that's for sure,' said Mrs G, three days later. 'Little bleeder. You should have seen the way he looked at me.'

'I did see the way he looked at you, Mrs G, and I confess his straightforward attitude to your criminality made me feel quite ashamed. I mean to say, what have I become?' A thought struck him. Little Preston Street? 'But golly, Ms G, are you really saying you would have *framed a dog*?'

'Trust me, dear. Tea?'

'Ooh yes, thank you.'

It was quiet in the office again. Twitten was typing notes while Mrs Groynes was busily knitting a set of matching black balaclavas in advance of a heist at a Shoreham fur warehouse planned for the weekend.

'Don't tell me the details,' Twitten had pleaded, so of course she'd supplied the exact location, the planned time of the raid, plus the names and addresses of all the personnel involved.

This being Friday, Inspector Steine was on the train to Victoria, polishing up his script for 'Law and the Little Man', which this week concerned the ever-dwindling height requirement in police recruitment (which had recently reached the worrying new low of five foot seven). The inspector's preferred topic – of the comically useless sniffer dog – he had been obliged to scrap, because once the dog-handler from the Met understood Steine's intentions, a stiff warning by telephone came from Scotland Yard. Evidently any public scoffing at decorated members of the brave canine detective force represented a significant breach of the Policeman's Code. Steine briefly considered making the argument for free speech, but buckled at once, in keeping with his usual pusillanimity. (In a file at Scotland Yard, interestingly, there was an assessment of Steine that said it all: 'It is impossible to overstate the weakness of this man's character.')

But having ditched the incendiary subject of police dogs being a waste of public money, Steine had chosen instead a subject that would ultimately get him into even more trouble. Fortunately, he was unaware of this as he studied his script on the train.

*I am sometimes asked 'Why is it, Inspector Steine, that while the police force complains of being so short of men, you continue to reject recruits who are anxious to join up?' The answer, I'm afraid, is that we have already lowered recruitment standards further than it is actually safe to do!*

'So, Bobby's back at the Yard now, is he?' asked Mrs G, as she completed the seventh balaclava and tossed it on a pile.

'He is. I gave him the entire credit for finding the writer Charles Prescott squeezed in behind that set of fake stairs in the studio. I felt it was the least I could do after you nearly destroyed his reputation.'

Mrs G let the comment pass. Destroying a dog's reputation didn't rank high on her list of concerns. 'But Bobby didn't actually work out this Prescott cove was the murderer, did he, dear? I mean, he had a bit of help from you.'

'Well, of course I had deduced already that Mr Prescott was the probable murderer; I just couldn't imagine where he had hidden. It was terribly clear after talking to Nigel that BBC radio scriptwriters are so downtrodden and under-appreciated that they will naturally be driven to desperate acts. But Mr Prescott had a very compelling personal motive. When the sound-effects man came up with one of the most graphic effects ever heard on the wireless – achieved, apparently, with a watermelon and an axe, which I have to tell you doesn't make the memory of it any the less disturbing – Mr Prescott was effectively sacked, even though it wasn't directly his fault that children were wetting their beds all across the country and the Director General received so many letters of complaint that he took the extreme emergency measure of going immediately on holiday.'

Mrs Groynes rolled her eyes. She considered asking where exactly the DG had gone on holiday and with whom and for how long and had he sent many postcards, but she knew from experience that sarcasm tended to pass Twitten by. So she said nothing. One of the drawbacks of befriending this young constable was having to listen to him bang on and bleeding on when he was carried away with an explanation. The bells and whistles were never optional.

'Now, some of this is personal extrapolation, Mrs G,' Twitten continued, 'but this is how I see it. When *Pirate Island* was cancelled, Mr Prescott was stripped of his BBC pass, so he decided simply not to leave the building. For the past *seven years* he has lived in the nooks and crannies of Broadcasting House, just biding his time until the perfect opportunity came to exact his revenge. Leftovers on trolleys have been his main source of sustenance, so it's been a diet of softened sugary biscuits, cold tea and dregs of shockingly bad warm white wine. He looks terrible, although I have to say, not that much worse than Nigel.'

'Is he mad, this Prescott?'

'Do you mean insane?'

'Yes.'

'Oh, completely.'

'And how did he do it, dear? What was the method?'

'He was very clear on that. He crept up behind Mr Val, stunned him with the coconuts, felled him with the ironing board and buried his face in the tray of sand.'

'Blimey.'

'This was all before everyone else arrived. And then, after he'd rung the bicycle bell to indicate Mr Val was still alive just before transmission, he squeezed himself into the tiny hollow space behind the flight of stairs used for sound effects. And it really is tiny. Only someone as bent and spindly as Mr Prescott could possibly have hidden there so successfully.'

'And that's where Bobby found him?'

'No. I said he did because it sounded better. But I'm afraid when we opened up the studio – which had been sealed off since the incident – Mr Prescott was sitting openly on the floor, babbling. Bobby actually gave him a lick on the nose. His mind had completely gone. It was a pitiful sight. And also a patent warning never to take up scriptwriting for the BBC, of course.'

Sergeant Brunswick's tread was audible now on the stairs outside the office. Twitten raised an eyebrow at Mrs Groynes' tell-tale craft project, but she shook her head. No need to tidy it away. Not for bleeding Sergeant Brunswick.

'Morning all,' said the sergeant, entering. 'Blimey, I'm glad that flaming dog has gone, aren't you?' He hung his hat on a peg, and took off his coat.

'Cup of tea?' asked Mrs G, bustling to the tea urn.

'Yes, please, Mrs G.' As he sat down, Brunswick looked over at Twitten, who was looking thoughtful. 'Don't tell me, son. You miss him.'

'I did feel jolly sorry for him,' said Twitten. 'It's hard when you notice everything and no one else does. It's a burden. I wish I could write to him occasionally, but I suppose there's no point.'

'Hark at him,' laughed Mrs G. 'Him and his burden.'

Brunswick looked around and spotted the handicrafts. 'Been knitting, Mrs G?'

'I have, dear. Just some bonnets for the orphan babies.' She held up one of the jet black, extra-large, sinister balaclavas for him to see.

'Isn't that a bit big for a baby?' he said, frowning. 'And is black—'

'How about a nice slice of cherry Genoa, sergeant?' she said with a smile, winking at Twitten. 'I've got a bit here with an extra big cherry I've been saving just for you.'

'Oh go on, then,' Brunswick said happily, having lost his thread. Twitten watched in grudging admiration as the frown magically vanished from the sergeant's face at the simple thought of an extra-large cherry with his name on it. You had to hand it to Mrs G. It worked every flipping time.

'There you are, dear.'

'Lovely. But what was I saying, son? Oh yes, I know. I'm glad that flaming dog has gone, aren't you?'

# MICHAEL JECKS – AFTER HENRY? NO COMMITMENTS

Edith Bremen stood at the rear of the stage, the lighting dimmed for once, sipping Prosecco, trying to express sophistication in grief, and knowing that she was failing miserably. It was not easy. Especially with that two-faced cow Irene Coles at her performative best, weeping, sobbing and wailing, while carefully preserving her makeup: the bereft woman in mourning. A perfect role for her.

It was rare for the Genesius Amateur Dramatic Society to mingle. In other am-dram groups, Edith had enjoyed the social life among aspiring thespians. Not here, though. Not since Henry and she had arrived. What a stupid name, anyway; Genesius was the patron saint of actors, a martyr who had lived as an actor or something. Why didn't they just call themselves Arundel Actors? It was all so bloody pretentious! And now, with Henry gone, she wasn't sure she could cope with them.

'Edith, how are you? I'm so sorry for your loss,' said Arthur Ransome. 'Such a terrible loss, and to . . . well, you know.'

She lifted her glass in a vague gesture that could have been gratitude, or perhaps a toast to Henry's memory. After all, this was a wake in his honour. A celebration of his life, they said. He would have liked that. The bastard. He walked out on her in the most selfish fashion imaginable. He didn't even leave them with a body to bury or cremate. Just . . . well, just *went.*

He would have enjoyed the sight of all this, she thought. All these *reptiles* fawning over his memory while maintaining their pretence of sympathy for her, his wife, and her new position as widow. Except to her they looked like jackals bickering over a fresh carcass. She should drop the am-dram group. Now he was gone, and she wasn't expected to help him at work, she could carry on with what *she* wanted. No commitments like the two-yearly shows, the matinees, the rehearsals. No, life would get simpler, more relaxed now, after Henry . . . And the tears threatened again.

'It must have been a terrible shock,' Arthur said, and took a quick slug from his glass as though it might fend off an angry response. His long dark hair quivered with reflected trepidation. He always looked so anxious nowadays, like a teenager asking for his first date.

That was at least easy to answer. 'Yes.'

After all, Henry had never shown the slightest inclination towards suicide. He had been under pressure recently, she could tell that; any woman married fifteen years would know when her husband was stressed, but that was part of the job. He was self-employed, a financial consultant, and there were always risks – lean months, lean years, the struggle of finding the annual fees to remain qualified – but suicide? Not Henry! She would never have thought him capable.

He would have enjoyed this. 'Good old Henry', the life and soul of every party, the first man always to hold up a sprig of mistletoe at Christmas, always first at the bar to buy a round of drinks, the man who was . . .

She viciously blinked the tears away. Not here. Not in front of Claire, Irene and the others.

'Still no, um, you know . . .?'

'What?'

'Nothing, nothing. I was just . . . Oh, look, there's Claire. I should just . . . I mean . . . You must have other people you want to talk to . . .'

She averted her gaze, and soon he had walked to the front of the stage to Claire, the obvious blonde-from-a-bottle. She was precisely the sort of amateur with whom Edith begrudged sharing a stage. Bubbly, friendly, affectionate with all the men, and a right bitch to the women, Edith despised her. But then again, she had a similar contempt for most of the other actresses. It was inevitable, given Henry's *problems,* as she liked to put it.

'How are you bearing up?'

'I can still hardly believe it, Charles. Anyone less likely—' She broke off.

'It is difficult, I know. You need time to mourn. Things will come clearer over time.'

'You think so?' She wasn't sure that mourning was exactly the term. She felt more like screaming and hurling multiple fragile objects at the wall.

'It grows easier. And you can find a new social circle. Perhaps learn bridge, or go bowling?'

'The last thing I need is more commitments,' she said. 'No, I feel a period of intense effort based on laziness and self-indulgence and gin and chocolate . . . And no diary entries. How could he do this to me, Charles? How *dare* he!'

Charles nodded understandingly. 'It will get easier. Honestly, it will. But you're empty, can I fetch you more wine?'

'Thank you, Charles.'

She knew he was fond of her. Not that he had ever tried to seduce her. She wasn't sure how she'd react if he did; she wasn't sure of anything anymore.

Poor Charles. Sad, lonely Charles. As the players' Hon. Secretary, he was always on hand to smooth over the little annoyances and irritations that could so easily flare and scorch the entire cast. An actor feeling he was upstaged; one partner jealous of the attention paid to another; a prima donna flouncing from the theatre because of a misspelled name on posters or fliers – she had seen them all. Charles was always there, and his skill at pouring oil on the waves of troubled waters was little short of miraculous. Edith watched him go to the makeshift bar with a sense of mild regret. He had gone through this, too. His wife had died in a crash.

Why hadn't she married someone like Charles? A school-teacher at a public college, where he taught maths and hockey, with an occasional foray into cricket when the other games master was away. He was tall, good-looking, and had a reliable income. When he retired, he would have a good pension. Whereas Henry . . . Well, self-employment meant constant money worries. Never any guarantee of the money coming in, especially now with restrictions on how salesmen operated.

'Darling, how are you bearing up?' Irene said.

While Edith had been watching Charles, Irene had approached Edith's side. 'You will let us know if we can help in any way, won't you? Such a loss. A terrible, terrible loss, darling.'

Charles had returned with her refill, and Edith took it with a calm stoicism. 'It is very difficult, of course,' she said coolly.

Irene's eyes flitted over the other players until they fixed on Claire, and her face hardened. She had long, masculine features, but her eyes were as cruel and vindictive as the Babadook's, Edith felt.

'I can imagine. *She* has a cheek coming here!'

Charles hastily tried to slip between them both and their view of Claire. 'Oh, I don't think . . .'

'You think I don't know?' Edith said. Her voice was, to her surprise, perfectly calm and restrained, but tasted like vitriol. 'After all, Irene, you were there before her, weren't you?'

'Look at her! Regular ice queen, isn't she?' Claire said to Stephan.

She liked the tall, Polish builder. It wasn't just his physique, she told herself, it was the accent. He sounded wildly exotic. The way he pronounced words made her go all wobbly. Better than Henry, the tight-fisted old goat. His upper-class voice was too plummy. Still, he'd been fun for a while. And it was one in the eye for Irene, the old cow, when Claire stole him from her.

Stephan was tall, ruggedly handsome, with hands that could just about encompass her waist. She had heard you could tell the size of a man's manhood by the size of his hands – that was Mel, in the wine bar. Mel had been dating a body builder, and her main comment was, 'Thick as my wrist – it was, honest!'

Claire was keen to find out if it was true.

She knew Edith's and Irene's eyes were on her, and she slipped closer to Stephan, turning her mournful face up to him, knowing that both would be watching, bitter and jealous. Everyone was jealous of her. Claire was young, attractive, everything they weren't. They'd never be able to appeal to a man like Stephan, big, muscled with shoulders like an ox, and with those big hands . . . she shivered in anticipation.

'It's just so sad,' she murmured. 'You can't tell, can you? What can tip someone over the edge. To think that he just undressed, and walked into the sea, knowing he couldn't live with things any more. It's just so sad.'

'Is sad. Is shame,' Stephan agreed, and recognizing the cue, he gently put an arm around her shoulders. She glanced down at his enormous hand and then back at him, allowing herself a brittle little smile. 'You're so kind.'

'You were friend of him, yes?'

'We grew close in *King Lear.* Everyone said my Cordelia was just wonderful. Henry was Lear, and he wasn't bad. For such an old man,' she added, glancing thoughtfully at Stephan's wrist.

'You were close?'

'Oh, you know,' she said with a light laugh, but then realized it sounded improper in the circumstances. She sniffed and added, 'He was older, more confident, a businessman with a real understanding of men . . . and women.'

She smiled blearily up at him, and was glad to see the blue eyes crinkle into a grimace of understanding. Suddenly the theatre felt horribly claustrophobic. Soon, with luck, she could persuade Stephan to take her home.

She really wanted to test Mel's theory.

It was Charles who saw him first. A slightly scruffy-looking man about halfway between forty and fifty, with mouse-coloured hair and an aura of bemused confusion, like a father presented with a new phone app and no instructions.

He walked down the centre aisle of the theatre until Deirdre, the manager, left her post serving drinks and made her way to him.

Charles eyed the stranger with a teacher's speculation. He prided himself on being able to judge people quickly, and in his view this was a friend, perhaps; certainly someone who must have known Henry. He had that sort of slightly shabby appearance that would suit many of Henry's clients, and all of them were convinced Henry was a perfect adviser. They knew by the way he took them for drinks to chat over their investments that he was reliable, stolid, not just some fly-by-night salesman, but a member of the Round Table and Lions. How could anyone mistrust a man who did so much for charitable causes? Charles had been taken in, just like them.

Deirdre was soon satisfied and began to lead the man to the gathering. Charles saw Arthur peering over. It was obvious that Henry's ex-colleague was wondering whether he ought to go and speak with the fellow, but decided that talking to one of Henry's clients might be considered bad form. Someone might think he was just trying to benefit from Henry's death.

'Edith, you do know that you can always call on me to come and help with things, don't you? If there's paperwork – or problems with the building; I can be quite a handyman. Let me know if there is anything you need fixing.'

'I will, thank you, Charles.'

Irene was pursing her lips with disgust. 'Look at her, the little tart. Making eyes at Stephan as if this was a drinks party. You'd think she'd have a little more consideration.'

'Like you?' Edith snapped.

Charles was quick to halt that flow. 'Come, now, Edith – this isn't the time or place to rake over—'

'As I said, Charles, I am fully aware of Henry's infidelity,' Edith said. 'Irene wasn't the first, but I suppose Claire was at least the last.'

Charles reflected that Henry's were not the only adulterous relationships he had seen blossoming during theatrical events. Actors tended to be outgoing, gregarious people, who would fall into and out of beds at the drop of a hat. Marriages had blossomed, and all too often failed, in amateur dramatic groups, but that was the nature of the beast. And bloody Henry had been a genuine beast. Out for himself, and the devil take the rest.

The newcomer had reached the steps at the side of the stage, and now he joined the wake. Deirdre offered him a glass, but he waved it away, glanced around the gathering, and then walked to Edith.

'Mrs Bremen? May I offer my sympathy? It must have been a shock to learn that Mr Bremen had died.'

She looked at him with a slight puckering of her brow. 'I'm sorry, I don't think I . . .'

'We haven't met. I am Detective Inspector Pauley.'

Charles put out a hand to try to lead the unwelcome guest away, but the officer was curiously immobile. He stood like a small stone plinth, and Charles gained the impression that even a good whack with his hockey stick would be unlikely to shift the fellow.

'Detective Inspector . . .?' Edith faltered.

'Yes, I am investigating the death of Henry Bremen.'

'But it's clear enough, surely?' Charles said. He was perhaps a little more forceful than he would usually have felt necessary with an officer of the law, but really, this man crashing in on Henry's wake was outrageous. The cocky devil may enjoy going and offending criminals, but breaking into the celebration of a man's life was ungracious, to put it mildly – which Charles usually did. He was not prone to angry outbursts. Teaching had cured him of that. If it had not, he would long ago have been committed to a mental institution, or imprisoned for murdering the whole of Class 5C.

'Is it, sir?'

Charles suddenly found himself pinned by an intimidating stare. The officer's eyes were quite a pale hazel, but there was an intensity about them that was thoroughly unsettling. He was reminded of Michael Bond's books, and Paddington Bear's unnerving, fixed, accusatory gaze.

He rallied. 'Well, of course it is. His clothes were found, weren't they?'

'As were John Stonehouse's, yes. There was no suicide note, of course.'

'No doubt it was blown away by the wind.'

'It was a still afternoon. And if there were a note, surely Mr Bremen would have thought to place a shingle on top of it to hold it in place?'

'A man who has decided to end it all will probably act less than rationally,' Charles said, with the haughty tone he used when explaining that striking a peer over the head with a gym slipper was not considered polite behaviour. 5C had taught him much.

'In my experience, sir, when a man decides to commit suicide and goes through the process, his actions are deliberate. It is rare for him not to leave a note to a wife . . . or loved ones.'

'Now wait just a minute!' Charles said warmly, and could not help but put a protective arm about Edith's shoulders. The fact that she did not draw away lit a warm sensation in his belly.

'Perhaps there was a reason why he didn't feel able to leave a note,' the officer said speculatively. He had turned slightly, and now was eyeing Claire.

'How dare you! You come here, to the man's wake, and make insinuations. I ought to throw you out!'

'I'm not entirely sure that would be a terribly good idea, sir.

School teacher arrested for obstructing an officer in the course of his duty . . . it wouldn't look good in the papers, would it?'

'What do you want?' Edith said.

'Just to ask a few questions. It seemed a convenient time to find out more about the people Henry knew, while all were gathered here.'

'Wait!' Charles's mouth had fallen open as the officer's words sank in. He was aware that the room had fallen silent. 'What are you saying? That you think Henry could have been murdered? That it wasn't suicide?'

'That's an interesting idea, sir. What brought that to your mind?'

'I do not wish to discuss this here,' Edith said somewhat distantly. She shivered, and looked away. It was bad enough that Henry had behaved as he did, without the police raking over her shame and embarrassment.

'That's fine, Mrs Bremen. We can do it later. At the station, perhaps,' Pauley said.

Charles felt he should take control of this discussion to protect Edith. 'What do you want to know? I'm sure there is no need to have Edith go to the police station.'

'No, I'm sure you're right, sir. Mrs Bremen, how much were you involved in your husband's business affairs?'

'Not terribly. He was the financial adviser, and I worked at the shop.'

'Which would that be?'

'Cotton's. The dress shop in Market Street.'

'And where were you on the day that Mr Bremen took his life?'

'At work.'

'Did he give you any reason to suspect he might end his life?'

'Of course not! I would have tried to persuade him not to be so . . .'

'Yes?'

'So bloody selfish!' she finished defiantly. 'He should have thought about me and how it would affect me. His death was a horrible shock, but worse is the fact that he never told me, he didn't *trust* me! I know nothing about his business, about our investments or pensions. I still have to go through the papers with Arthur.'

'Ah, yes. Arthur. That would be Mr Ransome, would it?'

'Yes. Arthur and Henry often collaborated. They weren't exactly partners, but Henry would help him with placing deals for his clients.'

'And he is here?'

'I'll take you to him,' Charles said. He removed his arm from Edith and led the way to Arthur, who stood looking wary and fretful.

'Mr Ransome,' Pauley said after introducing himself. 'Did you have any reason to suspect that Mr Bremen might end his life?'

'Good God, no.'

'But you were working with him professionally?'

'We sometimes collaborated, I suppose.'

'He would find financial institutions and invest your clients' money?'

'Occasionally, yes. Not terribly often.'

'But it's fair to say that for your larger clients, those with the most money, Mr Bremen had better contacts in banking and finance? He was better able to find investments for them?'

'Well . . .' Arthur glanced about him, aware that the rest of the dramatic group was hanging on every word for later repetition. 'Well, yes, but—'

'Would you say Mr Bremen was entirely trustworthy?'

'I would hardly have invested so much through him if I didn't!'

'So, if you don't mind, why have you recently stopped placing money through him? And, for example, telling some of your clients to pull your money out from him and reinvest elsewhere?'

'That was . . . look, is this really necessary?'

'When a man has been murdered, it's a good idea to find out what happened – and why.'

'That's the second time you've suggested murder. Why?' Charles demanded.

'Ah, well, suicide is self-murder, isn't it? But let's call it *homicide*, if it makes you happier, sir. Even if he killed himself, the question has to be, why? And a man who was handling large sums of money, well, to a suspicious mind, that might suggest the beginnings of a motive.'

'You mean Henry was not honourable? Really, Detective!'

Charles scoffed. 'Henry was a highly respected member of the community. What, are you trying to say he was embezzling money from his clients – and from Arthur's, too?'

'Well, sir?'

Arthur looked from the policeman to Charles, then over to Edith, and back to Pauley. 'Yes,' he said in a whisper. 'I think he stole the lot.'

Charles felt his mouth fall open again. 'Are you serious?'

'I realized only the day before his . . . you know. He had been running a Ponzi scam,' Arthur said. Seeing Charles's baffled expression, he sighed and explained in patronizing tones that reminded Charles of his own when trying to explain mathematical differentiation to 5C. 'A Ponzi is a simple scheme. You sell an idea to clients, take their money, and tell them you will invest it in financial vehicles. Perhaps the stock market, perhaps unit trusts – it could be anything. Just like Bernie Madoff did in the States. Rely on greed; promise high returns. Guaranteed ten per cent, say, perhaps up to thirty per cent. And you meet those returns. You pay out extraordinary dividends, based on their investments. But the trouble is, there are none. It's all a scam.'

'What?'

'The adviser takes all the money. He uses fresh capital to pretend he's paying out interest, but in reality every new client who pays him, that money goes in paying the supposed interest payments of previous investors. It's a classic fraud. All the new investors think their money is going into stocks and shares, but it's not. It just pays the dividends to existing clients, and to fund a lavish lifestyle for the adviser. That's what Henry was doing.'

Charles looked at Pauley. 'And you think it got too much for him?'

'Or someone whom he had defrauded, yes. It's a possibility, don't you think? For example, sir, where did you buy your pension? I assume you have one?'

'Me?' Charles gulped. 'The school has a defined—'

'But I believe you bought out of it and reinvested through a financial adviser. Who was that?'

'Henry.'

'I see.'

Charles could feel the stares of all the others focused on him.

'Wait a minute! I wasn't anywhere near the beach on the day he died! I can prove it! I was at school with—'

'Whereas you, Mr Ransome, were out,' the detective said mildly.

'I was with clients.'

'Who were where?'

'Well, close to where Henry died, I suppose.'

'And where would that be, do you suppose?'

'At the beach, of course. Or, in the sea near it.'

'You think so?'

'That's where his clothes were!'

'Yes. With no note and no body. It makes an interesting story, doesn't it? A man disappears, leaves a selection of clothing, all just at the time that he has been rumbled as a fraudster. But that begs the question of where the embezzled money all went, of course.'

'You think I stole it?' Edith said. She had joined them while Pauley was speaking, and on hearing his words her heart began fluttering. She felt light-headed, dizzy.

'No, Mrs Bremen. I'm sure your husband did, but I don't think you had any part in it. However, another man who was not his actual business partner, now *he* could have had an interest in the money.'

Arthur had been taking a restorative glug of Prosecco, but on hearing the policeman's words, he almost choked on it. '*What*?'

'You did say that you were not far from where Mr Bremen died during that day. Almost as though you knew where he was. If you had a falling out with him, of course, you might know where he had died.'

'You can't be serious! You suggest I had something to do with his death?'

'If you knew of his embezzling your clients' funds, it would suggest a strong motive, wouldn't it? Or perhaps you were aware, and just discovered that he had taken the lion's share and not divided it up equitably. That too might give cause for your desire to punish him – even kill him.'

Charles decided enough was enough. 'Detective Inspector, I really think you should leave now. You are distressing poor Edith here, and to be honest, I think your insinuations are out of order. I think you should go.'

'Ah, yes. The schoolmaster. I wonder, could you have had a motive to kill him?'

'What are you suggesting?' Charles said, but he could feel his stomach lurch as though to break from its moorings.

'Only that, if you had learned that your pension and all the extra funding, your life savings, which you had entrusted to Mr Bremen, had also disappeared, you may yourself have added incentive to exact revenge.'

'Oh, *really*!'

'And of course there is always the other possible motive,' Pauley continued, glancing at Edith pensively. 'Adultery is an unpleasant word.'

Charles felt his face flame with embarrassment. 'You . . . You say that I . . . I would never have—'

'No, sir. But we hear that Mr Bremen was quite noticeably affectionate with certain other people,' Pauley said, and suddenly turned to stare at Claire.

She said nothing for a moment. Then her chin tilted upwards in a defiant gesture, although she avoided meeting Edith's eyes. 'Well? I wasn't the first, and I don't expect I would have been the last, if he hadn't died.'

'Had your relationship ended?'

'Oh, I expect so. It was only a bit of fun,' Claire said. 'But how did you find out?'

Pauley grimaced. 'You went with him to local pubs and restaurants, he took you to the theatre, and you didn't think anyone would notice? Half the town knew, and from all I know of amateur dramatics, I would guess that almost everyone in this group would also have known.'

Charles tried to interrupt, but before he could, Edith spoke quietly. 'Well, then, Inspector. Since you clearly have some view as to who was responsible for my husband's death, perhaps it is time you told us whom you suspect, and put us all out of our misery.'

'Oh, I don't think so. I was really just satisfying myself about some aspects of his character,' Pauley said. He cast an eye around the group. 'You see, to my mind it all came down to the money and where that has gone. Was there a motive there for him to disappear? And I was left wondering about that, what could have led to the murderer having suddenly struck just now.'

He broke off and walked to the bar, pouring himself a large glass of sparkling water before continuing:

'I mean, was it the sudden realization of Mr Ransome that his business associate had walked away with his clients' money, or the fact that their partnership was based on a Ponzi scheme and Mr Bremen had taken too much; was it a client, such as a schoolmaster, a powerful sportsman, strong and capable, who took revenge for the theft of his life savings; was it the jilted lover, who was discarded like a used condom; or was it in fact the jealous wife, who resented being the home-maker while her husband was off playing the field with any available woman?'

He emptied the glass in one long, pensive draught.

'Well?' Edith demanded. Her light-headedness had faded and was replaced with simple anger. How dare this man come to Henry's wake and expose all this? Yes, she resented Henry. Who wouldn't? Charles put a hand on her shoulder, and she shook it away. No doubt Charles would have a claim on her, if Henry had embezzled his money – and what of the other clients? Would they *all* be able to sue her? Take her house? It wasn't *her* fault if he robbed them! Arthur, she saw, looked almost green, he was so pale. Could he have killed Henry, then? That little bitch, Claire, was surely too pathetic to do something like that. Irene? No, she would have killed Claire, not Henry. Besides, Henry was a big man, heavy and ungainly. As a corpse he would be an immense weight. It was surely more likely a man . . . and then her eyes went to Stephan, the heavily-built Pole, who looked as if he had spent much of his life as a labourer. He could have picked up Henry without trouble . . .

She returned her gaze to Pauley. 'So?'

'It was an interesting experiment. And I soon came to realize that there was one man, really, who had the best motivation to kill Henry.'

'Who?'

'Henry himself.'

Charles gasped in disgust. 'You mean to say you've gone through all this charade just to tell us that Henry did, in fact, kill himself? What the hell sort of nonsense is this? You come here, scraping up all the worst rumours you can, and—'

'I'm sorry, sir. You misunderstand me. What I mean is, Henry did kill himself – but then he reincarnated. I mentioned the money. It all went to a certain John Coventry. The proceeds of the frauds were all given to Coventry, as far as we can tell. The accountants will need more time to conduct a full audit, and no doubt some of the funds will have disappeared, but we have traced, as far as we can tell, the majority of it.'

Arthur drew a deep breath of relief.

'Yes, sir, our suspicions were unfounded. Bremen took the lot. So why give it all to Coventry? This fellow was listed as the client of a bank in Chichester, and tried to make a large withdrawal. The bank manager was suspicious and reported the transaction to us. As a result, Coventry was arrested by a policeman who recognized his face from the posters after Henry Bremen's disappearance. Coventry is Bremen. He is currently being held in Portsmouth, charged with a number of offences,' Pauley said. 'And, I confess, I felt sure you would all like to know what sort of a man he truly was. You all knew one or two aspects of his makeup. Now you all know rather more.'

Charles helped Edith out to her car. 'What now?'

'I don't know,' she said. 'I am still in shock, I think. Bloody Henry! He's still alive! He was going to saddle me with the debts, and reputation of being a criminal or a moron, while he went swanning off to the Bahamas or somewhere.'

'If I can help . . . you know I'll always be your friend, and . . .'

'Just now, the last thing I need is any form of commitment, Charles. Not now. Not after Henry.' She glanced back at the theatre, quiet now, and with the light off. 'Not now. Perhaps never.'

# LIZA CODY – CHARACTER ASSASSINATION

With jungle red nails
she lurks behind the stage door
checking her weapons.

She's invisible –
too old to be young enough?
She blames the writer.

Does she smile sweetly
or is she showing her teeth?
Will we ever know?

# FRANCES BRODY – BLOOD ON ICE

Not long after Winston Churchill died in 1965, Frank Nicholson married Sarah Williams. They had been courting for a year. Each had a savings bank book. Sarah held Premium Bonds and had a few streaks of luck in the monthly draws. They mustered a deposit on a redbrick terrace house with two bedrooms, an attic and a cellar.

Frank kept to himself that he had made a sensible decision – a forward-looking investment. He bought one hundred and twenty commemorative coins, Churchill Crowns, bound to increase in value. One side bore the Queen's head, the other side bore the head of Winston Churchill.

Frank kept his precious cupronickel Churchill Crowns in a postman's red bag, left behind in the cellar by a previous occupant.

Sarah and Frank first met on a bitingly cold January day, when she was on her way to a revivalist meeting and he to ice skate on the pond in Lansfield Park. They struck up a conversation. He lied and said, wasn't it a coincidence. He too was on his way to the revivalist meeting.

She said, 'You look as if you're going ice skating.'

'Oh, I am. On the way back.'

At the revivalist meeting, they listened to talk of fire, brimstone and salvation.

The next day, the ice melted. It was a year before the pond froze again. By then, Frank and Sarah were married.

Frank and Sarah were a happy couple. They had opinions on certain matters, and just one running disagreement. The matter was this: *Will ice or fire end the world?* Sarah said fire. Most certainly, fire.

Frank said ice.

All went well in the respectable redbrick house with two

bedrooms, an attic, a cellar and then two children, Elaine and Kathleen.

What started as a ripple became the storm of Frank's Big Mistake, his fall from grace, the shame of having his name in the evening paper, to be seen by all and sundry.

This is how it began.

One morning, Frank arrived early for work at the engineering and foundry works where he had served his apprenticeship. He spotted Carl the labourer stuffing scrap metal into a sack, and then hiding it in a corner behind a couple of crates.

Carl bit his lip as he looked at Frank, who was looking at him. 'Don't tell the gaffer on me, Frank. You're a family man. You know what it's like to make ends meet.'

True. But Carl had no ties. Frank pointed this out to him. Carl's children were grown up and gone. His wife had run off with the insurance man on the day her policy with benefits fell due.

Frank and Carl stood face to face. The outside door opened and shut. There was the ding of a clocking-in card being inserted in the slot. Frank heard himself saying, 'Just stop it off Carl. I'll say nowt this time.'

Frank did not tell the gaffer, or anyone. That night, he lay awake and thought of all the possibilities there were in the engineering shop and in the foundry. Men were left to their own devices in the old building where through gaps in groaning floorboards you could see down to the flames of the furnace blazing below.

Later, Frank asked Carl what the money from the scrap metal was for. It turned out that Carl had a dream.

Dreams can be catching. People don't tell you that, but it's true.

Carl told Frank that every year thousands of people disappear without trace. He wanted to bump into one of them, to find out how they did it. He had the notion that most of them were in South America, or on what must be a big island in the Pacific. The women there were beautiful and would be happy to marry an Englishman. Carl went to the library, read travel books, and consulted maps. He decided on Buenos Aires. He planned his route, which was to be a roundabout one so that he could thoroughly disappear. He would take the ferry to Calais, a steamer to India, a second steamer to Santiago, then to Argentina. He would buy a return ticket. In Santiago, he would cash in that return ticket. This would give him enough to live on.

Carl had already saved enough to give him the confidence to apply for a passport.

Two weeks later, Carl was gone, without revealing more details of his plans.

Frank pondered. He had started work at fifteen. He had the noose of a mortgage. He and Sarah and their daughters spent their annual family holiday in a big tent, belonging to Frank's cousin, pitched – with difficulty – near the river at Castle Howard, close to banks of nettles. Forming the spokes of a wheel, twelve or so adults and children placed their sleeping bags around the main tent pole.

Frank did not like sleeping round the tent pole. Sarah did not mind. She preferred this to holiday camps and boarding houses which struck her as vulgar. Also, you would not know who had slept in the beds before you. Frank pondered on privately owned caravans, owning a car, and not counting pennies. He would not contemplate 'Abroad'.

He pondered all the way to the conclusion that there was not much profit in carrying off scraps of metal in a bag. He could hardly risk returning after hours with wheelbarrow and sack. The obvious answer presented itself. A car. He could use the side entrance to the foundry, load up his boot and drive to a scrap merchant. He had a driving licence but was not sure how to approach Sarah about getting a car. Speculate to accumulate, that was how people prospered. The Churchill Crowns were off limits. Those coins were his long-term investment.

The following week, a solution presented itself. There was an influx of work. Frank and the bench moulder were asked to put in four nights' overtime a week for six months. With barely concealed excitement, he went home and told Sarah.

'We could do with the extra money, love, but don't let them work you to the bone,' said she.

Frank chose his moment the following night, while pound signs still flickered behind his and Sarah's eyeballs. He said, 'Jack Perkins will be making a downpayment on a car with his overtime money.'

'Oh aye,' said Sarah, as she went on reading the evening paper. 'That's his plan, is it?'

'It's his missus's idea. She fancies outings to the seaside and the country. Might be all right for them but what's wrong with a coach trip?'

His comment hit the mark. He could see that Sarah was thinking about it. She was a great one for thinking, working out the odds. It would take her a couple of days to consider and comment on something so momentous as car ownership.

For now, she ignored the topic. She changed the subject by reading certain items to him from the evening paper.

Although Sarah no longer attended revivalist meetings, she sent the children to Sunday school. 'Listen at this,' said she. 'Two youths bound over for stealing lead from a church roof. Bound over! Ought to be jailed. Common thieves, that's what they are, a menace to society.'

Under her glare, Frank shuddered. Sarah liked to pass her own sentences on wrongdoers, featuring life imprisonment, hard labour and stringing up by the thumbs. 'You work hard, I work hard. We don't clamber on to church roofs.'

'True,' said Frank. Sarah now worked in a haberdashery shop where, as far as Frank could make out, she cut satin ribbons to the required length and put hooks and eyes on display in order of size.

But here was the interesting thing. Mrs Clark, the shop owner, was changing her car and would give Sarah and Frank first refusal.

Six weeks later, Frank drove to work in a VW Golf. He parked in the alley by the side door.

Friday was pay day. As usual, Jack Perkins and Bob would go to Mary's Café for the set dinner.

Frank waited until they had gone through the core shop. He then opened the door on to the deserted alley. A batch of ingots had been delivered that morning, but Frank already had a bootful of scrap.

Pulling out of the alley, he almost collided with a lorry. His stomach churned as he thought what he would say if the dealer asked questions. The dealer did not ask. He weighed the metal and counted out the money.

In a daze for the rest of the afternoon, it was half past four when Frank realized that he had not touched his sandwiches.

After that first venture, he spaced out his trips, sometimes with scrap, sometimes lead, or copper, an ingot or two. He avoided aluminium, which weighed light.

Frank opened a new bank account and kept the passbook on top of the cistern. He found himself whistling 'South of the Border' as he wondered about his old workmate. Was Carl now on a steamer, or basking under a tropical sun with a cigar, a cool drink and a bathing beauty beside him?

Weeks passed. It was Friday again. Jack Perkins and Bob were on their way to Mary's Café. Frank picked up his small haul, went out and opened the boot.

Suddenly, Bob appeared round the corner. 'Frank! Gaffer's seen you from upstairs. I reckon he's on his way down.'

Frank's first thought was to get in the car and drive off, but he wasn't quick enough. His employer was at the side door. He seemed more upset and embarrassed than angry.

'Frank, I've called the police. Had to do it. If one feller gets away with it, they'll all be on the grab. I've been watching you, so don't deny it.'

At the police station, Frank sat in a cell. There had been no point in kidding them. He thought about keeping his mouth shut but somehow, it all came out. He signed a statement. They searched the house. Found the bank book on top of the lavatory cistern. He wondered if they found his Churchill Crowns in the cellar. If so, they said nothing. His receipt for the coins was still in the bag.

Sarah would shut the door on him. Divorce him. String him up by the thumbs. Seek custody of his girls.

A constable with nicotine stains all the way up two fingers came to the cell. He brought Frank a cup of tea and bread and cheese.

'What sort of sentence will I get?'

'Not up to me, is it?'

'Where will I be sent?'

'You're going nowhere yet. Your wife's here. She's standing bail, but don't expect to be out tonight.'

Sarah had been crying. They had five minutes, with a young WPC standing by. 'Why?' Sarah asked. 'We were doing all right.'

'I know.'

Then she surprised him. 'Will they take the car off us?'

'I expect so.' She had learned to drive and passed her test first time.

He didn't know what to say, and so he said, 'How do you think the world will end?'

'In tears, except that you've turned my heart to ice.'

The WPC tried not to look suspicious. Was this some sort of code?

'I blame myself,' said Sarah. 'I should have said no to a car. I shouldn't have wanted a caravan.'

'It's me,' said Frank. 'I'm the culprit.'

And while he was frozen with guilt, Sarah brought out the papers from the solicitor.

Frank stared. 'You're divorcing me.'

'No! The solicitor wants this form signing and witnessing. It gives me the car. I want to take the girls away until everything calms down.'

Sarah never missed a prison visiting day, even during the long summer holidays when she took Kathleen and Elaine to stay with Auntie Maura in Whitley Bay. Kathleen, the eldest, cried for her dad. Elaine wasn't fussed. An earwigger, she was excited to hear that another baby was on the way. But why did mum cry, worry about it and sit up late talking to Auntie Maura?

When Frank came out of prison, his probation officer helped him find work. He couldn't help with the other business. That was between man and wife.

All that was years ago. Sarah died. A tragic accident. When Frank came home from the hospital on the day his wife was pronounced dead, sparks lit the sky. Bonfire Night. Rockets exploded. Catherine Wheels spun.

For weeks, kids had stood in strategic positions with their Guy Fawkes. 'Penny for the guy, mister!'

Now Guy was wheeled off, to be consumed by flames. Frank had grown up thinking that this celebration was because Guy Fawkes had been brave to try blowing up the Houses of Parliament. Later, he discovered that the burning of Guy became compulsory by law, as a warning never to try again.

Every sound rattled his nerves. Sarah was right. Fire, not ice, would end the world. He went inside and shut the door, blaming himself for Sarah's death before her time.

Frank retired. It was difficult to go about the day-to-day business of living. He bought baked beans. He stacked the tins in a pyramid. When Kathleen came on her weekly visit, she tutted and fussed at her dad. Frank did beans on toast. Kathleen left him with slices of ham shank, a loaf and two tins of lentil soup. She told him to stop keeping stuff in the cellar and that he ought to have a lodger.

He never heard from his youngest daughter, Elaine. He wrote to her, but she did not reply.

Frank walked a lot. He was fit, for his age. He bought a new mop, intending to give the place a good clean.

The thought of getting stuck in cheered him, but by the time he brought cleaning stuff from the cellar, he had lost the will. He would get stuck in tomorrow.

A walk around the town centre could be draining. His town, *their* town, was largely gone. No milk bar. No Woolworths. So much pulled down and rebuilt. He would never be used to it.

The seasons, too, were more reliable then. It seemed, looking back, as if he had always been able to skate in Lansfield Park in winter. Now, the pond hardly ever froze. The park seemed a more meagre place altogether. He thought one tree may be dead, but still standing.

When bushes were cobwebbed with dew and grass white with frost, he sat on a bench remembering the pond as it had been in that long-ago winter, before everything went wrong. Sarah watching him, laughing, saying he made a spectacle of himself among the youngsters. He laughed too, for the joy of it.

On the way home, they had the old argument. *Will ice or fire end the world?* He said another ice age would come. Gradually the world would become colder. No one would notice at first. Winter would start a little sooner, end a little later. Odd cold days would increase in number and the temperature would fall. In tropical lands, changes would take place slowly. The sun would lose interest in warming the earth. Snow would fall, day after day. Gently. Ponds, rivers, oceans would ice over. People would huddle together to watch the snow and be lulled by it, enchanted by it, would die, and be covered over. Ice mountains would tower – lofty, magnificent. Sarah, angry at his predictions, quoted the

Bible. When they got home, she took out her Bible and pointed to a passage, reading,

'When the seventh seal was opened . . . the angel took the censer and filled it with fire from the altar and threw it on the earth; and there were peals of thunder, loud noises, flashes of lightning and an earthquake.'

Frank said, 'Ice.'

'Ice my foot!'

Now, Frank, an old man, well wrapped, sat on his newspaper on the park bench. A dog walker nodded and said good morning.

Frank was preoccupied. He was thinking that when he and Sarah had their arguments about ice and fire, they were not talking about the end of the world at all, but about a respite from the world as they knew it, about a great change that would come. He could imagine ice or fire, but not the end of the world.

Kathleen found out about her dad's long walks in the town, his meanderings in the parks and woods. She said, 'What if you fall?'

'I'll get up.'

'What if you can't?'

'Someone will help me up.'

'What if you break a bone? And don't say it'll mend because not at your age it won't. You should be careful.'

Frank knew that more 'What ifs' might follow. There were more 'What ifs' than bones in his body, trees in the wood or clouds in the sky. 'I'm very careful,' said he.

'We must find you a lodger. It'll be income. It'll be company. It'll be back-up for when we go on holiday, or what if we move and you don't come with us? What if there's no one here to pick you up? All the old neighbours have gone. Who would you turn to if I wasn't in reach?'

'But you are.'

Alert to Kathleen's ways, Frank knew that something was afoot. He did not know what. Kathleen put his stubbornness in the same bracket as having nineteen tins of beans in the cupboard.

'Get a dog,' she said, 'if you must go walking.'

He shook his head. 'No.'

'Go to the dogs' home. You're bound to be taken by one.'

'Don't want to be taken by a dog.' He was surprised at his

vehemence. He would have loved a dog, but it would likely outlive him. Kathleen. She wouldn't want it.

One day, Frank walked a little west of the town centre. He saw something he had not seen before. A building which had been a dance hall bore the sign,

ICE SKATING RINK

Frank stood quite still. He felt a kind of chill inside him. His body tensed. After a still moment, a flow of relief came as he relaxed again. He had heard of ice-skating rinks but never knew that there was one right here, in his own town. The very words had an odd effect on him. Ice Skating Rink. He stared at the bricks and mortar of the building, not able to bring himself to step inside. And then he went home.

That night, he did some gentle exercises.

The next morning, he went back and checked on the hours of opening. Weekdays, the rink was open from noon to nine in the evening. When Kathleen came on her weekly visit, he was too preoccupied to take much notice of her.

She said, 'Dad if you must buy beans, choose a large tin. Keep half in a dish. Small tins are uneconomical.'

Frank hoped that the ice rink would not be too dear. He did his exercises. He took out his skating boots and spent a long time cleaning them and polishing the blades.

He went to the rink the next day, as an observer. The ice was smoothly inviting. A woman and her child were teaching themselves to skate, clinging to the rail. Music played, lively and lilting.

On the way out, Frank said to the attendant, 'I skate but it's a good while since I was on the ice.'

He was afraid of being excluded. Afraid someone would say that he was too old, might fall, and they could not take the responsibility.

'My grandad skated until he was eighty,' said the attendant. Frank felt a great rush of affection for the attendant. It was like that moment at school, when you knew by instinct who would be your friend.

Frank stepped on to the ice, gingerly at first, holding on to the rail. After that, he skated a quarter of the way around the rink without so much as touching the rail. He was glad of the rest when he paused, held on to the rail, and gave hints to the mother and child.

He ached the next day.

The following week, he improved on his own record. He skated halfway round the rink, keeping close to the edge. The third week, he skated all the way across the rink to the tune of 'Sailing'. This was a moment he would never forget.

As he was leaving the rink, Frank felt a tap on his shoulder. Someone breathed in his ear and said, 'Hey-up, Frank. Father Christmas bring you a pair of ice skates, did he?'

Frank turned. He saw someone familiar, and looked the man in the eyes, noticed the grin. The name came to him. 'Tommy McDonald?'

Tommy grinned again. 'And I still don't know the answers. I know less now than I did then.'

Tommy had sat behind Frank at school, whispering, 'What's the answer?'

He once more repeated that question. They both laughed.

'I didn't have you down as a skater,' said Frank. 'What you doing here?'

'Been watching the grandchild fall down, pick herself up and start all over again. I pointed you out to her. I said you might give her a few tips.'

'Kids don't want to learn from an old geezer. She'll find her feet, find her style.' Frank didn't say that this would likely be his last visit to the rink. There came a time when you had to listen to your knees, and his knees were yattering.

'Anita's gone off with her pals,' said Tommy. 'Come for a swift one?'

'Go on then.'

Over a pint, two pints, Frank heard how Tommy and his family were getting on. His son Gary worked in the accounts department of a motor firm for Vauxhall cars and Bedford vans. He also heard the story of a young man called Daniel who was working temporary in the parts department. Daniel had been caught by the caretaker sleeping overnight in one of the vans. The caretaker did not report him but said he had better stop it off quick.

Frank knew it was easy for a person to find himself in the wrong. He thought of Kathleen going on about a lodger.

'Tell the lad he can stop with me, until he finds his feet.'

Daniel turned up. He's been in the forces, Frank told himself, going by the short back and sides, clean shave, polished boots and haversack. For someone sleeping in the back of a van, Daniel had made a good fist of keeping up appearances. He wore jeans and a donkey jacket. He was young. But these days, everyone looked young to Frank.

Frank knew what Kathleen would say. She would say, 'Well who is he? What do you know about him? Where does he work? Will he pay a month in advance?'

'Beans and a couple of eggs on toast?' Frank asked.

'Thank you,' said Daniel. 'I won't say no.'

Frank waited until Daniel had finished eating. 'How long will you need lodgings?' asked he, feeling inhospitable when the words came out. It was a Kathleen question.

'I'll only leave if I'm let go at work, or if you give me notice.'

As Daniel looked round, Frank saw the room in a fresh light. Kathleen was right. The sofa was shabby, the curtains out of date.

Frank heard noises. It was 5 a.m. He lay there listening, trying to identify the sounds. The cellar door. Footsteps on stone. He's looking to see what's worth grabbing, Frank said to himself. He won't find the Churchill Crowns. If I'm murdered in my bed, that would give Kathleen something to crow about. He could hear her. 'Dad! Do nothing unless you talk to me first.'

Frank made breakfast. His mind was never still these days. Often it was that question, 'How will the world end?'

Now he had said it. Aloud. Going gaga. The young lodger would turn tail sooner than he could open the door.

But Daniel repeated the question. 'How will the world end? That's a good one, and I can answer that. Not with a bang but with a whimper.'

'Ice or fire?' queried Frank.

'Why not both?'

That was obvious to Frank. 'Because the ice would put out the fire.'

'Not if the arrival of ice and fire are spaced across a millennium,' said Daniel.

He's an oddball, thought Frank. Sarah would have liked him. But he tried not to think of Sarah, and the day she came back.

When he woke again, Frank went on to the landing and listened. He thought the sounds came from the cellar. Had Daniel found the coins? Well, let him. Let him take them and skedaddle. Not worth risking your head battered in. Frank could not get back to sleep. He got up, dressed, and went downstairs.

Daniel had the mop and bucket. He was squeezing out the mop. 'Looks as if you could do with a hand.' Frank had forgotten how easy it could be to keep a place ship-shape.

Kathleen came when Daniel was at work. Frank told her about the lodger. She said, 'Well I'm glad you've finally listened to me. Is he clean?'

'Very clean. Look round for yourself.'

Kathleen undertook an inspection, starting in the attic. She didn't like going into the cellar but braced herself and was soon back.

'The Churchill Crowns are still there. A cellar's no place for Mum's engagement and wedding ring. I'm taking them. Your lodger will know a diamond when he sees one.'

'Judge not, less you be judged,' said Frank.

'Oh, give over. Next, you'll be telling me he knows how the world will end.'

'He does.'

She frowned. 'This Mr Magic Mop, is he in work?'

'Yes, he's in work. Wait and meet him. He'll be here a little after six.'

Kathleen wouldn't wait. She paused at the door. 'You should have let me give him the once over. Find out where he's from.'

Frank already had an inkling where Daniel was from. The North-East by his accent. Frank knew from the look in Daniel's eyes that he'd been in trouble. Perhaps he was on the run. Frank poured himself a cup of strong tea. He lit a cigarette. He remembered his own sick to the guts feeling, that fear. Knowing you've been found out. No one will look at you in the same way again.

That evening, Frank went down to the cellar. He called up the steps to Daniel.

Daniel came down. 'What's up?'

Frank had forgotten how fast someone could go up and down stairs 'Nowt's up.' Frank lifted a handful of coins. 'These are Churchill Crowns.'

'I saw them.'

'I thought you might have. The longer I keep them, the more value they have.'

'For your children, grandchildren.'

'For a rainy day.'

Frank felt better for telling about the coins. He trusted Daniel.

Daniel was sociable, went with Frank to the rink, hired skates himself, saved Frank when he was almost knocked over by a group of youngsters acting the fool.

It seemed a miracle to Frank that in the depths of the cold winter, Lansfield Park pond froze. He heard about it on the local radio news and felt a rising excitement.

Daniel was reluctant, but Frank insisted. He was well wrapped up. It was early. He may have the pond to himself.

There were a few hardy souls in the park. A dad and his kids were making a snowman. A couple of teenagers tested the ice.

The booth where a person could hire skates was closed, so Daniel could not skate. Frank needed no assistance. He placed his newspaper on a bench, sat down and put on his skates. He would do better on ice than on land. He was glad when the shivering youngsters left the pond.

Frank called to Daniel. 'Whistle "I Am Sailing"!'

Daniel whistled. As he stood and whistled, he watched Frank. As he was watching Frank, Daniel saw the first crack in the ice.

Frank did not notice the first crack. He did not notice the second crack. 'Keep whistling,' he called. 'You don't know what you're missing!'

When Frank stumbled, Daniel held out an oar, picked up from the moored boat. There was a rough edge to the oar that drew blood when Frank grasped it.

Frank struggled to keep his balance. Daniel stabbed at Frank with the oar.

Frank let out a cry. 'Watch it! What you doing?'

Daniel stopped whistling. 'Ending your life. The world ends with ice, doesn't it? That's what you told my mother.'

To anyone watching from a distance, it would look as if the oar was offered as a lifeline.

'My mother's world ended on your cellar steps on the day she came back to plead with you again. I've missed her every day of my life.'

'Who are you?' Frank neared the edge of the pond as Daniel held out his hand.

'I'm your wife's son.' Daniel grabbed Frank's arm. 'Tut, tut, Frank, you're too slippery. I can't do it. Perhaps because you murdered my mother.'

'I didn't kill her! That was lies. She fell down the cellar steps.'

'You convinced the police and the coroner but not Auntie Maura. Not Elaine. They knew. They weren't believed.'

Daniel moved the oar. The crack in the ice grew.

People had noticed the commotion. Someone shouted, 'Grab the lifebuoy!'

That was when Daniel slid into the icy water, making what appeared to be a brave, last-ditch attempt to save his wet and shivering landlord. He grabbed Frank by the shoulders, and then put his arms around him and his mouth to Frank's ear. 'Mum had come to ask you just once more for us all to be together.'

Frank had cut his hand. He grasped a shard of ice. 'Save me!'

Slowly, Daniel brought Frank to the edge of the pond, knowing the deed was done.

They each had a place in the ambulance. Attention was on trying to revive the older man, a vain attempt.

Daniel turned down the medal for bravery.

He turned down Kathleen's offer of a bag of commemorative Churchill Crowns, taking just one, as a keepsake, to place by his mother's headstone. He would miss his mother every day of his life. He could still see Sarah so clearly, remember her smile, her touch, and her kiss on his forehead on his first day at school.

## ABIR MUKHERJEE – FULL CIRCLE

I've told her about the floors. Told her at least twice, but does she care? Does she listen? No, just nods and says 'yes Mrs, yes Mrs,' and then just goes on as before, leaves them all wet until there's an accident. Until I break my neck, and then what? Then what'll happen? Oh, she'll be fine, of course. I'll be in the hospital and she'll have another job by tea-time.

It'd be all right if it was just the floors, but it's not, is it? It's the beds too, and the sills and the kitchen counters. I swear she doesn't wipe them down at all. I should get George to move one of those cameras he's fitted into the kitchen next time he's over. Get him to keep an eye on her cleaning. It's not as if the one he put in the lounge does much. Just sits there spying on me as I watch the TV. Ideally he'd move the one in the bedroom too, but he won't agree to that, *just in case something happens*. Destroying my privacy. Probably thinks he's showing me what a good son he is. But I shall insist on him moving the one in the lounge. Get some value out of the thing at least. Spy on Maria and her cleaning instead of on me. Not that it matters. It's all rather pointless now.

Oh Andrew, how I wish you were still here.

I suppose I shouldn't be too harsh. She's lost her husband too, and she's already late for her next house. Already out the front door with her coat half off. And she probably wouldn't even understand. Her English is still terrible. It's been over a year now and she still just gibbers Ukrainian into that phone of hers and then points it at you with a look of expectation. And how anyone is supposed to read the translation given the screen is cracked nine ways till Sunday is beyond me.

To be fair, I did tell her. I did say, 'How do you expect me to read that?' And what did she say? 'Sorry Mrs Screen broken coming from Ukraine.'

I see she didn't eat the sandwiches I made her.

'Too much hurry, Mrs.'

*Too much hurry.*

There she goes, on her bike. 'Three more house today, Mrs.'

And you have to respect what she's been through, fleeing the bombs and leaving her family. Her son in the army. Same age as George. Still she should put her coat on properly. She'll catch her death.

I should eat the sandwiches. Waste not, want not. Take them out into the garden, have them under the awning with a cup of tea. It's brightening up outside. Be a shame to waste the sunshine . . . and the sandwiches.

Why is it so hot? October next week and still it's in the high twenties. That old garden thermometer of yours reads twenty-two, but then you bought it in Morocco so can it really be trusted? Hard to believe it's autumn. Muggy like July. Good job George isn't here. Him and his lectures on sun cream and skin cancer. *'Can't be too careful at your age, Mum.'* It's all Celia's doing. The woman won't leave the house without slapping on the factor 50. Even at night. And now she's got George and the kids doing it too.

The sandwiches are dry. Maria's fault. She should've eaten them when I'd made them. She didn't and now I'm the one forced to eat dry sandwiches. I should complain to Mrs Whatshername, the other Ukrainian woman, the one who's been here twenty years and runs the show. Next time she turns up in that silver Mercedes and smelling of Chanel, I'll do just that.

Except I won't, will I?

That reminds me. I should've given that money to Maria. Blast it. She left in such a hurry that I plain forgot. Well it's too late to worry. No point in crying over spilt milk . . . especially if Maria's cleaning. I'll just post it to her, care of Mrs Whatshername. Just put it in an envelope and post it along with all the other letters: to the bank; the electricity company; to Reverend Pleasance; and to Mr Grey at Sydenham & Marsh.

Everything in order. That's the way.

Everything in order.

Except for the garage.

Should have had it cleared out. Should have paid Salim a little extra to do it. Half a day's work at most. But your boxes are still in there, Andrew. Your files and letters and suits. Doesn't matter what George says (or rather Celia, for no doubt 'tis her idea), I won't just throw it all out.

Where is Salim, anyway? He was here earlier, raking the leaves. In the potting shed, probably. Goodness knows what he does in there.

'Salim!'

'Salim!'

*Yes, there he is.*

'No, nothing urgent! I was just wondering if you wanted a cup of tea?'

*Shame.*

It pains me to think what he's been through. I should've offered him the sandwiches. He could have had them with the tea.

Nice to hear the kettle singing on the range. If George had his way, it'd never sing again. If George had his way I'd be using the electric one Celia brought round. Ugly, plastic thing. The kettle, not Celia, ha ha.

He's right though. The range costs a fortune to run these days what with Ukraine and Gaza and Covid . . . *Inefficient,* George calls it. *A relic.* If he and Celia had their way, it'd be ripped out and a modern electric oven put in. And they probably wouldn't stop there. Why not the whole kitchen? Or the whole house? Such is the way of the world.

Where's Salim's mug? Should be on the lower rung of hooks. Next to the ones reserved for the handymen. Maria's probably moved it again. I should've had words with her. Well Salim will just have to have his tea in one of the handymen's mugs.

*Shame.*

Hard to believe he's almost fifty. Hard to believe he spent almost twenty of them in prison. Reverend Pleasance says, we are all in need of forgiveness. *All of us.*

I should take Salim some biscuits too. Shortbread, from the tin. They're the expensive ones, but it doesn't matter.

'Salim! . . . Tea!'

Where is he? The shed, most likely. He's always in the shed.

'It's here, on the garden table!'

There he is.

Best leave him to it. Lots still to do today before . . . But it *is* nice out. Shame to waste it.

'Come, Salim. Come sit with me for a while.'

I shall miss the garden. The roses and the hyacinths and the purple wisteria for those few blessed weeks in May. Remember how you once said that on rare occasions, when it's in the mood, wisteria sometimes blooms twice in a season? Thirty years in the house, Andrew, thirty years of waiting for that second, bloody bloom and it's never come. Still, there was joy in the anticipation, the thought that *this* year, maybe, just maybe, it'll happen.

Oh Andrew, I do miss you, you silly old fool.

The look on Salim's face. Like he's scared of me. Like I'm some strange creature he needs to be wary of.

'Sit here. I won't bite.'

I should really have spent more time with him. I should have at least *tried* to get to know him.

'How's the tea?'

*'It is good, Mrs Worthing. Very nice.'*

There's sweat on his temples. I should have bought him a hat. Too late in the season now to get much use out of it but he could have used it next year. Maybe there's one of yours, still in the garage?

'No, no, the biscuits are for you. Try one.'

*'Thank you, Mrs Worthing.'*

Surprising how slender his fingers are. Like yours, Andrew. The fingers of a surgeon, or a cellist, or at least they should have been. Not the fingers of a convict. Not the hands of a man who's spent twenty years in prison.

He doesn't remember me.

'How are you getting along with the high hedges?'

*'Good, Mrs Worthing.'*

It's understandable. It's been almost thirty years. I didn't recognize him at first either, and he was the centre of attention. Why would he remember me? I was just a face looking at him. One of many.

'Remember to trim the tops. I want a nice even line.'

*'Yes, Mrs Worthing.'*

Shame. It was just the way of things in those days. You didn't question it.

Why is it so hot? It feels like ants crawling over my skin.

'I'm going inside, Salim. You finish up your tea. Bring the cup to the kitchen when you're done.'

Fifteen minutes.

Need to get a move on.

'Salim. I'm going out. Is that all right? Just leave everything in the garage when you're done.'

Last check. Back door locked. Windows closed. Phone. Purse. House keys. Car keys.

What am I doing? It's the bus today. The car keys need to stay in the bowl. Easier for George that way.

Fifteen minutes till the bus. Time for one last look around. I have lived my life in this house. The best part of it at least. The part that mattered. The part with you.

The bannister is loose again. It doesn't matter now.

How bare the bedroom looks without the photographs. Just grey outlines haunting the walls where they once hung. Maybe they'd have been all right, but there's no point in taking the risk. Better me boxing them up with a note for George than some removal men throwing them all in a crate, or worse, Celia throwing them in a skip.

There's Salim, in the back garden, on his ladder, tending to the wisteria. Shame it was at the back. It would have been nice to have it along the front of the house, like at The Gables across the road, but they like the light, don't they, and the houses on this side are north facing. Remember, Andrew, when Mrs Thompson passed and The Hollies came up for sale, and you said we should buy it, just for the aspect? The wisteria would shoot up there, you said. But I'd grown to love this place by then. I couldn't give up our home just for the aspect.

Look at him out there, up on the ladder. Even now it's painful to look at him. To know what I know. The best years of a man's life.

The curtains. Closed or left open? Closed. Definitely closed.

Back down the stairs, one last time, holding on to the wobbly bannister for dear life. Back through the living room. Your chair is still in pride of place, facing the TV. I couldn't bear to move it. It was as much as I could manage just to throw out your old copies of the *Radio Times*, with the ticks marked next to the programmes you wanted to watch.

The Aga is cooling. Gas turned off at the mains, just like the nice chap from the servicing company showed me. The kitchen is starting to feel cold. Like the warmth is leeching out of it. Never mind about the rest of the house. This is enough. This is where it all happened. Oh Andrew. I wish you were here.

I should switch on the light in the upstairs hallway. Who knows how long it'll be before George comes here, and we don't want burglars.

*Remember to double lock the front door!*

You never did tire of reminding me, did you, Andrew? And so it became second nature to me, even after you'd reached the stage of having to go back and check, once then twice, and then not at all. That was the hardest part. When you stopped reminding me; when you just stopped. Well it is double locked, don't you worry.

I shall miss the street. Only fifteen houses, but a real community. Or at least it used to be. It's not the same any more. Some of the younger families at the far end haven't even come round to introduce themselves, but that's the whole world these days, isn't it? Impersonal. Even the children don't play in the close any more. Too busy with their screens and their phones. Not that it's their fault. It's the parents. All of them, too scared to let their precious children out of their sight even for a minute.

The lawn at the Hawthorns needs a trim. Not like Mr Althorp to let it get untidy. I do hope he isn't poorly. And the bins are still out at Churchill Cottage. Twenty-four hours now. Not the first time, either. They really should bring them in timeously. It makes the whole street look untidy. I know they're busy, what with both of them working and looking after the twins, but they'll have Mrs Peterson and the residents' committee after them if they're not careful. I'd bring them in for them if I didn't have the bus to catch.

Mr Mondol at Avonmore is in his front garden. Lovely family. And to think of the eyebrows that were raised when they moved into the street. But that was a long time ago, and to your credit,

Andrew, you took a stand against it. *Live and let live*, you said, and you were right. Their children. So well behaved. The little one, Priya, a doctor now, and the boy, Aroon, something high flying in the city. They still come and visit me sometimes when they're home, bringing little parcels of sweets or food from their mother. You always liked her cooking, didn't you, even though it was far too spicy for me.

*'Hello, Mrs Worthing. You are looking radiant today. Off to Buckingham Palace for tea with the King?'*

That Mr Mondol. Such a joker. And that mischievous smile of his. He reminds me a little of Salim, though less burdened by the cares of the world.

'Naturally, Mr Mondol. It is Friday after all. I must be getting along now.'

No sign of the bus.

No surprise there. Everything's going to the dogs these days. A fish, they say, rots from the head, and that's what's happened to this country. Politicians, all of them, only in it for the money. At least the weather is good. Beach weather. Remember the service the council used to run for us pensioners? A pick up from the end of the street and off to the seaside for the day. Remember the time we had too much to drink at the King's Head on the seafront? It's a wonder we made it home at all. The council ended the service last year. Economic cut-backs.

Anyway, here's the bus now, wheezing up the hill.

Lots of seats. That's good. A nice quiet journey, hopefully.

The High Street isn't what it used to be. Just charity shops and empty windows now, and ones selling those electric cigarettes of course. You can't move for them. You remember the walks we used to take, Andrew? Through the town down to the beach? You'd have hated to see what's happened to the place. Remember the sweet shop? The little one on the corner run by that family who'd come over from Kent? The wife was lovely but the husband never said much. They said he'd been a miner at one of the last collieries over there. Took a truncheon to the head on the picket lines. Of course, we never believed it back then, did we? That the police would do such things. We watched the news and we saw the pictures but even then, we never believed it. We blamed the miners for everything that was done to them.

How is it possible, Andrew, to go through life being so sure of your footing, of thinking we were on the side of the angels when in reality we were nothing of the sort? The older I get, the more those certainties of our youth become uncertain. Were we wrong to trust them? The government, the police, even the Post Office. Why did we always take the word of the strong against that of the weak?

Do you remember the time Mr Mondol's boy Aroon came over to play with George? He must have been about ten at the time. A Sunday it was in July. Hot, like today. I remember taking bowls of ice cream through to them. They had that film on, the one with Michael Caine and the red coats. George cheering when a Zulu was shot, and Aroon asking him why? Why was he supporting the baddies?

*'They're not the baddies,'* George had said. *'They're us.'*

*'They're the baddies,'* Aroon had maintained.

I remember thinking how strange. I didn't understand what the boy meant at the time. I just thought the poor lad didn't quite understand, but of course, he did. It was I who didn't. I think I understand now.

Too late though. All too late.

And that, dear Andrew, is my greatest regret.

Remember the court case? Remember how excited I was, opening that letter? Jury service. What a thrill. Me, doing my bit. Something to tell the ladies at church the next Sunday. And then, on the morning of the first day, making my sandwiches and you driving me to the station. I can still remember the butterflies in my stomach walking up those steps and through the doors of the Crown court. It was positively fun, and then it all changed. I mean you don't expect it to be rape.

I remember seeing him for the first time, brought up to the dock. A brown man, head down, shuffling along. I think some of the others were ready to convict him then and there. I remember the girl, too. Poor thing. In those days they made them come to court didn't they? Nothing but a slip of a girl. Seventeen at the time. Sixteen when it happened. I remember my rage. She was so pale, so broken. Just skin and bone and lost innocence. Just a girl. How could anyone do . . . *that* . . . to her?

There's my stop. Time to get off. A press of the button, a little wave to the driver and careful on the kerb stones. That's it. Slow and steady.

She couldn't identify him. But who could blame her? All she remembered was a dark-skinned man grabbing her by the throat as she walked home from the station. The police though, they were sure. A tall, handsome chap by the name of Inspector Clarke took the stand. He said they had picked him up less than a mile away, in a state of agitation, alcohol on his breath. There was no such thing as DNA back then, but they had a confession. Freely given, they said, though he and his defence counsel refuted it. They said it had been obtained under duress, that the police had beaten him and forced him to sign it. They said he didn't drink. That the police had poured spirit on his clothes. A tissue of lies. No one believed him . . . well almost no one. There was one old gentleman on the jury who wasn't convinced. He said you couldn't trust the police, but the other men soon bullied him into submission.

I thought him a savage. A barbarous devil who had no business being in civilized society. And so we pronounced him guilty and Salim went to prison for twenty years.

The gulls are out in force today. The holidaymakers too. The coastal path is thick with them. Still, there are quiet places. There are always quiet places. It's a bit of a walk, but I have time now.

I never really thought of him again after that, nor the girl after a while. I didn't even recognize him when he came to the door as part of that rehabilitation programme. It was only later, much later, that he told me his story. About the wrongful conviction. About his sentence being quashed. About that Inspector Clarke who had, sixteen years later, gone to prison himself for fabricating evidence in a whole number of cases. Perverting the course of justice. It was only when I looked it up on the internet and saw Clarke's face that I remembered. Clarke, the handsome, mild-mannered policeman. We had all believed him. I mean, why wouldn't we? He was a police inspector, and that man in the dock was just some foreigner. We trusted the police in those days.

It's hard to believe, on a day like this, that there can be so much wrong in the world. From up here it all looks so peaceful, so idyllic, so *English.* The England we were brought up to believe in. In some ways Salim hadn't even been a real person to me then. Just an evil to be stripped from our streets and put behind bars. I admit I was glad when the judge handed down such a harsh sentence.

The truth came much later; twenty years on and over a mug of tea in the back garden. When Salim told me his side of things: of how the police had picked him up on his way home from college; of the things they had done to him; of his time in prison; of all that he had lost . . . fiancé, family, home. *Everything.*

And so here I am, Andrew. Making atonement for my sins. I've instructed Mr Grey at Sydenham & Marsh. Had a new will drawn up. Don't worry, I'm leaving George what's left in the bank. It's more than enough, not that George will see it that way. But the house, that will go to Salim. He has spent more time tending to it and the garden than anyone else in recent years, so why not?

This is the spot. There are a few souls in the distance. Not quite as secluded as I hoped, but good enough. Look at the sea down there, Andrew. Shimmering like it did that time we went to Burgh Sands.

One small step.

I do hope you understand, Andrew. It's taken me a long time to understand right and wrong. A lifetime you might say, and this feels right.

Eyes closed, I think. A last inhalation. The whole world reduced to the air in my breast.

I understand now, Andrew. I understand now.

# MICHAEL Z. LEWIN – SHOWTIME

'OK, here's the note again.' The musical director hit a key half a dozen times.

'I'm just a bit nervous,' the blonde in black said. 'But I do love to audition.'

'The note,' playing it again. 'Ready? And . . .'

'Like the beat beat beat of the tom tom,' the blonde began.

Andrew made his way to Rusty, who was sitting on an aisle in the Cambridge Arts Theatre – where all the Footlights shows of the 1960s premiered in the spring.

'What do you think?' Andrew asked.

With a wry smile, Rusty tilted his head.

'OK, not her, but we've got some pretty good people.'

'Yes,' Rusty agreed. 'But don't even ask.'

'You appear in college revues, Rusty. Even got a good personal notice in the newspaper. And as a Committee member don't you have a moral obligation to audition?'

'Moral?' Rusty said with a laugh. 'Since when did morality become a factor in this show?'

'You've made your point about all that,' Andrew said.

'And it's been ignored.' Rusty sighed. 'Maybe over here you guys just work differently from how Mammy and Pappy raised me up.'

'I don't know about that,' Andrew said, 'but I thought you Yanks made a big deal out of team loyalty. As a Committee member you *ought* to put yourself forward for the show.'

Rusty just said, 'No.'

'Is it the material? Write sketches for yourself.'

'Not the material.'

'The people already cast?'

'Nope, they're pretty good.'

'So, what then? Me?'

'Of course not, mate.'

'Andrew!' came the call from the centre of the auditorium. It was Dick.

'I've got to go. But *please*, Rusty, think about it. Dick loved you in the Clare revue and I know he thinks you'd have a perfect slot.'

Andrew left.

Dick . . . Rusty thought. The director of the new show. *He* was the problem.

The blonde did not get a call-back. Not many from outside the Club membership did but there were a few pleasant surprises. Christie, for instance, with his prepared piece about how starting with a flawed premise but reasoning illogically from it at least gave you a chance of being right.

Rusty wanted good people in the show, of course he did. Footlights activities aimed at the spring revue through the whole year. 'Smoking Concerts' twice a term gave performers and writers a chance to try out new material in front of the rest of the Club. Implicit was a hope that their sketches would be selected for inclusion in the annual show or, perhaps, that they would be invited to audition for it.

And Rusty hoped the show would be a success, for Andrew's sake and for the sake of a couple of other friends. The more successful the show, the greater the chance that it would serve as the career launch pad so many hoped for. And so many before this year had achieved. So, in general terms, he wanted the show to do well.

But not Dick. He wanted Dick to fall into a hole in the road. 'Police are looking into it,' as the quickie went. No, he did not like Dick. He did not respect Dick – even as a director. And the word 'moral' anywhere near Dick was a travesty. Basically, Rusty wanted Dick to curl up and die. Was that because Rusty was a Yank and they were all violent?

Or was it because Dick had dated Rusty's sister's best friend, Harriet, and exploited her. He used her body, took her savings, and then ditched her, laughing when she told him she loved him. 'If you love me so much, then top yourself,' he'd said.

How did Rusty know all this? Because in the clubroom Dick

had told the story the day after, loudly. And laughed. 'It's the swinging sixties, for God's sake,' he'd roared.

Harriet didn't try to top herself but, in a daze after her showdown with Dick, she'd walked in front of a lorry. She wasn't dead but she'd been in a coma for a week.

Dick was an out-and-out wrong 'un. And there was no way that Rusty would take direction from such an asshole.

At the Gardenia that evening Blossom asked Rusty how auditions had gone. Her question was greeted with a shrug. A bloke's way of 'saying' I don't want to talk about it?

But he couldn't concentrate as she considerately moved the conversation to a reprise of their respective tutorials and assignments. She was coming up to exams – though he was not. And as a physicist, he had nothing to contribute to her preparations for Part One of the English tripos. So, he asked about what was on his mind. 'How is Harriet?'

'No better,' Blossom said. 'Still unconscious.'

'I wish I could make Dick unconscious,' Rusty said.

But she knew. And he knew she knew.

Turning to the chalk board they each ordered the lasagne special for 7/6. The Gardenia had been affordable for students since 1947. A sign on the wall said so.

And that done, Rusty asked, 'How's life with *The Faerie Queen*?'

Blossom laughed. 'Careful, sunshine. I might tell you.'

Rusty laughed too but saw that for a moment she *was* thinking about Spenser's epic sequence of stories. Which had a lot of morality about them. He knew – or at least had gathered – that much. Moralities were widely considered in Cambridge. Except, it seemed, at the Footlights.

But then they were both jolted out of any knightly musings as Dick came into the restaurant with two blokes and two women. His coterie.

'Oh fuck,' Rusty said. 'I'm bad enough company without him in here.' He didn't *want* to be bad company. Blossom was dynamic, special and his love.

But still he watched as Dick and the others were led to a table across the room. That was something. Until Dick, instead of sitting, made his way to Rusty and Blossom's table.

'Rusty!' he bubbled. 'And the lovely Blossom. I hoped I'd be able to have a word with you today.'

'What word would that be?' Blossom said quickly, trying to throw herself between Rusty and his demon. 'Antidisestablishmentarianism?'

Dick roared. But he was a roarer. 'Will you be up in the clubroom later on?' he said, fixing Rusty with his slightly bulging eyes. But without waiting for an answer he turned to Blossom. 'Make sure he is, will you, Peach Blossom?' More laughter. But then he left them alone. And their food arrived.

'A dark rum, please,' Rusty told the waitress, although they'd declined spirits when asked initially about drinks.

'And a peach schnapps for me,' Blossom said. 'And put it on the bill of the table over there.'

Rusty had to go to the clubroom anyway that evening. Casting the show might be the dominant topic around the membership but there were other, less glamorous tasks for the Club Secretary's attention. Letters to Club alumni – an innovation – were to be approved. And Edgar – the clubroom's barman – had details to add about the party he was throwing to celebrate his daughter's imminent wedding. The Secretary should spread the news of Edgar's generosity.

And Rusty also wanted to talk with Wilf, one of the few other Club scientists. He led Blossom to where Wilf was talking to Matt.

'Look at this,' Wilf said, taking a piece of paper that Matt had been writing on.

Expecting dialogue for a new sketch, Rusty instead found half a dozen economically drawn cartoons. 'Matt?'

'This is the whole of my response to the exam questions I had today.'

'He wants to be rusticated,' Wilf said, excitedly.

'*Not* rusticated,' Matt said. 'I want to be sent down. Expelled. Refused to be allowed to return.'

'Will they do that?' Blossom asked

'They will call me in and offer to *understand* my difficulties and then make it easy for me to reappear next term. But my parents won't let me drop out unless the college *refuses* to take me back. I'll try to explain that in words simple enough even for a dean to understand. I require expulsion. I have a life to lead.'

'Remember,' Rusty said, 'if you decide to raise sheep on a farm, don't plant them too deep.'

'My life? Just a joke for you?' Matt said.

'Not a joke. A series of jokes.'

'At least it won't be a quickie,' Matt said. He picked up his piece of paper, his empty pint glass, and rose. 'Drink anyone?'

The other three declined the offer.

But as Matt left, Lee approached the table, a little unsteadily. 'Hel-*lo*, Blossom my dearie,' he said. 'Interest you in some wine?' He pulled a bottle from one jacket pocket and two empty wine-glasses from the other.

'Not without a brain transplant,' Blossom said.

With a shrug, Lee put the bottle and glasses back into his pockets and moved towards another table and another girl.

'How about *that*?' Wilf said.

'Lee's too drunk to remember he's tried that on me before. Twice,' Blossom said.

'I meant Matt,' Wilf said, though he looked after Lee who was already pulling the wine bottle from his pocket again.

'Gotta wish Matt luck,' Rusty said. 'Someone who knows his own mind.'

Wilf glanced longingly at Blossom but said, 'Yeah,' to Rusty.

'I want to pick your mind,' Rusty said.

After a moment Wilf said, 'About?'

'Something I could make a rope from that would then dissolve quickly in water.'

'Huh?' Wilf said.

When they were walking back to Blossom's college, they crossed the Cam. Rusty stopped them on the bridge.

'What?' Blossom asked after it was clear the pause wasn't just for another kiss.

'Look. Water.'

'It's traditional,' she said after a moment, 'for bridges and suchlike.'

'You saw how friendly Dick was trying to be tonight.'

'And well-behaved,' Blossom said. 'My breasts felt positively invisible. He wants you to be in the show. *Wouldn't* it be an opportunity?'

'Might be.' But Rusty was thinking of other things than a potential step to a dazzling future. 'Suppose . . . If I could lure Dick on to a punt with me . . .'

'You what?'

'And if I had some breezeblocks in my rucksack . . .'

Blossom became quiet.

'And if we were downstream, and it was dark, and there were no other punts around, I could whack him on the head with the punt pole. And I could tie him to the breezeblocks with the kind of rope Wilf described and I could drop him overboard. Once the rope dissolved, no one would know to look for the breezeblocks at the bottom of the river. They'd just think that he fell into the water and hit his head. End of Dick, and justice done. When Harriet wakes up, we could tell her that the nasty man was dead and gawn. And she could get on with her life.'

'Unless the shock just made her look for more traffic,' Blossom said.

'But isn't that what *should* happen to Dick?' Rusty said. 'A life for a life?'

'Going biblical on me? I think you should have a look at the later Cantos of *The Faerie Queen*.'

Rusty shrugged.

'Besides,' Blossom said, 'Wilf said the rope would take days or maybe even weeks to dissolve completely in just water, depending on its temperature.'

'Mmm, yeah. Not ideal.'

'I suggest that you make your rope out of braided sheep's intestines. Or pig or cow. The point is that it would be strong enough for your purpose, but then the fish in the Cam would eat it all, releasing the breezeblocks and leaving the body to float.'

'Yeah . . .' Rusty said, eyes brightening. Then, 'And you think it would work?'

'Bound to,' Blossom said.

He kissed her. 'Not just a pair of pretty breasts.'

'Nope,' Blossom said. 'My legs are good too.'

* * *

But everything changed before Rusty had a chance to decide if he *really* wanted to look for a butcher who'd sell him animal guts. And to think through how he would braid intestines to make a long enough rope.

Later that night a huge ruckus had taken place in Petty Cury outside the stairs to the Footlights clubroom. A man had attacked Dick as he left the club at about half-past midnight.

The beating was brief but severe, the attacker using a truncheon – according to witnesses, who all stepped away although one of the women ran to a payphone to call for help. The police and an ambulance arrived almost simultaneously and the attacker gave himself up quietly. None of the witnesses could identify him.

According to the stop press in the Cambridge paper next morning Dick's skull had been fractured along with his shoulder bone and a femur. The attacker was the brother of a comatose woman already in hospital.

'You've seen this?' Rusty said, waving the paper as he joined Blossom for lunch on a bench in St Edward's Passage.

'It was all they talked about over breakfast,' she said. 'You'd think all their exams were on current affairs. But how are *you* feeling about it?'

'I shot and gutted a deer before I was eighteen,' Rusty said. 'Whatever one's fantasies of justice and revenge, the truth is that physical violence is dehumanizing.'

'Otherwise known as wrong?' Blossom said.

'Do you have an exam today?'

'Not till tomorrow morning, fortunately. But being this close to something so ugly may influence some of my interpretations about the virtues of chivalry.' She passed him a packet of crisps and watched with a smile as he struggled with the little blue salt bag inside. 'And what are you going to do today, Mr Secretary?'

'I suppose I'll watch auditions, if they continue. But the show's main concern will be to find a new director.'

'You?'

'I have enough nightmares, ta. Andrew's the obvious choice.'

'But . . . mightn't this open the way for you to audition after all?'

'Silver lining in a pool of blood? Doesn't feel right.'

'Well, Yankee Doodle, see how you feel tomorrow.'

'I'd really like to know more about what happened last night, and why,' Rusty said. 'Did you know Harriet had a brother?'

'I never heard of him. But your clubroom will be alive with the sound of gossip.'

Rusty waved the newspaper. 'I'm trying to shake more facts out.'

'Let me,' Blossom said, taking the paper from him. 'What's printed here does leave a big hole.' She pretended to read. 'Police are looking into it.'

# RUTH DUDLEY EDWARDS – PUBLISH AND BE DAMNED

'Have you heard George died?' boomed Baroness Troutbeck, Mistress of St Martha's, the Cambridge college known in some circles as Heterodox Central. The Baroness's first name was Ida, but nobody who valued their survival ever called her that. She was Jack to all and sundry.

Robert Amiss moved the phone further away from his ear. 'George who?'

'Fortescue, of course. The hero who made a fortune out of being cancelled. Haven't you read the obits?'

'I've been in France, avoiding the news and trying vainly to get started on my new novel.'

'The funeral's on Saturday. Be there.'

'Why? Of course I've heard of him, Jack, but I never met him.'

'I need you there. There's an air of mystery about his last will and testament. And besides, you'll enjoy it.'

Amiss had long experience of how the baroness's natural secretiveness conflicted with her desire to get her interlocutor unquestioningly to obey her orders. Mysteries appealed to her, as they did to him. In days gone by, he'd done some sleuthing on his own account, but somehow or other, he'd morphed into Jack's sidekick.

Knowing her as he did, Amiss managed to press the necessary buttons to extract some of the story. George, an old Cambridge pal of hers and, he guessed from her tone, one of her exes, had suffered grievously for making what was anathematized as an 'inappropriate' joke during a literary lunch organized by his publishers.

Many of those present had been amused, but not Titania Osborne, who claimed that George's attempt at humour had been injurious to her mental health. Recently recruited by Torsten

Redknapp, the new MD of Swansong, the publishing house for which George had written many books, she had the title of sensitivity reader. 'Which,' said the baroness, 'she interpreted as giving her licence to eradicate any attempt to challenge her own ideological prejudices.'

Amiss groaned. 'I can see what came next.'

'Exactly.'

So much fuss was made about George's quip, she explained, that Titania had threatened to organize a hunger-strike if he wasn't fired. Redknapp had summoned George to come to the office. When he said by way of introduction, 'Let me educate you,' the normally mild George had flipped. Saying he wasn't going to be patronized by a dim-witted constable from the thought police, he stormed out. Redknapp responded with an email telling him the days of pale, male and stale authors were over and he was henceforth a non-person with Swansong. On the advice of Human Resources, Titania was promoted to the new position of Chief Inspiration Officer.

'Could Redknapp really just fire him? What did George's agent have to say?'

'Allegra Runcible? She admitted times were so difficult she had no stomach for the fight, said she had to go with the flow and since all the publishers were running scared, no one would want to take him on. "Cosies aren't cool", she said. Which at the time was true.'

'If not exactly far-sighted. So what did George do?'

'Rang me up and told me he was going off for twelve months to reinvent himself. A lot happened after that.'

'Like?' asked Amiss patiently.

'Can't natter on. Must to fly to the Lords to beat up the bishops. Read the obits and I'll meet you at the Wolseley for devilled lamb kidneys on Saturday at 8.00 a.m. I'll have the train tickets.'

From the obits Amiss learned that George was sixty-seven, an amiable, easy-going, childless widower with many friends. After a spell in the forces as a rifleman, he'd made a very decent living for thirty years publishing a book a year in each of his two series. Mr Reliable who never missed deadlines, he was on the Jane Austen wing of crime writing, an heir to the Golden Age, with two likeable protagonists and ingeniously and meticulously plotted stories that did well with libraries and aficionados of the whodunit everywhere.

'My thousands of loyal readers can be sure I would never give them nightmares,' he had said in an interview before his fall from grace. 'Though it's true I know how to handle a gun, none of my murder victims ever has their head blown off. Deaths in my books are almost decorous. You will encounter no graphic orgies, the vicar will not turn out to be a sociopathic cannibal, and helped by my amateur sleuths, the forces of law and order, even including the obligatory stupid policeman, will eventually get their man. Or woman.'

After his defenestration, he had issued a statement saying he was going abroad and 'doing a Greta Garbo' for a while, and then maintained radio silence.

As always, however, George was industrious. By the time he came back on the scene, he had regained the rights to all his books and had them handsomely repackaged and republished online, where they were selling well.

He had also self-published another book of a very different kind, which he announced with a lavish London party and a PR campaign about why a respected cosy writer had gone over to the dark side. It was a thinly veiled satire on the publishing industry in general and literary London in particular in which the murderer set about killing those who, in his words, 'in the name of social justice but usually because of pusillanimity, had made free speech, the bedrock of our profession, the enemy of ideological purity and sacrificed it to the gods of bigotry'. The pen portraits of unprincipled publishers, cowardly agents and hypocritical leaders of hitherto respected literary institutions were so recognizable, well-written and the methods of despatching them so disgusting yet blackly funny, that George gambled that the victims wouldn't take the risk of suing and becoming a laughing stock. If they did sue, on the other hand, the attendant publicity would be worth its weight in gold. Like all George's books, this one had clever plot twists, but it embraced everything he had hitherto deplored. The sex was explicit and perverse, the violence wanton and sickening. One online reviewer summed it up neatly as revolting and terrifying enough to have both Thomas Harris and Bret Easton Ellis throw up. Possibly over each other.

It became a sensation.

George's hunch had been right. The targets pretended they would not stoop to reading *Woken*, and he made millions. He purchased an exquisite Regency manor house in Suffolk complete with every luxury from hot tub to ice house. His hospitality was legendary, particularly his summer parties. Publishers, enticed by money even more than ideology, queued up to invite him to write another blockbuster for them, but he explained it was a one-off. He had written it as a form of catharsis and now he'd got the darkness out of his system, he'd return to writing cosies. He claimed he had no hard feelings about making peace with those who had ill-treated or ignored him and invited old enemies as well as friends. After a short illness, he had died peacefully at his home.

Amiss, in a dark grey suit from his office days, had just sat down when the baroness appeared at the table in a black crepe suit with a matching fur jacket. 'Real or faux?' asked Amiss.

'I don't approve of faux anything.'

'Don't tell the activists.'

'Wait till you see the hat. I've left it in the cloakroom as it's too large to put on a chair.'

'Of course it is.'

There was a brief altercation over Amiss's refusal to try the devilled kidneys. 'I know you're a slow learner, Jack, but you should by now have grasped that I can't be bullied into eating organs,' he said. 'I'll have the kedgeree. Now can we talk about George and why we're trekking off to Suffolk?'

'Several reasons, not least that George is one of my most generous benefactors.'

'It didn't mention that in the obits.'

'No. He decided the announcement should wait until he was dead. He's been planning the funeral and its subsequent festivities for ages and the entertainment includes the reading of his will. There should be an announcement of the St Martha's Orwell Chair he promised me.'

'What other delights are ahead of us?'

'This message arrived the day after he died,' she said, producing it from her handbag. '"George Fortescue, who shuffled off the mortal coil yesterday, invites you to his home on Saturday to listen to good music and appropriate readings. You can celebrate his last joke while consuming, inter alia, large amounts of caviar and champagne and listening to his last will and testament. He hopes anybody who is anybody in the book world will be there."'

'Will they be?'

'I suspect it's an offer they can't refuse.'

'Including Torsten and Titania, do you think?'

'I fear not. Being a power couple whose insistence on ideological purity was steadily bankrupting Swansong, they were persuaded to take leave to "pursue other opportunities". When last heard of, they were preparing to go to South East Asia to explore culture thanatology. For all I know, they're still there.'

'The string quartet was excellent, so was the poetry but the Bible reading seemed a bit odd,' said Amiss during a pause in the proceedings as he and the baroness took a break from reunions and sneering at celebrities they both despised. 'What was going on with Elijah and chariots of fire and his protégé Elisha having bears eat little children because they mocked him for being bald?'

'I will admit that when I visited George on his deathbed, it did seem as if he'd gone a bit Old Testament. He was trying to find the right quotes about people getting their just deserts and hadn't been able to find the right one.'

She waved the waiter over to refill her glass. 'Here comes the lawyer.'

The will was workmanlike in style but dramatic in substance. George had thought long and hard, he said, about how to disburse his money to defeat the forces of wokery, and had decided he wasn't up to it and so left the job to someone else. He left his millions to a trust fund to be chaired by his oldest and doughtiest friend, the Great Disrupter, Baroness Troutbeck. She and he had compiled a list of the just, who were to be consulted and supported, and the unjust, whose plans were to be foiled.

'One of your more interesting secrets,' said Amiss. 'I only wish Titania and Torsten were present to hear it.'

* * *

The lawyer completed his duties by calling on the baroness to say a few words. 'She will also read you at George Fortescue's express request the communication which was delivered to me this morning by courier.'

The baroness's thanks to George and promises of war against the enemies of free speech were brief, not least because like everyone else, she was consumed with curiosity.

'They threw me down a metaphorical well,' she read. 'So I reciprocated with a real one.'

It didn't take long for the police to decide to search the ice house, which had been built in the shrubbery over a large and deep pit. George had announced a change of heart and invited Titania and Torsten over the day before they were due to leave the country so that 'apologies can be made and we can put things right'.

Rather disingenuously, it must be said, he'd hinted that he was prepared to fund their trip overseas. Lust for lucre overcame their reservations. But when they turned up, he made it clear that they were the people he expected to apologize. When they refused repeatedly in tones of outrage and threatened to exact ferocious reprisals via social media, he dispatched each of them with a single shot.

'I wonder what this will do for his sales,' remarked Amiss, as they conducted their post-mortem by phone a few days later.

'They'll soar higher than ever, depend on it,' replied the baroness. 'Besides, as George pointed out, Titania and Torsten had only themselves to blame. He gave them the clearest possible trigger warning.'

# ALINE TEMPLETON – THE KINTSUGI VASE

I like to think of myself as a moral person. Oh, not obsessive, or anything – I just pop in occasionally to the local church, and according to the vicar God's pretty hot on not judging other people and if you do, he might not be so forgiving about the bad things you do yourself.

So I always tried to think the best of Ned Kenton, despite the way he treated the lovely Rosalind France.

They were world-famous. Saying you'd never heard of them and their great love story would be like saying you'd never heard of Antony and Cleopatra's – and with that pair I always sort of doubted it would have lasted for fifty years in show-business, like the France-Kenton marriage did.

With her deep auburn hair, genuinely green eyes, porcelain complexion and chiselled cheekbones, Rosalind regularly had the 'most beautiful woman in the world' tag attached to her. Ned, whose hazel eyes were so dark you could only see the gold flecks in close-up, had a sexy touch of the irresistible 'bit of rough'.

Naturally there were rumours from time to time, mainly about Ned when he was pictured wining and dining yet another leading lady, but it was noticeable that when the same one featured too often, the photos would quite suddenly stop. Oh, for all that she looked like a Dresden shepherdess, it was clear that when Rosalind put her dainty foot down, Ned would twitch back into line.

Well into her seventies, she was still beautiful. She had scorned the nips and tucks and Botox, scorned too the cosy 'National Treasure' style; there was a haunting beauty in the perfect bone structure and the unfaded green eyes.

I was much too young to have seen them in the early days when they were doing Shakespeare together, of course, but in the old films I watched so avidly – *Much Ado About Nothing* and *The Taming of the Shrew* – she gave as good as she got, matching him for weight of personality, and then some. The female of the species is famously deadlier than the male, and underneath all that machismo Ned was a bit weak.

I read every fanzine I could lay my hands on, watched every film they had made together or separately and even managed to see them on stage after they'd reached the age when contemporaries were settling for less demanding TV work.

They had a second home in the village where I grew up, a sort of Miss-Marple-style village not far from Stratford, a Queen Anne property with a little private theatre added for the amusement of their house parties. Called The Doll's House after one of Mrs France-Kenton's most famous successes, it was lent to the locals sometimes.

When I was sixteen I had a tiny part in a play being put on by the local am-dram society – *Silhouette*, I think it was called – and when I heard she was actually going to watch it, I was sure this would be my big chance. She'd spot me as a young actress of stunning talent and she'd decide to take me under her wing.

In my determination to be noticed, I broke every dramatic rule: forced my way to centre stage whenever I came on, blocked the lead players, ad-libbed a bit to pad out the slender part, then fluffed my lines and to my eternal shame forgot the cue the next speaker was waiting for. There was a long pause, in which I could feel my face getting so hot that I thought it might explode and I wanted to die.

After the ordeal was over, Rosalind French came backstage and with practised grace and charm praised what it was possible to praise. That didn't include my performance which she tactfully ignored, but she gave me a kindly smile and a pat on the hand on the way out.

'Very creative, darling, but less is more. If you haven't the instinct, don't try. It won't make you happy.'

It was the best advice I ever had. I felt broken, naturally, as only a teenager deprived of her dream can be, but she made me realize I didn't really want to be an actress, I just wanted to be *her.* Once I wearied of playing the tragic heroine, I was grateful.

I went into the beauty business instead. Well, that's a fancy way of saying that I had my own hairdressing salon – creative in its way – and it brought me a good income and a settled family life. When arthritis made standing a problem, I trained as a manicurist and whenever Rosalind France came back from London, she'd summon me. She had exquisite hands, with long, slim fingers and perfectly almond-shaped nails.

I loved going to the house. It was grand, but in a shabby-chic way. While I set up in her bedroom with a full range of varnishes, Rosalind – she was Rosalind to me now – would go to the safe that was concealed by a little sketch of her as Desdemona by some posh artist – can't remember who – and she'd take out a tray of breathtaking rings: emeralds featured strongly, and there were gems of every colour and semi-precious stones in wonderful designer settings.

Then we'd discuss which she'd choose to wear and select a colour accordingly. Every so often there'd be a new addition that usually appeared after a flurry of stories about Ned and some up-and-coming actress, kind of like an apology. A look of unspoken understanding would pass between us, and she sometimes made a sly little joke about the actress in question.

We talked a lot, over the years. There probably weren't many people she could trust not to go to the press and sometimes when there were marriage breakdown stories circulating, she'd sigh and shake her head.

'They don't understand,' she would say. 'It doesn't mean anything.'

One day, I was so angry with the man, I burst out, 'But how do you keep it together, when all this goes on?'

She smiled – the famous smile that made her face seem lit from within. 'Let me show you something.'

She fetched a vase that stood on a pretty walnut bureau. I'd noticed it before, of course: it was an elegant shape, celadon green, but it looked like someone had broken it and then stuck it together again but where you'd use superglue, they'd used gold. It was kind of crazy, but splendid.

She picked it up carefully. 'This is my most treasured possession. Ned gave it to me for our silver wedding. It's a Japanese technique called Kintsugi, and the vase is more beautiful now and stronger than it was before it was broken.' Her green eyes glowed as she said, 'You see, my true love hath my heart, and I have his. Everything else is trifles, light as air.'

The way she spoke brought a lump to my throat. He was a right sod, Ned Kenton, but I believed her: he'd always come back.

Then there was a story that ran longer than usual in the gutter press. The lady, if you could call her that, was a very successful loud-mouthed American star with a reputation for ruthlessness.

I was worried, frankly; whatever Rosalind said, the woman had her claws into Ned. But then, there was another stunning addition to the tray of rings: a huge yellow sapphire, flanked by pavé diamonds.

'Wow!' I said.

She laughed. 'It's a whopper, isn't it? We'll need to choose the colour carefully.'

We chatted about their plans for the summer. The long-range forecast was good and they planned to spend most of it here together. 'With climate change, London's impossible in summer,' she said. 'It'll do Ned good to relax – he's doing too much.'

It was a shock when not long after they arrived we heard Ned had had an accident one evening – a fall from the terrace overlooking the gardens on to the paving stones fifteen feet below. A fatal fall.

He'd been walking with a stick lately, the staff working at the house said he'd been drinking all afternoon and the balustrade was low – so it was sad but not that surprising.

The big shock came when Rosalind was arrested for murder. I couldn't bear to read the press stories; I didn't believe it for a minute. I could picture her face as she said, 'My true love hath my heart and I have his' – that shining sincerity! It had all been whipped up by that American – well, bitch, if you'll excuse the expression.

Public opinion was divided: Ned was known to be a heavy drinker but there were those who'd always think the worst of a possessive wife and there'd been enough doubt to make the police take an interest.

It was difficult to imagine Rosalind France imprisoned but I didn't have to imagine. Just before the trial, I got a phone call from her lawyer, asking me to come to see her. Of course I agreed; I took my manicure kit, guessing she wanted to look her elegant best as the photographers had their day.

It wasn't that, though. In the drab little room she was like an exotic bird caged; she was still beautiful but there were heavy shadows under her eyes and she looked nervous.

'Would you be prepared to speak for me in court, darling? You know more about me than anyone else.'

I immediately said, 'Of course,' though I was a bit scared – never, I'm happy to say, having had anything to do with the law.

Then she told me what she wanted. I could say whatever I liked, she said, but she wanted me to talk about the Kintsugi vase, and what she'd said at that time. 'Do you remember that?'

Her voice was anxious. I said, of course I did, and she went on, 'And you know how darling Ned always sent me apology presents, and how he sent me that yellow diamond just a few weeks ago?'

Of course I did, and I was more than ready to go into detail about that, and particularly the significance of the Kintsugi vase. She kissed me when we parted.

The crowds outside the Old Bailey were terrifying, but the police whisked our car through and then I sat in a waiting room while they got the show on the road. Surprisingly, I wasn't really nervous: I knew what I was going to say, and after all I had once had aspirations to be an actress; this was my chance to appear before an audience.

With Rosalind's words of long ago ringing in my ears, 'Less is more', I didn't go over the top, just answered the questions straightforwardly, and the Kintsugi vase being brought forward as an exhibit gave me the opportunity to stress how it showed the true strength of their long marriage.

Secretly, I liked to think my testimony was what got her acquitted, but of course she was amazing under questioning; I was allowed to slip back in to see it, and to hear the unanimous 'Not Guilty' from the jury foreman.

She was whisked away after that – abroad, they said. She sent me the most magnificent bouquet of flowers I had ever seen, and a magnum of Bollinger, but it was some time before she came back to the village again.

When I got the message to come to do her nails, I was delighted.

I'd wondered if the whole court business would make it awkward, but no. Rosalind chose the yellow diamond – 'My absolute favourite,' she said, and we chatted about her travels after the trial and about what she'd be doing now.

'Of course, darling,' she said, 'I wouldn't be going anywhere, if it wasn't for you. The way you delivered your evidence – perhaps I was wrong to tell you not to go on the stage. It was a magnificent performance.'

I laughed. 'I've been happy with my life. And stating the truth isn't really like acting, is it?'

Rosalind looked at me sharply. 'Goodness, darling, you didn't really believe all that, did you?'

My jaw dropped. 'The vase—' I faltered.

She got up, laughing, and went over to the bureau. She picked up the vase, much less carefully this time, held it above her head and threw it with force at the stone fireplace where it shattered in pieces.

'It was the embodiment of Ned's lies and excuses. I only stayed with him because our marriage was a legend and I was damned if his parade of sluts was going to ruin it. I've wanted to do that for a long time, but I'm glad I didn't now!'

She came back, sat down again and held out her hand. 'Oh look, I'm sorry. I've gone and smudged a nail. Can you fix it, darling?'

'Yes,' I managed to say. She went on to talk about how hot it had been while I finished the job, then I packed up my kit.

After I refused the first call to go back, I never heard from her again. She did a lot more travelling after that and a couple of years later I heard she'd died of a heart attack in Paris.

Over the years I was regularly called by hopeful journalists, but I never spoke to any of them and I never told anyone about our last conversation. The 'not guilty' verdict had been given and that was it.

After all, I'd tried all these years to think the best of Ned Kenton in the teeth of the evidence, so in a way, it was only fair that I should do the same now for Rosalind France. They were a theatrical legend, after all, and legends have never really had their basis in reality.

# SIMON BRETT – CAST, IN ORDER OF REAPPEARANCE

Simon Brett writes: *With thanks to Lucy for the title . . . and so much more . . .*

The two things that worry actors most are what they look like and remembering their lines. Which of those is scarier generally depends on the size of the individual actor's ego. Charles Paris, never having had matinee idol good looks, was not too bothered about his appearance. Remembering lines, though, became, as he grew older, an increasing anxiety.

Actors, like writers, don't really retire. Oh, some make grandiose statements about retirement – to the media if they're famous, to their friends if they're not – but they don't really mean it. They still nurture the hope of that call from the National Theatre asking them to give their Lear, of a whole career of mediocrity salvaged by one blistering final performance. In an actor, again like a writer, hope is the last thing to die.

Charles's surface cynicism would assert that he had long ago extinguished all such dreams but, as in all of his profession, the little flicker of a pilot light still glowed.

Learning lines is a matter of practice and this is one of the areas in which the theatre can be a cruel business. Obviously, the less an actor works, the less he practises learning lines. So, he not only has the humiliation and frustration of being out of work, he also knows that one of his essential professional skills is being eroded by inactivity. And there is the additional fear, felt by everyone as they get older, that all memory skills are in decline.

It happens to successful actors, too. Particularly those who've made it in the movies. Holding in one's head the lines for a short cinema take is not too tricky. But many have come unstuck when they return to the theatre and have to memorize the words for an entire evening.

That was not a problem for Charles Paris. His acting experience had included film, but not at a level for him to be described as a movie star. Any kind of star, really. Though he had been a professional actor all his adult life, the big breaks had never come his way. It wasn't a matter of talent. He was at least as good at his job as many who had gone on to much greater fame. But, for Charles Paris, that kind of thing had just never quite happened.

Which was perhaps why, in the twilight of his career, he had ended up in a touring revival of a rather creaky stage thriller. The process had started with a call from his agent, Maurice Skellern. Which was, in itself, a rare event.

'Charles! How're you doing?'

'Sorry? Who is this?' It was a game the actor had played many times before.

'It's Maurice. Your agent.'

'Ah, sorry. Didn't recognize the voice. It's been so long since I last heard from you.'

'Now, Charles, that's unkind. You know how busy I am, always beavering away on behalf of my clients.'

'Other clients. I haven't noticed you beavering away much on my behalf recently.'

'That's very ungrateful, Charles.'

'Is it? When did you last put my name forward for a part? When did you last send me along to a casting session?'

'Charles . . .' Maurice Skellern sounded appropriately wounded. 'I'm constantly putting your name forward. But when the producers don't bite, I feel it's kinder for me not to say that I mentioned you than to tell you they weren't interested.'

'Oh yes?' was the instinctive cynical response. And yet there was a sliver of doubt within Charles that what his agent was saying might be true. Names are quickly forgotten in the performing arts. It only takes a few months of not working.

Maurice changed the subject. 'Have you seen the new Netflix series *On a Cruise*?'

'No,' said Charles. 'I don't have Netflix.' He had been slow to catch up with the streaming phenomenon. He found the pleasure of watching other actors working was finite.

'Boy playing the lead, Jared Kinsella . . . he's one of my clients.'

'Ah.' One of Maurice Skellern's most infuriating habits, on the rare occasions when he did ring Charles, was talking about his other clients. By definition, his other more successful clients.

'Getting very good ratings,' said Maurice.

'I'm glad to hear it,' said a tight-lipped Charles Paris. 'Was there any particular reason you called me this morning?'

'Of course there was, of course there was. I wanted to tell you that my beavering away on your behalf has paid off.'

'Oh?' Charles tried to bleach the monosyllable of all intonation but he couldn't suppress the little bubble of hope within him.

'Yes, I've engineered an offer of work for you.'

'Really?' Still keeping things cool. Obviously, it wouldn't be the National Theatre offering him Lear, but there were plenty of other good parts out there for mature actors. Something classical maybe . . . a Chekhov, a Wilde, an Arthur Miller . . .? Or some ground-breaking original play by one of the hottest new writers . . .?

'It's a tour of a stage thriller,' said Maurice Skellern. 'Not actually Agatha Christie, but "School of".'

'Oh.' Not for the first time, Charles's dreams shrank to accommodate reality. 'What's it called?' he asked wearily.

'*Dead as a Doornail*.'

Charles groaned inwardly. It was one of those titles – like 'Deadline' and 'Body Count' – that had been used far too often in the world of crime fiction. 'It's a tour, you say, Maurice?'

'That's right,' came the enthusiastic response. 'Three months, week runs at each venue.'

'And, as usual, zigzagging across the country like a demented fly?' Charles had done enough tours to know that they never followed the logical route of minimizing the travel time between venues.

Since his agent didn't reply, Charles went on, 'Any chance of it going into the West End?'

'It's not that kind of tour, Charles.'

No, of course it wasn't. He might have guessed. 'And this was a job that you actually got for me, Maurice? "Beavering away on my behalf"?'

'We-ell . . .'

The hesitancy made it absolutely clear. 'I see. So, someone from the production just rang you up out of the blue?'

Another 'We-ell . . .' Followed by: 'But they wouldn't have rung me if I hadn't been beavering away on your behalf . . . you know, putting your name about, dropping words in the right ears . . .'

'Hm . . .' The sound was larded with cynicism. 'Where does the tour open?'

'Rugland Spa.'

'All the Number One venues, eh?' It was said with no less cynicism. 'Well, I'll think about it,' Charles added.

'"Think about it"? Think about what?'

'Whether I want to do the job or not.'

'Don't be silly, Charles. I've already told them you'll do it.'

'Oh.' Maurice always assumed that Charles would say yes to any offer. What made it galling was that he was usually right.

The agent reverted to his reproachful tone. 'And, of course, I'm not expecting you to say thank you to me for getting you the job.'

Charles was made to feel guilty enough – though God only knew why – to mumble a 'Thank you.'

'You really should try and catch *On a Cruise*,' said Maurice. 'Wonderful showcase for Jared Kinsella's talents. It'll be feature films next for him, Hollywood . . . That boy is really going places, you know, Charles.'

'Funny, Maurice, that, throughout my career, you have never said I was "going places".'

'Now that's very hurtful, Charles. You are certainly going places.'

'Oh yes? Like where?'

'Rugland Spa,' said Maurice.

Charles Paris had history with Rugland Spa. He'd worked there a long time before, in another stage thriller, also as creaky as a wicker coffin. That one had been called *The Message is Murder*. Having read the script for his most recent booking, Charles couldn't see that, from the literary viewpoint, *Dead as a Doornail* was much of an improvement.

The venue where he would be working had undergone improvement, though. Rugland Spa's old Regent Theatre, in the commercially valuable Maugham Cross area of the town, had been a target for developers for some decades. Expensive refurbishment after the Second World War had not done enough to revive the building in its original Victorian form. Many changes of management and dwindling audiences, coinciding with the end of the weekly repertory system, meant that the site had been snapped up for redevelopment in the 1980s.

The plans were to knock down the Regent and adjacent buildings to make room for a shopping mall with a block of 'affordable' apartments on top. (It goes without saying that, in reality, the new flats would only be affordable to people with a lot of money.)

But a provision in the development's planning permission insisted that the build should include a performance space, 'so that Rugland Spa's fine tradition of theatre should be continued'.

The resulting structure did not have any of the Regent's old Victorian magic. It was a functional and soulless space, more reminiscent of conference room than playhouse, which the local council had rechristened the 'Rugland Spa Community Arts Hub'. Like all such ventures, its future was very shaky. It hosted a few professional touring play productions, and one-nighters for bands and stand-ups. The space was used by the local am-dram and Operatic Society and was the venue for an increasing number of conferences. It would not require a very sophisticated prophet to predict a near future in which the Hub's business involved no theatre at all.

Still, it was opening its doors to the touring production of *Dead as a Doornail*. Which meant that Charles Paris, after some very bleak months, was in work.

And, whereas back in the day in *The Message is Murder*, he'd only been playing the dead body whose murder was being investigated, in *Dead as a Doornail* he actually had some lines.

'Hi, Frances. It's me.'

'Oh. Charles. Only the fact that it's too corny stops me from saying "Hello, stranger".'

'Rap over the knuckles duly registered. And deserved.'

Charles and Frances were still technically married. At one time they had been traditionally married. They'd lived together and had a daughter Juliet. But the demands of an actor's itinerant life – not to mention the allure of Bell's whisky and young actresses – had led to a parting of the ways. Frances and their daughter had stayed in the Highgate family home, and Charles had decamped to Hereford Road, off Westbourne Grove.

When he'd moved in, the area had been pretty run-down, but its proximity to the burgeoning Notting Hill had brought it up in the world. The description of the kind of bedsit in which Charles lived had been dignified by estate agents to 'studio flat'. And the rental he was charged had risen proportionately.

There had been many attempts at reconciliation between Charles and Frances. He would promise fidelity and a reduction in the drinking – and, on each occasion, at the time he spoke the words he really meant them – but every time, somehow, he backslid. At last, to save herself future pain, Frances said she didn't want to see him again.

Her resolve, like his, though, had a habit of backsliding. Neither could ever quite make their estrangement endure. The marriage remained semi-detached.

'How're you doing, Charles? Have you got any work?'

'Remarkably, yes.'

'Oh? You got the call from the National about your Lear?'

The private joke was so old, it hardly justified acknowledgement.

'Not quite so rarefied, I'm afraid,' Charles replied. 'Three-month tour of a stage thriller.'

'Oh well. Three month's income, anyway. Longer with rehearsal payments.'

'Yes.'

'What are you playing?'

'The Suspect Whose Work As A Doctor Gave Him Access To The Medication An Overdose Of Which Caused The First Murder Victim To Die.' It wasn't the first time he'd played a doctor. He had been in the famous 'Out, damned spot!' scene in a production at Salisbury rep. ('With the only medical help on offer coming from Charles Paris's Doctor, it was no wonder that Lady Macbeth topped herself.' *Wiltshire Times*)

'Ah,' said Frances. 'And did you do it? Are you the murderer?'

'Now, come on, you know the rules, Frances. If I told you that, I'd have to kill you.'

'Spoilsport. Any chance of a West End transfer?'

'You gotta be joking.'

'Ah. Any star names?'

'Depends how you define "star". If you mean a superannuated poseur who played the lead in a television series in the 1990s, then we've got one in the role of the detective, who glories in the name of "Inspector Pargeter".'

'Who're you talking about?'

Charles offered a clue. 'Played Sergeant Wickens in umpteen episodes of *Duty Patrol.* And has lived in the afterglow of that celebrity ever since. All-round good guy, stalwart of chat shows, famous for his charity work, Lord's Taverners, Garrick Club, that kind of thing. Will have great appeal to the geriatrics of Rugland Spa, I would imagine.'

'*Duty Patrol?*' Frances repeated. 'The series was so unmemorable I've completely forgotten who was in it.'

'Trafford Duke,' Charles revealed.

'Yuk!' Frances's shudder transmitted itself down the phoneline.

'That's not the usual response to him. All-round good guy, like I said.'

'The usual response must be from people who haven't met him.'

'I didn't know you had.'

'A first night party for something you were both in, way back. Disgusting groper. Even came on to me.'

'Showed he was a man of taste,' said Charles, trying to ingratiate himself.

Her icy response told him the attempt had failed. 'No woman is flattered by the attentions of a habitual groper.'

'Ah.' Charles tried again. 'Well, I'm sure a lot less of that is allowed to go on now, post-#MeToo.'

But, again, he'd said the wrong thing. 'Have you found that then, Charles?' asked his still-icy wife.

'No. Well . . . Um . . .' was all he could muster by way of comeback. 'Anyway,' he went on quickly, 'I don't think Trafford Duke's name would guarantee a West End transfer these days.'

'Probably not. How long till opening night?'

Charles gave her the when and the where. Until his faux pas, he'd rather enjoyed re-establishing banter with Frances. They'd always entertained each other. Now, surely, after so much water had flowed under the bridge, they could get back together on a more permanent . . .?

'Rugland Spa, eh?' Frances echoed. 'Well, there's a coincidence.'

'Oh?'

'I'm going to be staying in Malvern that week.'

'Oh?'

'With a friend.'

Charles felt a knee-jerk pang of jealousy. But why? She didn't say it was a man. As the retired head of a girls' school, Frances had lots of female friends, former staff members, former pupils. She could be staying with any one of them.

'Rugland Spa's just over the border in Herefordshire,' she went on. 'I could get a cab and come to your First Night.'

'Cab? Won't you have your car with you?'

'No. And my friend doesn't drive.'

Non-driving friend, Charles reassured himself. Perhaps elderly. Malvern was a sort of retirement area. Probably some teacher Frances had known from her own schooldays.

Her next words dashed that hope. 'Even if he did drive, he wouldn't want to come. Loathes the theatre. Concert hall or nothing for him. Wants to go to Malvern for its Edward Elgar connections. And some concerts.'

'Ah.' The natural, the logical thing would be for Charles to ask more details about this 'friend'. But something within stopped him.

'Oh, well, if you could make it for the First Night . . .' he said feebly.

'I'll check.'

With whom, Charles wondered, annoyingly.

'So, are you in rehearsal yet?'

'Start Monday.'

'In Rugland Spa?'

'No, London. Go out there for the week before we start.'

'Right.'

'So,' he said after a slight pause, 'since we're both in London . . . perhaps we could meet up for a drink or . . .?'

'That'd be nice,' said Frances. But she didn't reach for her diary to fix a date.

And, after the phone call had ended, Charles reflected that they'd both been in London for the past six months. Possibly even a year. And he hadn't suggested meeting up for a drink during that expanse of time.

Frances's caution, he concluded wryly, when it came to dealing with her husband, was justified.

Scripts are full of boobytraps for actors. Some lines, often in Shakespeare, are frankly unsayable. Charles Paris had once played the unenviable part of Fabian in a tacky production of *Twelfth Night* as part of the Ludlow Festival. Equally unenviable were some of the lines allocated to the character. The one he recalled with particular loathing was: 'Sowter will cry upon't for all this, though it be as rank as a fox.' He had asked for the line to be cut but the director, a Shakespeare purist, would not hear of it. So long as the words were spoken as if they were the components of a joke, he reassured the reluctant actor, the audience would be bound to laugh.

Charles could still remember, with pain, delivering the line every performance to an uncomprehending and stony silence.

Then there were lines which got cocked up in rehearsal. As in the same Ludlow production, when the actor playing Sebastian inadvertently spoonerized the speech: 'I prithee, foolish Greek, depart from me.' His reading of 'I prithee, ghoulish freak, depart from me' prompted much merriment among the company. And planted the dangerous seed of giggling each time the line came up.

Intonation, too, could cause inappropriate changes of meaning. Charles remembered being told of an actor booked to record an audio commercial for a well-known make of remedial footwear. The text was thought by the advertising agency to be unambiguous, but the wrong message came across when the actor read, 'If you think *your* feet are bad, you should see Dr Scholl's!'

Another script hazard that had scuppered many a rehearsal was the Repeated Cue. Often, particularly in stage thrillers, the same character will have to say the same line more than once. 'So, who do you think the murderer is now?' might be a good example. In the early stages of rehearsal, the Repeated Cue can be picked up with the wrong response, thus moving the play's action forward or back by a significant amount of time.

The trouble was, it didn't only happen at the early stages of rehearsal. Then, the cock-up is greeted with hilarity by the entire company but, if it occurs too often, the director will be the first to lose their sense of humour.

And the fact that it has occurred at all prompts a visceral fear in the cast that it could happen during a live performance. Such nightmare visualizations only add to the endemic paranoia of the acting profession.

They had a laugh-provoking misreading on the first day of *Dead as a Doornail* rehearsals, which took place in a shabby room above a gothic church near Shaftesbury Avenue. (London is littered with unlikely spaces that get booked for play and television rehearsals.)

The unfortunate actor who committed the blunder was the youngest member of the cast, a buxom little redhead called Vikki Roman, playing the Suspect Whom The First Murder Victim Had Been Blackmailing Over Some Compromising Photographs.

Old habits died hard and, at readthroughs, Charles Paris still scanned the female company members for potential romantic encounters. But even he had to admit, rather unwillingly, that a forty-year age gap would have to rule out any such aspirations with Vikki Roman. Mind you, the expression Trafford Duke cast on the girl suggested he had no such inhibitions.

Charles probably wouldn't have had that thought if Frances hadn't mentioned the older actor having come on to her. Because that morning, Trafford Duke was his customary bonhomous self, humble about his celebrity, asserting that theatre was always his first love, looking forward to being part of a company again, smiling at everyone, the all-round good guy.

The way Vikki Roman had kowtowed to him over pre-readthrough coffee suggested she wasn't averse to his interest. Surely, she couldn't be impressed by his television fame in *Duty Patrol*? She wasn't born when the series went out, and it had rarely been repeated. Maybe her parents had been fans and built up for her the privilege of working with Trafford Duke . . .? Or maybe she was just attracted to any kind of celebrity . . .? Looking for someone to give her a leg up on the showbiz ladder . . .?

The line in the readthrough that tripped Vikki Roman up was:

'Let bygones be bygones.' Clearly not an expression she had ever heard before, what she read was: 'Let big ones be big ones.'

When the company hysterics had subsided, Trafford Duke was heard to observe, chuckling, 'Very appropriate, young Vikki. Because you have got delightfully big ones!'

Charles Paris, who sometimes had difficulty keeping up with the latest sensibilities of political correctness, would – mercifully – have known better than to make that remark. And the shocked silence in the rehearsal room suggested that the comment hadn't gone down well with the rest of the company.

'Trafford, it is entirely inappropriate to make jokes about women's breasts.' It was the director who voiced the consensus opinion. Barb Benson. Charles was only meeting her for the first time that morning, but he'd checked her CV out online and been impressed. She'd done some innovative and challenging work. Site-specific spectacles. Verbatim theatre. Feminist versions of the classics. Original feminist scripts. She'd just got very good reviews for a new play at the Royal Court which had taken on the subject of masculine 'coercive control'.

She was also – Charles didn't do social media, but he heard from other cast members – very active and militant on various platforms in defence of women's rights. Enthusiastic about the practice of naming and shaming.

Some people might have questioned why, given that track record, she was directing a tour of a broken-backed thriller like *Dead as a Doornail*. But Charles Paris had been around the profession long enough to know exactly why she was doing it. For the money. This was an approach for which he had great sympathy. Everyone has bills to pay. In the theatre, unless you were incredibly lucky or incredibly pig-headed, you had to go where the work was. Even if that involved the occasional bit of slumming. And he reckoned, in her taking on *Dead as a Doornail*, he was witnessing their director slumming.

There was something undefined about Barb Benson. Age? Probably early fifties. Orientation? Could be straight, could be gay. The important thing, so far as Charles was concerned, judging from her introduction to the day's rehearsal, she knew how to direct.

And also, from what she'd just said to Trafford, she was not afraid to stand up to her leading actor.

'Oh, come on,' was his wheedling response. 'Can't anyone take a joke anymore?'

'We can take jokes,' said Barb firmly. 'But we can't take insults. Trafford, will you please apologize to Vikki?'

'Oh, for God's sake . . .' he grumbled.

Vikki Roman failed to do her bit for feminist solidarity by protesting, 'It doesn't matter. I'm not offended.'

'See?' said Trafford, feeling vindicated. 'If the lovely Vikki herself doesn't mind . . .'

Barb Benson's voice remained steady as she said, 'It is not just a matter of Vikki's opinion. We are a company who are going to be working together for some months. And if we start rehearsals by accepting blatant sexism, then we're very definitely going to be setting off on the wrong foot. We all have boundaries which must be respected. So, I ask you once again, Trafford, will you please apologize to Vikki?'

The old actor looked around the company, hoping for some expression of support. Finding none, he mumbled, 'Very well. I am appropriately rapped over the knuckles and will aim to do better in the future. Sorry, Vikki.'

There was a tang of irony in his voice, sending up his stance of penitence, but he had actually said the relevant word. Charles was impressed by the way their director had handled the situation. She had clearly defined who was in charge. And her #MeToo credentials were firmly in place.

It was the end of the last day's rehearsal in London. Over the weekend, the cast would all travel in their different ways to Rugland Spa, starting Monday morning on a week of technical and dress rehearsals. Charles Paris found himself in a Soho pub with Camilla Bruton, who was playing the Suspect Whose Writing Career Could Be Destroyed By The First Murder Victim's Revelations Of Plagiarism In Her Bestselling Novel But Who Then Turns Out To Be The Second Murder Victim.

She had been writing in a diary when he entered the pub and, seeing her empty wine glass, he'd offered her a drink. Charles had worked with Camilla a couple of times before, though neither had much recollection of the shows they were in together.

There had never been any sexual spark between them. Charles

remembered her, like many female actors (he still, incorrectly, thought of them as 'actresses'), as being neurotic. She enjoyed staging big scenes, a Drama Queen both on and off the stage.

Like his career, hers had not exactly flourished and her death just before the interval in *Dead as a Doornail* wasn't going to give it much of a boost. But they got on well enough. Being able to be pleasant to people you don't have much in common with is one of the essential skills for a jobbing actor. Charles came back from the bar with a large Pinot Grigio for her and a large Bell's for himself.

'So, how do you think it's going?' asked Camilla, her rueful-ness suggesting she herself wasn't that impressed.

He grimaced. 'Hard to say at this stage.'

'Stop hedging, Charles. It's a total Titanic of a show.'

'Well . . .'

'Oh, go on. Admit it.'

'I think Barb's doing a good job.'

'She's doing as good a job as circumstances are allowing her to do. But we have to face the facts. The only operation that can save *Dead as a Doornail* is a Total Leading Actor Transplant.'

'Well, I'm not sure . . .' Though Charles often entertained bitchy thoughts about his fellow thespians, something within him rebelled against speaking them out loud.

'Trafford is terrible,' Camilla continued. 'He doesn't even have a passing acquaintance with the lines. When you're onstage with him, you never know what cue he's going to come up with.'

'We've still got a week,' said Charles, in feeble mitigation.

'A week during which he'll get totally confused by all the technical stuff and regress even further.'

'Maybe not,' said Charles hopefully. But he wasn't convincing himself and he certainly wasn't convincing Camilla.

'He is such a bastard,' she said with sudden vehemence.

'Trafford?'

'Who else? And he's doing it again.'

'Sorry? Doing what again?'

'Coming on to women. Have you seen the way he flirts with that Vikki?'

'He's of a generation that would regard such behaviour as being "gallant",' said Charles, wondering why he was defending the randy old bastard. Probably, he concluded without satisfaction, because he was part of the same generation.

'And the girl's as much to blame as he is,' Camilla went on. 'Playing up to him, simpering at his compliments, laughing at his jokes. You wonder why feminists bothered when all their achievements are let down by a girl of that age.'

Charles decided that 'Hm' would be an uncontroversial response.

'What's more, he looks straight through me. I don't know whether he's genuinely forgotten or if he's just pretending we've never met.' Camilla was seething. 'God, I'd like to kill the bastard!'

Charles was relieved to find that the nearest pub to the stage door of Rugland Spa's Regent Theatre was still there, though now, of course, it was the nearest pub to the stage door of the Rugland Spa Community Arts Hub. But, mercifully, all the upheaval of the Maugham Cross redevelopment had left it unchanged. Which appealed to Charles. He liked scruffy pubs. Maybe because they reflected his own gloomy self-image.

At the end of the Monday, the first day's rehearsal in the new venue, Charles found himself having a drink with Trafford Duke. They were both on pints – rehearsal was thirsty work. Charles would move on to the Bell's later in the evening.

The day's work, so far as Charles could see, had been a disaster. The change of location from London to Rugland Spa seemed to have loosened Trafford Duke's hold on the few lines in *Dead as a Doornail* that he had committed to memory in London. Rehearsal had been all stops and starts. The fuse of Camilla Bruton, most of whose few scenes involved being interrogated by Inspector Pargeter, got shorter and shorter as prompt after prompt was demanded. Actual detonation didn't happen that day, but it was only a matter of time.

Even the even-tempered Barb Benson got close to losing her rag on a couple of occasions, as Trafford Duke paraphrased yet another line. But somehow the director curbed the instinct to remonstrate.

Given the kind of day it had been, Charles was surprised to find that, in the pub, the offending actor seemed completely relaxed. Cheerful, even. As ever, the all-round good guy.

'I always love it,' he said, speaking with all the sincerity he would have used on a chat show, 'when a production gets on to the stage for the first time. Old magic of theatre, you know. Something indefinable that can never be replicated in a rehearsal room. That's the moment when a production comes alive for me.'

Charles hoped that was the moment when his lines might also come alive for him. Not on that day's showing, though.

He dared to say, 'And, hopefully, the lines will soon come.'

'Oh yes,' Trafford agreed breezily. 'In the context of actual performance, it always all comes together. Doctor Theatre sorts it out.'

'Doctor Theatre' was professional jargon for the way debilitating flu or other ailments could be shrugged off while an actor was actually performing, only to return with renewed virulence the moment the curtain call was over. But, though the good Doctor had an impressive success rate with physical illness, he had never been known to produce a remedy for unlearned lines.

'Pretty little bit of skirt, that Vikki,' said Trafford, abruptly changing the subject.

Charles grunted a non-committal reaction.

'I always manage to get the pretty ones.' A complacent smile.

'Hm.'

'Never got married, you know.'

'Oh.' Charles couldn't think why he was being treated to all this information.

'Not for lack of opportunity, obviously.' Trafford Duke chuckled. 'But, as they say, why buy a book when there's a perfectly good lending library in the town?'

Charles thought people didn't actually make that kind of sexist comment so much nowadays, but he kept his views to himself.

Anyway, Trafford didn't need any prompts to continue talking about his success with women. 'I always did all right with the fairer sex. Just luck, I suppose,' he added in a tone which meant he regarded it as anything but luck. It was all down to his fatal charm.

Charles could think of no appropriate comment.

'And I never liked being tied down. Soon as marriage was mentioned, that was me off. Plenty more fish in the sea.' Another fruity chuckle. 'And I was always ready to "use sex like a shrimping net".'

Charles recognized the reference. Noel Coward's *Hay Fever*. Myra the vamp was described as 'using sex like a shrimping net'. The phrase didn't really fit the context in which Trafford had put it. Wasn't worth pointing out, though.

'Seem to recall you did rather the same, Charles,' Trafford insinuated.

'Did what?'

'Had a taste for young actresses. Put it around a bit – eh?'

'Oh, I wouldn't say—'

'Don't apologize, dear boy. One of the perks of being an actor, always was – all that available crumpet. However much the current generation whinge about "boundaries" and "taking advantage" and "inappropriate behaviour". If a woman's up for it, well, you're in clover, aren't you? And, if she isn't up for it, then it's the man's job to persuade her she really is up for it.'

'I'm not sure—'

'Glad to have a kindred spirit like you in the cast, Charles. We're cut from the same cloth, you and I.' Trafford Duke looked at his watch and downed the rest of his beer. 'Must be off. Can't keep a young lady waiting, can I? And, equally, can't greet a young lady without having had a shave. I do have standards, you know.'

'Right.'

'So, it's back to the dressing room for a quick run over the stubble with the old cutthroat. I've used one all my life. Nothing gives as good a shave as that, you know.'

'Ah.'

'See you in the morning.'

That expression was one of the bonuses of being in work. You had people to say 'See you in the morning' to.

But the glow was momentary. Left alone, as was often the case, Charles felt depressed. It had really hurt hearing the old actor putting the two of them in the same category. Despite his proximity to becoming a National Treasure, Trafford Duke was an old groper. Whereas Charles Paris was . . . Was what?

He could not deny that his behaviour in sexual situations hadn't always been as proper as it should have been. Maybe there had been occasions when he'd taken advantage of someone younger. And, even when he knew he wasn't hurting them, when both parties just wanted a bit of fun which would end with the tour, he couldn't feel guilt-free. There was always the hurt he was causing Frances.

No, his track record in relationships wasn't great.

Nor, when it came to that, was his success in his chosen profession much to write home about. He winced as he recalled some of the reviews he'd received over the years. Why was it he could only remember the bad ones? ('Charles Paris's Leontes made me wonder why he'd chosen the theatre as a profession, when there are so many vacancies for people to stack shelves in Sainsbury's.' *Norwich Evening News*)

No great shakes as a detective either, he brooded, piling the misery on himself. His amateur investigations had been a sequence of wrong trees barked up and wrong suspects accused. On the rare occasions when he'd got the perpetrator right, it had been more by luck than judgement.

He'd never achieved what he'd always thought of as 'the full Poirot'. That was the case which he had solved with perfect logic and explained to the Suspects (who had been gathered in the Library), with the guilty party identified before the police had even arrived.

Obsessed with failure, Charles Paris went up to the bar and ordered a large Bell's. It wasn't his last of the evening.

The following morning, he was full of hangover and self-reproach. His mood wasn't improved by a phone call with his wife. All mobiles were dutifully switched off during rehearsal, so he got her message in the coffee break and called back.

'Just wanted to sort things out about your First Night.' She sounded impossibly cheerful and breezy.

'Oh yes?'

'Next Tuesday – is that right?'

'Yes.'

'Good. I had the Monday fixed in my mind. Which I couldn't have done because we're going to a performance of "The Dream of Gerontius" in Malvern.'

'Ah.' Charles resisted the urge to ask for a definition of the 'we'. He had already built up quite an animus against Frances's anonymous 'friend' and could now add the damning fact that the man regarded 'The Dream of Gerontius' as entertainment. It wasn't to Charles's taste. He had once spent a month in a concert hall one evening listening to it. But, even as he had the recollection, he knew he was being mean-spirited.

'Well, I'll be there,' said Frances. 'Get a cab over. What time's the kick-off?'

'Seven o'clock. Early because it's also the Press Night. Though why they still do that . . .'

Back in the day, Press Nights started early so that the critics could return to their typewriters in time to file their copy for the next day's papers. Now, though text could be sent from anywhere on a mobile phone, the tradition is still maintained.

'Anyway,' Charles picked up, 'meet for a drink afterwards?'

'Quick one.'

'Show should come down about nine-twenty.'

'I'll book a cab for ten to take me back.'

'Great.'

'Where do we meet?'

'Pub near the stage door. Can't remember what it's called but it's the only one for miles. Pleasingly unimproved.'

'You mean "scruffy".'

'Yes.'

'You've always liked "scruffy", haven't you, Charles?'

'I suppose I have. Always preferred it to "shooshed-up", anyway.'

'Hm. How're rehearsals going?'

'How long have you got, Frances?'

'OK. I get it. Spare me the blow-by-blow. Well, I'll see you then, Charles. I'll have a large Bell's with two lumps of ice on the bar waiting for you.'

'Thanks.'

'That is, assuming you're there.'

'I'll be there, Frances. Have I ever not been there for you?'

'I think that's a rather silly question to ask, Charles, given past history. Goodbye.'

Yes, it had been a very silly question to ask. The phone call hadn't helped his hangover one bit.

Charles couldn't understand Barb Benson's behaviour. She showed enough moments of inspiration to suggest she was a very good director. She was inventive in creating theatrical effects and she gave good notes to the actors. She was capable of making *Dead as a Doornail* a far better production than its script deserved.

Yet, when it came to stopping what was preventing it from being a far better production, she did nothing. So far as Trafford Duke was concerned, she sat on her hands. It was still basically the lines that were holding him up. He retained at best a nodding acquaintance with them. So, rehearsals proceeded in fits and starts. The company could never get a proper run at anything.

But, though Barb had shown herself to be unfazed by his star status when she called him out over his sexist remark to Vikki Roman, she kept unnervingly calm beyond the moment when any other director would, either in private or in front of everyone during rehearsal, have taken her lead actor to task about his ignorance of the script.

Charles Paris couldn't work out what was going on. Barb Benson seemed to have an agenda of her own. Taking the money, he supposed.

The only time that he did hear her lose her temper, it wasn't with Trafford Duke. It was with the Rugland Spa Community Arts Hub Box Office Manager. 'No!' the director was shouting at the poor man one day at the end of rehearsals. 'I don't care whose favourite seats they are! I need to book the entire front row for the Press Night!'

Charles Paris had lived with himself long enough to know the relationship between his happiness and alcohol. When he was in work and that work was going well, he was only a recreational drinker. When he was out of work or the work he was doing was going badly, he and alcohol became more mutually dependent.

He also knew well the relationship between his nerves and alcohol. A couple of large Bell's before a show diluted the panic. But they could also dilute the performance.

Again, if he was doing good work, work he believed in, work he believed he was doing well, he would lay off the booze on performance days. Promise himself a couple of large ones at the end of the evening, when he felt he'd earned them. And his acting often benefitted from the abstinence.

When he thought what he was doing was rubbish, though . . . or when he thought he wasn't doing his job very well . . . his attitude changed. Then he drank to exacerbate the self-loathing. He could find some kind of perverse justification in the thought that he'd given a bad performance because he was pissed. In some strange way, it seemed to let him off the hook.

It was therefore a bad sign that, at lunchtime on the day of *Dead as a Doornail*'s First Night, he went into the pub to have three large Bell's. And no food.

When he got back to the Green Room, some of the cast were gathered round a television screen on which an interview Trafford Duke had given for that morning's local news was being played back. Though far too young to have seen him in his television pomp, the female presenter, Clarice, was unctuous in her flattery.

'And would it be fair to describe you as a "National Treasure"?'

'It would be flattering, Clarice,' Trafford replied with easy charm, 'but I don't know whether it would be fair. And, anyway, I don't think I'm quite old enough for that title.'

'You were awarded a CBE for your charity work.'

'Yes. I really like to keep quiet about it, but one does do what one can to help the less fortunate.'

'And there are rumours that a knighthood might follow.'

'Clarice, I never listen to rumours.'

'And it's opening night tonight at the Rugland Spa Community Arts Hub.'

'It is indeed. *Dead as a Doornail*.'

'Everything ready, Trafford?'

'As ready as it can be, Clarice, at this stage of a production.'

'Are you looking forward to the First Night?'

'The customary mixture of frantic excitement and sheer terror, that's what I'm going through. But I must say, Clarice, that it's wonderful working with such a highly talented young cast and such an inspiring director.'

Saying all the right things, thought Charles with his customary edge of cynicism.

'Well, I must say,' Clarice went on, 'the show is provoking a lot of press interest.'

'Is it? I wasn't aware of that.'

'Oh yes, it's all over social media.'

'Ah.' Trafford Duke held up his hands in mock-horror. 'I don't do any social media, Clarice. Afraid some of the things written there might be hurtful to my fragile actor's ego.'

'You should have a look, Trafford. You'll find you have quite a substantial fan base online.'

'I wouldn't know about that,' said the modest star. 'I'm just a jobbing actor, delighted at the bonus of being in work.'

'Well . . . Trafford Duke – maybe soon Sir Trafford Duke—'

'Oh, no, no.'

'It's been a privilege and pleasure to talk to you . . .'

'As it has been for me to talk to you, Clarice.'

'So, lots of luck with the show tonight.'

'Thank you so much, Clarice.'

Smooth bastard, thought Charles Paris, not without admiration.

Getting the lines right in *Dead as a Doornail* was important. This was not because they were good lines. The playwright's dialogue creaked as much as his plot. But the lines had to be said right because of the nature of the play. A stage thriller is packed full of information to help the audience to keep up with the plot. And, as in all storytelling, the secret is controlling the flow of that information. The narrative mechanism only works if details are fed out in the right order.

Trafford Duke's attitude to his lines ensured that the mechanism didn't work. Gratified by the round of applause which greeted Inspector Pargeter's first entrance, he appeared to think that the audience had given him carte blanche to say whatever came uppermost in his mind at any given moment.

He also developed a trick which had been used by many canny older leading men. The late Rex Harrison had perfected it in his later stage career. It was basically a Look. A Look of reproach to be delivered after the stage went quiet. And it was delivered to the actor who had to speak next after Inspector Pargeter's most recent line. Since the actor in question had no idea what cue they would be presented with, they were justifiably flummoxed.

And the audience came away with the impression that the

hiatus had been caused by the younger actor. National Treasure Trafford Duke, they thought, was giving his customary star performance. What a pity the producers couldn't have afforded better actors in the supporting cast.

More than once during that First Night, Charles Paris was the undeserving recipient of the Look. Well, perhaps he wasn't quite as undeserving as the rest of the company. His lunchtime intake at the pub, bolstered by a hidden half-bottle of Bell's in his dressing room, had rendered his own grip on the lines a little tenuous.

Though the logic of *Dead as a Doornail*'s plot was shot to pieces by the time they reached the interval, there was no evidence that the audience minded. Maybe most of the mature residents of Rugland Spa, The Trafford Duke Fan Club, had come to see their favourite Sergeant Wickens from *Duty Patrol* and weren't too bothered what they were seeing him in.

Among the company, though, the feeling prevailed that the show was going all right. Surprisingly, Barb Benson wasn't backstage to give them interval notes. She was apparently busy seeing some people out front.

Trafford Duke was particularly ebullient. And none of the actors whom he'd made to look stupid took issue with him. He was the star, after all. Without him, whatever his shortcomings, they'd be out of work.

Only one of them cracked when he went too far by announcing to the assembled Green Room, 'Well, I think we're getting away with it.'

It was, needless to say, Camilla Bruton. Being the Suspect Whose Writing Career Could Be Destroyed By The First Murder Victim's Revelations Of Plagiarism In Her Bestselling Novel But Who Then Turns Out To Be The Second Murder Victim, she had been neatly poisoned at the end of the First Half. So, her evening's work was over and she suffered no inhibitions about shouting at Trafford Duke.

'You've been getting away with things all your life! And you think you are so bloody famous you can go on getting away with things! Well, let me tell you, Trafford, there's going to be a reckoning. Very soon. And you'll discover that there are some things even you can't get away with!'

With that parting shot, Camilla Bruton stormed off to her dressing room.

The target of her spleen just shrugged a sort of masculine 'bloody women, what can you do about them?' shrug.

The usual Green Room interval chatter resumed.

The major cock-up happened about half an hour into the Second Half. It was a Repeated Cue incident.

And it happened soon after the Third Murder. The scene had opened with considerable discussion about the recent death of the Suspect Whose Writing Career Could Be Destroyed By The First Murder Victim's Revelations Of Plagiarism In Her Bestselling Novel But Who Then Turns Out To Be The Second Murder Victim. Inspector Pargeter spelled out certain potential scenarios as to who could have organized her poisoning. (Or, rather, Inspector Pargeter should have spelled out such scenarios. In the words of Trafford Duke, these became a little more fanciful.)

In particular, Inspector Pargeter gave quite a grilling to the Suspect To Whom The First Murder Victim Had Confided He Was Going To Cut Him Out Of His Will In Favour Of A Cat's Home. The actor in this role reacted by saying, 'I had nothing to do with it! Why is everyone always picking on me?'

At this point in the action, an explosion is heard from offstage. All the company but one rush off to investigate, led by Inspector Pargeter. The person left onstage is the Suspect Who Needed A Kidney Transplant And For Whom The First Murder Victim Would Have Been An Ideal Donor. He had stayed behind to check the First Murder Victim's desk for forged share certificates, when he was shot in the back by someone offstage, and died behind the sofa.

When the other cast members returned, they did not notice his body, but got on with Inspector Pargeter's interrogations. Shortly afterwards, the Inspector was summoned offstage to take a telephone call. (The setting of *Dead as a Doornail* pre-dated mobiles.)

At this point, when the other suspects turned on her, the Suspect To Whom The First Murder Victim Had Confided He Was Going To Cut Him Out Of His Will In Favour Of A Cat's Home said, defensively, 'I had nothing to do with it! Why is everyone always picking on me?'

The next line belonged to the Suspect Whom The First Murder Victim Had Been Blackmailing Over Some Compromising Photographs, who was, of course, played by Vikki Roman.

And this was where things went wrong. Rather than saying the right line, 'We aren't picking on you. We have logical reasons for calling you a murderer', she had said, 'Oh, won't you pipe down! You're always complaining.'

This, unfortunately, was the response to the same cue from twenty minutes earlier in the play. The cast, with rabbit-in-headlight eyes, instinctively started playing back the earlier scene.

And the Suspect Who Needed A Kidney Transplant And For Whom The First Murder Victim Would Have Been An Ideal Donor, who had dialogue in the earlier section, had to reappear from behind the sofa and pretend that the audience hadn't seen him being shot.

By now, even the Trafford Duke Fan Club had realized that there was something wrong. But they weren't worried. Sergeant Wickens from *Duty Patrol* could always find a way out of any situation, however challenging.

The trouble was that Sergeant Wickens, in his identity as Inspector Pargeter, was still offstage taking his telephone call, so unable to find a way out. When he eventually got his cue to return, rather than being absent for two minutes, he'd been away for the best part of a quarter of an hour.

Order was eventually restored, though not the order in which *Dead as a Doornail* was meant to be played.

The Suspect Who Needed A Kidney Transplant And For Whom The First Murder Victim Would Have Been An Ideal Donor just hoped no one in the audience noticed that he'd been murdered twice.

The way the structure of *Dead as a Doornail* worked, the Suspect Whose Work As A Doctor Gave Him Access To The Medication An Overdose Of Which Caused The First Murder Victim To Die was not onstage at the final curtain. No, fortunately, Charles Paris was not another Murder Victim. Having been proved by Inspector Pargeter to be innocent of any crime, the good doctor had gone off to take his evening surgery.

This meant that Charles Paris had time before the curtain call to nip back to his dressing room for another bracing slurp of Bell's.

He was at the top of the stairs about to turn right when he saw the door opposite him was open. Camilla Bruton was sprawled forward in her chair. From her wrists, blood had flowed on to the makeup table in front of her.

Charles did not go into the room. He knew how unpopular amateurs entering crime scenes were with the police.

But he took note of the bloodied cut-throat razor on Camilla's table.

Feeling suddenly confident, he moved along the corridor to the Number One dressing room. Trafford Duke's, obviously.

He didn't know exactly what he was looking for, but he recognized it when he found it.

A letter in Camilla Bruton's handwriting, which he recognized from seeing her with her diary in the Soho pub.

The first lines of the letter confirmed his suspicions.

But his reading was disturbed by sounds from along the corridor.

Barb Benson was standing in the doorway of Camilla Bruton's dressing room.

The director was shouting, 'She's just done it to screw up my plans and draw attention to herself!'

The Green Room was full. The *Dead as a Doornail* cast, sensing a crisis, had hurried offstage after one curtain call. The backstage crew were there. As was Barb Benson, fronting a group of women who Charles recognized had been sitting in the front row. Also present were some people he hadn't seen before.

Everyone seemed to recognize the new authority in Charles Paris. They listened in silence as he spoke.

He nearly began by saying, 'You may wonder why I've asked you here' but resisted the temptation. Still, there was a feeling about the occasion of Suspects gathered in the Library.

'What we're dealing with here,' he said, 'is a case of murder. A very simple case of someone seeing an opportunity to get out of a very awkward situation. Though he never acknowledged it, never even recognized her, Trafford Duke had history with Camilla Bruton.'

'This is absolutely preposterous!' the National Treasure protested.

'In this letter . . .' Charles produced it from his jacket pocket '. . . Camilla spells out her grievances. Many years ago, when she was just starting out in the business, Trafford Duke took advantage of her in a manner which would now be described as "coercive behaviour". She didn't report him at the time, but, as we all know, attitudes to that kind of thing have changed. So, Camilla sent Trafford this letter, saying how he'd driven her into a mental breakdown, from which she had never recovered.

'Trafford realized two things about the letter. One, that in the current post-#MeToo climate, if its contents ever got out, he was ruined. And, two, that the contents of the letter could also have been read as a suicide note.

'Having spent time with Trafford, Camilla knew that he always shaved with a cut-throat razor. And he knew she knew. So, he planned to set up a scenario which would look as if she had cut her own wrists.

'But when could he do it? As Inspector Pargeter, Trafford was onstage almost every minute of the play . . . or he would have been if *Dead as a Doornail* had run the course it should have done.

'But Trafford had an accomplice in the cast. Vikki Roman.'

'I don't know what you're talking about,' the actor in question protested.

'Oh, I think you do, Vikki. You were the one who had to respond to the line, "I had nothing to do with it! Why is everyone always picking on me?" You had it in your power to take the play back a quarter of an hour. Thus giving your lover time to murder the woman who could destroy everything he had built up over so many years!'

There was a shocked silence.

Never, in his career as an amateur detective, had Charles Paris felt so supremely confident. He had achieved his ambition. He had solved the murder before the police arrived. He had done 'the full Poirot'!

Then he noticed someone in the Green Room doorway, wiping red off her arms with a towel. It was Camilla Bruton.

'Well,' said Barb Benson, 'despite attempts to upstage me, I have achieved what I wanted to.' She turned to Camilla. 'Typical of you to have wanted to put on your own spectacular. When you first talked to me about what Trafford had done, I thought you had agreed to join in with me and the others.' She gestured to the women who'd been sitting in the front row. 'But oh no, that didn't bring you sufficiently centre stage, did it, Camilla? You had to feed your inner Drama Queen by setting up the mock suicide.'

Camilla was about to respond but a look from the director quelled her.

'And, as for you, Charles. God knows what you were on about. I think you've spent too much time reading Golden Age crime fiction. All that gobbledygook of an explanation. Or maybe it was just the drink talking.'

He wished there was a hole in the floor small enough for him to hide in.

'But none of it really changes anything. Camilla's over-dramatic gesture was making the same point as I am. And some of what you said, Charles, was getting near the truth, too.'

She turned to face the show's star. 'Because this is all about you, Trafford. I was so angry when Camilla told me how you'd treated her that I reckoned she couldn't have been the only one. Checking out shows you'd been in, contacting actors who'd worked with you. Then trawling social media, it didn't take long for me to build up quite a list of women who had had the same experience of your taking advantage of them. Reckoning your fame gave you immunity from any complaints. In fact, your coercive behaviour, Trafford.'

She gestured to the women who'd been in the front row. 'I'm sure you don't remember their names any more than you claimed not to have remembered Camilla's, and I'm sure you never expected any of them to reappear in your life. But let me tell you . . . every one of the women here is prepared to stand up in court and say how you treated them.'

Trafford Duke suddenly looked as pale as Charles felt.

'And I must pass on particular thanks,' Barb went on, 'to Vikki.' She pointed the girl out. 'Who agreed to take part in the production of this terrible play and to stop you from being suspicious about what was really going on. I hope he didn't come on to you too much, Vikki.'

'God, no,' came the reply. 'I wouldn't let him touch me. I do have some standards, you know.'

'Good.' The director grinned grimly. 'Anyway, I'm pleased with the outcome. It may not have been by the most direct route, but all of these women will have their day in court.

'As, also . . .' she turned a sweet smile on the National Treasure '. . . will you, Trafford.'

Charles noticed that the people in the Green Room he didn't know were busy writing on iPads. And he realized they were journalists.

In the pub, the two ice lumps in the large Bell's had melted to give the whisky the pale colour of lemonade.

'Was there a woman in here who bought that?' Charles asked the barman.

'Yes. Cab came for her . . . what? Ten minutes ago?'

'Did she leave a message?'

'Just the Bell's.'

'Ah.'

Frances had gone back to bloody Gerontius.

He downed the diluted whisky in one. It didn't taste as good as it would have done half an hour earlier.

So, he'd never achieved 'the full Poirot'. No endorsement of his skills as an amateur sleuth. Another old review rose to the surface of his memory. ('When Charles Paris's Inspector was put in charge of the case, there must have been wild jubilation at the Unconvicted Murderers' Club.' *Romford Recorder*)

Charles Paris felt alone. But then he'd always been alone.

He asked the barman for another large Bell's.

# SIMON BRETT – THE DETECTION CLUB: A PERSONAL MEMOIR

I've been a proud member of the Detection Club for more than forty-five years, fourteen of those as President. Over that time, I've had the pleasure of meeting some truly fascinating people. As in every other area, it is people who make life worth living.

And crime writers have such varied backgrounds. Most other professional bodies – those of lawyers, doctors, accountants, politicians and so on – are made up of people who have had a roughly similar experience of training. But there is no training to be a crime writer. When I was growing up, there was literally none. Now, many universities have Creative Writing courses, but I've met few crime writers who have benefitted from such targeted education. Most of the ones I know just wanted to write crime fiction and went ahead and did it.

Of course, a lot of them used expertise and experience from their day jobs to enrich their work. Many legal thrillers are written by lawyers. Medical crime novels are often written by doctors. Fictional journalistic investigations are often created by journalists (most of whom call their first crime novel 'Deadline', in the belief that no one's thought of it before).

And a few police procedurals are written by policemen, though most are written by crime writers who, in time-honoured tradition, make it all up. Colin Dexter was someone with whom I enjoyed many Detection Club dinner conversations. I once saw him being interviewed and asked the inevitable: 'Do you do a lot of research to get your police procedure right?'

'Oh no,' he said, 'I think it'd spoil the story.'

On another occasion I saw Ruth Rendell having the same question put to her during a Q & A. 'The only time I have been in a police station in the last thirty years,' she responded majestically, 'was when I was done for speeding.'

Most readers of this volume will be aware of the Detection

Club Initiation Ceremony, featuring Eric the Skull. Dorothy L. Sayers had a major influence on the original script for it, and the text has undergone many changes and tweaks over the years. But one continuing element has been the moment when, in candlelight, the red-robed President asks the Candidate for Membership to place their hand on Eric the Skull and say what, in the context of their crime writing, they hold sacred.

I became a member of the Detection Club surprisingly early in my writing career, in 1978 when, I think, I had only published three books. But, in fact, although my name appears on the membership list for 1978, I wasn't actually initiated until the next year. Back then – it seems inconceivable now – I still had a day job. I was a comedy producer at London Weekend Television and, the evening when I was invited to my first Detection Club dinner, I was committed to being in the studio, producing some dire sitcom.

So, the first dinner I attended was on 7 March 1979. Although my wife was invited to accompany me, I went on my own that first time, anxious to find out what this strange organization might be about.

I must say, then as now, my welcome as a new candidate was warm and generous.

As I recorded in my diary, 'To Garrick Club for Detection Club dinner. Sat next to Antonia Fraser, met Julian Symons, Dick Francis, Harry Keating, Sheila Mitchell, Katharine Whitehorn, etc. etc. Pleasant evening. Home 11.00.'

What I didn't mention was my initiation, which for some reason didn't happen until the summer of 1979. But, ever since that dinner more than forty-five years ago, I have suffered from l'esprit d'escalier, defined, as I'm sure everyone knows, as 'thinking of the perfect reply too late'. When the then President, Julian Symons, asked what, in the context of my crime writing, I held sacred, I came back with some pompous answer about 'protecting the integrity of character from the depredations of plot'.

What I should have said, of course, was: 'I hold sacred the first drink at the end of a day's writing, hoping it never becomes the first drink at the beginning of a day's writing.' A development, incidentally, that I have more or less avoided.

Eric the Skull has featured in my life in other ways. While I was President, on quite a few occasions I was driving with the precious relic in my charge. And I had this fantasy of my car smashing into a bridge and bursting into flames. Which prompted the headline: 'CRIME WRITER WITH TWO SKULLS KILLED IN MOTORWAY INFERNO.'

Another occasion I remember with Eric . . . For those of you who don't know, Eric is a real human skull, always assumed to be male, though some authorities say it actually should be called 'Erica'. For the Initiation Ceremony, he – or she – is carried on a red cushion and in his – or her – eye sockets are small battery-powered red lights.

For some fifty or sixty years, no one had any problem with this. Then, with the arrival of new cultural sensibilities, some Detection Club members began to wonder whether our treatment of a human relic was appropriate to the dignity of the original skull-owner. At an AGM that I chaired, this issue came up for discussion,

Civilized debate – debate is always civilized in the Detection Club – ensued. And, though the general view was that the use of Eric the Skull was legitimate, some members felt that the use of the lights in the eye sockets was an irreverence too far.

My suggestion – that the light should be removed from one eye and the members who objected should sit on that side of the room, while those who approved should sit on the side of the skull whose light was on – was rejected. So, the issue was put to the vote.

The continuing use of Eric's lights was carried. And Michael Hartland, then Secretary of the Detection Club, wittily concluded the minutes of the AGM with the words, 'The eyes had it.'

Eric the Skull played yet another part in my life. A very bright radio producer called Liz Anstee suggested to me the idea of writing a play about the origins of the Detection Club. And I wrote one entitled – would you believe – *Eric the Skull*. I was very pleased with the way it worked out. Fenella Woolgar played Dorothy L. Sayers, Janie Dee was Agatha Christie and – in a little in-joke – Mark Williams, who plays Father Brown on television, was cast as his creator, G. K. Chesterton.

At those early dinners in the 1970s and 80s, I met some

wonderful people. I remember once sitting next to Eric Ambler. The conversation didn't exactly flow, because he was by then profoundly deaf, but I did feel honoured to be next to such an iconic figure. I liked his books and I greatly admired the title of his very unrevelatory memoir, *Here Lies Eric Ambler*. There seems a kind of symmetry about the fact that I am now one of the executors of his literary estate.

And then, of course, there was P. D. James. She wasn't one of those who stinted on her research, she was a stickler for doing the thing properly. Her work in the Home Office had put her in contact with many important figures in the police and she was meticulous in getting the facts right.

Meeting Phyllis was, for me, one of the great pleasures of the Detection Club. And our paths kept crossing at crime conventions and charity events. But the time I really got to know her was when we spent two separate weeks co-tutoring Arvon writing courses on Crime Fiction in the relatively spartan conditions of a house called Totleigh Barton deep in Devon. Phyllis was then in her seventies but mucked in with everyone else and had infinite patience when talking to the course participants about their work.

Those weeks always ended up with an evening of readings. One of my treasured memories is of Baroness James of Holland Park actually *singing* her witty poem about Colin Watson's invented whodunit village Mayhem Parva to sixteen very fortunate aspiring writers in a barn in the middle of Devon.

When the course finished I drove her back to our house where we had lunch. 'Well,' said Phyllis, 'we were bloody good. They were lucky to have us.'

What people who didn't know Phyllis personally could not appreciate was how mischievous she could be. Her public image as a right wing, Anglican public servant disguised how funny she could be. I remember once having a conversation with her about the questions we least liked being asked in Q & As, and we agreed the most annoying were: 'Where do you get your ideas from?' and 'Are you writing anything at the moment?'

Then Phyllis told me of an incident when she had a call from her agent, saying that a Dutch television company wanted to film her at home. They would arrive at eight thirty in the morning, set up the cameras, do the interview, and be away by ten. Phyllis agreed to do it.

As arranged, on the appointed day they arrived at eight thirty but, because they were a television company, they laid cables across and trod mud into the carpets of her immaculate house in Holland Park Avenue. They moved around all the precious artefacts in her study and spent an inordinate amount of time adjusting the lights to the director's satisfaction. Eventually, just after noon, Phyllis was sat down in her chair opposite her interviewer.

'Miss James,' asked the Dutch journalist, 'are you writing anything at the moment?'

'Well,' said Phyllis, with some asperity, 'I would be!'

Margaret Yorke (real name Margaret – or Peggy – Nicholson) was a very strong character, with decided opinions about everything. A bit daunted when I first met her at a Detection Club dinner, I came to be very fond of her. She was a great defender of our libraries and a persistent letter writer. A lot of what she wrote in those letters, it has to be said, were complaints.

I remember, when I was Chair of the Crime Writers' Association, my wife Lucy and I organized the CWA Annual Conference in Chichester. It ran from a Friday to Sunday and was, as anyone who's done it will attest, an onerous job. So, when, on the Sunday, we had said goodbye to the last guest, Lucy and I heaved huge sighs of relief and waited for the response.

No emails back then, of course, so any comments, positive or negative, came by phone call or post. On the Tuesday morning, on to our hall floor fell a letter in Margaret's distinctively small writing. I opened it with trepidation but was relieved that it gave high commendation to the programme of speakers and entertainments Lucy and I had organized.

I later discovered that, from the same source and by what must have been the same post, a letter had been sent to the CWA Secretary, complaining about the deficiencies of the hotel in which the members had been accommodated. Very Margaret Yorke.

She also had an original turn of phrase. I remember her once describing a man of whom she disapproved as 'a dubious factor'. It's an expression I have appropriated more than once in my own writing.

The last time I saw Margaret, she was in a very upmarket convalescent hospital, only one step down from a stately home. 'I put aside money for this,' she confided in me. 'I wanted to go out in a degree of style.'

Then she said, 'I know there's going to be no happy ending to this. No trumpets blaring to recognize my miraculous recovery.'

But it was spoken philosophically, by someone reconciled to the approaching end.

Another regular at Detection Club dinners was Gavin Lyall. Delightful if a little taciturn himself, he frequently brought with him, as a bonus, his wife, the wonderful and witty Katharine Whitehorn. I had worked with her quite a bit in my days as a BBC radio producer and we never failed to have a wide-ranging and enthralling conversation.

Gavin's background was as a journalist and he wrote excellent espionage thrillers, distinguished by their depth of research, particularly into the world of aviation. I remember meeting him at a Detection Club autumn dinner in 1989. The big news of the day was the fall of the Berlin Wall. Knowing Gavin to be a shrewd commentator on international events, I asked him for his view of what had happened. 'Put it up again! Put it up again!' he said. 'I'm halfway through a book.'

And, indeed, the prospective ending of the Cold War did suddenly make his kind of espionage thriller look dated.

I saw Gavin at another Detection Club dinner early in 1990 and I asked him tentatively what had happened to the book he had been halfway through. 'I've scrapped it,' he replied. 'I am now writing a book set in 1903, *when at least you knew where the next war was coming from!'*

I was honoured when, in 2003, I was asked by Katharine to speak at Gavin Lyall's memorial service.

Talking of the members' partners who, incidentally, have always been welcomed to Detection Club events, I remember an incident at a dinner in the Garrick Club. It was a steaming hot summer evening and, as we all rose to leave, Lionel Davidson's wife fainted. There was a nanosecond of silence, while every crime writer in the room contemplated how they could use the incident in a book, before everyone rushed forward to help her. (She was, incidentally, absolutely fine in a few minutes.)

Lionel was a charming and intriguing character, one of the few writers to win three CWA Gold Daggers. I used to relish his conversation at Detection Club dinners. He kept saying he had a very good idea for a stage thriller which the two of us should write together. He would call me about it. Because of my admiration for his thrillers, I was very excited by the prospect. But, sadly, the call never came.

Lady Antonia Fraser was a member of the Detection Club, elected for her series of crime novels about Jemima Shore. And on some occasions, she would come with her husband, Harold Pinter. Having grown up knowing the plays and their atmosphere of menace very well, both my wife Lucy and I did find it slightly daunting if we ended up sitting next to him. But he couldn't have been more affable, talking about his digs in Worthing when he was a jobbing actor and, of course, his great love of cricket.

Tim Heald was another great cricket enthusiast. He, a great friend with whom I used to play regular squash and, as we got older, Real Tennis, was a frequent presence at Detection Club dinners. I remember, as he passed his sixtieth birthday, he became rather obsessed by mortality, which was an unusual mood for him, who always thrived on being the life and soul of the party. As we talked, it became increasingly clear that he was having these thoughts because his father had died at the age of sixty-four. He continued to talk about death, while I wondered what ghastly health condition he might have inherited.

When Tim reached his sixty-fifth birthday, a definite change occurred. He was much more relaxed, the Tim Heald I used to know, and he stopped harping on about mortality. At that stage, I felt emboldened to ask what was the cause of his father's death.

'Oh,' said Tim, 'he was run over by a taxi outside Buckingham Palace.'

Now, there are some conditions which I'd have thought are hereditary, but some which definitely aren't.

There are a couple of individual lines I remember fondly from Detection Club members. At a dinner celebrating the delightful Peter Lovesey's eightieth birthday, he began by saying, 'I don't feel eighty. Feel fairly fit. I think it's the long walks. I set out in the morning, and then I forget where my house is.'

An excellent joke from Peter – and one I'm prepared to steal shamelessly.

And I always greatly enjoyed the company of the President I succeeded, H. R. F. – 'Harry' – Keating. I remember him once giving a post-prandial address in the Middle Temple. He began by saying, 'Over dinner, I was discussing with my host, Mr Justice Brown, what was the right amount to drink if one is going to deliver an after-dinner speech . . . and I've just realized that I've got it wrong.'

Another line I've been guilty of snaffling.

I can't say how honoured and delighted I am that this book exists. Many thanks to Martin Edwards, who has now taken over the Presidency from me with such aplomb and success, but whose idea this anthology was. And who has had the time-consuming task of editing it.

In conclusion, I'd also like to thank all of the Detection Club members, past and present, whose company has so much enriched my life.

Simon Brett

# Presidents of the Detection Club

G. K. Chesterton: 1930–1936

E. C. Bentley: 1937–1949

Dorothy L. Sayers: 1949–1957

Agatha Christie: 1958–1976

Julian Symons: 1976–1985

H. R. F. Keating: 1985–2000

Simon Brett: 2000–2015

Martin Edwards: 2015–

# About the Contributors

**Catherine Aird** is the pen-name of Kinn McIntosh. She is the author of the Calleshire Chronicles, a series featuring Detective Inspector C. D. Sloan, which began with *The Religious Body* in 1966. She has also published several collections of short stories. A former Chair of the CWA, she was honoured with an MBE in 1988. She has received the Golden Handcuffs award (now known as the CWA Dagger in the Library) and also the CWA Diamond Dagger.

**Simon Brett** was educated at Dulwich College and Wadham College, Oxford and subsequently worked as a producer with BBC Radio Light Entertainment and London Weekend Television, before becoming a full-time writer in 1979. He is the author of over a hundred books, including the Charles Paris, Mrs Pargeter, Fethering, and Blotto & Twinks series of crime novels, and his radio and TV series include *After Henry* and *No Commitments*. Another former Chair of the CWA, he has received the CWA Diamond Dagger and an OBE for services to literature.

**Frances Brody** is the pen-name under which Frances McNeil, who has written several books under her own name, publishes crime fiction. She has written extensively for radio and also for television and the theatre. In 2009 she published *Dying in the Wool*, a historical mystery which introduced Kate Shackleton. Kate, a photographer with a flair for amateur detection, became a popular series character. In 2021, she launched the Brackerley Prison series, set in the 1960s, with *A Murder Inside*.

**Ann Cleeves** published her first crime novel in 1986. A series about amateur detectives and birdwatchers George and Molly Palmer-Jones was followed by a police-focused series featuring

Inspector Ramsay. DCI Vera Stanhope was introduced in *The Crow Trap*, which was originally intended as a stand-alone but developed into a series adapted for TV as *Vera*, with Brenda Blethyn in the title role. Her series featuring Jimmy Perez and set on Shetland was equally popular, while *The Long Call*, the first book in her latest series, has also been adapted for television.

**Liza Cody** is an artist trained at the Royal Academy Schools of Art as well as a crime novelist. *Dupe*, her first novel, won the John Creasey Memorial Dagger, and launched a series about the female private investigator Anna Lee, which was televised with Imogen Stubbs in the lead role. She has also published the Bucket Nut Trilogy featuring professional wrestler Eva Wylie, as well as stand-alone novels such as *Rift*, *Gimme More*, *Ballad of a Dead Nobody* and *Miss Terry*, and numerous short stories. She has won a CWA Silver Dagger, an Anthony award, and a Marlowe award in Germany.

**David Stuart Davies** worked as an English teacher prior to becoming a full-time novelist, playwright, and editor. A leading expert on Sherlock Holmes, he published novels and non-fiction books about the great detective, as well as a play, *Sherlock Holmes – The Last Act*. His crime fiction included a series about a private investigator called Johnny One-Eye. He was for many years editor of *Sherlock* magazine and the CWA members' monthly newsletter *Red Herrings*.

**Martin Edwards**' novels include the Lake District Mysteries and the Rachel Savernake books, most recently *Hemlock Bay*. His non-fiction includes a multi-award-winning history of crime fiction, *The Life of Crime*. He has received three Daggers, including the CWA Diamond Dagger, as well as two Edgars, and four lifetime achievement awards. A former Chair of the CWA, he is consultant to the British Library's Crime Classics and was recently commissioned to write a locked room mystery audio drama for *Doctor Who*.

**Ruth Dudley Edwards** is a well-known journalist and writer of non-fiction, whose awards include the CWA Gold Dagger for non-fiction and the James Tait Black Memorial Prize. As a writer of humorous mysteries, she has won the Last Laugh award and been shortlisted for the CWA John Creasey Memorial Dagger and also, on two further occasions, for the Last Laugh award. Her crime novels satirize establishments ranging from the House of Lords to the worlds of academe and modern art.

**Kate Ellis'** first novel, *The Merchant House*, launched the long-running DI Wesley Peterson series set in Devon. She has also written five crime novels in an ongoing series featuring another cop, Joe Plantagenet, set in fictionalized version of York, and a trilogy set in the immediate aftermath of the First World War as well as many short stories. She won the CWA Dagger in the Library in 2019. *The Devil's Priest* is a stand-alone historical mystery set in Liverpool.

**Christopher Fowler** worked as a copywriter before founding a successful film marketing company. He published over fifty books on a variety of topics, including the posthumous memoir *Word Monkey*. His achievements in the field of crime fiction were recognized in 2015 by the award of the CWA Dagger in the Library. He was best-known for the Bryant and May series, a homage to the Golden Age of detective fiction that ran to twenty-one books and achieved international acclaim.

**Elly Griffiths** is a pen-name for Domenica de Rosa. She had a career in publishing and wrote four novels under her own name before turning to crime fiction in 2009 with the first book in the Ruth Galloway series, *The Crossing Places*. Her second series is set in 1950s Brighton, while *The Stranger Diaries*, which won an Edgar in 2020, introduced DS Harbinder Kaur, who also proceeded to establish herself as a series detective. Elly received the CWA Dagger in the Library in 2016.

**John Harvey** has enjoyed a long and varied literary career, and high among his achievements are the Charlie Resnick crime stories, set in Nottingham, which began with *Lonely Hearts* in 1989. The series was adapted (by John himself) for television as *Resnick*, with the Oscar-nominated actor Tom Wilkinson playing the jazz-loving Charlie, and for radio. John's other major characters include Frank Elder and Jack Kiley, who features in 'Fedora', for which John won the CWA Short Story Dagger. He received the CWA Diamond Dagger in 2007.

**Michael Jecks** has been Secretary of the Detection Club since 2016 and is a former Chair of the CWA. He has published about fifty books since making his debut in 1996 with *The Last Templar*, which was the first in a series of over thirty Knights Templar mysteries. He has also written three books set during the Hundred Years War, while *Rebellion's Message* launched a series of Tudor mysteries featuring Elizabethan cutpurse and adventurer Jack Blackjack.

**Alison Joseph** began her career as a documentary director, making programmes for Channel 4. Her principal crime series features a nun, Sister Agnes, and her other books include a series featuring Agatha Christie as a character. She has written extensively for radio, adapting Maigret novels by Georges Simenon and books by S. J. Watson and Craig Russell, as well as writing original radio dramas. She is a former Chair of the CWA.

**Michael Z. Lewin** is an American-born author perhaps best known for his series about the private detective Albert Samson, based in Indianapolis. Lewin himself grew up in Indianapolis, but has lived in England for more than forty years. Much of his fiction continues to be set in Indianapolis, including a secondary series about the cop Leroy Powder. A series set in Bath, England, features the Lunghis, who run their detective agency as a family business. Mike is also a former Secretary of the Cambridge Footlights.

**Peter Lovesey** had already published a successful book about athletics when he won a competition with his first crime fiction novel, *Wobble to Death*, which launched a series about the Victorian detective Sergeant Cribb. Since then, his many books and short stories have won or been shortlisted for nearly all the major prizes in the international crime writing world. He has been presented with Lifetime Achievement awards both in the UK and the US and the Detection Club anthology *Motives for Murder* was published in his honour in 2016.

**Abir Mukherjee** pursued a career as an accountant before writing *The Rising Man*, the first book in the Wyndham and Bannerjee series set in Raj-era India. Published in 2016, the book won the CWA Historical Dagger. *Death in the East* subsequently won the same prize, while *Smoke and Ashes* and *A Necessary Evil* reached the shortlist.

**Michael Ridpath's** first novel, after a career in finance, was *Free to Trade*, a bestseller about the murky world of bond trading which was translated into over thirty languages. The success of that book enabled him to become a full-time writer, and he published seven more thrillers with a financial background before starting a new series set in Iceland. He has also written spy novels set in pre-war Europe and stand-alone thrillers such as *Amnesia*.

**Andrew Taylor's** crime novels include a series about William Dougal, starting with *Caroline Minuscule*, which won the John Creasey Memorial Dagger, the Roth Trilogy, which was televised as *Fallen Angel*, the Lydmouth series, and stand-alone novels such as *The American Boy*. He is currently working on a series set in the late seventeenth century. He has won the CWA Historical Dagger three times and also the Diamond Dagger, as well as receiving awards in Sweden and the US.

**Aline Templeton** grew up in the East Neuk of Fife and was educated at St Leonard's School, St Andrews, and Cambridge University. She has worked in education and broadcasting and has written numerous stories and articles for national newspapers and magazines. After publishing seven stand-alone books, she started a series set in Galloway and featuring DI Marjory Fleming. Her latest series character is DI Kelso Strang.

**Lynne Truss** is a novelist, radio broadcaster and dramatist who began her media career as a literary editor. She spent six years as a television critic for *The Times* before moving into sports journalism for the same newspaper. In 2009 she wrote a book about her experiences: *Get Her Off the Pitch: How Sport Took Over My Life*. Her championing of correctness and aesthetics in the English language led to her 2003 bestseller, *Eats, Shoots &*

*Leaves: The Zero Tolerance Approach to Punctuation*. Her crime writing career began in 2018 with *A Shot in the Dark*, which launched the Constable Twitten series.

**L. C. Tyler**, a former Chair of the CWA, has published nine books about hapless crime writer and amateur detective Ethelred Tressider and his unsympathetic literary agent Elsie Thirkettle. The series has twice won the Last Laugh Award for the best comic crime novel of the year. He has also written a stand-alone, *A Very Persistent Illusion*, and a series of historical mysteries about seventeenth-century lawyer and spy John Grey. 'The Trials of Margaret', a short story that he contributed to the Detection Club anthology *Motives for Murder*, won the CWA Short Story Dagger.